"WHY DO YOU HIDE?"

"You're not the prim and proper lady you pretend to be."

"Why do you say that?"

"Because it's true. I see it right there, in those bottomless eyes of yours." He leaned a little closer, so his breath fanned her neck as he spoke.

"You're imagining things, Adam. There's nothing in my eyes except—"

"Fire. Your eyes damn near boil over with passion sometimes. Your skin . . . it just about simmers. I feel it when I'm close to you . . . like this."

He was close. Too close. And she did feel as if her skin were on fire.

"I think, Brigit Malone, that deep down inside, you're a hellion."

FAIRYTALE

MAGGIE SHAYNE

AVON BOOKS ◆ NEW YORK

AVON BOOKS
A division of
The Hearst Corporation
1350 Avenue of the Americas
New York, New York 10019

Copyright © 1996 by Margaret Benson
Inside cover author photograph by Karen M. Bergamo
Published by arrangement with the author
Library of Congress Catalog Card Number: 95-95180
ISBN: 0-380-78300-2

First Avon Books Printing: May 1996

AVON TRADEMARK REG. U.S. PAT. OFF. AND IN OTHER COUNTRIES, MARCA REGISTRADA, HECHO EN U.S.A.

Printed in the U.S.A.

RA 10 9 8 7 6 5 4 3 2 1

Once Upon A Time . . .

Adam

—◆—

SEVEN-YEAR-OLD Adam Reid raced through the forest, zigging and zagging like a mad bumblebee, arms spread out at his sides. The summer breeze turned into a wind that whooshed past his ears and tangled his hair. He pretended he was flying. He liked pretending. Even though his father was always telling him how bad it was, how foolish. He got the strap for it sometimes, when his tall tales got a little too tall.

But only if his father had been drinking.

He buzzed around the base of a giant maple tree three times, then came to a halt when his keen eyes picked out a barely visible path beneath its broad, leafy limbs. No longer interested in playing bumblebee, Adam lowered his arms. He hunkered down and squinted at the almost invisible trail in the mossy ground. No matter how many times he came out here, he never failed to find a new adventure to pursue.

Adam loved these woods. He wasn't sup-

3

posed to be here. The forest was not on his father's property, but on the state land that bordered it. And he'd been warned repeatedly to stay away. But that hadn't stopped Adam.

Now he began following that trail, wondering what it might be. Deer trail, he decided, his seven years of wisdom assuring him it was so. Maybe he'd see a big whitetail if he went really slow and quiet.

The path meandered for a ways, wriggling this way and that in S-patterns and loops and figure eights. Then it vanished into a patch of mean-looking blackberry briars, with deceptively pretty white blossoms that smelled so good he wished he could taste them. But when Adam squatted on his haunches, he saw that the thorny, flowering briars sort of arched over the trail. If he bent really low, he could still follow it. So he did.

Bending almost double, even crawling on all fours here and there, he continued to follow the path. It was like a covered bridge now. Or a tunnel. The ground beneath him slanted upward, taking him over a small hill and partway down the other side before the brambles finally thinned out. He emerged on a grassy slope that seemed to be one side of a big old hump in the ground. And about halfway down that grassy hump, he saw a dark hole, sinking back into the mound. It looked like ... Adam ran closer and stopped, bracing his hands on his knees and breathing fast from excitement. It was! A cave! He'd discovered a cave. Maybe pirates had holed up here. Or a dinosaur! Or cave men, a zillion years ago. Neat!

Without hesitation, Adam crawled inside. The opening wasn't big enough to go in standing up. It was kind of dark, and a lot cooler than it was outside. But Adam wasn't afraid. Not much, anyway. He had his penlight, which he was never without. Just like his jackknife. He flicked the light on now, and ventured deeper. The farther he went, the wider the walls opened out, and the ceiling got higher, too. He came, at last, to what looked like the very back of the cave. A room about the size of his tree house, and big enough so he could stand up. This was the best discovery he'd ever made.

He played in there for hours. He explored, and carved his name in the stone walls, and yelled really loud to hear his voice echo, until he got tired. And then he decided to take a short nap before heading home. It was a long walk, after all.

So he sat on the ground and leaned back against the cool wall, and he closed his eyes.

When he opened them again, Adam wasn't sure if he'd been asleep or not, or if he had, how much time had passed. Not wanting to be late for dinner and risk another walloping, he hurried to the cave's entrance. He had to crouch low again, of course, but he made good time, scuttling closer to the bright yellow sunlight he could see up ahead. He stepped out, stood up straighter, and brushed the dirt from the knees of his jeans. Then he brought his head up, blinking first at the brightness of the sunlight, and then in shock.

This was not the same place he'd been to before. This was . . . this was *different*.

Everywhere he looked there were flowers like he'd never seen before, blossoming in every color he could imagine and a few he never had! And they filled the air with their smells. Wonderful smells! There were pebbles and stones on the grassy ground. But they were no regular stones. Every rock he saw glittered. Like . . . jewels or something! Adam turned to look back at the cave entrance, wondering if there had been another tunnel in there, one he hadn't noticed. He sure as heck hadn't come out the same way he'd gone in.

Okay, then. He'd take a look around, really quick, and then he'd go back inside and find the right way out. If he dawdled out here much longer he'd be in hot water with his father for sure. But gosh, this place was too much to resist. Like something out of *The Wizard of Oz*!

He ventured farther, and took a closer look at the trees. Squinting, moving closer, he looked again. Heck, there were pictures in the bark! A moon. Some stars. A sun. A fairy.

What the heck?

Adam moved through the trees, curious, amazed. This was no normal forest. This was . . . this was . . .

"This is Rush, young man. And you are most certainly *not* supposed to be here."

Her voice was like music. Like bells. Adam whirled to see a woman . . . a beautiful red-haired woman whose belly was swelled like she'd swallowed a basketball. He guessed she must be expecting a baby. She wore the kind of glittery, gauzy dress you'd expect to see in a

fairytale, and her eyes were just about the bluest he'd ever seen in his life.

Something moved behind her and Adam narrowed his eyes. Then he thought he was going to drop dead in his tracks. He blinked, rubbed his eyes and looked again. *She had wings!* Fragile-looking, like a dragonfly's wings. You could see right through them, but they were there.

"Who *are* you?" he managed to ask her.

"Máire," she said, smiling. It sounded like "May-ruh" to Adam. But he didn't have time to ponder it long. She was leaning closer, squinting at him. "Few mortals can see the doorway to this place," she told him. "It's enchanted, you know."

Adam looked around, nodding. "Yeah, I was starting to figure that."

"Maybe you *are* supposed to be here." She tapped her chin with one dainty finger. "After all, there's no such thing as coincidence. So, there must be a reason for your coming here, mustn't there?"

"Uh—I don't think so, ma'am. I—I ought to be getting home." He took a step backward.

She sighed. "Yes, that's probably for the best."

Adam agreed. He didn't want any part of any enchanted forest or any fairy godmothers or whatever the heck she was. Sheesh, he'd read about fairies. They could be dangerous. He turned, feeling lucky he was going to get out of here unscathed, but then he got a chill right up his spine. Because he didn't see the cave. He'd wandered too far.

"Oh, don't worry. I'll show you the way." The lady took his hand in hers, and then she went

still, and stared down at him, her eyes sparkling, her eyebrows lifting in surprise. "*Now* I know why you're here!" She smiled, looking at him like she was seeing something awfully sweet. One of her hands rested lovingly on her swollen belly, and she ran her other hand through his hair. If she pinched his cheeks, he was outta here, he decided. Then her smile faded, and she even looked a little sad. "You must be a very strong little boy. And a brave one, too."

"Well, sure I am," he confirmed, wondering how she could tell.

"Tell me, young Adam. Would you like to see your fate before you go?"

"My . . . *fate*?"

"Your future. I can show you, if you want."

Adam swallowed hard. His heart was racing, his hands were sweaty, and he really wanted out of here. Now. But he'd be awfully dumb to pass up a chance to see his future, wouldn't he? He'd particularly like to know if he'd missed dinner, and whether he was going to get beat when he got home tonight because of it. Trying for a nonchalant shrug, he said, "Okay."

The lady smiled again. She drew him off through the trees a little ways. Then she stopped and pushed aside a dense tangle of branches. "Look through here," she told him.

Adam looked.

There was a pond there, with water as blue as the winged lady's eyes. This side of it was dense with dark green reeds. But there was no mistaking the splashing and the laughter he heard coming from beyond them. And when he squinted harder and looked, he saw a woman.

Bunches of long black curls trailed over her back and shoulders. She was playing in the water like a little girl, only she was no little girl. He couldn't see all of her, which was a good thing because he didn't think she was dressed. Looked like she was skinny dipping to him.

All of a sudden she went still, and turned her head in his direction. Her eyes were black as coal as they met his through the gaps in the reeds. And Adam felt a shudder work its way right to his toes.

Then Máire let the branches snap back into place, cutting off his view.

"Who is she," he asked.

"You mean, who *will* she be," the woman corrected him. He frowned hard at her. "She *will be* your future, Adam. Your fate. She'll come into your life when you least expect it, because she needs you to show her the way."

"What way?" He was more confused now than he'd been when he'd spotted her fairy wings.

"The way to her sister, and then the way back home."

"Oh," he said, as if he fully understood, though he didn't.

"Whatever you do, Adam, you mustn't let yourself fall in love with her. She'll break your heart if you do. She has to leave you in the end. Don't forget."

"Don't worry. I don't even *like* girls." Adam turned and yanked the branches aside again, but when he looked now there was only more forest. No pond. No woman.

"What the heck?" He turned back to Máire

again, but she was gone as well, just like the vision. And right beyond the place where she'd been standing was the cave he knew would lead him home again. Though Adam was certain it hadn't been there before.

Brigit

March 21, 1978
St. Mary's Orphanage
Maybourne Row, Brooklyn
9:00 p.m.

"READ IT AGAIN, Sister Mary Agnes."

Sister's gentle smile added creases to her lined face. One withered hand ruffled Brigit's curls. "All right, little one. But this is the last time."

Brigit snuggled more deeply into the small wooden bed. Her pillow was lumpy, and her blanket none too thick. She ran her hands lovingly over the intricate embroidery on the book's cloth cover, her fingers tracing the elegant scroll of the title, *Fairytale*. Her parents must have loved her very much, to have made such a wonderful book for her. Brigit knew that because Sister told her so often. She opened the book to the first vellum page, with its brilliantly colored, hand-painted illustration. The one showing the mystical forest, with the crystal water in the center, and way off in the distance, the

11

castle spires. Brigit looked at the picture for a
long time, before pushing the book into Sister's
powdery soft hands.

"Once upon a time," Sister began, "not so
very long ago, two princesses were born. No ordinary princesses, though. These babies were
special. These babies were fay."

"And that means fairy, right Sister Mary Agnes?" Brigit didn't need to ask. She knew the
Fairytale by heart. But her comments and questions had become a part of the ritual.

"Yes, Brigit. That means fairy." Sister Mary
Agnes turned the page, and let Brigit take a
good long look at the next picture. This one was
of the beautiful fairy princess holding her twin
daughters in her arms. One had raven's wing
curls just like Brigit's, and the other had hair as
yellow as spun gold.

"Their mother was Princess Máire, the only
daughter of the Fay King Padráig. And their father was Jonathon, the mortal man who'd come
through the invisible curtain to find her. 'Twas
the hand of Fate that led him there, for the enchanted realm is invisible to most mortal eyes."

Despite the thinness of her blanket, Brigit felt
warm when she thought about Máire and John,
and the love they'd had between them. So
strong it had crossed worlds to find fulfillment.
Sister Mary Agnes often said Brigit was too
young to think about love the way she did. But
Brigit didn't think so. She thought nine was
plenty old enough to understand matters of the
heart. Sister would think so too, if she knew
about Brigit's dream. One dream which came to
her over and over again. A lovely dream in

which the fairy princess Máire appeared to her and whispered, "Would you like to see your fate, little one?" And Brigit always answered yes, and waited as Máire parted some mists with a wave of her dainty hand, and pointed. When Brigit peered through she saw a man. A golden-haired man who looked very sad and confused, and she felt an instinctive urge to try to comfort him. He needed her, that man with the hurt in his deep blue eyes.

But she couldn't tell Sister about that dream. She'd never understand.

Sister had turned the page, and was reading again. "Their home was the forest of Rush, which lies beyond the mortal world. And the princess's daughters were born at a time of peace. But alas, by the twins' first birthday there came a period of great turmoil in Rush. For even in the enchanted realm, evil exists."

A little shiver raced up Brigit's spine. The vellum made a whispery sound, and Sister's voice came again, as raspy and soft as the paper.

"The Prince of the Dark Side was never content to live in the part of the enchanted realm to which his family had been consigned. That part beyond Rush, where daylight never ventured. Always, those dark ones had coveted the fay forest and kingdom. They'd raised up an army of trolls and goblins and all manner of dark beings, and together, they laid siege to the castle of the king."

Brigit didn't look at that picture. It was too scary. A mishmash of nightmarish creatures storming those pretty castles, wielding swords and maces and looking as fierce as death itself.

"Princess Máire was killed in the battle, and poor John was beside himself with grief. Only wise King Padráig knew what must be done. He ordered John to take the wee princesses away from Rush. To part the invisible curtain once more, and to return with his daughters to the mortal world, where they would be safe from the Dark Prince's blade."

Brigit nodded. "And before Jonathon left . . ." she prompted.

Mary Agnes smiled and turned another page. "Before Jonathon left, King Paddy gave him two books, fashioned by Princess Máire with her own hands. She'd been blessed with the second sight, Máire had. She'd been able to see into the future. And she'd crafted the books for the time when her daughters would have to get by without her."

"And is this one of them, Sister?"

Sister made her eyes very big, as she always did when Brigit asked the question. "It might very well be, Brigit."

Brigit nodded. It was fun to think her mother might have been a fairy princess.

"The king told John to see to the children's safety. For one day, when they were grown, they would be called to return, the eldest to take her place on the throne of Rush. And the younger to assist her in regaining it. As firstborn— though only by a minute—the eldest had inherited the largest share of her mother's magic. And when the time came, she would regain some memories of the kingdom. The youngest, though, would likely remember none of it. The

accepting of her fate might well be more difficult for her."

Mary Agnes flipped to the last page, the page depicting Princess Máire, with her cascades of red-orange curls and her glittering gown. Her love-filled, sea-blue eyes seemed to stare at Brigit from the page.

"Trials and turmoil await you, little princesses. But when things seem hopeless, turn to the *Fairytale* to remind you of who you are. And remember, if you be true to your heart, happiness will greet you at the end of your journey."

As always, Sister Mary Agnes left the book open to that page and laid it in Brigit's lap.

Brigit traced Máire's beautiful face with her fingertips, blinking tiredly. "Do you think she really was my mother?"

Mary Agnes sighed. "I only know what I know, child. Father Anthony found you and another tiny girl sleeping at the altar one morning. And each of you had a book just like this one. Yours with the name Brigit inside, and the other with the name of Bridín. And tucked into a little pocket sewn within each cover, was a pendant for each of you."

Brigit fingered the necklace she never took off. A dainty pewter fairy, embracing a long, narrow crystal, with points at both ends.

"The note Father Anthony found beside you said simply, 'My time on this earth is ending. Please, take care of my girls. Jonathon.' "

"And what happened to Bridín?" Brigit knew, but asked again anyway. Sister's tales seemed more real when Brigit made her tell them right to the end.

"Bridín was adopted right away, darling. But you'd taken ill, and were in no condition to go with her. One day, though, you'll find a fairytale all your own. One day you'll have your happily-ever-after."

"Will I really, Sister Mary Agnes?"

For years Brigit had trusted utterly in the *Fairytale*. She'd had to, because she'd had nothing else. And she adored the woman who told it, knew Sister Mary Agnes would never deliberately lie. But Brigit wasn't a baby anymore. And the longer she remained here at St. Mary's, the harder it became to believe in fairies or enchanted kingdoms or . . . or especially happily-ever-afters. She closed her eyes as Sister's crinkled palm slipped repeatedly over her hair.

"You will, Brigit. I promise you will. No girl with a gift like yours will be alone for long."

Brigit frowned, her eyes popping open again. "I have a gift?"

Sister Mary Agnes lifted her head to stare at the picture, and Brigit followed her gaze, still unsure what was so special about it. The rectangle of construction paper hung a little crookedly above the painted white headboard of the bed. Brigit had discovered her knack with a paintbrush for the first time today, when Father Anthony had brought boxes of brushes and paints and paper for the orphans here. Sister Mary Agnes had seemed to think she'd witnessed her first miracle. She'd been a little breathless earlier, when she'd caught Brigit in the act of balancing on a stack of pillows while trying to Scotch tape her painting to the wall. To cover that crack in the plaster.

"Yes, child. Make no mistake, you have a gift."

"Who from?"

The tears that came into Sister Mary Agnes's eyes made Brigit frown. Why did she get so choked up over a construction-paper lady? It was just a copy of a picture Brigit had found in an art book. Some lady with two first names. Mona Lucy or something like that.

"From God, Brigit."

Ah, well, there was no understanding grown-ups. Even Sister Mary Agnes, though the sister was better than most adults, in Brigit's estimation. She rolled over, sliding her storybook under her pillow as she did every night, and pulled the worn blanket up over her shoulder.

"You're a blessing, child. You've brought an honest to goodness miracle right here to May-bourne Row. In a shelter nearly falling down around our ears, beside a church with chipped paint and folding chairs instead of pews. A miracle, Brigit."

But Brigit was tired, and thought Sister Mary Agnes was overreacting a little. Or maybe she sensed that Brigit's belief in the *Fairytale* was getting shaky, and now she was trying to invent a new one. Give her something else to hang on to. How could a picture be a miracle, anyway?

"Sleep, love. And tomorrow we'll show your painting to Father Anthony. He'll know what to do."

She crossed herself before leaving in a rustle of black fabric.

Only, for Sister Mary Agnes, tomorrow never came.

Bridín

~❦~

March 21, 1978
Binghamton, NY
9:00 p.m.

BIG GUYS ALL dressed in black stood around the place like sentries guarding a border. One in the hallway outside her rooms. Two outdoors, below her bedroom window. Bridín didn't mind them. They treated her like gold, being that she still wore her pendant. They didn't dare do otherwise. If any of those dark ones tried to hurt her—if they so much as touched her—they'd suffer. Die maybe. She couldn't be sure, since none of them had ever tried. They were afraid of her, those big, dark beings. So the Dark Prince had needed mortals to care for her. Weak ones, whose minds he could control.

The nurse, Kate, of course, had no idea who the guards really were or who they worked for. She simply believed what she'd been told, that Bridín was sickly, and not quite right, and needed constant guarding and protection and

care. Her kindness to Bridín didn't come from fear, the way *theirs* did. Hers came from her heart. She was good inside. Bridín was surprised the Dark Prince would tolerate her presence.

But he did, and Kate adored her, was constantly trying to please her. Always bringing games and toys for her. Making sure she got to eat the things she liked, and often sneaking in ice cream for dessert. She even rented film reels and a projector now and then, and showed Disney movies on the stark, white wall of her room. But even so, Kate couldn't see the truth. Despite all Bridín's efforts to reach her, her mind remained clouded by the Dark Prince's magic.

They'd let her keep her book. They'd had no choice about that, because it was protected by magic. They couldn't touch it anymore than they could touch her. Even though poor, confused Uncle Matt still believed it was the book that had driven her insane in the first place.

She wasn't insane. And she knew that Uncle Matt was no longer thinking for himself. His mind was just as weak as Kate's had been, that was all. It had been easy for the Dark Prince to take over, so she couldn't hate her uncle too much. He'd tried to give her a home after her adopted parents had been killed. And really, if she'd only been older and wiser, she would have known better than to make such a fuss when her dreams told her their car accident had been no accident. That the Dark Prince was behind all of it. That he was trying to orchestrate things so that Bridín would never be able to return to Rush. Really dumb of her to blurt all that. But she'd only been eight then. And the

visions . . . the memories had come as a terrible surprise.

She was older and wiser now. Nine. And she knew better than to try to explain her visions to just anyone. Better she not even admit to them, when she could hide it, since doing so only re-inforced Uncle Matt's belief in her insanity.

So Uncle Matt went about his business, which took him all over the world, and Bridín rarely saw him. He was convinced he was providing the best possible care for his poor, confused little niece. Convinced by the control the Dark Prince exerted over his mind. As for Bridín, she re-mained here, a prisoner in her uncle's home, held captive by forces her uncle didn't even be-lieve could exist.

She was wiser now. Wise enough to know she had to bide her time. She'd just stay here until she was old enough to return to Rush. She'd just pretend to have resigned herself to life as an in-mate in her own bedroom. At least that way, her enemies would have no reason to take further action. And it wasn't as if she could leave here, even if she tried. Oh, the others could come and go as they pleased. The unaware mortals could cross through the invisible barrier the Dark Prince had erected around this place, and not even feel it there. And those men in black, the prince's henchmen brought over from the other side, could pass freely as well. Evil didn't harm evil. But no fairy could pass. The force of the negativity would crush her. The house that looked to mortal eyes like any other house was in truth a pretty cell to Bridín. But when the time was right, she'd find a way to escape.

She looked across the table at Raze, who'd been sitting in quiet contemplation of the Monopoly board for some time now. Of the handful of mortals in her uncle's employ, he was the only one not completely blinded by the Dark Prince's spell. She'd reached Raze, enchanted him, and gradually made him see the truth.

Who'd have believed the formerly homeless man, the bum who used to sleep in the park across from the orphanage, would turn out to be the strongest of them all?

"Aren't you gonna shake the dice? It's your move, you know."

Razor-Face Malone snapped to attention and ran one hand over his graying stubble. "Sorry." He scooped up the dice and tossed them. Then promptly moved the boot, which was her token, instead of the race car, which was his.

Bridín covered his hand with hers. "Raze, what's the matter? I know something is."

His pale blue eyes met hers. So sad! Bridín felt a shiver go up her spine, but ignored it. Nervously, she fingered her pendant, sliding it back and forth on its thin silver chain.

"Okay," he said softly. "I'll tell you. I have to, sooner or later. Bridey . . ." He looked straight into her eyes. "I'm leaving. They're sending me away, tonight."

She felt her eyes widen, felt them burn. "Leaving?"

He nodded, looking as upset by this as she was.

"But Raze, you can't! Where will you go? What will you do?"

He smiled, to reassure her, she knew. "Just

like you to worry more about old Raze than yourself," he told her. "I'll manage. I got by just fine before, and I can do it again."

Swallowing her tears, Bridín brought her chin up, forced a smile. Tried not to think about Raze returning to the life he'd led before he'd been brought here. A lonely man scraping a living from the streets. He was older now. He'd never survive that way again. "Well," she whispered. "It was only a matter of time before they wised up. I should have been expecting this."

"Yeah." He put the boot back where it had been, and moved his race car.

"Are you in danger, Raze? Do you think *he* knows your mind isn't his anymore?"

Raze gnawed his lower lip for a moment. "I think he suspects that his hold on me is slipping. I think he believes he's getting rid of me before you have a chance to get through." He met her eyes, gave his head a shake. "But you did, Bridey. I know the truth. I won't let him brainwash me again."

"I know."

Raze reached a hand across the table, covered hers with it. "I'd rather be shot than leave you. You know that. I'd stay if I could."

"I know that, too." Bridín would not cry in front of Raze.

Though he was like a grandfather to her, he was as much a child as she was—more so, in a lot of ways. She loved him. Crying would only hurt him more, and she refused to do that. "We'll see each other again," she told him.

"Sure we will. I'm not going far, you know. I'll stay close, try to find a way to see you, make

sure you're okay. I just don't know why he had
to catch on."

Bridín shrugged. "Me neither, Raze. But
everything happens for *some* reason, right?
Maybe . . ." She let her words trail off, and
vaguely knew the dice she'd been holding had
fallen to the floor. But she wasn't seeing them.
She wasn't seeing anything that was here or
now. Instead, she saw flames. She heard cries.
And she knew something she hadn't known before.

"Bridey? Baby, you okay?" Raze was there on
her side of the table now, gripping her shoulders. She ought to be smelling the minty oint-
ment he used for his achy joints, but she was
smelling smoke instead. Raze yelled for Kate,
but she barely heard that beyond the roaring
and crackling of the flames, and the screams of
the children. She knew she was shaking all over
and staring off into space. She felt the sweat
trickling down her face, and stinging her eyes.
She screamed, very loudly, shrilly, endlessly.
And she knew it was her voice, but it didn't feel
as if it was. She felt apart, separate, as the vision
unfolded in her mind. Episodes like this one
were what had made her uncle question her sanity in the first place, and left him ripe for the
subtle influence of the Dark Prince's power. But
she watched the vision, despite her terror of it.
She explored its every aspect.

Kate's gentle hand gripped her arm, and she
felt the sharp jab of a needle. It overwhelmed
the feeling of that searing heat on her skin. And
in a few seconds, the vision faded away.

It was such a silly way to treat people of
magic, she thought, as the drug began to fog her

mind. She knew it was happening to others, in other places. The mortal world just didn't understand them, so they locked them up, and labeled them crazy, and tried to medicate their visions away. Made no sense at all.

The nurse was picking her up, but she squirmed, reaching for Raze.

"Please," she heard him say. "Let me."

And then she was shifted into his bony arms. Good. She had to talk to him, and she wouldn't be awake much longer.

"I know the reason," she whispered, hooking her arms around his neck, resting her head on his shoulder.

He stopped walking and looked down at her. Of all the people in the world, Raze was the only one she dared share her visions with. Because he was the only one who no longer discounted them as imaginary. He was the only one she trusted not to report all she said back to the Dark Prince. He'd seen her book, too. He'd told her he thought it was something sacred.

"It's my sister, Raze. Just like in the story. She's real. I . . . wasn't sure before, but now I know."

"Another vision?" he asked, and his voice was a low whisper. He started walking again, staying a few steps behind Kate as he carried Bridín from her playroom, through the double doors and into the room where her bed lay waiting.

"She's in danger," Bridín rasped. "You have to go to her, Raze. You have to save her. Tonight."

The old man blinked, but she didn't see disbelief in his eyes. Only surprise.

"She's still at the orphanage. St. Mary's. You remember. There isn't much time."

Raze nodded.

"You have to believe me, Raze. It's real. I know it is."

One of his hands smoothed her hair. "Now haven't I always believed you?" His smile reassured her, and she relaxed a little. "I'll see she's all right, Bridey. Don't you worry."

Bridín's eyes fell closed, but she popped them open again. "She doesn't know . . . about me . . . and you can't tell her. Not yet."

"But—"

"If she tries to come to me now, they'll get her. They'll find a way to get her locked up somewhere, like me. They'll think she remembers, and they'll do anything to stop her if they believe she might try to go back."

Raze didn't ask who "they" were. He knew. Bridín sensed he'd understood everything she'd ever told him. She didn't know how she'd broken through the Dark Prince's spell over him, but she was sure she had.

"But what about you, Bridey?"

She sniffed, lifted a hand to stroke his whiskers. He was lowering her into her bed now. She didn't want to let go of him. But she had to. "Keep her away from me, Raze. It's me they're watching. I'm the one they see as a threat right now, not Brigit. We have to keep it that way."

"But—"

"When the time is right, I'll know. And I'll get a message to you both. I'll send you some kind of sign. I'll know how to find you. You know I will. I can do it."

Raze nodded as the nurse came to the other side of the bed to pull the covers over her.

"Poor little thing, always ranting like this," Kate said softly, her cool palm stroking Bridín's forehead. "She thinks she's some kind of fairy, you know."

And Raze nodded, because he knew it was what was expected of him, and one never knew who might be watching. "I know. It's a shame."

"Just when we think she's coming out of it, another delusional episode," Kate went on, and she lovingly tucked the covers around Bridín.

"Come on, Raze," she said when she'd finished. "Time for you to go. Bridey needs to rest."

Bridín met Raze's eyes, and nodded. "Go. Go to her. Do it for me."

He nodded back at her, then turned to Kate. "Be kind to her," he said, and there was no plea in his voice. More like a command. It was very unlike his usual, gentle tone.

"She's my special angel, Raze. I'll take good care of her. Go on, now. Mr. Darque is waiting downstairs with your last week's pay."

"Darque?" Bridín whispered, her eyes widening a bit, though she was barely awake now. "He's here?" He, like Uncle Matt, rarely put in an appearance. Bridín knew why. He was busy running the kingdom of Rush. *Her* kingdom.

Raze turned back to Bridín. "Don't worry, Bridey," he whispered. "He can't hurt you. You know that."

"I know . . ."

"If you need me, child . . ."

"I'll let you know. I promise." Her eyes fell closed, at last.

Darque

RAZOR-FACE MALONE WAS gone. Expelled, because his will had been stronger than Darque
had realized. Malone had been quietly repelling
the spell for some time now, and Darque would
have known that, had he been here. The fools
he'd left to watch over things should have seen
it, sensed it. But of course, they hadn't.

Maybe the child had got through to Malone.
Unlikely, but possible, Darque knew. He probably should have simply killed the old man.
Would have . . . but the child adored him. Killing Malone would only solidify that fairy child's
hatred of him. And that was not the plan. Not
at all.

He'd keep her here, his prisoner, until the
fight had gone out of her. And then he'd use
her. He'd use her to regain control of the kingdom he saw as rightfully his own. The kingdom
his family had been banished from a thousand
years ago. Banished. Condemned to life in a part
of Rush where the sun's light never ventured.
Renamed, even. The family name dropped, out-

lawed, forgotten. They'd become the Dark Ones.

Darque stood over the bed of the sleeping child, and looked down at her. He shouldn't do so. It was unwise, because looking at her beautiful, innocent face might soften his heart, and he could not afford to allow that to happen.

When his father's armies had stormed the kingdom of Rush nearly a decade ago, the fay king had been defeated at last. This child's mother, heir to the throne, had been killed. And the twin daughters, next in line, driven from the realm of magic altogether. But his own father had lost his life in that battle as well, and still they hadn't regained power in Rush. Oh, he held the throne, yes. But there was constant rebellion. Countless pockets of those loyal to the fay, hidden in the forests, always stirring the citizens to battle.

He wanted his rule solidified, dammit. He wanted power over all of them, and he wanted peace. A verdant land filled with citizens who'd be loyal to him unto the point of death.

And he'd have it. He'd have all of that, and more.

He'd have it, because he had her. She'd return to Rush, one day, though she believed it his desire never to let her. The only way she could return would be at the side of her twin sister. Such was the way of the magic, that the twins could only reenter Rush if they did so together. Which was why he must keep them apart, just until the time was right.

They'd return, though, eventually. This one ... he looked down at her golden curls again, and quickly averted his eyes, hardened his

heart. This one would return at the point of his sword. He'd find a way to liberate her of that enchanted pendant, and she'd no longer have any protection from him. He'd have her kneeling at his feet, for all the kingdom to see. And then those damned fay folk would bow to him as well . . .

. . . or watch their precious princess die.

Brigit

April 1988
A Brooklyn slum

TEN YEARS HAD come and gone for Brigit since
that horrible night. Ten years, and she'd been
living on the streets with the homeless people
like her. She was nineteen, now, but God, she
felt so much older. Older than Raze. Older than
Sister Mary Agnes had been.

Brigit remembered it as if it were yesterday,
every word, every line in Sister Mary Agnes's
face, and the sound of her aged voice rustling
like dried leaves at the hand of the wind, as she
read that ridiculous *Fairytale* night after night.
Brigit still knew every word by heart.
Sometimes she'd open the book, reading it in a
whisper late at night when she couldn't sleep,
and she'd imagine Sister Mary Agnes there beside the bed, draped in that black habit from
head to toe.

So many vivid impressions, all instigated by
one tiny scrap of paper. Why had she saved the
thing anyway?

Against her will, Brigit scanned the clipping, reading the words again, reminding herself why she had to go through with this scheme of Mel's. Her hands trembled, and tears blurred her vision, but she blinked and made herself read.

"Fire swept through St. Mary's last night, destroying the church and leaving the children's shelter heavily damaged. So far only one death is reported, that of Sister Mary Agnes Brockway, seventy-two, formerly of Queens. One child is still listed as missing, and Father Anthony Giovanni, parish priest, theorizes the nine-year-old girl ran away in panic. He does not believe the child's body will be recovered by fire fighters as they search the premises today. 'Brigit is a special little girl,' he told reporters at the scene this morning. 'Too special to be taken like this.' "

Special?

Brigit folded the yellowed newspaper clipping exactly the way it had been folded before, and returned it to its spot in the bottom of the cardboard box where she kept her clothes. The physical act of putting it away helped her to put away the memories as well. None of them mattered. Not now. They might as well be as fictional as the *Fairytale* that lay in the box beside the clipping. The elaborate creation of some kind soul determined to placate a lonely little girl.

Sister Mary Agnes herself might have created the book, for all Brigit knew.

She'd called Brigit's talent a gift. A miracle.

"If she could see me now, she'd turn over in her grave."

"What's that?"

Brigit turned, looking through the sagging

doorway with its peeling gray casing. The folding card table in the next room seemed to be holding Raze up as much as the stool beneath him. Even beyond the stubble, and in the shadow of his ever-present Mets cap, she could see the grayish tinge to his face. The green shirt that had once been part of someone named Bob's uniform, hung on Raze as if he were a stick figure. He coughed, and Brigit thought the rickety table would collapse.

She swallowed her doubts, lifted her chin, and went to him, running her hands over his frail back until the spasm passed. He was old. When had Raze become so old? He'd always been the strong one, he'd always been the one to take care of her, right from the start. That awful night at St. Mary's when all the other children had obeyed the sisters and joined hands and made their way out of the burning shelter. All but Brigit. She'd let go. She'd gone back, looking for Sister Mary Agnes. And she'd ended up trapped in an inferno more terrifying than anything that Dante fellow had dreamed of.

Her hands tightened on Raze's frail shoulders. He'd heard her screams that night. He'd come after her. Somehow, a man she assumed was one of the bums who slept in the park across the street, had pulled her out of that hell. And she'd been with Raze ever since. She'd been convinced that because he'd saved her from the fire, because he'd taken her from the orphanage, that somehow made her his little girl. And she'd loved the old man with all her heart from the instant he'd rescued her. He'd wanted to return her to Father Anthony. But she'd cried and

pleaded and begged to stay with Raze, and he'd
been too soft-hearted to send her back.

Razor-Face Malone had become the only family she'd ever had. He'd saved her life. So now
she'd do what she had to do to save his.

"Come on, Brigit," Mel called from his spot
in the corner. "Break's over."

She nodded in response to the slightly whiny
voice. Mel sat on the bare floor, back against the
naked lath wall, legs crossed. His gray chauf-
feur's cap was too big for his puny head, but
managed to look jaunty anyway. And besides,
it covered the bald spot.

"The quicker you finish up, the quicker you
get a warm bed and some medicine for Raze."

"You don't have to keep reminding me of
that."

"I think I do," Mel said, getting to his feet.
"Hell, with your talent, you should have been
into this scam years ago. You could'a been *rich*
by now." He gave a sharp, slanting nod and a
wink. "You stick with me, and you'll get that
way soon enough. I got *connections* now."

"No."

He shrugged and paced the room. He was
better off than she and Raze. But he got that way
because he was a crook. Oh, she knew, she
wasn't much better herself. But aside from
pinching a few groceries and a wallet here and
there, she'd been fairly honest, out of respect for
Sister Mary Agnes, and the things the nun had
taught her. *Not* for any other reason. Not because of morality or values. Hell, with the way
the world treated people like her and Raze, she

didn't figure she owed anyone anything. She'd do what she had to do to survive.

And when she wasn't surviving, she'd race through the alleys and vault mesh fences and cartwheel in the gutters. Because she had to. Raze said she had too much energy and she'd explode if she didn't let it out.

Not today, though. Today she was tossing Sister Mary Agnes's teachings aside, using all that pent-up energy to make her hands obey her mind. She was taking the step that would brand her as much a criminal as Mel was. And still, there were men far worse. At least Mel had never *hurt* anybody. His game was the con, though he had yet to score big, as he put it. Deep inside, Mel was good. If Brigit didn't believe that so firmly, she wouldn't be doing this.

Lately, though, he'd been keeping some bad company. These *connections* he kept talking about. One of them was a man named Zaslow, a man Brigit knew was evil just by looking at him—as if she really were half-fay and could read a man's heart by plumbing the depths of his eyes. This entire scam had been Zaslow's idea. Fencing stolen artwork was, Mel claimed, Zaslow's specialty. So when Mel had offhandedly mentioned Brigit's "gift" in one of his endless efforts to impress the man, a plot had been born.

Raze coughed again, and Brigit caught her breath. He was getting worse.

"I know, I know," Mel said, a touch of mockery in his voice. "You're only doing it this one time. You keep telling me. But you wait 'til you have that money in your hands, kid. You wait

'til you *smell* that green, and then we'll see if you're so damn noble.''

Brigit closed her eyes. There was no sense talking to Mel. He'd been a small-time con all his life, and he'd convinced himself she was his ticket to wealth untold.

But she vowed, she *swore* on Sister Mary Agnes's memory, that she would only do it once. Just this one time, and only because Raze's life depended on it. She didn't like being even remotely involved with a man like Zaslow. It made her feel soiled and low.

Raze hadn't wanted her to do it, even this one time. He'd fought tooth and nail against her going along with this thing. He said it was wrong, plain and simple. But Brigit didn't see that she had any choice in the matter. Raze was dying.

He was dying. That talent she had for seeing things in a man's eyes had shown her that when she'd looked into Raze's. And she'd known then that she'd do whatever it took to save him.

She sighed and crossed the floor of the condemned apartment to the easel that seemed as out of place here in this ruin as a diamond in a dimestore. A color print of the Matisse was Scotch-taped to the crumbling wall. She clamped her jaw against the memories the sight of it evoked; memories of Mona Lisa on construction paper, hanging crookedly above a small wooden bed, and of the awed expression Sister Mary Agnes wore when she stared at it. Better not to let the thought of that horrible night enter her mind now, or her hands would

start shaking. She had to finish. Now, while the afternoon sun was still slanting in through the broken windows, giving her so much light to work by.

Brigit drew a breath, squared her shoulders, took one last glance at the Matisse nude, and then surveyed what she'd done so far on canvas. It would be a perfect likeness. She didn't know how she knew that, she simply did. And she didn't know how she could wield the brushes and match the colors the way she did, either. There was no technique to it. She'd never had an art lesson in her life. She just studied the image she wanted, kept it focused in her mind's eye, and . . . and painted.

Raze coughed again, a deep, racking cough that sounded painful. Brigit picked up a palette and a brush.

Bridín

—·—

1995

IT WAS TIME.

Bridín knew it, sensed it the way birds sense the proper time to migrate. It was time to get out of this place. It was time to find her way back to Rush.

She needed help. She needed her sister and Raze. The time had come to get a message to them. And the method came to her just as easily as the knowledge did. Brigit might not understand it, when she saw it. But Raze would. And he'd know the time had come. And even if he didn't, it wouldn't matter. Bridín would simply send the message on its way with a fairy's wish clinging to its tail, and the same protective spell as the one cast by her mother over her book and her pendant, coating it like fairydust to keep the Dark Prince from going anywhere near it.

When she'd finished perfecting every last detail of the intricate painting that would be her message to her sister, Bridín clasped her pewter

37

fairy pendant in her right hand, lifted it, and pointed its quartz crystal toward the canvas. In a strong, steady voice, she chanted:

> *"By the powers of the fay*
> *Darker forces, keep at bay.*
> *To my sister, wilt thou flee*
> *Bring my Brigit back to me!"*

Bridín felt the magic surge through her, down her arm into her hand, and from her hand into the crystal. It zapped from the glowing stone— a pale amber ray of light that suffused the entire painting for just an instant, and then vanished. Bridín sank into her bed, exhausted.

There. It was done. Soon she'd be with Brigit again. And together, they'd find a way for Bridín to get back to Rush. They'd raise up an army there, and they'd send the Dark Prince back into the far reaches of the forests where he belonged. She'd free her people from his evil rule. She would.

PART TWO

If This
Be Magic . . .

Chapter One

❦

Present day

"I'M TERRIBLY SORRY, Mr. Reid. I didn't know."

Adam got to his feet, carefully lifting the painting, his hands touching nothing but the frame. He eased it back onto its hook above the golden oak mantel. Then nudged it a millimeter at a time until it hung perfectly straight.

Damn cleaning service. Damn strangers, sometimes a different one every week, coming in to clean the place. You could tell them a hundred times, leave them a thousand notes, and they would still forget. He missed the old days. He missed the full-time maid he'd had to let go. He missed having enough money to pay for her even more.

Hell, he was only hanging on to the house by a thread. But to lose it would be to admit defeat ... defeat to a man he'd learned to despise. And that was something he couldn't do.

He didn't care to analyze his other reasons for clinging to this oversized money drain. Like the

woods out back, it was something he didn't care to explore further.

He turned to the woman who was still trembling a little in reaction to his bellow when he'd walked into the study to see his prized possession on the floor. "No one," he said slowly, resisting the urge to snatch the brass-handled poker from the rack of implements near his side, and shake it in her face. "*No one* touches this painting. Tell your boss that if one of her people forget that again, I'll . . ."

He gave his head a shake. He sounded like an obsessed fool. Then again, that was exactly what he was, wasn't he? "Never mind. Just get the hell out of here."

"Yes, Mr. Reid. I'm sorry. I wasn't told."

She backed through the tall double doors, pulling them closed, probably in a huge rush to get out of his sight. He couldn't blame her, could he?

He swallowed the panic he'd felt when he'd first come into the room to see the bare spot on the stucco wall above the fireplace. Everything else had been in place. The brass candle holders and the antique Navajo pottery on the mantel didn't seem to have been moved. He bit his lip, and stared up at the painting. He ought to get rid of the damned thing before it drove him completely nuts. Short trip, he knew, but there was no sense rushing it. Getting this thing out of his sight might slow the deterioration of his common sense considerably. But he couldn't sell the painting. He wouldn't.

It wasn't the quality of the work that had so captured him the first time he'd seen it hanging

in the Capricorn Gallery on the Commons a year ago. Though it was very good, it was the subject that enchanted him.

A forest where flowers unlike anything real bloomed in riots of color. Where every boulder and every pebble were gemstones. Every swirl of tree bark, a work of art. Hidden among the twisting foliage, timid creatures of no known species peered at the spectacle in the central clearing. They only appeared when one looked at the painting from just the right angle. He'd owned it for weeks before he'd spotted all of them . . . and he wondered even now if there were more to be discovered. In the distance one could see towering castle spires, gleaming like silver beneath a jewel-blue sky. And in the clearing, in the very center, a pool of crystalline water with dense green reeds concealing the woman who bathed there. She was only a hazy outline. Tiny bits of flesh visible here and there between the reeds, slanted ebony brush strokes for her eyes, and swirling ones for her long, untamed hair. None connected. Just bits. An abstract figure. Scattered jet and peach-toned pieces of a jigsaw puzzle. But if you stood back and squinted, you could almost see her.

And when you looked at her that way, she seemed to be looking back.

When he'd first laid eyes on the painting, he'd wondered if maybe he was finally having the breakdown he'd been expecting for so long. But that concern hadn't stopped him from buying it. Nor had his shortage of funds.

The woman . . . and the place. The mythical forest where she bathed. They were the ones

he'd seen in that ridiculous dream he'd had
when he'd been . . . what? Seven? Didn't matter.
He'd been convinced it hadn't been a dream at
all. That he'd actually visited this place while he
was on one of his reckless treks into the forest.
He'd been convinced for a time that he'd stumbled upon some secret doorway to an enchanted
glade. That he'd talked to a fairy. That he'd seen
his own future.

Unfortunately, he'd felt compelled to run his
mouth about it until his mother had suggested
therapy and his father had taken the strap. . . .

Smack!

*You're a man, Adam. My son, do you understand
that?*

Smack!

A man does not believe in fairytales!

Smack!

*A man knows the difference between the truth and
make-believe!*

Smack!

Do you think you know the difference now, Adam?
Yes!

*I don't. But you will, Adam, you will if I have to
take every bit of hide off your ass. You will.*

Smack! Smack! Smack!

"Mr. Reid?"

The woman's voice broke the memory. Adam
carefully unclenched his fists, stopped grating
his teeth, reminded himself that the stench of
stale liquor on hot breath wasn't real. He
blinked twice, and shrugged it off as easily as
he always did. It was no big deal. It didn't
bother him anymore. Not in the least. His father's brutal methods had made Adam tough, and

they'd certainly taught him the difference between fantasy and reality. Dear old Dad. Probably didn't even realize he'd done Adam a favor
by being so cruel. He hadn't hung around long
enough to see the results. He'd sold everything
he owned, including the house and property,
and he'd walked out on his wife and only son.

But Adam had his revenge, sort of. He'd made
his own money, bought the place back. Brought
his mother here to live out her days in peace,
without a hard-drinking, hard-hitting husband
to worry about. She'd died here, and Adam
liked to think she'd died content. But he knew
deep down, she'd never got over her husband's
betrayal.

He knew exactly how she'd felt. Because the
fact was, he was on the verge of losing it all over
again, due to a remarkably similar kind of betrayal.

But he wasn't going to think about his ex-wife
or her uncanny similarities to his old man right
now, either. Right now he was thinking about
that damned dream. Hell, that's what he spent
most of his time thinking about.

His childhood dream had to have had a basis
in something he'd read or heard somewhere.
And Adam's obsession to find the myth or tale
that was its source had made him one of this
country's top experts on fantasy and myth. Hell,
he'd made a career out of the knowledge he'd
gained. He'd published books on the subject of
fairytales and their origins.

But even so, he'd never found the story that
must have inspired his dream.

Or the woman.

Though he knew it had all been nothing more than a fantasy, he'd let the search for its source consume him. What could a seven-year-old have seen or read or heard that would have instigated a dream that real? That vivid? So lucid he'd been sure it hadn't been a dream at all. There had to have been *something*.

When he'd seen the painting, he'd become more convinced of that than ever. Someone else knew about this mythical land. Certainly the artist knew. Even knew the name of the forest in Adam's dream. At the bottom of the painting, cleverly woven into the lush greenery so that it was all but hidden, was a single word. And Adam supposed most people would have assumed it was the artist's signature, if they'd even been able to discern it. But Adam knew better. The word at the bottom was *Rush*.

No myths or legends he'd studied had come close to describing the land he'd believed he'd visited back then, or the woman he'd seen. None mentioned this forest of Rush by name. His obsession to find the source of that fantasy grew stronger every day. Christ, he ought to be grateful for his father's stern intervention, or he might be a *real* basket case by now, as real as the dream had seemed to him at the time.

He looked at the painting again, and again a small chill raced up his spine at the powerful similarities to his childhood delusion. The artist had captured Adam's dream right down to the tiniest detail. Right down to the pictures in the tree bark. Right down to the hypnotic power of the woman's eyes.

Somewhere, there was an explanation for all

of that. And if it took the rest of his life, Adam would find it.

No time to dwell on it now though. He had a class in twenty minutes.

"So, according to this ancient Celtic manuscript, what characteristics would you expect to find in your average fay-female? If you read the assigned chapters, you'll know this stuff. Come on."

Adam sat on the edge of his desk, watching hands pop up all over the room. This group was nothing if not enthusiastic. Even if they were a bit too imaginative for his tastes.

"Miss Monroe, let's hear your opinion."

The twenty-year-old aspiring swimsuit model beamed at him, shifted in her seat, her skirt sliding a little higher on her thighs. Nice thighs, too. She was taking this class for easy credits. He let her get away with it mainly for the view. Carla Monroe bending over was a rewarding experience.

She ran a finger along the scooped neckline of her blouse, tracing her cleavage, drawing his eye.

He wondered if she was more interested in screwing him for the challenge or for the grade. Had to be something. It was always something where women were concerned, wasn't it?

"They're brimming with energy," she said slowly, drawing the words out. "Particularly *sexual* energy."

Too bad she was a pink slip waiting to happen, or he might oblige her. Too bad he needed his tenure here so damned badly. A year ago, it

wouldn't have mattered. A year ago, he'd had money to burn. Or he'd thought he had. He'd been blissfully unaware of the ways his young wife had of moving money around. By the time Sandra and Adam's pal Rob had sailed for parts unknown, they'd taken him for damn near every penny.

The only thing in this world worse than a thief, he mused, was a female thief. A beautiful female thief. A beautiful, ruthless female thief who didn't bat an eye at the prospect of ripping out your guts along with your money.

He swallowed hard, but the bitterness remained like bile in his mouth. "True, Miss Monroe. This work suggests that. What else?" He glanced around the room. "Michael?"

"Their power over mortal men is the most interesting thing," Michael said. He took his wire rims off as he spoke, twirled them between his fingers, then slipped them back on. "That one passage was . . . almost scary."

A murmur of laughter rose from the students. Adam flipped open the book and read aloud. "Many a man has died of longing for one such as her. For her skin has the flavor of honey which contains a magic all its own. Once a man's lips taste her nectar, he is bound to her for all his days. Be forewarned, then, for her spell cannot be broken. Look for the sign . . . the sign of the cradle moon above the mound of Venus. Be it pale, you might yet escape with your heart and mind intact. But be it crimson, she is of royal blood, and too strong for a mortal man's resistance. Even a glimpse into the eyes of such a one may spell your ruin. For if she looks upon

you with longing, your days are numbered. Run while you can, 'ere she captures your soul and leaves your body vacant, to waste away unto death with longing for a love you can never have."

The laughter died as he read, and when Adam looked up, it was to see rapt interest on the faces of his students. And someone whispered, "Maybe it's not a myth."

"Yeah," someone else stated, forgetting all about waiting to be called on. "Hell, you said this Celtic text is, what? Nine hundred years old? Maybe it's . . . you know . . . nonfiction."

The murmur of agreement that rose in the room made Adam grate his teeth. Then he stopped grating them, and the book in his hand hit the desk with a bang worthy of any shotgun. "For crying out loud! You—" His reproval was interrupted by the ping of the little timer bell he kept on his desk. He sighed, lowering his head, drawing a new, calming breath. Reminding himself they were just kids.

He'd been a kid once. He'd had some pretty farfetched notions himself.

Not gonna think about that. Not now.

"Okay, time's up. What do you say tomorrow you come in here with some *intelligent* theories, hmm? Like maybe, what sources the author might have drawn on to come up with his version of fairy lore."

He closed the book, turned his back, dismissing them with the gesture. But the exodus was quieter than usual. Calmer, and he peered over his shoulder to see intense expressions on many young faces. Christ, they weren't actually con-

sidering the possibility the text was anything but fiction, were they?

Imagination could be taken too far. It could be dangerous.

It can leave bruises, right Adam?

Shut the hell up.

Not to mention obsessions. Like your obsession.

He ignored the voice in his mind. The one that sounded like his father's voice. It didn't bother him again, as he dropped the heavy book into his briefcase, followed by a file folder full of essays and the wind-up timer. Which left the desktop as barren as the surface of the moon. Clean. Orderly. The way he liked it. He locked the drawers, pocketed the key.

His own theory was that the newly translated discourse on the qualities of fay folk was a collage of other myths and legends. Some imaginative soul had picked bits and pieces from stories he'd heard, and put them together to make his own version. It had the flavor of classical Greek tales of sirens, luring sailors to their deaths with the beauty of their songs. Maybe there had been a little Arthurian inspiration, as well. The Lady of the Lake with her ethereal beauty, nearly human in appearance, but too beautiful to be mortal.

Adam grinned a little as he thought there may be a bit of succubus lore tossed in for good measure. Drawing a man's soul from his body into her own, leaving him to wither and die of longing for her. Sounded like a new spin on a succubus to him. Hell of a way to go, too.

He set the case on the shiny surface of the desk, deciding to list his possible sources on the

board for discussion in tomorrow's class. No doubt once he got the ball rolling, the kids would come up with several more. He turned around, picked up a new piece of chalk, and began writing in bold, noisy strokes across the spotless blackboard. SIREN, he wrote. And beneath it, SUCCUBUS, and beneath that, LADY OF THE LA—

He paused with the chalk a hairsbreadth away from the board. A tiny chill crossed his nape, cold fingers spreading down into his spine, and he knew he was no longer alone. He turned his head, then his body. A woman stood in front of his desk. And there was something . . . familiar about her. Something he couldn't quite put his finger on.

His gaze dropped slowly to the spot about hip level where pale denim crawled tightly into the juncture of her thighs. Then it rose, over the barest glimpse of smooth-skinned belly where the blouse didn't quite reach the jeans. He saw her navel, and he thought of honey.

Man, he'd been too long without sex.

He told himself to look up faster, but his stubborn eyes continued the slow scrutiny and he realized he was secretly savoring it. He wasn't normally such a hound. She must be emitting some kind of musk that spoke directly to his libido. She could be a troll for all he knew. He hadn't taken more than a brief glance at her face yet. Because, hell, why rush it? The black t-shirt fit her as if it were made of spandex. It molded and hugged her high, round breasts. And Adam figured if she didn't want to be looked at, she wouldn't be wearing it. So he looked. And then

he moved up a notch, to see the pendant around her neck. A pewter fairy, wrapped seductively around a quartz crystal point.

He lifted his brows, wondering if she were a new-age yuppie or a potential student. If she were a student he probably shouldn't be eating her alive with his eyes right now. Because she might be one of those types who screamed sexual harassment if a man so much as crooked an eyebrow in her direction, and she might get him fired. No fear of that with Carla Monroe. She practically begged to be looked at. But this woman might be different.

The thought gave him the jolt he needed to bring his gaze up where it belonged. To her face.

But then his mouth went dry. A fist seemed to drive itself into his gut, forcing all the air from his lungs in a harsh, noisy exhale. Because she was incredible, and because her eyes sucked him in like quicksand, and because he had the oddest feeling that he knew her. Or should know her. Or . . . or *something*.

Her eyes were hidden behind small round wire-rims, but they were still huge and dark and exotically slanted. The glasses did nothing to conceal their almond shape or invisible power. Ebony. He couldn't tell the pupils from the irises. A fringe of paintbrush-thick lashes surrounded them. Like black holes surrounded by cilia. They would entrap and absorb everything that came too close, and there would be no escape.

He blinked and shook himself, feeling awkward and even a little dizzy. As if he'd had a few too many drinks. Which made no sense at

all, since he'd had nothing stronger than coffee.

What the hell was the matter with him, anyway?

"Mr. Reid?"

He cleared his throat and told himself to get his act together. "Yes. What can I do for you?"

"I'd like to enroll in your class."

Several answers sprang to mind, the first and most obvious being that she ought to be in the admissions office and not in his classroom. The second being that she ought to be anywhere in the goddamn universe other than his classroom.

But what he said was, "Sorry. This class is full. Check back next semester." If he didn't know better, he'd almost think he was afraid of her. All five feet and possibly 100-pounds-soaking-wet of her.

When her gaze fell in apparent disappointment, he was finally able to look away from the eyes that had seemed to envelop him and hold him captive. To distance himself, take in the full picture of her face. Like stepping back for a better view of that painting he'd found at the Capricorn. Exactly like that. So much like that, he shivered involuntarily.

Her face was heart-shaped. Her hair, endless cascades of riotous, gleaming black curls. She could have been any age, nineteen to thirty-nine. Impossible to tell. One delicate hand rose, and she fingered the pendant she wore, moving it back and forth on its chain.

She was nervous.

"It's very important that I take this class," she said, and her voice reminded him of water chuckling over stones. Deep and smooth and re-

freshing. But he wasn't too entranced by it not to notice the silt of desperation stirring beneath the surface.

"Why?"

"I'm . . ." She lifted her chin, met his eyes again. "I'm . . . it doesn't matter . . ."

Her words trailed off, and she averted her eyes almost guiltily.

"This is going to sound like a line," he said slowly, ignoring every warning bell going off in his head, though they were damn near deafening. "But I have the feeling I know you. Have we met?"

"No."

When she wasn't looking at him, his equilibrium seemed to function just fine. "Now how can you be so sure? You haven't even told me your name."

She shook her head slowly, her raven hair falling over her face. "What does it matter? The class is full." She started to turn away.

And he felt an inexplicable urgency not to let her go. "Wait a minute," he said, and she stopped. "Look, you never know when someone will drop out. Give me your name. Your phone number . . ."

She lifted her gaze to his, and he went tongue-tied all over again, and was forced to let his words trail off.

"I know I've seen you before . . . somewhere," he whispered.

She narrowed those gleaming black eyes on him, and this time he got the feeling it was she who couldn't look away. He felt her try, then surrender. She stared into his eyes, and then a

tiny frown appeared between her dark brows, and she stared harder. Adam experienced the most peculiar sensation of . . . *invasion*.

And then her eyes widened.

Adam snapped his fingers and pointed at her. "Aha! You recognize me, too, don't you?"

She shook her head, taking a single backward step. "No."

"You do so. I can see it in your eyes. So come on, tell me, where did we meet?"

She closed her eyes, lowered her head. "It can't be . . ."

"Gee, was it that bad?" He dipped his head in an effort to see her downturned face, and tried to inject a little lightness, because frankly the woman looked as if she'd seen a ghost. "It *was* that bad? Hmm, maybe I'm better off not remembering."

"I have to go."

"Oh, come on. Give me another chance, huh? Isn't there a rule somewhere that says you can't blame a guy for stuff he doesn't even remember?"

She shook her head, turned toward the door.

"Okay, what if I can find a way to make room for you in the class?" Damn, what made him say that?

She went still, her back to him. And Adam had no idea why he felt such an incredible longing to go to her, to touch her. It was powerful stuff. Made him think of that damned text he'd just been reading to the students.

"I've . . . I've changed my mind," she said softly, her voice a little hoarse.

And it hit him then, clear as day, that she was

lying to him. She wanted *something*, all right, but taking his class wasn't it. No doubt in his mind. Though how he knew that, he still wasn't sure. What he did know was that nothing was more dangerous than a beautiful, dishonest woman. Especially one who looked the way she did. She was probably ruthless to the bone. Deadly to him. He felt her subtle threat right to his soul. But he felt this sudden, inexplicable allure, too.

Sirens and rocks, he reminded himself.

And even as he was nodding in agreement with his mind's silent warnings, his body was moving toward her. His hands were closing on her shoulders. "Tell me how you know me," he said softly. "It's gonna drive me nuts if I can't remember."

"I can't," she said as her chin fell to her chest. It was a whisper, so low he barely caught it. Something wasn't right here, and his curiosity rose up to challenge his wariness. It didn't put a dent in his attraction to this strange, familiar woman, though. "Maybe if you'd just tell me who you are . . ."

She turned to look up at him once more, shook her head from side to side, sparkling moisture adding a sheen to her eyes.

"Are those tears?" he asked her, running the tip of his thumb over her dampened cheek as his stomach clenched oddly at the sight of her crying. "Look, if there's something wrong, maybe I can—"

She lifted her hand, laid it gently upon his as he touched her face, and stared so deeply into his eyes, he felt his world begin to tilt on its axis. Very slowly, he trailed his fingertips down the

side of her face, tracing the curve of her cheekbone, and the hollow beneath it, and the line of
her jaw. And she closed her eyes, and he felt the
hand upon his tremble.

And then she jerked away, eyes flying wide.
"No," she whispered, and backed away as if his
touch burned her. Then even more softly she
said it again. "No. You'll be far better off if you
stay away from me, Adam Reid." She turned
and ran out of the room. And though she
seemed agitated, desperate to escape, Adam
later couldn't recall hearing her footfalls when
she raced down the hall. Which was odd, because footsteps in that hallway tended to echo
nonstop.

Chapter Two

◄►

HIM! MY GOD, it was him!

Brigit ran all the way to her car, but when she tried to fit her keys to the lock, she dropped them. And then she just stood there, fighting to control her suddenly rapid breathing. Her hands vibrated, and she braced them on the warm metal of the car, arms rigid, head lowering between them. She tried for a deep, steady breath but it became an open-mouthed gasp. Her heart hammered. Her pulse thundered in her ears.

This wasn't possible!

But it had happened. Only moments ago, she'd looked into the eyes of the man she'd dreamed about, on and off, for as long as she could remember. Always the same dream. It never changed, only grew longer, more intense. Her feelings about it had changed, though. They'd matured into something completely different. She used to look through the mists and see a troubled man, and she'd want to comfort him. But with the years, she'd seen so much more. Her dreams of him revealed a tortured

man. One in more pain than any human should
have to bear. And more. A virile man, with
enough passion in his eyes to burn her alive. A
man in need . . . of her. In every way a man
could need a woman.

All of that had been there, visible in his eyes,
in those dreams Brigit had always had. Dreams
where the fictional Máire had whispered that he
was her fate.

God, what did it all mean?

Those same things had been in his eyes again,
just now, when they'd met hers up there in that
classroom.

He needed her. And he didn't even know it.
Worse yet, she hadn't come to him to help
him. She'd come to hurt him even more than
he'd already been hurt.

God, what was happening? Had that lifelong
dream of hers been some kind of premonition?
Was there any such thing?

The very idea terrified her, so she put it from
her mind and tried to focus on simple things.
Immediate things. Crouching down to recover
the keys. The dirt and gravel she scraped up
along with them. Getting the door open. Ad-
justing the visor against the brilliant, late summer sunlight and slipping on her dark glasses.
Starting the motor.

She drove down the steep inclines of the university area's streets, then turned and headed
for the Commons. By the time she'd parked and
left the car, she was telling herself that there had
to be a way out of this mess. There had to be.
She and Raze hadn't come this far to have it all
ruined for them now.

This was maddening! She wanted to stand in the middle of the sidewalk and scream at the top of her lungs! She wanted to tug at her hair and spin in rapid circles until she fell to the ground from dizziness! She wanted to smash something!

What was she going to do?

She couldn't go through with it. Not now that she'd seen the man. Adam. His name was Adam Reid. His eyes were the deep, glittering blue of a midnight sea under a harvest moon, the dark, bottomless blue of sapphires, and when she'd looked into them she'd seen his very soul.

No. She wouldn't do it to him. She told herself that again and again as she stifled her maddening frustration and walked the last couple of blocks to the Commons. Then she paused, and stood still for a moment, eyes closed, head tilted slightly back. She listened, and she sniffed the air, waiting for the magic of this small strip to get to her, to calm her.

A hundred feet away, a jazz band played, and the saxophone solo wafted straight to heaven. When summer sighed, its warm breath brought the scents of fresh-baked doughnuts, because she was standing near the bakery, and more subtly, the scents of flowers. Violets and hyacinth.

That was better. Brigit opened her eyes, a little calmer now, a little less likely to smash the first breakable object she got her hands on out of sheer frustration. It wouldn't do. She had a reputation in this small college town. Among the merchants, she was liked and respected for her innovative ideas and determination to succeed.

Among the students, she was admired and sought after for long heart-to-hearts and advice. The town's residents saw her as a success story. A young single woman caring for her aging father, running a successful business, and doing both with ease. They called her a good example. An inspiration.

She'd fooled them all, hadn't she? No one who looked at her would see an orphan, much less a wild thing of the streets. No one would see an accomplished criminal, a master art forger who'd sold her soul to get where she was today. No one would see the wanton that lived inside. The feelings that burned in her sometimes late at night. The ones she doused and drowned and suffocated, only to have them return to haunt her over and over. The ones she'd never confessed to anyone. Not even Raze.

The ones instigated by those dreams of the man with the pain and the passion in his eyes. But she saw them. Her dreams of that man had grown up over the years. Now, when she dreamed of him, she went to him. And he looked up into her eyes and he knew her. She knew he did. He'd slowly get to his feet, and he'd reach for her, and she'd go slowly, willingly into his arms, tilting her head up for his kiss. Never a timid kiss. His mouth would cover hers, and his tongue would plunder, and his body would send silent messages to hers. He'd set fire to her blood as he kissed her. And in the blink of an eye, she'd see them naked, clinging to one another in a frenzy of lovemaking so intense it left her weak. She'd wake from those dreams breathless, shivering and damp with

sweat. And because the dreams kept coming, more often and more potent all the time, she knew the wanton inside her must be growing stronger and more restless.

Sister Mary Agnes would be appalled if she knew about those dreams. It was times like this that made Brigit glad her twin sister was only part of the *Fairytale*, and not a real woman. Certainly not the fair angel she'd become in Brigit's mind. The living, breathing image of feminine perfection. Of goodness.

Or if she were real, thank goodness she didn't know what kind of woman Brigit had become.

But she tamped that thought down, too, and moved forward, and thought about how stupid it had been to dress in faded jeans and a crop top in order to try to fit in at the university. To pass as a student. The scents of flowers grew stronger and more varied as she approached her place—*her place*, the little flower shop called Akasha which she had bought, which she *owned*. She smelled daffodils and narcissus.

To Brigit the mingled aromas were the smell of peace, of security, of happiness. She even managed a small smile and picked up the pace. Sun glinted from the glass walls of the little greenhouse, which projected from the rear of the narrow brick building like a house's back porch.

The spell shattered to bits, though, when she reached the front door and saw the man sitting on the step. He wore a suit and a tie, but he was filth in human form. He was a nightmare from the past. He was the embodiment of her many sins, finally come to demand their wages.

"Out to lunch, Brigit? Well, I'm glad you're back. I've been waiting."

"Zaslow. You said you'd give me until to-morrow," she whispered, glancing up and down the walk at passers-by, feeling as guilty as if they could tell at a glance why this man was here, what he wanted, what she'd done. Who she really was underneath the civilized fa-cade. A wild thing.

That other part of herself was one Brigit thought she'd buried a long time ago. She was the one who'd lived on the streets with Raze, who'd learned to pick pockets with the stealth of a cat when the need arose. Or to spend fifty cents in a grocery store, and leave the place with fifty dollars' worth of food, and who'd done it without compunction if it was what it took to stay alive. She could steal from the cleverest, and fight with the dirtiest, and do it better than anyone. That was the other side of Brigit. The side she tried so hard to pretend no longer ex-isted. The side without inhibitions or fears.

"I changed my mind," Zaslow said, bringing her back to the present as he got to his feet. Step-ping aside, he nodded toward the door. Zaslow was a big man. Barrel-chested and broad, but not flabby. Intimidating.

There was little choice. Brigit fished her key from her pocket and unlocked the shop. As she stepped inside the chimes above the door tin-kled a magical welcome, and the countless other sets hanging from every possible appendage fol-lowed their example. The smells of hundreds of plants embraced her, as they always did. But the usual, soothing effects were nowhere within

reach. She felt the filth of the man's presence soiling the sunlit air around her, and the smell of her own fear overpowered the calming aromas of the plants.

She fought for calm as she walked behind the counter, instinctively wanting something solid between them. She nudged her glasses up higher on her nose. Placing her palms flat on the cool marble surface, she met his interested gaze on the other side, and she dipped down deep in search of courage before she spoke.

"You can't make me do this."

"I can and I will."

She'd always known he was evil. Men like him were a breed apart from most inhabitants of the planet. They were hollow inside. Empty. Without a soul. It was all right there in his eyes. She couldn't look into those eyes for more than a few seconds. So much evil there, and more than that. There was certainty, confidence. He was convinced she would do exactly as he'd ordered her to do. But she couldn't do it . . . not anymore. Not to Adam Reid.

"I'm not a thief," she whispered, though she knew in her heart that wasn't quite true.

A little anger sparked in his pale gray eyes, but he banked it immediately. He kept his voice level and chilling. "You think just because Mel made the switches, you're innocent? You think those people you and he stole from would agree with you? Do you, Brigit?"

She closed her eyes, sought the peace she could find if she concentrated hard enough. It didn't work, though. Right now, nothing could soothe her.

"I didn't mean for it to go as far as it did," she whispered. And she was explaining it more to the violets than to Zaslow.

"You only wanted to do it once. The Matisse. I know, Brigit. Mel told me everything."

She jerked her gaze up to Zaslow's big chest. No higher. His eyes made her go cold inside. And that close-cropped salt and pepper hair reminded her of porcupine quills. "Mel's the one who told you how to find me?" She couldn't believe it was true. Crook or not, Mel was a friend. The only one from her past she still kept in contact with.

"Before I was done with him, he was begging to tell me what I wanted to know." Zaslow rubbed the knuckles of one hand with the palm of the other.

A sick feeling welled in Brigit's stomach. Mel! Yes, he'd been a criminal, and yes he'd convinced her to help him with the scheme, and ended up leading her by the hand down a path that was barren of morality. But she'd always had a choice. It had been her decision, not Mel's. And when she'd had enough, Mel hadn't even argued with her. She'd written to him, called him once or twice. But she hadn't seen him in almost five years, not since she and Raze had left the city and come to this place she'd known was a haven from her first glimpse of it. Her salvation. Her new life. She'd thought she'd left the past behind.

She saw the cruelty in Zaslow's eyes, and shivered. "What did you do to him? Did you hurt him? Is Mel all right?"

Zaslow only shrugged and turned away from

her. He slowly paced the length of the shop, his fingers idly stroking fragile leaves. Bending now and then to sniff at a blossom. "You didn't expect it to be so lucrative, did you, Brigit? But how could you know, at the tender age of nineteen? Hmm? You didn't have a clue how much money an original Matisse would bring on the black market. And the owner not even realizing it was stolen—man, that was the beauty of it. That was the beauty. Best scam I was ever into."

"But I didn't—"

"You made enough that first time to get you and the old man some decent clothes, get you cleaned up, so you didn't look like bums when you took him to see the doc. Made enough to get old Razor Face into a good hospital, and pay for all those tests. But bills have a way of reproducing, don't they Brigit?" He came back to the counter and stood there, searching her face as if looking for an answer. When she didn't give one, he went on. "Yeah, they do. Just like goddamn rabbits. I know how it is. And then there were the treatments, and the specialists and the medicine. And hell, Raze had to have a place to come home to when they let him out, didn't he? He had to have a bed, and some heat, and regular meals, right? Hey, I'm not saying you got greedy. You did what you had to do to survive." He absently fingered the geranium that thrived in its basket on the counter. Lifting one snowy white blossom to inspect it, he nodded once, and snapped it from its stem without so much as blinking.

His figure blurred, and Brigit had to close her eyes because of the red-hot stinging in them.

"I'm sorry, Sister Mary Agnes," she whispered.

"So you did a few more." Zaslow kept talking, ignoring her pain. He popped the little cluster of blossoms into a buttonhole on his lapel, fussing with it until it hung just the way he wanted. "So what? It's not like you went out and killed someone or robbed a bank, now is it? The owners never knew the difference. No one got hurt. It isn't as if you wanted a free ride, after all. You just made enough money off your little forgery enterprise to run away to this yuppie college town. Enough to buy this pretty little flower shop, here. Made yourself into a respectable lady, didn't you Brigit? Member of the small business association and everything. You go to community meetings and talk to troubled kids. Donate money to the homeless. Volunteer at the soup kitchen on weekends. What is all that, your penance or something?"

She lifted her fingers to her temples, rubbing brutal circles there, lowering her chin to her chest. "Will you please just leave me alone? Please?"

His hand was suddenly clasping her chin, thumb and forefinger digging into her cheeks, forcing her head up. He leaned over the counter so his face was close to hers. "You're no better than I am, Brigit, so drop the act. You're a thief. And you're gonna do this for me. I promise you that."

"No." She tried to pull away from him.

He released her abruptly, and she stumbled backward, knocked her head against the shelf behind her. A coleus plummeted from the shelf, exploding on impact at her feet. Purple and

green leaves, broken stems, black soil, and bits of pottery covered the floor and dusted her feet. Fragile roots lay exposed.

"I got enough dirt on you to put you in prison for thirty years." He wasn't yelling. Just speaking very calmly as he straightened his tie, and gave his cuffs a gentlemanly tug.

"If you turned me in, you'd go to prison, too, Zaslow."

"Wrong little lady. I've *been* to prison. That last painting you forged for me . . . the buyer turned out to be an undercover cop. I did my time, and I did it with my mouth shut. They tried everything to get me to tell them the name of my forger, but I wouldn't do it."

Brigit shook all over and remained where she was, back to the wall literally as well as figuratively. "Not out of loyalty," she whispered. "You only kept my name out of it so you could use me again."

"Why doesn't matter. You owe me, Brigit Malone."

"I can't—"

"Then I'll turn you in. And what do you think will happen to the old man then? Huh, Brigit? What do you think Raze will do? You think he can get by on the streets now like he used to? Hell, he can barely feed himself."

"Don't do this."

"It's done. You get close to Reid. You get inside his house, get a look at the painting, and then you make a nice replica for me. Since Mel's . . . unavailable, you make the switch for me. Bring me the original. You do everything I say,

exactly as I say. Otherwise, I see to it the cops find out everything I know."

She thought of Adam Reid, though she tried to blot his image from her mind. She thought of the pain in his eyes. Passion and pain, all entwined together in eyes that glistened like gemstones. He'd frightened her and drawn her all at once. She'd never looked into anyone's eyes and felt the things she'd felt in his. She'd glimpsed goodness. Yes, she'd been sure it was there. But buried beneath so much bitter pain and anger that it might never surface again. There was danger in Adam Reid's eyes. Dark, threatening danger.

It would have been easier to give in, easier to save herself from Zaslow's threats, if Adam Reid had been a stranger. But he wasn't. He was the man she'd been making love to in her dreams her whole life. He was the man she'd always thought would one day need her like no one else ever had . . . or ever would.

Squaring her shoulders, she met Zaslow's evil, contaminated gaze. "I tried," she breathed, though she was sure he wouldn't give in. "I went there today, just like you told me to, and he wouldn't even let me in his class. How am I supposed to get into his house if I can't get into his classroom?"

Zaslow shrugged. "That's your problem, not mine."

Brigit's throat felt like sandpaper. He wasn't going to back down. "Why does it have to be *that* painting?" It was a desperate attempt to divert him. "Why not pick another one, any one you want? A Rembrandt. A Picasso. Anything

else. Why do you want an unknown painting by an anonymous artist anyway?"

"Because that's what my . . . my *client* . . . is paying me a hundred grand to get. Look, this guy hired me to steal *that* painting. He didn't say how, he only said do it. Making a substitute is my idea. Best way to handle the job. This way, Reid never even knows he's been ripped off, my client gets what he wants, and I get paid. Look, Brigit, this is not the kind of guy to settle for substitutions. Now I'm done talking to you. You gonna do this or am I gonna bring you down hard?"

She sought for excuses, and clung to the one that was the most genuine. "I can't do it without a print, Zaslow. If you don't believe me, ask Mel. He always got me a print to work from. I need something in front of me as I work."

"There are no prints of this piece," he growled. "Don't you think I checked?"

"Then how do you expect me to—"

"Like I said, you get *close* to him." His filthy eyes traveled to her toes and back again, and she felt dirtied by their touch. "Shouldn't be a problem for you, Brigit. You're a hot little number. Hell, I'm tempted to try you myself."

Her stomach churned, and she thought she'd vomit.

"Reid is healthy, male, and straight, honey. So why don't you just make him an offer he can't refuse?"

She shook her head, banking her revulsion. She wouldn't do it. Not in a hundred years. She couldn't even think of it, seeing Adam Reid's tortured blue eyes in her mind again. Yes, she'd

forged paintings before, but she'd never had to look her victims in the eye. She'd never had to see their pain and know she'd be adding to it. She'd never had to get close to them, much less do what Zaslow was suggesting, only to betray them. Like slipping a blade between the ribs of a friend.

"Or, you can use this." He pulled a folded newspaper from inside his jacket, and shoved it in her face. The classifieds. With an ad circled in red.

"Boarder wanted. Estate on Cayuga Lake. Reasonable rates." There was more, but she didn't bother. She threw the paper down and stared up at Zaslow. He could send her to prison maybe, or at least ruin her business, destroy the entire life she'd built here by shouting her secrets from the rooftops.

But even if he did, Raze would be all right. She'd set aside money in his name. No one could touch that. Not even if she was caught. And it would be enough to see him through.

So let Zaslow do his worst. She met his gray eyes, not flinching from their cold emptiness this time. She wasn't a lonely, frightened little girl anymore.

Very calmly she said, "I can't. I *won't*."

He leaned across the counter, his vile breath fanning her face. And the menace in his eyes sent ice-cold terror right to the pit of her stomach. "We'll just see about that, won't we, Brigit?"

Then he turned and strode away. The chimes jangled as he slammed out of the shop. Brigit didn't relax until he'd walked so far she could

no longer see his retreating form through the windows. And then she sagged to the floor behind the counter, and just sat amid the spilled, dark soil feeling stunned, drained.

The soothing smells of Akasha wafted slowly into her psyche, like a balm to her soul. The wind chimes she'd hung all over the place tinkled magically. And she knew, no matter what consequences she might face, that she had done the right thing.

Chapter Three

THE HOUSE WASN'T theirs. Not yet. They were still renting, while they waited for the loan to be approved. With her sterling reputation, thriving business, and healthy financial state, Brigit had been looking forward to a quick approval.

But it wouldn't happen now, would it?

No, Brigit realized as her bare feet sank into the grass at the edge of the driveway. Her shoes dangled from the two fingers of her left hand. No, the loan wouldn't be approved, not if Zaslow was as good as his threats. Not if he exposed her as a thief. A forger. A criminal.

She bit her lip as the wind stirred the dead leaves at her feet, and carried their scent up to twirl it around her face. The porch swing swayed, emitting a lonely creak. It was a small porch, little white railing all the way around. She'd always wanted a porch swing. And a neat white house with black shutters. It was the kind of place she'd dreamed about when she'd been a lonely little girl at St. Mary's. The kind of place she'd imagined she might live in one day, when

she had a real family. The family she'd fanta-
sized about had never come to adopt her. But
she had the house now. And she had Raze. He
was her family.

She liked to think that if her sister were real,
she'd have found a place like this, and a dream-
world family to go along with it. *If* she were real.
Seemed less likely all the time, though.

Brigit had tried once, a few years ago, to check
into the records in Albany, to find out for sure
if she'd had a twin. But she'd been told the records were sealed and that was that. She'd probably never know.

There were window boxes on the front of her
little house. She'd grown riots of pansies in them
every summer since she and Raze had moved
in here.

She tried to swallow and couldn't, so she settled on blinking her eyes dry and mounting the
steps. The screen door squeaked when she
opened it, banged closed again when she let it
go. The stairs right in front of her led up to the
bedrooms. The living room lay on her left, the
dining room on her right. Raze wasn't in either
of them.

"Raze? Are you here?"

No answer. She dropped the shoes to the
floor, frowning, and walked the full circle,
through the living room, into the kitchen that
took up the entire rear third of the house,
around into the dining room and back to the
front door. Growing more worried by the second, she called out again. Raze was getting old.
The thought of him hurt ... or sick ... turned

her stomach to a vat of bubbling corrosives. She headed upstairs.

"Raze?"

Brigit's heart jumped into her throat when there was still no answer. She checked both bedrooms and the bathroom, panic taking a firm hold.

There was a thud below. Seconds later, a motor roared and revved like a frustrated bull. Brigit lurched into motion, racing through the hallway and swinging around the corner and down the stairs. The front door stood wide open, and she launched herself through it. "Raze! Where are you? What's—"

The car's tires spun on the dry pavement, sending the stench of hot rubber into the air. She glimpsed two forms in the front seat, and the one on the passenger side was stooped. The face silhouetted, the whiskers familiar and dear. The car sped away, red taillights shrinking rapidly.

"Raze!" Brigit screamed, racing down the steps, across the front lawn and into the street, running for all she was worth. As if she stood a chance of overtaking a speeding car. "No! Nooo!"

Only when the vehicle was no longer visible did she stop. Her entire body trembled, and her knees were shaking with the effort of remaining locked. Tears burned twin trails down her face. God, she had to do something!

She turned, making her way back to the house, though it was an effort with the dizziness of shock and the way her body seemed to want to turn to liquid. Looking up from the bottom of the front steps, she stopped in her tracks.

There, on the door, was Raze's Mets cap, pinned to the wood by the blade of a knife. A small square of white paper fluttered there, too, like a butterfly trying to escape the pin. It was held over the cap by the same blade. Sinking slowly to her knees, trembling all over, Brigit realized what was happening. She didn't even need to see words scrawled carelessly across that slip of paper. But she leaned closer, and read them anyway. Two words.

Do it!

Nothing more. But what more was needed?

Adam paced the admissions office like a prisoner awaiting a parole board decision. Maxine, at the desk, was in no such nervous state. She seemed to derive incredible amounts of pleasure from the slow dipping of her doughnut into her coffee. Getting it just soggy enough. Then snatching it up to her mouth to catch the moist end before it fell into a blob on her desk.

So far she was two for three.

And in between bites, she glanced into her huge black book, where everything that went on in this office was recorded.

"Well?"

"No record of a new student signing up for your class yesterday, Adam. Sorry." She moved the doughnut to the cup again.

"She *didn't* sign up," he snapped, then regretted it when her hand froze in mid-dunk, and a large portion of doughnut dissolved and disappeared into the murky black depths of her coffee. "Sorry. But I told you that once. She

came to ask about signing up and I told her I
was out of room.''

Maxine lifted the doughnut from the cup,
shaking her head and clucking her tongue as she
surveyed the damage. She peered into the cup,
brows furrowing. ''Well, what did you tell her
that for? You're not, are you?'' One finger
plumbed the coffee sea, in search of survivors,
he figured.

''I thought I was, but then I checked my roster
last night and realized I have room after all.''
Bald-faced lie, yes, but he was desperate.

Desperate, and damned if he knew why, to
see that woman again. He hadn't slept. Instead
he'd tossed and turned in his bed all night, al-
ternately sweating and shivering, seeing her face
every time he closed his eyes.

Something about the woman had grabbed
him by the throat and wouldn't let go. And if
he didn't get to the bottom of this he was going
to go insane!

''Adam?''

He cleared his throat, straightened his tie. ''I
was hoping she left her name or an address or
something. She must have had to sign in
somewhere. All visitors do, don't they?''

Maxine's forefinger emerged from her coffee
cup at last, with a globule of doughnut mush
coating it. She popped it into her mouth. And
when she pulled her now clean finger out again,
it was with a loud smacking sound.

''Well, there's nothing in my notes. What did
you say she looked like?''

What did she look like? Adam lowered his
head, picturing her again in his mind. It was

easy. Because her face wasn't strange to him. It was eerily familiar, and that was part of what was driving him nuts about this. He knew he knew her. He just couldn't place her. "Small," he said, and his voice was a little softer than it had been before. "Delicate." The word slipped out before he gave it much thought. "And she has these *eyes* that just . . ."

He brought his head up. Maxine had lost interest in the doughnut. Her attention was all his now. Brown eyebrows which had never been dyed to match the copper-red hair rose in twin arches. "Well, now. Isn't that interesting? She had eyes, you say?"

Her voice was full of speculation, and her double chin damn near quivered with amusement. "Ebony eyes," he said, careful to keep his voice cool and detached. "Hair to match, long and curly. When she left, she seemed a little . . . distraught."

She'd been distraught all right. Almost as if looking at him—*touching him*—had shaken her as much as looking at and touching *her* had shaken *him*. Why, though? Why?

What did she really want with him?

A little voice inside whispered a warning, once again. But it was quieter now. This need to see her again had all but drowned it out. Still, he heard it, recognized it. A woman with this kind of power over him—one he sensed was lying—was the last thing Adam needed in his life right now.

But despite the very real, icy fear that writhed in the pit of his stomach at the thought of seeing her, Adam was convinced he could handle this

thing. He could keep his feelings in check, talk to her as if she were just a stranger. Hell, he only wanted to see her long enough to make her tell him where they'd met before.

Liar!

As much as he detested dishonest women, he figured he could stand her that long. Unless she decided to lie about that, too.

Maxine puckered her brows and sighed. "I just don't remember seeing anyone like that in here yesterday. Sounds . . . pretty, though." Reaching for her doughnut with one hand, she flipped a few pages in her book with the other. Then stopped abruptly. "Well, what do you know? Here she is. Hmm, that's not my writing. She must have stopped in while I was out to lunch. You were right, someone stuck her name on the visitors list."

"Well?"

She turned the book around and Adam leaned down. Brigit Malone. Akasha, The Commons. That was all it said. "What the hell is Akasha?"

"Akasha?" The male voice from behind Adam made him turn around to see his best student, Michael Sullivan, lounging in the doorway. "Oh, come on, Mr. Reid. Akasha. You know, the fifth element. The omnipresent spiritual power that permeates the universe and all that."

Adam frowned. "I was talking real life, kid, not religious myth."

"Skeptic," Michael accused. Then he shrugged. "Well, in real life it doubles as a flower shop on the Commons. Great place. You ought to check it out."

Adam nodded slowly. "I think I will."

"Uh, can you do us a favor and wait 'til after class? Everyone's waiting on you, Mr. Reid. I got elected to come looking."

Jerking his wrist up to eye level, Adam blinked in surprise. He was never late for anything. He was the most notoriously prompt, the most organized man on campus. He never got distracted like this.

"Anything wrong, Mr. Reid?"

"No." He looked at his watch again, confirming he was ten minutes late for his own class. Distractedly, he started for the door.

"You're forgetting your briefcase, Adam."

He turned to Maxine, saw her plump finger pointing to the floor where he'd set it down. Shaking his head, he bent to pick it up.

"You're not yourself," Maxine whispered at him. She sent him a wink. "Must be those *eyes*."

Maybe it was. More likely, though, it was this niggling feeling, half-anticipation, half-dread, when he thought about seeing her again.

He managed to get through class, but he was thinking about seeing her, getting the answers to his questions, the whole time. He couldn't seem to carry a thought to completion before he lost the thread. Couldn't seem to concentrate, wasn't focused. The kids tossed their theories at him as to the origin of the Celtic text, and he listened. Didn't argue, didn't question. Just listened.

It seemed to take forever, but the class finally ended. His timer bell pinged and he walked out, just like that. Papers strewn over the desktop. Drawers unlocked. And ten minutes later, he was at the front door of Akasha.

The sign said CLOSED. But as he peered through the glass, he saw movement, so he tried the door and found it unlocked.

He stepped through and into what seemed like another world. The place sparkled. The place actually sparkled. And it wasn't just the crystal prisms turning slowly in the windows, and reflecting rainbows of color that danced with a life of their own, touching everything. It wasn't just the many windows that seemed not only to admit golden sunlight, but to enhance it somehow. Or the plants that lined every available bit of space. The place smelled magical. A mingling of incredible perfumes, plants and flowers, and some sort of incense, too, he thought, permeated it. And the sound of it sparkled, too. Mystical music floating softly on fragrant air, touching him, caressing him. Those wind chimes that came alive with the slightest change in the air currents, whispering, tinkling whenever he moved.

He stood still, just inside the door, lost in sensations for several moments, before he gave his head a shake and reminded himself why he'd come here. To see her and figure out why he felt he knew her. It was important, somehow. He'd sensed that from his first glimpse of her.

No one stood behind the counter. He heard something. A sniffle. A sob. Adam was still holding the door in one hand, and he let it go now, stepping farther inside, scanning the aisles in search of her. The door swung closed, tinkling the chimes overhead as it passed.

"I'm sorry, but I'm not really open today."

It was her voice, but not deep and resonant as

it had been yesterday. It was tear-choked and hoarse. It came from somewhere beyond the slightly opened door in the back. And he moved toward it, an odd sensation snaking around in his stomach.

"I just came in to take care of a few things," she went on, guiding him in, drawing him nearer. He thought of sirens, and wondered if he were about to crash on the rocks. "And then I'm going . . ."

He nudged the door open and stepped through it, into the warmth and light and humidity of a small room made completely of glass. Her greenhouse.

She stopped speaking as if she sensed him there. Lowering the watering pot to a bare spot between several ferns, she lifted her head, met his gaze. And behind the round glasses, those black eyes were as mysterious as ever, more so even, because they glimmered beneath an ocean of tears. She wore a green silk blouse, tucked into a modest black skirt that hung loosely on her, and skimmed the tops of her knees. Her wild hair was caught up in a tight French braid that hung down to the middle of her back. This was her costume. He knew it instinctively. Yesterday she'd taken it off, and tried to look like one of his students. And he thought maybe she didn't even realize that she'd been more herself in jeans and a crop top with her hair wild and free, than she was now in her uniform of propriety.

And why the hell was he thinking as if he knew her better than she knew herself? He hadn't even met her, yet, technically speaking.

"And then you're going . . . ?"

She blinked, averting her face and removing her glasses long enough to swipe the back of one hand over her wet eyes and tear-stained cheeks. "Never mind. It's . . . not important."

"Looks pretty damned important to me."

He moved closer, because he couldn't stop himself. And she stood perfectly still, watching him, quickly slipping those glasses back on as if to hide behind them. Fear and—God, was that longing?—mixed in her eyes, and he almost believed she couldn't have moved away if she'd wanted to. He reached out, unable to control the impulse to brush at a tear she'd missed—or was it simply because he had to touch her again? He ran his thumb across her cheek, his other fingers spreading gently over her face. And there was something. Something that sent his heart slamming against his ribs and made his throat close off. Something potent and startling and unexpected. Though it shouldn't have been. He'd reacted much the same yesterday, hadn't he? It was as if he fell under some kind of spell every time he looked into her eyes. And yet he couldn't seem to resist looking into them anyway.

The way her eyes widened, the way she sucked in a sharp gasp and pulled away from his touch, he was well on the way to convincing himself she'd felt it too, whatever the hell *it* was.

His hand hovered in the air for a moment longer. Then he lowered it, feeling like a fool. And he searched for something to say. What did you say to a beautiful, weeping stranger?

"Is there anything I can do to help?"

She held his gaze with those moist, mesmerizing, soul-searching eyes of hers . . . and very slowly, she nodded.

Chapter Four

SHE TRIED NOT to look into his eyes. She couldn't afford to feel his pain, or to see the other things coming to life in those deep blue gemstones. Other things. Like the way he looked at her. As if he were seeing the epitome of his fondest dream. As if she were something precious, rare, something he'd never thought he'd see.

She was nothing. Less than nothing. A criminal unworthy of even a passing glance from this man.

Brigit strained, for once, to find the girl she'd been years ago. The one who had been willing to do whatever was necessary to survive. The one who'd felt—as lousy as the world had treated her—that it had no right to expect anything better in return. The one who'd lived in a condemned building, and who'd sold her soul without batting an eye, to save the life of the old man who'd once saved hers. Right now, instead of denying the existence of that wild thing inside her, she longed to hide behind it. To be ruthless and clever and devious, the way she'd been

then, when she'd done whatever was necessary to survive.

She had no choice but to do it again. And it was going to be the hardest thing she'd ever done. She told herself it shouldn't be. That she need only think of Raze in the hands of that monster Zaslow, think of the things Zaslow might do to him if she failed. It would give her the strength to go through with this. She'd do whatever she had to. She'd forge the damned painting.

How, though? How the hell was she going to lie her way into Adam Reid's house? Into his life?

She dared a glance at him. He stood there, waiting for her to speak. Okay, then. There was no more putting this off. She knuckled her eyes dry again, and replaced her glasses with careful deliberation. She straightened her spine.

"Sorry," she said. "I don't usually greet my customers with tears."

He tried for a smile, but it was unconvincing. He wore the baffled, confused expression he'd always worn in her dreams of him. "Maybe I should come back another time."

"No. I'm fine now, really."

He looked at her, one golden brow arched in disbelief.

"Really," she told him. And he nodded, though she didn't think he believed her. "So what are you doing here? Is it about the class?"

"Yes." His lips thinned, and he tipped his head back, looked at the deep blue sky beyond the glass ceiling, then lowered it again, shoving

one hand backward through his luminous, honey-coated hair. "No."

Brigit tilted her head. "Which is it?"

"I . . ." He licked his lips, then shook his head. "It doesn't matter. You didn't want to take the class anyway. Did you?"

She lowered her head to hide the jolt those words caused her. He was too perceptive. How could she ever hope to deceive him? She wondered what had brought him here, and wished she had the powers Sister Mary Agnes had woven into the fairytale. She'd simply wave her hands and whisper a mystical chant, and she'd be given instant access to his mind, his home. To his life. To his painting.

He was a frightening man. Such conflicting emotions passing through those eyes of his. From near reverence to wariness and suspicion when he looked at her. And always that old, well-worn anger simmering just below the surface. Crossing him would not be pleasant. Especially if he caught on. And fooling him would not be easy.

She fingered the pendant she wore, and ordered herself to calm down.

He was looking around the greenhouse now, turning slowly, so she could better appreciate the lines of his face. Harsh and angular. A straight Roman nose and wide-set almond-shaped eyes. He had the eyes of a wizard, she thought. Hypnotic, mesmerizing. Eyes like an oracle. They seemed capable of seeing everything, right to the soiled hubs of her soul. And the thick, sensual lips . . . the ones she'd tasted so often in her dreams.

He turned then, caught her staring at his mouth, and one corner of it twitched. His eyes registered sensual awareness, followed by a flare of alarm. Both of which he concealed almost immediately. "This is quite a place."

She thought of her mission, thought of the classified ad Zaslow had shown her. And tried not to think about Adam's lips, and not to look at his eyes.

"Thanks. It better be, I guess. I'm stuck here for a few weeks. That's why I wasn't opening today, in fact. I need time to pack up some things . . ." She let her voice trail off as his sharp eyes narrowed, probing hers. And she couldn't help it when she looked away.

"Why's that?" he asked, his voice soft and wary. As if he were fully expecting—even awaiting—the lie she was about to tell.

She was not a good liar. She'd always been far better at thievery and forgery than outright, face-to-face deception. Her entire life, as far back as she could remember, she'd never been able to tell a lie to someone's face without seeing Sister Mary Agnes, arms crossed over the front of her black habit, one foot tapping the floor, staring her down until she squirmed. For a while, she'd seen that vision face to face. Now she only saw it in her mind, but it was no less effective. She writhed inside.

"Radon," she blurted.

Oh, yes. She'd nearly forgotten the other reason she never lied. Because she was so utterly terrible at it.

He crooked that one golden brow again, his eyes still piercing her. "Radon?"

She nodded, turning away from his knowing stare, absently straightening the amaryllis at her right, letting her eyes drink in the perfection of its large white trumpets rather than face this man as she lied to him. "My house is built over an old shale bed, and it turns out there's radon seeping into the basement. It causes cancer, you know."

"I remember hearing that somewhere."

Of course he did, she thought. It was last week's lead topic on "20/20." "I have to move out until it's safe again."

"That shouldn't take long, should it? A couple of days, maybe?"

She paused, biting her lip, her back still to him. "Well, then there's all that construction. The entire basement needs to be . . . er . . . radon-proofed."

"Of course it does," he said, and the sarcasm was so subtle, she couldn't be sure it was there.

She grated her teeth, and made herself face him, trying to read his eyes, but he'd put up some kind of invisible shield. One she thought was as effective as the glasses she wore. She was shocked that his eyes told her nothing. That had never happened to her before.

"I don't suppose you've considered staying in a hotel?"

She shook her head quickly. "Can't afford it. All that construction and all . . ." He probed again, silencing her, but this time she held his gaze. She was determined to see whether he believed a word she'd said, or was just letting her make a fool of herself for his amusement. And still his eyes revealed nothing.

Except that, bathed in the sunlight streaming down from above, they turned from dark, mesmerizing sapphire, to a lighter shade with flecks of turquoise appearing here and there.

"Your shop is nice," he put in. "But it's small. Where are you going to sleep?"

She shrugged. "I'll just spread a sleeping bag on the floor."

He drew a breath, shook his head. He looked into her eyes, probed, then looked away again. "Are you going to tell me it's a coincidence, Brigit?"

She heard a ripple of anger in the words, but oddly enough, it sounded more like a plea. "Coincidence?"

"Just yesterday I placed an ad in the Ithaca *Times*. Room and board, cheap, or in exchange for light housework. I don't suppose you saw it?"

He wouldn't release her gaze. She tried to look away and couldn't. He knew she'd seen that ad. He knew she was fishing for an invitation. God, he saw right through her!

"Yes," she admitted. She faced him squarely, waiting for the disdain to appear in his eyes. It didn't. There was relief instead. Silent gratitude for something as simple as the truth. Impulsively, she added more. "To be honest, that's why I came to the university. Not for the class. Just to . . ."

"Check me out."

Lips thinning, she nodded. Now that he knew she'd lied to him, she'd never get into his house. God, how could she save Raze now?

"And what's the verdict?"

Her head came up fast, and she bit her lip. "What?"

"Do I pass inspection, Brigit? Am I the kind of man you think you could . . . live with?" There was a slight tilt of his lips, as if he were trying to lighten things up. But it didn't reach his eyes. They were more intense than ever, and she had the feeling the question meant a lot to him.

"You mean . . . you'd let me?"

"Assuming you have time for a little light housework. With the shop to run and all, maybe you'd rather not . . ."

"No! I mean . . . yes." Her voice softened. "Yes, I'll have time. I'll make time. I have to . . ."

God, if she wasn't careful he'd see how vital this was to her! She cleared her throat, met his eyes, shivered at the potency of the impact whenever she held his gaze for more than an instant. It was electric. Magic. Reviving her forbidden dreams of him, and making her body shudder with awareness and raw, erotic hunger. Their gazes held for far too long. She was reading things in his eyes, and showing him things in hers . . . things that shouldn't pass between strangers. Unspoken longings and erotic promises. All slipping from somewhere inside her before her conscious mind regained control. She blinked rapidly, embarrassed at the intensity of that long glance. From the corner of her eye, she saw him give his head a fast shake, as if trying to wake himself up from a brief slumber.

"Akasha's hours are a little unorthodox," she said, to cover the awkwardness. "We open in the afternoon and close at eleven P.M. It seems

to fit the schedules of the students much better than nine to five would. I have free time in the mornings."

He nodded, seemingly lost in confusion. Chaos. Determinedly keeping his gaze on the floor he said, monotone, "So would you like to see the place?"

When she didn't answer because she was busy studying the way the sunlight illuminated the swirls of paler blond and darker gold in his hair, he looked up again, met her eyes. And for just an instant she thought she saw knowledge in them. That he knew damned well she was still being less than honest.

A ripple of fear raced up her spine, into her nape, and she shivered involuntarily. How could he melt her soul with the heat and wanting in his eyes one minute, and chill her with suspicion and mistrust in his eyes the next?

He didn't hold her gaze this time. It was a brief, chilly clash before he focused on the plants, feigning interest in them. "Well?" he went on. "Are you still interested?"

She paced slowly away from him, pushing one hand through her hair as if deep in thought. And then she turned to pace toward him again, stopping halfway, gnawing her lower lip, making him want to do the same. A lush begonia hung between them, its leafy, twisting strands interfering with his view of her, and for a second he resented it, because he enjoyed looking at her so much.

And then he went still, and he felt his blood slowly freeze over in his veins. Because he sud-

denly knew why she seemed so familiar to him. She was the woman in the painting. The woman he'd seen in his childhood delusion all those years ago. She was . . .

No! No, she couldn't be. She was not the woman he'd obsessed about for the past twenty-five years. The resemblance was no more than coincidental. Because the thing that had instigated the obsession had never really happened. It was just a story he'd heard somewhere, and incorporated into his dreams. He hadn't *really* seen this woman bathing in a pond in an enchanted forest. He hadn't *really* been told that she was his fate. That she'd come into his life so he could show her the way home, and that if he fell in love with her, she'd break his heart.

But then again, he'd never *really* believed it had only been a dream, had he? Not deep down inside, where it counted. And right now, there wasn't a kernel of doubt in his soul or body that this was her. It was only his practical mind that rebelled.

She turned to look at him from beyond the plant's twisting vines. Just the way she had before, in the dream or vision or hallucination or whatever the hell it had been. His knees threatened to buckle and he couldn't seem to draw another breath. In a second he'd be gasping. Chilled beads of sweat broke out on his forehead, and his goddamned hands were shaking.

And he suddenly remembered the question he'd asked her just now. Whether she'd come with him, to his home. Whether she'd stay for a while. And he was terrified she'd say yes, and just as terrified she wouldn't.

His mind all but begged her to come with him. Into his home. It scared him, the amount of tension that coiled in his stomach as he awaited her answer. She'd lied to him, for God's sake. And he had a feeling she still was, despite her uncanny resemblance to his lifelong fantasy. She wasn't even a very *good* liar. Radon. Right.

But he'd taken the bait. Not because he'd believed her, but because he'd wanted to. And he supposed it was a good thing he did. Because when she looked into his eyes, he didn't think there was a way in hell he could say no to her.

Christ, she hit him on so many levels she left his head spinning. She was his obsession. As if someone had breathed life into his childhood dream. As if a magic wand had been waved and she'd just walked right out of his head, and into his life. He'd searched for her for so long . . .

No. Not for her. For the source of that fantasy . . . the myth that had to have inspired it. You never searched for her!

Was that true? Because it certainly *felt* as if he'd been searching for her. He'd thought the painting was as close as he'd ever get to finding her. But now she'd stepped off the canvas. And he wasn't capable of letting her just walk away. Not without knowing her, trying to find out what all of this meant.

On an entirely separate level, he resented her. Because she had this incredible power over him, and because she was lying. She was up to something. His need to know everything there was to know about her was something he understood. Her desire to entangle herself in his life, though, was baffling. Every defense mech-

anism he'd developed through the betrayals
he'd been dealt had jumped to full alert. Alarm
bells were going off in his head, warning him
that he was walking right into yet another heartache.

And yet he was powerless to resist. When he
wasn't looking at her, he could convince himself
that he was going in with his eyes wide open
this time. But when he looked into those eyes
he felt as if he'd tumbled headlong into a trance
state, and that he'd be her willing slave for the
rest of his life if she so much as asked it.

The effect she had on him reminded Adam
sharply of the descriptions of fairies in that
newly translated Celtic text, and countless others. The enchantments they could place on the
man of their choice. The way he'd waste away
from sheer unfulfilled longing. A passage of
John Keats came to mind. Adam tried to shake
it away.

Ridiculous!

And yet he heard the words echoing in his
mind.

> *I met a Lady in the Meads*
> *Full beautiful, a faery's child,*
> *Her hair was long, her foot was light*
> *And her eyes were wild.*
> *I set her on my pacing steed*
> *And nothing else saw all day long,*
> *For sidelong would she bend and sing*
> *A faery's song.*
> *She found me roots of relish sweet,*
> *And honey wild, and manna dew,*
> *And sure in language strange she said*

> "I love thee true."
> And there I shut her wild wild eyes,
> With kisses four.
> "La belle dame sans merci
> Thee hath in thrall!"

She came toward him, touched his shoulder, and he jerked at the erotic impulse that hissed through him, shaking the verse from his mind. He'd never thought of his shoulder as an erogenous zone before.

"Adam?"

"Yes?"

Stop looking into her eyes. It's that simple. Just don't look at her and you'll be fine.

"Did you hear me?" she asked in a voice like silk. "I said I'd like to come with you."

His vision blurred as he deliberately misinterpreted her words, and let himself fantasize, just for a second.

"To the house," she added quickly, almost as if she could read the pictures in his mind. "To see the room."

"I'll take you," he told her, and then he turned away, leaving her to interpret that whatever way she wanted. He headed for the door, his neck damp and prickly, and his heart doing things that might be described as palpitations.

"All right."

She was with him, right beside him, and he hadn't even heard her footsteps.

Her hair was long, her foot was light . . .

Shut up, he thought. Just shut the hell up, Keats.

* * *

Adam Reid didn't live in a house. He lived in a fantasy. From the steep, curving drive to the majestic pines that lined it, to the electric-blue sky above. Beautiful. And when she caught sight of the house, she lost her breath. It reminded her of a medieval monastery, tall and square, and made entirely of huge blocks of reddish-brown stone. The house wore an ivy coat, Brigit noticed, and she thought it must need it to ward off the chill of all that stone. And then she frowned, because for just a second, looking at the rows of arched windows had felt a lot like looking into someone's eyes. And what she'd read there had been sadness. An old hurt. Just like the one that lived within the soul of Adam Reid. The one he kept hidden beneath layer upon layer of bitterness, wariness, and anger.

"Here we are," he said, pulling his aging Porsche to a halt and killing the motor. It was the first time he'd spoken since they'd left the Commons. There had been something in the car beside the two of them. An invisible, pulsing tension so tangible she thought it might be a living thing.

"It's beautiful," she told him. She opened her door and got out. And as soon as the wind hit her, she knew there was something very special about this place.

Beyond the house, she could see Cayuga Lake, its swirling waters stirred by the wind's fingers. And to her left, a miniature mountain's towering pines made love to the deep blue sky.

The girl she'd been so long ago seemed to yawn and stretch from her enforced slumber. Summoned to wakefulness by the magic of this

place, perhaps. Brigit had managed to lock that wild thing away, to make her a prisoner of the controlled, responsible woman she'd become. But now the girl sniffed the scent of the lake and of the pines on the wind. And she suggested, in a mischievous whisper only Brigit could hear, that it would be wonderful to run barefoot through those tall grasses at the base of the hillside. To cartwheel and somersault all the way down that slope. To frolic naked in the lake, as its vigorous waves tossed her to and fro. Or to stand fully clothed in a rainstorm, right there on those cliffs that jutted out over the water.

For a moment, she envisioned herself doing just that. Standing on the cliffs, soaking wet, her hair whipped by the wind, her arms outspread as she welcomed the storm, taunted the lightning. It wasn't the respectable owner of Akasha standing there in Brigit's vision. It was an untamed hellion. And there was a glint in her eyes, and she was laughing aloud as she dared Adam Reid to take her in his arms and kiss her the way he really wanted to.

Brigit slammed her eyes shut, mentally thrusting the wild thing back into her cell and locking the door. There was no room in her life for that wanton anymore.

"Are you all right?"

Blinking him into focus, she managed a firm nod. She wasn't all right. She was falling apart. God, where was her hard-won control now? Everything had been taken out of her hands! Raze's well-being. Her own decision to become a mature, responsible, socially acceptable woman. Maybe even her ability to remain that way.

And her deeply rooted feelings for this man. Her dream man.

"You looked . . . odd."

"It's this place," she said, and turned to look out over the water again. "It's magical."

"I used to think so."

When she looked at him, one corner of his mouth had pulled into a sad, perhaps nostalgic smile.

"Come on. You're going to have to see the inside before you decide."

But she'd already decided. She'd stay here. Under any other circumstances, she'd have run from this place as fast as she could, and vowed never to return. It would be difficult to keep her facade in place here. Nature knew the wild thing inside her. Nature seemed to be calling to her, rousing her, and beckoning her to take over.

Brigit would just have to deal with it, though. If she did manage to get through this and save Raze, she would have a life to go back to. A business to run. A place in this community to fill.

He took hold of her elbow, and propelled her away from the cliffs, back along the path she didn't even remember walking, to the front of the house. Wide stone steps and an arched wooden door with stained glass. His keys jangled, and then he opened the door and ushered her inside.

A huge room spread out before her, white stucco, big windows. A wide mahogany staircase split into opposite directions halfway up, and ran into hallways on either side. At the bottom of the stairs, on a pedestal stand, a sparse

fern with yellowing leaves made her grimace. She instinctively went to it, touched one withering strand, rubbed it between her fingertips.

He led her through the high-ceilinged foyer, from which she could see the rows of bedroom doors upstairs. He never slowed down. And she should have wondered why he was making a beeline to the double doors at the far end of the room. But that wouldn't come until later.

He flung the doors open with a flourish. "This is my favorite room. Technically, it's the study, but to me it's more like a haven. Come in."

Brigit stepped into Adam's haven.

And then she froze in utter shock. Her gaze riveted to the painting that hung above the mantel. She couldn't look away. She couldn't move. She couldn't even draw a breath.

"Beautiful, isn't it," he asked in a soft voice. He stood close beside her, and she assumed he, too, was staring at the piece. But she couldn't look at him to be sure.

"It's . . . it's not possible . . ."

She felt Adam's eyes on her. "Brigit?"

She shook her head, trying to remind herself not to speak her thoughts aloud, when what she felt like doing was screaming at the top of her voice. The painting was the perfect image of the first page of her precious *Fairytale*. The one Sister Mary Agnes had read to her every night. The one she'd clutched to her heart, even when she'd expected to burn to death in the fire. The one she'd clung to as Raze carried her to safety, and that she'd cherished ever since. The one bright spot in an otherwise heartbreaking childhood.

And here was its opening page, on Adam

Reid's wall. The picture of the forest, and that magical pond in its center. With the castle spires visible if you squinted at the silvery clouds. And the pictures in the swirls of tree bark.

Only in the book, there had been no woman bathing in that pond.

"I think she looks like you," Adam whispered. He sounded almost reverent.

"No. Not me." Brigit wanted to close her eyes, because the woman in the painting was staring straight into her soul. Oh, she looked like Brigit all right. But she wasn't. Brigit knew her, knew exactly who she was. She was the image of the wild thing Brigit kept locked inside.

And all of a sudden it occurred to her that *this* was the painting she was supposed to copy.

She actually staggered backward. She felt the blood drain from her face, felt her eyes widen and her lips part on a silent exhalation.

"Brigit?" He caught her shoulders, steadying her, and only then did she realize how very close she'd been to collapsing in sheer shock. Gently, he scooped her up, cradling her to his chest for all too short a time. And she couldn't stop her arms from linking around his neck. She couldn't prevent herself from burying her face in the crook between his shoulder and his neck. Because he'd held her this way so many times before, in her dreams.

She felt him shiver, heard him draw a harsh breath. And only a moment later, he lowered her onto a sofa. He hurried away and returned in seconds with a glass of water, which he pressed into her hands. His hands covered hers, and warmth suffused her, right to the core. He

didn't remove them right away, and she saw him blinking down at his hands on hers, as if trying to solve a puzzle.

He finally sighed, and took his hands from hers, and Brigit sipped the water. Adam studied her.

"I've shown that painting to a lot of people," he said at last, taking the water from her hands and setting it on the glass-topped coffee table beside yet another dying houseplant. This one a geranium. "None of them has ever reacted like that."

"It . . . it wasn't the painting," she told him, though she knew full well it was.

"No?"

"No. I've just had a few rough nights. No sleep. And I skipped a couple of meals, and I guess it's probably catching up with me."

He nodded, but skepticism darkened his dark blue eyes. She'd better get used to the idea that lying to him was to be used only as a last resort. He saw through every fib she concocted. She sat up a little, and he turned, sliding closer until he sat right beside her. His gaze went back to the painting on the wall.

"Have you ever seen it before, Brigit?"

Her throat went dry at his question. That insight again. But it couldn't possibly be *that* sharp. "I don't think so."

God, why would he ask that? And what was he doing with this piece of her childhood?

"It's incredible, though," she said, trying to keep the emotions out of her voice. "Who is the artist?"

He shrugged. "It's anonymous. See, way

down near the base, where the water ripples? There's a word there. The dealer at the Capricorn thought it was the artist's signature. But I disagree."

Brigit tilted her head and looked for the word. When she saw it her heart tripped over itself.

Rush.

"What . . ." Her voice emerged as a croak. She cleared her throat and tried again. "What do you think it is?"

"The title of the piece," he said slowly, softly, not taking his eyes from the work. "I think it's the name of that place. Rush."

"How do you—" She shouted half the question, going rigid and jerking her head around to face him. Then she bit her lip, stopping herself from asking how he could know the name of that forest. The answer was simple enough. He must have heard the *Fairytale*, too. And so had this anonymous artist.

She felt an acute sense of disappointment. All this time, she'd honestly believed that story was hers and hers alone. That—even if it hadn't been created by a fairy princess for her twin daughters—maybe Sister Mary Agnes had made it up, just for one lonely orphan. It took away the magic, knowing it had been an ordinary fairytale that hundreds of others had shared.

She closed her eyes to prevent him from seeing the way the revelation had hurt her.

"It touches me," he told her. "Did from the first time I saw it hanging in the gallery downtown. I wouldn't trade it for anything."

That brought her gaze back to him. And if there was guilt in her eyes before she lowered

them again, then it was no wonder. A tidal wave of the stuff had risen up to engulf her at those words. He wouldn't trade it for the world. But he was going to trade it. For a fake.

"You feel better now? Strong enough to continue the tour?"

She met his eyes again. "I don't need the tour," she told him. "The place is wonderful, Adam. If you'll have me, I'd like to move in."

He smiled, and she thought it was genuine. "When?"

"Tonight."

Chapter Five

"I'M IN." HER voice was a harsh whisper.

"Well, now, that *was* fast. You're better at this than I thought you'd be."

"I'm not sure I can go through with this," she said softly. "It's more complex than anything I've tried before."

"You'll do it, Brigit."

There was a pause, tension, as her breath rushed in and out a little faster than before. "I need to know more," she said at last. "Who is this client? Why does he want—"

"No sense asking, Brigit. I don't have the answers either. You just do your part and don't worry about the rest."

"Adam Reid is an intelligent man," she said slowly. "He's going to catch on."

"You'll just have to see to it he doesn't. *Distract* him, Brigit. Come on. Use your imagination."

"You're a pig!" She all but spat the words.

The reply was low, vile laughter.

"I want to talk to Raze," she said, her voice

choked now. No longer assertive or sure. It was pleading instead.

"Then I suggest you get the job done."

There was a click, and then silence. Brigit swore very softly and there was a coarseness to her voice that suggested tears. And then she set her receiver down, too.

Adam didn't hang up until the other two had. He drew his brows together in a frown, and wondered just what on earth he'd got himself into. This woman who looked like his fondest fantasy was conspiring against him. Plotting with someone else . . . to do what? He couldn't even begin to guess. Hell, if they were planning to con him out of his fortune, they were almost a year too late. Sandra had seen to it there wasn't anything left worth stealing. And it was a sign of his own hardened heart, he supposed, that he missed the money more than he missed her. Hell, no wonder she'd left him.

Brigit was up to something, though, and he had an instinctive feeling in his gut that she posed far greater danger to him than his wife ever had. And it was too late to back out now, whatever it was. Brigit had arrived later that same night with three large suitcases and a bulky garment bag. And he wondered why she was in such a damned hurry to get under his roof, and what the hell she was planning to try to pull on him. He'd find out. He'd find out if it was the last thing he ever did.

Easy to say, now, he thought. With her in his ex-wife's bedroom, out of his sight. But when he was near her and she started working him over with those eyes of hers, his common sense

seemed to take a powder. Because of her likeness to the woman who was the center of his obsession, he realized. He had to find a way to get past that. He had to get a handle on his rampant interest in her. Distance himself. Find out who she really was and why she'd nearly fainted when she'd seen the painting. She must know something about it. She had to. It was the only rational explanation. If it killed him, he would find out what. And while he was at it, he'd find out what she was after here.

To do that, he realized, he'd have to spend time with her, and do so without falling under her spell. Away from her, he was sharp and objective and insightful. Near her, he became a helpless puppet, incapable of thinking beyond the moment. The beauty in her eyes. The shape of her mouth. The satin curls and raven lights in the hair she kept bundled up tight, which was a crime in itself.

Adam closed his eyes, grated his teeth, and banished the apparition from his mind. God, he'd conjured her image with no more than a thought. And there he'd been again, stricken what felt like a mortal blow from the sheer force of her presence.

This kind of attraction just wasn't natural. But it was understandable. He rationalized that it was only because of this longtime obsession. Only because he saw her as its center, its essence. If she were a blue-eyed blond, he told himself, he'd feel nothing for her. But he had to wonder if that were true.

He stared for a long moment at the telephone on the nightstand. And finally, with a sigh, he

gave up trying to untangle the reality of the conspirator in the next bedroom, and the fantasy woman who'd haunted his soul for nearly all his life. He needed to stop thinking about all of this, just let it go. His head throbbed and his nerves stood on their quivering ends. He wasn't thinking about newly translated texts, or tomorrow's class, or his tenure, or his finances. He wasn't thinking about the approaching winter and the need to have the heating system replaced, or the ominous clunk in the Porsche's transmission. He was only thinking about Brigit Malone.

Impulsively, he turned to the French doors. With the darkness outside and the lights on within, their smooth glass became a mirror. He could see nothing outside. Only the perfect reflection of his own, gloomy bedroom. And the image of a man in abject—if inexplicable—misery.

As if in an act of defiance, he cranked both handles and slammed the doors open wide. The autumn chill had taken a respite today. Tonight, even the breeze had died away. The night's air laid oppressive and silent over the world, heavy as a woolen blanket. Heat surrounded him, smothered him as he stepped out onto the wrought-iron deck he'd had built along the entire length of the house's back side. From here, he could look out over the lake. Usually there would be a refreshing breeze waiting to greet him.

Tonight there was only a humid, sweaty hand. Invisible. Holding him in its fist until he could barely draw a breath. Holding him prisoner the way his obsession did.

Adam stared out at the dark water, seeing no movement. Only able to make out the crooked-finger shape of Cayuga by the darker shade of the water compared to the land around it. He turned toward the south, so he faced the forested hillside. Its shape swelled toward the sky, and he remembered playing there as a child. He remembered what he'd seen there, where he'd gone.

Someplace that had shaken his world to its fragile core. Someplace that had twisted his insides up so much he hadn't dared go back. Not in almost thirty years. And part of him, way down deep, knew that he hadn't stayed away out of fear of his father's brutal reprisals. Because he could have explored those woods again, after the bastard had abandoned them. There had been time before the new owners had tossed Adam and his mother out of their home. And more time after Adam had bought the place back again. But he hadn't. Because he knew, somewhere inside him, that he was terrified of what he might find out there. He'd never been sure whether his mind could handle going into that forest again, and seeing the magical doorway that led to an enchanted realm. And he was equally unsure he could handle not seeing it, as little sense as that made. That, perhaps, was the basis for his obsession to find the source of his fantasy. The fact that he'd never been able to fully convince himself it hadn't been real. Oh, he pretended to believe that. But the doubt still lingered.

Blinking, bringing his focus back, he looked at where he stood. He'd stopped walking right

outside Brigit's bedroom. The French doors that matched the ones in his own, stood right in front of him. Closed, but bare. Sandra had liked all the windows in her rooms left uncovered. No need for drapes or blinds, she'd insisted. This was the second floor, after all, and only the lake lay beyond the glass, and far below. There was no way anyone, even if they were on a boat, could see inside.

He wished now that he'd had the windows covered after Sandra had taken off. It had never seemed important, somehow. At least, not until this very moment.

He closed his eyes, opened them again. It didn't work. Brigit was still there. Pacing the bedroom like a caged lioness, tear tracks scalded into her cheeks, lashes still damp. She hugged herself, as if to ward off a chill, though Adam belatedly remembered he'd forgotten to turn the central air back on in her room. It must be stifling in there.

She wore the clothes she'd been wearing earlier. Black skirt almost to her knees. A shimmery green silk blouse, tucked into it, and a wide black belt around her tiny waist. The belt buckle was a golden sun with wavy rays sticking out all the way around. Her earrings matched. And her hair was pulled into a knot at the back of her head, though the heat and humidity had coaxed several curls loose. Even the glasses were still firmly in place.

The only other difference was that she'd kicked off her shoes now. She paced in black-stockinged feet.

The double doors, bare as they were, gave

him a wide-angle view of the entire bedroom.
He saw open suitcases on the darkly stained
four-poster bed. Draped across one of them was
a vanilla nightgown which consisted of little
more than a length of satin and two spaghetti-
thin straps.

She paced in a repetitive pattern, then broke
it, and walked through the open door to the
bathroom. And in spite of himself, Adam took
a few more steps. Steps that brought him to that
arched window. And he could see so very
clearly, the water spewing full force from the
faucets, foaming as it hit the nearly full shell-
shaped tub. He wondered briefly why the window wasn't coated in steam. Then she stepped
into his line of vision, and he only wondered
how the hell he was going to make himself turn
around and walk away.

Hot. The place was hot and humid. Heavy,
thick air. Didn't the man have air conditioning
in a house this size? She hadn't noticed this
sticky heat downstairs. Then again she hadn't
remained down there long. Unable to look him
in the eye, because of the guilt she knew he'd
see in hers.

Besides, she'd been in a hurry to get the big
garment bag out of his sight. With his piercing
eyes, she could almost believe he could see right
through it to the canvases that were hidden inside. The ones that were the exact size and shape
of the painting downstairs in his study. The
painting he'd said he wouldn't trade for the
world. The one she was going to steal from him.

She felt sick to her stomach, and lowered her

head until her chin touched her chest.

If I survive this, I'll kill that bastard Zaslow!

Brigit blinked in shock at the potent anger she'd heard in that voice from within. The voice of her other self. The wild one. She quelled it quickly, because the anger she heard in it frightened her. No. She wouldn't kill him. She was a sensible, civilized woman. She wouldn't *kill* anyone. She'd just do what she had to do, and find some way to go on.

God, she was so worried about Raze. She'd wanted to talk to him, to hear his voice. Zaslow could have allowed it. He was being deliberately cruel, and enjoying it. Either that, or . . . or he'd done something to Raze. Hurt him so badly he was unable to talk . . .

Tears spilled from her eyes again at that thought, but she pressed the back of one hand to her lips to keep from sobbing, and rapidly blinked the tears away. She couldn't afford to think that way. Not now, not here, with Adam Reid's sharp gaze always probing for secrets and lies. And finding them.

Now . . . now she needed a cool bath . . . and rest. She needed rest. Her wits were already dulled from lack of sleep. She'd need to be sharp if she hoped to fool Adam.

She wondered if now that she'd met him, he'd still appear in her dreams at night. Those erotic dreams woven by that wanton inside her. Brigit lost control of the wild thing when she was sleeping. And her control during the hours of wakefulness would be sorely tested, she thought, now that she was living under Adam's roof. Even now, she felt a ripple of desire for

him flitting up and down her nerve endings. She hoped the spell of those dreams would be broken now that she'd met the real man. But somehow, she doubted it. If she had those kinds of dreams about Adam Reid tonight, she wasn't sure she could get up and look him in the eye tomorrow morning.

Brigit brushed her fingertips across her damp forehead, pushed sweat-soaked tendrils of hair off her skin. She lifted one hand to begin unbuttoning her blouse, as she walked into the bathroom to check on the cool bath she was running. The tub was like an ivory seashell, with little steps cut into one side. No curtain around it. No frosted glass doors. It was open, and she squirmed a little at the idea of feeling so exposed as she bathed. The one inside disagreed. *She* found the idea tantalizing.

Brigit wished *she'd* go back to sleep and stay there.

Still, she supposed it would be all right. There was only one arched, floor-to-ceiling window in here, and nothing but the lake beyond it. She could see nothing now, of course, but by daylight, one would be able to see the incredible view from the comfort of the tub. She could almost envision some purely sexual creature soaking in that shell of a tub, like a pearl. Sipping champagne and staring out at the lake and the hills and the greenery. The blue sky above. From way up here on high. Queen of all she surveys, Brigit thought.

And oddly, she thought of the painting again. Of the woman bathing in the midst of all that natural beauty.

Brigit glanced at the tub, and thought she should have settled for a quick shower.

Oh, go on! Who's going to know?

That one inside her was yearning to try a little decadence on for size. And Brigit was tempted to let her. She'd never lived in a place like this . . . never had the chance to feel such luxury. She went back to the bedroom for a vial of essential vanilla oil. And while she was there, she removed her glasses, and placed them carefully on the bedside stand. A little more of the wild one's impishness possessed her as she hurried back to the bathroom and poured a generous amount of oil into the cool water. Impulsively, she leaned over the tub to inhale its fragrance.

This was not what he'd had in mind when he'd decided to come out onto the balcony. Nor when he'd decided he ought to keep a close eye on her. She was doing nothing more suspicious than running a bath, and he ought to leave.

Right now. He ought to leave.

He didn't, because there seemed to be some kind of magic at work here. He watched her as she shook her hair loose. The first time he'd seen it down, wild and untamed, since that day in the classroom. Her glasses were gone now, too. And—and she'd somehow lost the appearance of the shy, the controlled, the staid plant shop owner. He realized with a little jolt of surprise that his instincts about her had been right on target. The primness had been an illusion. He saw that now, in the simple way she ran her fingers through that mane of hair, arching her back and tipping her chin up. She was a creature

of pure sensuality. She was desire, in a physical form. Venus. Aphrodite. And the transformation seemed to come from within her.

Her back was toward him as she slid the green silk blouse from her shoulders and let it fall to the floor. And why had he somehow known her skin would look luminous? Satiny? That the curve of her spine would be perfect and enticing, beckoning him closer?

Her hands moved around to the front, and a second later, she was pushing the skirt away. Stripping away the vestiges of civilized woman she'd been wearing. Pushing the skirt down over her hips, letting it pool around her feet. Standing there in a forest-green camisole with black lace trim. Further evidence of the woman she was pretending so hard not to be. Her panties had high-cut legs. And she wore black stockings that only came to mid-thigh.

She lifted one leg, propping her foot on the edge of the tub, and she pressed her hands to her thigh, and Adam shuddered with a primal twinge. Those hands, small, efficient hands, rolled the stocking down, all the way to her ankle, then worked it off her petite foot and dropped it carelessly on the floor.

Sweat broke out on Adam's forehead. His breathing was deep, ragged. And he was hard. He told himself to look away, to leave this deck right now, before it was too late. But he couldn't do it. It was almost as if some spell were keeping him there, as if she'd truly mesmerized him, cementing his feet to the spot, refusing to release the hold her body had on his eyes. His physical self refused to obey his mind's commands. In

fact, his body refused to do anything at all, except respond to the slow revelation of hers.

By the time she'd removed the other stocking, he was throbbing. Aching.

But it wasn't over yet. Not yet. Because her hand came up, and pushed the thin strap down from her shoulder. And as she undressed, she moved through the bathroom, looking it over, taking it in. The other strap was lowered.

Jesus! He bit his lip, leaning forward in anticipation.

She pushed the camisole down, wriggled her hips through, and let it fall at her feet. And without a second's hesitation, she shoved off the high-cut panties as well, and his tongue darted out to moisten his lips, and he thought he'd stopped breathing.

The luscious curve of her spine dipped inward at the small of her back, then eased and vanished between two perfect buttocks. Smooth and rounded just enough, he thought. Swaying oh-so-slightly as she moved to the tub.

"God damn," he whispered.

She bent over to shut off the water, then lower, swishing one hand through it.

He choked out a hoarse, involuntary curse, his erection so hard it was painful.

And she whirled to face the window, startled, and Adam went utterly still. Maybe she'd heard him. He was given a brief, tantalizing glimpse of small, firm breasts with upturned nipples that looked as succulent as honeydew. Looking at those confections made his mouth water, and his heart pounded in his chest like a jackhammer. That silver necklace winked and glimmered

from between her breasts, and the pewter fairy that embraced the diamondlike quartz crystal took on a new degree of sensuality. One he'd remember whenever he saw it from now on.

He saw something else. Something red, a small mark on her lower abdomen. Only a glimpse. No more, as she snatched a towel and yanked it over her body, frowning hard at the glass, seeing nothing, he knew, but her own reflection.

He stood motionless on the other side. And though he knew she couldn't see him with the light on inside and the pitch darkness without, he got the feeling that she knew he was there. Sensed his presence somehow.

Or did she?

Impossible to tell. Because she turned her back, and she let the towel fall away. Quickly, she stepped into the tub and sank down into the water, hiding her body from his hungry stare.

And only then was Adam finally able to convince himself to walk away.

At breakfast, she was once again the reserved, the wary, the shy woman he'd first known. She wore a loose-fitting crinkle dress of deep blue, with yellow stars dotting it. She'd belted it at the waist with a braided yellow belt, and there were tiny golden suns and cradle moons hanging from the belt, moving when she did. And, of course, that necklace hung around her neck. He'd come to the conclusion that she never took it off, and he wondered why.

Her hair was in a tight French braid all the way down to the middle of her back, again, and

her round wire rims were perched over those mystical eyes. She was hiding. This was her facade. He knew the real woman. He'd seen her last night. But he'd known her even before then. He'd met her almost thirty years ago.

"Sleep well?"

She lifted her gaze from her empty coffee mug to meet his. "Fine, thank you. Although . . . I thought I heard something on the deck outside my room."

He crooked a brow at her. "Really?"

"Probably an animal."

A barb . . . meant to stick him. No doubt about it, she had known he was out there last night. Why not just say so, then? Why not call him on it?

Because she had to stay here, in order to pull off whatever con she was working up to. And if she admitted that she knew, then she'd have to leave, wouldn't she? No self-respecting woman would stay. It was easier to play word games, to throw missiles and see if they hit any targets.

Well, he wasn't rising to her bait.

"I'll take a look around out there tonight before you go to sleep, if it will make you feel better."

Her round eyes met his, wider than ever. She said nothing. He almost got lost in those eyes, but caught himself in time, and averted his gaze. Distance, he reminded himself. Objectivity.

"Coffee?"

"Just hot water." She pulled a tea bag from a deep pocket and dropped it into her cup. He poured the water for her, replaced the pot, and sat back down.

The space between them wasn't empty. There was something there, something alive and crackling and hot. He could feel it, and he was sure she could as well.

"I have classes most of the day," he said. "I won't be back until tonight."

"Oh. Well, I won't see you, then. I don't close Akasha until eleven."

He nodded, wondering what she'd do while he was gone today. Wondering if he should even leave.

"What . . . do you want done? You know . . . to the house."

He shrugged. "If you can manage to keep the rooms I use everyday in something close to livable conditions, I'll be happy. I don't expect you to do the whole house. The service is gonna send someone once a month to do the major cleaning."

She didn't seem satisfied with the answer. She sat there, dipping her tea bag in synchronized movements that started to work on him as surely as a hypnotist's pocket watch.

He cleared his throat, jerked his eyes away from her hand, stopped fantasizing about how it would feel on his warm, hard flesh. "You can clean up the breakfast mess, I suppose. You remember where the kitchen is?"

"Yes."

"And if you get a chance you can straighten my bedroom."

Again her head snapped up and her eyes sparked. "Where—"

"Right next to yours, Brigit." He enjoyed her surprise, and allowed himself a smile of tri-

umph. "The room you're sleeping in belonged to my wife. She made sure it was the nicest one in the house. I thought you'd like it."

"I do." She lowered her gaze, sipped her tea. Then she frowned and met his eyes again. "What happened to her?"

The words that formed in his mind were *none of your damned business.* But the ones that fell from his lips were different ones. "Last I heard, she was in Venezuela."

Those eyes of hers flickered, but held his by sheer force. An invisible force. One that made him answer questions he had no intention of answering.

"She left you?"

He only nodded, telling himself to finish his coffee, to break eye contact so he could regain some control here.

"I'm sorry," she said so softly he almost believed her. "That must have hurt."

It had hurt. It had torn him apart. Not that Sandra would have had any way of telling. He was an expert at keeping his feelings to himself. And it wasn't so much losing *her* that had given him all that pain. It was the loss itself. The feeling of being stabbed in the back by someone he'd been foolish enough to care for, to trust, yet again.

Hell, he should have known better. Wouldn't happen again, though. He'd finally got the point.

"Adam?"

He looked up, having lost the thread of the conversation.

"Are you all right?" she asked him, as if she gave a damn.

Those eyes worked their magic, sucked him in. Damn, he wanted her. Maybe this whole thing wasn't such a great idea after all.

And the way she was looking at him, he could almost believe this mind-blowing desire might be mutual.

And that made it even more potent. He stood abruptly. "I have to go."

Glancing through the glass that lined three walls of the breakfast nook to judge the weather, he yanked his suit jacket from the chair where he'd tossed it.

"It's going to be a beautiful day," she told him, reading his thoughts it seemed.

"Dark clouds on the horizon."

She shook her head. "The rain will hold off until tonight."

He frowned at her. "Amateur meteorologist?"

Her smile was quick and blinding. "Good guesser," she replied.

He shook his head, not returning her smile.

"Have a good day, Adam."

He stopped at the doorway that led out to the foyer, wondering at the odd tingle that had raced down the back of his neck at her words. The feeling of warmth, of . . . optimism . . . that seemed to sink through his pores. As if it were more than a wish.

Damn. He'd better try getting some more sleep tonight. "You, too," he muttered, and then he hurried away from the woman and her mysterious vibes. In the foyer, he took a moment to snatch his raincoat from the rack near the door,

his way of thumbing his nose at her predictions, he figured. But before he left, he turned, looking back toward the room where he'd left her.

She was humming, her voice angelic, her tune, haunting and strange. His throat went dry. He reached for the doorknob, and just before he turned away again, his gaze fell on that fern at the base of the stairs.

He frowned hard. It didn't look quite as brown and withered this morning. Now what the hell was up with that?

Chapter Six

IT WAS NOT pleasant, what she had to do. But she had no choice. She waited until she was sure Adam had left, until she heard the sound of his car driving away, and then she went up to the bedroom, lugging her equipment downstairs and through the double doors into the study. She spread a drop cloth on the floor, and set the tripod atop it. Then she stood the canvas up. She'd donned a smock for the occasion, and she pushed her sleeves back automatically. And then she stood poised, and still, and silent. She focused on the painting above the mantel. Not just with her eyes, but with her very soul. And she waited.

As always, it happened. Her hands chose a color, and squeezed a daub of it onto the palette. She didn't look at the tube of paint. Her gaze never wavered from the painting as she sought to cling to that state of soul-deep concentration she had to achieve in order to work. Without looking away, she grabbed another color, and squeezed it beside the first. She dipped her

123

brush in one, and then the other, and then back again, and she rolled the bristles against the wood until she felt the mixture was just right. Her eyes still on the painting, she lifted her brush.

With the first stroke, she heard Sister Mary Agnes's voice, rustling like dried leaves in a wind, reading the *Fairytale* aloud as she had so often.

Once upon a time, not so very long ago, two princesses were born. No ordinary princesses, though. These babies were special. These babies were fay.

Brigit caught her lips between her teeth as they silently mouthed, "And that means fairy . . ." She bit down harder, and tried to tune the memories out. She needed to focus. But her hands continued wielding the brushes as if operating without her control, and the voice in her mind went on, skipping ahead.

Father Anthony found you and another tiny girl sleeping at the altar one morning. And each of you had a book just like this one.

It wasn't real, Brigit told herself. It was a fairytale.

One with the name Brigit inside, and the other with the name of Bridín.

"And what happened to Bridín," Brigit allowed herself to whisper. "What happened to my sister?"

Ridiculous. It was a fairytale, and there was no more to it than that. A story Sister Mary Agnes had used to give her comfort. And why was she thinking about the nonexistent Bridín so much just now, anyway? While thoughts and questions about the mysterious twin popped

into her mind every once in a while, and always
had, lately she'd been besieged with them. It
seemed Bridín, real or make-believe, was a constant presence in Brigit's mind these days. Why?

The painting. Something about this painting.
God, it was all tangled up with her disjointed
memories and that stupid fairytale she was beginning to wish she'd never heard! Sister Mary
Agnes should have known better than to fill a
child's head with fantasy and tell her it was real.
Didn't she realize how confusing it could be?

Her hands moved faster, brushstroke upon
brushstroke coating the canvas. Her arms
worked furiously, and a thin sheen of sweat
coated her forehead.

Confusing? No, it was maddening! Because
Brigit had never known exactly where to draw
the line between the story and the actual facts
of her own life. Had her mother really died, for
example? And had her father only given her up
when he, too, was about to lose his life? Had
there ever really *been* a twin sister? Or was all
of that just part of the fairytale Sister Mary Agnes had passed on to her?

She hadn't let those questions surface with
this much insistence in years, because they only
brought frustration. Her files were sealed. She'd
never know. There was no way she'd ever
know.

She blinked then, and her flying hands slowed
a bit.

Maybe there *was* a way. Why hadn't she considered it before? Adam would know. He was
an expert in fairytales, wasn't he? He'd published books on the subject, taught classes at the

university. He probably knew every fairytale ever told. And she already knew he'd heard of hers. If he hadn't, he wouldn't have likened this painting to the forest of Rush. Where else would he have got that name? The fact was, he'd probably read accounts of the _Fairytale_ she'd always thought of as hers alone. And he would _know_. He could likely even tell her its origins, and point out hidden symbolism in the words. But most importantly, he'd know whether the twin sister was, indeed, just part of the story.

But how could she ask him? She certainly couldn't tell him the truth. That _she_, orphaned Brigit Malone, who'd taken the last name of a homeless old man because she hadn't had one of her own, had once believed herself to be the daughter of a fairy princess. He'd laugh her right out of the house. And she couldn't show him the book. Not now. She'd already told him she'd never seen this painting before. If he saw the book, he'd know that was a lie. Though the illustration in her book and the painting on his wall were different, they were also, obviously, the same. And she'd pushed his tolerance for lies too far, already.

She could ask him about the story, though. And since she was so bad at lying, she'd keep her version of things as close to the truth as possible. Without making him think she was totally insane, anyway.

She brought her gaze down, away from the painting on the wall, and focused on the canvas in front of her.

Perfect. She'd captured the background. The stunning blue of the sky and the silvery shapes

of castle towers in the distance, hazy and unfocused. So a viewer might wonder if they were real, or just shapes in the clouds.

The world in the painting was a magical place. A place that couldn't exist, except in the vivid world of imagination. The artist's. And Sister Mary Agnes's. And even her own.

A shame . . . such a shame . . . a place like that couldn't be real.

And when she looks into your eyes, sir, you're helpless to disagree. A man will grant her every wish, answer her every query, for his will melts under the power of her stare.

Adam closed the book and sat at his desk, staring down at the leather binding. If he didn't know better, he'd swear the author was describing Brigit Malone. The woman who'd taken up residence in his house . . . and more importantly, in his mind.

He shouldn't be thinking about her. Okay, he should be, but he should be thinking about what she could be up to, rather than what she looked like naked. The slender length of her limbs and the lightness and grace of her every movement. The spirals of hair curling against petal-soft skin. Those eyes. Those breasts. That glittering pendant dangling in between.

Adam groaned under his breath. Dammit, he was a fool. What he ought to be thinking about was the little detour he'd taken on his way in to work this morning. The one that went past her house, out on Sycamore. It had been a simple task to look for her address in the phone book. Simpler yet, to take a run by the place.

There was no sign of any construction going on in the neat white cottage. No sign at all. But that shouldn't have surprised him. He'd known she was lying about that from the second the words had left her succulent lips.

He pulled his car onto the roadside, and went to the front door. Breaking and entering would have been the last thing Adam Reid would consider doing, under normal circumstances. However, things were far from normal between him and his houseguest. He had to know about her. He couldn't help himself.

First he knocked, just to be sure no one was home. And then he peered through the window, cupping his hands on either side of his face to block the morning sun.

And a merciless hand gave his guts a ruthless twist. Because he spotted ordinary things, ordinary furnishings and a small television. But then he saw the other things. The telltale signs. The brown leather work shoes on the mat beside the door. Size eleven or so, he figured. The soft brown flannel shirt. The man's CPO jacket on the coat rack.

He didn't walk off the porch, he staggered from it. And only when he'd stood braced against the Porsche, gasping for air, had he noticed the damned mailbox. "Malone, R. F. & Brigit."

A man. She lived with a freaking man. And they shared the same last name.

Jesus.

"Jesus," he muttered again now, as he sat at his desk, remembering. Wondering if R. F. Malone was the same man he'd heard her talking

with on the phone last night. How the hell had
he let himself fall into this? He was tangled up
with a married woman. And he was so goddamned hot for her he couldn't think straight.
She had some kind of hold over his mind.
Maybe it was deliberate, all part of whatever
scheme she was hatching. He didn't know. Until
now, he'd thought he could let her stay until he
found out.

Now though, he wasn't so sure. He had a feeling the best thing to do would be to go home,
right now, and throw her out on her ear.

Home. Yeah. He'd had a plan when he'd left
there this morning. He'd intended to be back by
noon, but he'd lied to her, deliberately told her
he'd be gone all day long when he'd had every
intention of arriving early, surprising her. Catching her red-handed . . .

Doing what, he wondered? Somehow, lifting
the silver seemed beneath her.

Anyway, his well laid plans had gone to hell
when old man Sneichowski had called a staff
meeting, and made it a priority. Adam had no
choice but to attend. This job was too damned
important to risk incurring Sneichowski's wrath.

Brigit put away her paints, cleaned her
brushes, and carried the canvas upstairs to hide it
in the back of the huge closet again. She managed
to clean up the breakfast dishes in record time,
but she hesitated at the idea of going into Adam's
bedroom. The idea was so disturbing . . .

Why?

Grating her teeth, she told herself that a little
housekeeping was the least she could do to

make up for what she was going to take from
him. She stiffened her spine, and walked down
the broad hallway, past her own room, looking
over the gleaming hardwood railing on the
right, down into the study below. Her gaze lingered on the painting for a moment too long.
She turned at Adam's bedroom door, put her
hand on the knob, and walked in.

And then she became lost in sensations. Because his scent lingered here in this place. Subtle. But here. Surrounding her, touching her
skin.

The rumpled bed drew her gaze, and she
moved toward it, unable to stop herself. She put
her hands on the wrinkled sheets that bore the
imprint of his body, and imagined she could still
feel his warmth there. That bed, with its covers
flung back, looked incredibly inviting.

She stopped herself from crawling into it.
Barely. It took longer than it should have taken
for Brigit to realize what was happening. That
wanton inside was in the driver's seat, running
the show, acting out her carnal fantasies. Whispering how erotic it would feel to strip to the
skin and slide between the sheets that had so
recently been wrapped around Adam's flesh.
Brigit put an end to that at once, stiffening her
spine and strengthening her resolve. She pushed
that other one into her cell and closed the door.
And then she efficiently made Adam's bed, refusing to pay any attention to the images of him
in it, of the two of them in it together, that hur-
tled through her mind.

When the job was finished she turned away,

relieved. Her hands trembled. Her breaths came unsteadily. Her heart raced.

Swallowing hard, she bent to pick up his discarded robe. But as she did, she saw a fat book under his bed. And that made her pause.

Brigit licked her lips. She knew perfectly well she shouldn't be doing this. She shouldn't. But something drove her, probably the irreverent imp that lived in her soul, and she folded the robe to her chest with one arm, and reached for that book with the other.

An album, she saw as she tugged it out. A photo album. Her legs folded under her, and she pulled it into her lap. His terry robe ended up slung over one shoulder as she opened the cover and began studying photographs. Family photographs. And she knew instinctively that this album hadn't belonged to Adam. It had belonged to his parents. There were baby pictures, dozens of them. And she knew by the golden hair and intense sapphire eyes—those wizard's eyes—that they were of him. And later, school pictures. Year by year, she saw Adam grow. There was his kindergarten class photo. He stood proudly in the front row, beside a little girl with lopsided pigtails, and he must have been fighting that day, because he had a hell of a shiner.

And on the next page, a similar shot, this one of a cluster of first-graders. And again, he was easy to spot, because of the big, purple bruise high on one cheekbone.

Something broke inside Brigit as she continued turning pages. Something ached and cried, and an anger was born. She flipped the pages

faster, and her throat closed off. Adam's handsome young face appeared bruised in too many of these pictures. Here a shadow on his jaw. There a split lip. Here a tiny line of stitches in his forehead. One had his arm in a cast.

Confusion knitted her brows tightly, as she examined every page, until she knew the faces of Adam's parents as well as she knew her own. And curiously, the bruises stopped showing up in Adam's photos at about the same time his father stopped appearing in any of them. The last half of the book was filled with photos of a teenage Adam, and the young adult. Several shots of him with his mother. At his graduation from high school. From college. No bruises. No father.

The explanation was obvious. Tears filled her eyes, and she tipped her head to one side until her cheek rubbed against the terry robe on her shoulder. She inhaled, to smell him in the fabric. This was the source of all the pain she saw in his eyes, then. This was the wound that wouldn't heal.

She could heal it. She knew she could, if he'd let her. Only . . . she'd have to injure him again before she finished, wouldn't she?

"You enjoying yourself?"

She'd been looking forward to seeing him again, so she could ask about her fairytale. Only now, that was the farthest thing from her mind. She didn't want to see him at all. Not like this. There was anger in his voice, and blazing from his eyes when her head snapped up and she faced him. But she understood that anger now. She knew about his old hurt.

And there really wasn't a thing she could do about it, was there? No. Not when she'd come here to hurt him just a little bit more.

She closed the album, slid it back under the bed, and slowly stood up. "I'm sorry," she told him. And she thought he must know it didn't apply to her snooping.

She held his gaze, lifting one hand to swipe the tear from her cheek. The anger in his eyes flickered, lost power.

"You told me you were going to open up the shop today," he said. "Why didn't you?"

"I . . . got distracted."

"I can see that."

"That's not what I meant," she replied with a quick, guilty glance at the album under the bed. "The construction people called, and there were problems to be sorted out. Decisions I had to make." She licked her lips. The lies were not flowing smoothly. Not easily. And his skeptical, piercing stare wasn't making it any easier. "By the time I got everything sorted out with them, I just didn't feel up to much of anything."

Liar! he wanted to shout at her.

But that wasn't all. There was more than her lies happening here. He'd expected to catch her up to no good when he'd come home. What he'd found, instead, had almost put him on his knees. She'd been curled up on his bedroom floor, absently rubbing his bathrobe against her satiny cheek, occasionally turning her nose to the fabric and inhaling, closing her eyes. She'd been crying. Staring down at something in that old album that had been under the bed since

before Mother had died, and crying in silence.

Why?

She was lying, dammit. Lying about everything. Married, in all likelihood! He'd come here
with every intention of telling her to leave. Go
back to good old R. F., whoever the hell he was,
and stay out of his life forever. So why wasn't
he?

She stepped closer to him. Closer still. And he
only stood there, watching, waiting. She
stopped when her body was so close to his there
was barely space between them. He felt her heat,
and more. A sort of tingling that seemed to leap
from her flesh to his. As if she couldn't help herself, she lifted one hand. When her fingertips
touched his cheekbone, he sucked in a breath.
But he didn't move. Her touch traveled over his
face, until her fingers skimmed the tiny scar on
his forehead. And then she pressed her palms
to either side of his head, tilted it downward
and stood on tiptoe to press her lips to the very
same spot.

She released him then and hurried from his
room. He heard her car start up seconds later.
And then it roared away, down the drive, fading
in the distance.

What in the name of God was going on with
her?

Frowning, Adam wondered just what there
was in that old photo album that had got to her
so much. And though his family history was
something he tended to avoid like the plague,
he reached for the album now, flipped it open,
and scanned the pages, trying to see the photos
through Brigit's eyes.

And then it hit him. The bruises. The way

she'd touched his face, kissed that scar on his forehead.

Ah, hell, she knew.

He heard her car pull in hours later. Hard not to, as noisy as it was. A tide of relief washed over him, that he'd chosen the perfect time to be away from the house. Sitting out here, on the cliffs. Telling himself that he shouldn't be so mortified she'd learned about his secret. Hell, it didn't make him less of a man, did it? He'd have fought back, if he'd been older. Hell, he'd have probably killed the old bastard.

It was the thought of her sympathy he couldn't stand. He'd rather have her take him for whatever meager assets he still had, than to call her scheme on account of pity. He couldn't handle that.

Nor could he look into her eyes knowing she'd seen those photos. Not yet, anyway. So, like a coward, he'd come out here to hide from her. He sat staring down at the roiling waters of the lake, waiting for the storm she'd predicted to move in. She'd been right about that.

So in tune is she with nature, that even the weather cannot hide its face from her seeking eyes. Whatever she wishes to know is eventually revealed to her. Such is the nature of the fairies.

He shook his head at the utter nonsense reverberating in his head. Passages from that Celtic text. He'd been reading it too much. Determined for some reason to get through every page of it as soon as possible.

As if it were anything but another tale to add to the collection.

"Adam?"

He didn't turn. He only went stiff at the sound of her voice. "How did you know I was out here?" If she gave him some mystical answer about *just knowing* he was going to scream.

"I looked for you in the study. Saw you through the windows."

"Ah."

"I came out here to apologize. For going through your album before. It was . . . it was wrong. I'm sorry."

He said nothing, but a second later she was sitting beside him on the flat stone ledge that jutted out over the lake's rocky shore. "The view from here is incredible."

He turned to look at her, then. Surprisingly enough, there was no pity in her eyes. No hint of the secret she'd discovered. No sign she'd use the knowledge against him. He saw acceptance in her eyes, instead. Maybe understanding. Nothing more.

The incoming wind whipped tendrils of her hair loose. He wanted to undo the braid that held those satin locks captive. He wanted to pull her glasses off and set them aside so he could really look into her eyes.

"There's a storm coming, you know," she said, turning her face into the wind. And almost as if she'd read his thoughts, she took the glasses off and set them down.

"I know."

She nodded.

"She hated storms," he said, and it was as if the words just leapt from his tongue without permission.

"Your wife?"

He met her eyes, wondered how she saw things even he didn't see. "Yeah."

"Has it been . . . very long?"

Why was it, he wondered, that whenever he spent time with Brigit, he wound up answering questions he'd have decked anyone else for even daring to ask him. "Almost a year since she walked out. Along with my best friend, and most of my money. One big happy family." He continued staring out at the whitecaps, and the foaming lake. And he heard her thoughtful sigh.

"No wonder you're bitter."

"Not bitter . . . just a little poorer. And a lot wiser."

"Wiser? In what way?"

"I know better than to trust again," he said, and he knew she'd disagree. She needed him to trust again, didn't she? She needed him to trust her, if she was going to pull off whatever it was she was planning.

"That's a hard line to hold . . . a lonely way to live."

"Lonely is better than used, Brigit. Besides, who the hell is there to trust, hmm? Who would you suggest I start with? You?"

She met his eyes, held them steady. "No. Not me."

He studied her face. So perfectly lovely. So open and honest. So goddamn deceiving. Sitting there in the darkness with the wind in her face, telling him not to trust her. What the hell was it about her, anyway, that drew him so much?

"I get the feeling," she whispered, tilting her head and raking his face with her eyes, "that

this bitterness started long before your wife left you, though. I get the feeling it started a long time ago. In your childhood."

He lowered his chin to his chest. So she wasn't going to let it go after all. "The only thing I learned in my childhood, Brigit, was not to believe in fairytales."

She laughed, but it was a sad sound.

"What's funny?"

She reached up to tuck a loose lock of hair back into place, and he caught his own hand lifting, reaching out, as if to stop her. Or to untwist her hair and watch the wind shake it loose. He stopped himself in the nick of time.

"Not funny, ironic. Fairytales were the only thing I *did* believe in." The wind blew a little more of her hair free again. "I wonder which is worse," she said softly, thinking it through out loud, he thought. "Believing so strongly and having the fantasy shattered? Or never having the chance to believe at all?"

She reached up to push the hair into place again, and this time he covered her hand with his own, stopping her. And she turned her head, met his eyes. So much pain there. And he had to know. He had to.

"Tell me," he heard himself whisper, and the sound of the words was swallowed up by the wind, but he knew she heard them all the same. "Tell me what you believed in so strongly. I really want to know."

She lowered her chin to her chest. "If you'll talk to me about what you learned not to believe in," she replied.

Watching the way her lips moved nearly did

him in. But he blinked and gave his head a shake. "I don't talk about that," he told her. "Not to anyone, Brigit. Don't ask me to."

"Do you talk about your father, Adam? Do you talk about what he did to you?"

He wanted to look away, and he couldn't. "No," he said. "Because it doesn't matter anymore."

"He hurt you. He's still hurting you. That matters."

"Not to me, it doesn't."

"To me, then."

Adam closed his eyes to block out the sincerity in hers. He wasn't going to talk to her about this. He wasn't. He . . .

"You know, they say abused kids can grow up to be abusers."

"Yes," she said softly. "I've heard that."

"But not necessarily, you know?"

"Of course not. Lots of abused kids grow up to be wonderful parents."

"You know why?" Why? Good question, he thought. Why am I blurting my most secret feelings to this woman? This stranger? And yet his mouth kept right on moving. "Because they know what a little kid longs for in his heart. They know how bad it is for a kid to go without the one thing he craves. All it takes to put a kid right in paradise, is for his parents to love him, Brigit. It's so damned simple. Why can't more adults see that?"

He felt her hand covering his where it rested on the stone.

"I don't know," she whispered. "Maybe they're blind."

"They are. I'll tell you something, Brigit, when I have a son, I'm going to love him with everything in me." He opened his eyes, saw her staring at him, and saw her tears. "Don't pity me."

"I'm not. I'm jealous of you."

He lifted his brows.

"You'll be a wonderful father, someday, Adam," she told him. "Your children will be lucky, and beautiful, and your family, deliriously happy. I envy that. I really do."

No pity. No poor baby routine. Maybe it was okay that he'd opened up to her a little bit. Maybe having her validate his fondest dreams would make them more real, more possible.

Or maybe she'd throw them right back in his face someday. He'd forgotten her lies for a few minutes, hadn't he? And somehow she'd tricked him into sharing his oldest pain with her. How had she done that?

"I don't want to talk about me anymore," he said, looking away from her.

"All right."

His relief was intense. Almost as if, had she insisted, he'd have had no choice but to go on with the conversation. To tell her every secret he had. Which was crazy, of course. She was still looking at him, still searching his eyes. And when he looked into hers he couldn't stay angry over her supposed invasion of his mind. Instead he fixated on her mouth, and decided if she didn't start using those lips to talk with, he was going to find another occupation for them.

"Tell me," he coaxed, drawn into her eyes and stuck there like a fly trapped in a spider's web. Saying whatever foolish words popped into his

mind, because he was too entranced by her to censor himself. She was spinning some kind of magic, damn her. And he was eating it with a spoon. "Tell me about the fairytales you believed in."

She smiled very slightly, not smugly. Maybe it was more of a self-conscious smile. "I wanted to tell you anyway. So that maybe, you could tell me where the story came from. There are parts of it . . . parts that are important for me to understand."

"I will, if I can." Anything, he thought vaguely. Right now—out here with the dark clouds skittering over the half moon, making shadows on her face, and the wind coming off the lake, whipping more tendrils of her hair loose until they reached toward him, caressing his cheeks like loving fingers—right now, he'd do anything she asked of him.

She leaned back, hands flat on the ground behind her, and her legs stretched out in front, one crossed over the other at her ankle. She wore no stockings tonight. Her lean legs were bare and smooth and tempting him to touch. To taste. He realized she was barefoot. And he thought about kissing her again, from her toes to her hips. He fought the impulse with everything in him.

God, she was beautiful. Like an angel. Or something else ethereal and elusive and mysterious. Something you could glimpse and observe and long for, but too precious ever to hold.

But he wanted to hold her. He wanted it so much he couldn't look away. Utterly mesmerized by her eyes and the deep, sultry sound of

her voice, he listened to her as she began to tell him her story.

Her eyes focused on the roiling lake. But her gaze was turned inward as she began, "Once upon a time . . ."

Chapter Seven

"WHERE THE HELL did you hear that story?"

The harsh tone of his voice startled her, and she snapped back to the present, out of the past that had been swamping her mind as she recited the *Fairytale* from memory. "I told you. It's just a story I heard when I was . . ."

"It's just the one story I've been searching for my entire life," he yelled back, and it shook her to know he wasn't raising his voice just to be heard over the wind. He was angry. "Just a story I've never been able to find, Brigit."

"But—"

"Once more, where did you hear it?"

His face was hard. Granite lines and angles and shadows. And the wind came in stronger than before, whipping his hair into chaos. Roiling storm clouds obliterated the moon's glow, now. But they were nothing compared to the ones raging in his eyes.

"An old nun," she said softly, "told me that story on the nights when I was too afraid or too lonely to sleep. I used to think it was true. That

143

I was really . . ." She let her voice trail off, shaking her head slowly at the expression he wore. "You don't believe me."

He said nothing, just got up as the first raindrops plunked and smattered the flat stone under his feet.

"Come on inside. You'll get soaked."

"But, Adam, you've heard that story before. I know you have. You knew about the forest of Rush."

"What?"

He seemed so alarmed that she blinked in surprise. "You said you thought 'Rush' was the name of the forest in the painting. Adam, that's why I assumed you'd heard my *Fairytale*."

"*Your* fairytale?"

She lowered her head. "Well, I used to think it was mine. That someone had made it up just for me. I only realized it wasn't when it became obvious others had heard it, too. You . . . and the artist who did your painting."

She looked up at him, standing above her, staring down at her with an expression that combined so many emotions she couldn't name them all. Disbelief. Confusion. Rage. Suspicion.

"Adam, I don't know what you suspect me of here. But I only told you about the story because I wanted to know if the version you'd heard included the twin daughters."

His eyebrows bent into question marks. "I'm damned if I'm going to stand out here in the rain and discuss something I know is impossible. A goddamn lie. There's no way you heard that story."

"It's not a lie." The rain fell harder. "Adam,

that fairytale was the most important thing in
my life for a long time. I clung to it when I had
nothing else. And if you know anything about
it, about where it comes from or . . ."

He stared at her, and she felt his eyes probing
her soul. Felt his doubts. And something else . . .

"The only thing I know about it, Brigit, is that
it doesn't exist."

Brigit got to her feet, leaning close to him as
the wind came harder. Raising her voice to be
heard over its deep moans. "If you heard the
story, and the artist heard the story, how can
you say it doesn't exist?"

"I *didn't* hear the damned story! I—" He
pushed a hand through his damp hair. "I'm going inside."

She closed her eyes, refusing to watch him go.
Damn! She hadn't meant to cause him any more
pain. And she obviously had. She'd been worried he'd see through the lies she told. Now he
was seeing lies when she spoke the truth. Why
was he so certain her fairytale didn't exist? What
kind of cruel joke was this, anyway? He knew
the story, but claimed he'd never heard of it?
And what had he meant when he'd told her it
was the story he'd been searching for all his life?

Oh, God, and what did any of this matter?
She'd been foolish to let herself get distracted.
She was here to do a job, not to find answers to
the mysteries of her birth and bloodlines. Not to
find out, once and for all, if she might really,
truly have a sister.

She closed her eyes, released a long, slow,
shuddery breath, and with it, forcibly, a bit of
her tension. The sound of the rain was a com-

fort, and she stood still, feeling its coolness soaking her clothes, her hair. It didn't matter that she didn't know who she was. Or where she came from. Or what she was supposed to be doing in this lifetime. It didn't matter.

She shouldn't be asking anything from Adam Reid, anyway. Not when she was about to deceive him and steal from him. Let him go inside. She'd stay here. And maybe the rain would cleanse her stained soul. She tipped her face up to the droplets, felt them cooling her heated skin. And she couldn't stop the tears of shame from falling from her eyes, but they mingled with the rain and were hidden.

Shit, this was too far-fetched to be for real. Now, more than ever, he knew that Brigit Malone was lying. Trying to convince him she held the answer to his childhood delusions. Trying to make him believe she'd heard the tale . . . that he'd finally found the source for those fantasies that had nearly got him beat to death by his own . . .

Not nearly beat to death. It was a few broken ribs, for Chrissakes! A half-dozen stitches in the back of the head. Kids get hurt worse than that playing high school sports.

He hadn't been in high school, though. He'd been in second grade. He remembered thinking that if this was love, he wanted no part of it. And he'd held that lesson in his heart, ever since. Love and pain were one and the same in his scarred mind. And whether it made practical sense or not, the lesson was too well learned to

ever be forgotten. Hell, he ought to thank the old man for teaching him so well.

It doesn't matter.

Adam stood at the bank of windows in his study, and he stared out to the stone ledge. She was still out there. Had been for hours. He'd turned out all the lights so he could see her in the darkness and the rain. The yellow stars and moons on her dress made it a little easier to spot her.

She'd remained as she'd been, standing there and letting the rain pummel her body. He'd had to come inside. Jesus, she'd been so sensual, especially before she'd risen. When she'd been lying beside him on that cool rock protrusion, with her eyes closed and her dress getting wet. All he could think about was lowering his body on top of hers, of kissing the rainwater from her skin . . .

Not of the lies she was telling or of the reasons behind them. She couldn't have heard the story when she was a kid.

Why not, Adam? You apparently did.

Only he didn't remember it as a story. He thought he'd actually gone there. Seen that place called Rush, firsthand. Talked to a pregnant fairy named Máire, for God's sake.

Yeah. And what are the chances of Brigit making up a name like that? What are the odds she'd come up with the same name you dreamed? Hmm?

But he hadn't gone there. It *had* been a dream, instigated by a tale he must have heard . . . but one he couldn't have heard, because he'd searched the world over for it, and he'd never found it.

Brigit must know about his dream. She must know details. How, though?

Made no sense whatsoever. There was no conceivable reason for her to deceive him this way. And even if she somehow knew all the details of his childhood delusion, and was making up all this about having heard stories of Rush, there was one thing she couldn't fake. Couldn't lie about. Her likeness to the woman in his fantasy. The woman he'd been told was his fate. The woman who was supposed to break his heart, because he had to let her go in the end.

In a dream, he reminded himself, turning to glance at the painting, the enchantress from his childhood fantasy. Only in a dream.

And that old doubt came whispering through his mind like a cool, bracing wind. *It wasn't a dream, Adam. And it wasn't a delusion. It was real, and deep down inside, you know it. No other explanation makes sense.*

A shiver worked up his spine. The practical part of his mind dismissed that whimsical voice, ignored it, but his heart couldn't do the same. What if it were true? What if his experience hadn't been a fantasy? And what if she were really . . .

His gaze returned to the ledge outside. She stood with her arms stretched out to her sides, head tipped back to the rain. And she turned in an excruciatingly slow circle.

She is a faery's childe, and her joy is the rain. From it she draws comfort . . .

Jesus, he snapped inwardly. Quit thinking in terms of that damned Celtic text!

But he couldn't stop thinking of it, because

she was the embodiment of all it described. Damn, could she really be . . .

Finally she stopped turning, let her arms fall to her sides, and turned to walk along the path, and out of his line of vision. She was coming back to the house.

Maybe, he reasoned, as he built a fire in the grate and tried to convince himself it was for his own benefit, not hers, maybe there really were more things in heaven and earth than were dreamt of in his philosophy. Maybe.

So either she was telling the truth, and had no more idea than he, where the story had come from. Or she was lying in a deliberate attempt to perpetrate some complex scam.

Or maybe all of this was real. Part of his mind wanted to play with that theory, examine it, and dwell on it. But most of his mind rebelled. He wouldn't let himself linger in those long-forbidden areas of his mind—realms he'd deemed off-limits, like the woods where it had all begun. But it kept coming back to him, teasing his brain the same way sounds on rooftops around Christmas Eve teased children's minds the world over. Tempting his imagination to dare explore it.

She'd told him a tale of Rush. And in it, Máire had twin daughters. Brigit and Bridín. She'd asked him about that part of the tale, whether it was included in any versions he might have heard. Why? The only logical answer was that she, Brigit, believed she might *be* the Brigit in the story. And that somewhere, she had a twin sister named Bridín.

If that were true, then the pregnant Máire he'd

dreamt of had shown him a vision of her own soon-to-be-born daughter. And told him she was to be his fate.

He blinked, recalling that fairy lady's words to him when he'd been a little boy. "She needs you to show her the way . . . the way to her sister, and then show her the way back home."

He gave his head a shake to silence that bell-like voice he remembered so well, but it went right on. "You mustn't let yourself fall in love with her. She'll break your heart if you do."

A cold chill crept into his nape, and he shivered. As he passed the geranium on the end table, he paused, doing a double take. The thing's leaves were vivid green. And if he wasn't mistaken, those tiny nubs he saw were flower buds.

His stomach knotted a little. Just yesterday the plant had been withered and brown. He remembered the way she'd paused beside it, rubbed her fingers over the drying leaves.

Brigit, his mind whispered. She must be . . .

"She must be the owner of a nursery on the Commons, stupid," he said aloud. "She must be applying her talents to save my pathetic houseplants. And that's all."

But overnight?

Tomorrow, he decided, dropping to his knees in front of the hearth and adding larger bits of wood, he would do some research on Brigit Malone.

He woke to screams so harsh and so frantic they made his heart freeze in his chest. And then he smelled the smoke.

"Oh, shit!"

He dove out of bed in his shorts, and took only the briefest second to feel his bedroom door for heat before flinging it open, lunging into the hall, and leaning over the railing, automatically checking the fireplace. He immediately saw what was wrong, and his entire body sagged in relief. There was no fire. Something had plugged the flue. Smoke billowed gently from a smoldering log on the grate and floated upstairs. Brigit had stopped screaming, so she must realize now that there was no danger.

He took the stairs two at a time, and used the brass pail and the matching shovel to scoop the offending log out. Smoke spiraled off the charred lump. He rapidly shoveled up a few other smoke-belching embers, and added them to the pail, then carried the mess outside, into the rain, and dumped it right into the first puddle of water he came to.

He left the front door open, and opened all the windows in the study before going back upstairs again. And then he tapped on Brigit's door, wanting to check on her before going back to bed.

There was no answer.

Frowning, Adam pushed the door open and stepped inside. But she wasn't in the bed. He flicked the light on, and then crossed the floor to open the French doors, and allow fresh air in to cleanse the room's slightly smoky air. And that's when he saw her.

She sat on the floor in the corner, knees drawn to her chest, eyes wide but, he thought, unseeing. She was pale, and trembling, and tears had burned tracks into her cheeks. She clutched a

book to her chest with white knuckled hands. And she wore only that vanilla satin nightgown. One of the thin straps had fallen from her shoulder, and the way her knees were bent, the bottom of it was bunched up around her hips. She looked, he thought sadly, like a frightened little girl. And that was what did him in.

A shiver ran up Adam's spine at the fear in her eyes. He'd never seen anything so desolate in her before. She always seemed so vibrant, so full of life. But right now, her eyes were vacant. Dead.

He crouched in front of her, his hands automatically closing on her shoulders. "Brigit? Hey . . . come on, talk to me." He shook her a little. "Brigit?"

Her eyes seemed to focus on him. But her breathing was still ragged and too fast.

"It's all right, angel," he told her. And then he blinked, surprised the endearment had fallen so naturally from his lips. And then he decided it fit her. "There's no fire," he soothed. "Just smoke. The chimney was plugged. It's no big deal."

She closed her eyes, released a shuddering sigh. "I was so afraid . . ."

"It's all right." He sank to the floor beside her. It was a good spot. The night breeze rapidly filled the room with rain-washed air that swept through, whisking the smoke back outside with it before blasting more fresh air in.

She pressed close to his side, her head on his shoulder. "Sister Ruth told us to hold hands," she whispered. "But I let go. I went back . . . for Sister Mary Agnes."

A cold chill raced up his spine as she whispered the words, and he wasn't certain she was even aware who she was talking to. His arms went around her in an effort to stop her shivering, but it didn't work.

"B-but I couldn't find her," she said. "There was so much smoke . . . and then the flames . . ."

"There's no fire, Brigit. You're safe." He clasped her nape, turned her head so he could look into her eyes. They were still closed, so tightly it was as if she were fighting not to see something. But he had a feeling she was seeing it anyway. "Open your eyes, Brigit. Dammit, look at me. There's no fire, you understand?"

Her eyes opened, but he wasn't sure if it was in response to his command or to her own nightmares. They opened wide. Too wide.

"I couldn't get out! I couldn't breathe!"

A lump came into his throat, so large he nearly choked on it. This was no dream. No nightmare. This was a real memory.

"You're safe now," he told her. He took her hands, pressed her palms to his own face. "Look at me, will you? It's Adam. There's no fire. You're safe, Brigit."

She blinked several times. "Adam . . ." She sat up a little straighter, searching his eyes, then she covered her face with her palms and muttered, "Oh, God, oh, God." Her entire body shook with the force of her sobs. She drew her knees to her chest, wrapped her arms around them, and she rocked back and forth.

There was the slightest hesitation on Adam's part. Slight . . . as his wariness kicked in to analyze her behavior. Real trauma, or clever ploy?

No. She wasn't acting. Whatever was happening to her, or had happened to her, was real. And frightening. And like it or not, it was tearing his heart out to see her in this state.

Adam got to his feet and bent over her. He slipped one hand beneath her legs and one around her back, and he picked her up, took her to the bed. He lowered her onto it. She rolled to one side, her back to him, and drew herself into a little ball. She reminded him of the woolly bear caterpillars he used to search for as a child. The way they'd curl themselves up when he touched them. An act of self-preservation. She was every bit as scared right now as those insects had been. She trembled, and every few seconds a sob racked her body. She still clutched that book to her breast, whatever it was.

Adam swallowed hard. He looked at the door, even then knowing he couldn't leave her. Not like this. He whispered a prayer to St. Francis of Assisi, and then he laid down on the bed beside her. He snagged a handful of covers, pulled them up to cover them both.

It was right. He knew it was a second later, when a sob choked her, and she turned to him. When she curled up against him, burying her face in the crook of his shoulder, pressing so close and curling her body up so tightly it was as if she'd like to crawl inside him. As if she'd like to hide there, from her memories.

And dammit, he knew that feeling all too well. He had a few memories of his own that could put him in a similar state. And he couldn't turn away from another person who'd had a childhood full of nightmares. He couldn't do it.

He wrapped her up in his arms and he held her, and all his pent-up breath left him in a rush. The rigidness left his shoulders and his spine. He stopped grating his teeth. This was right. This was where he needed to be, right now. He stopped fighting it, and let his instincts have free rein. His hands stroked her hair, and rubbed her back, and squeezed her tighter. He whispered to her that it was all right, that she was safe, that he wasn't going anywhere.

Her trembling body relaxed in his arms. Her face lay tight to his unclothed chest. He felt her hot tears there, and her warm breath. He felt her quivering lips each time she parted them on a sob. The scent of her hair and that of her tears mingled to create a bittersweet perfume he'd remember always. Her skin slid beneath his hands like silk.

He kept it up until she cried herself to sleep.

And then he wondered what demon had possessed him to end up in bed with this woman. Was he so far gone that, even knowing she lied with nearly every breath, he was still this ... this ...

Enchanted.

Yeah, that was the word for it, all right. If he didn't know better, he'd think he was under an enchantment.

And maybe that's exactly what it was. And maybe it was about time he remind himself that if all of this really *were* true, if his childhood fantasy had really happened, and if Brigit Malone were truly the woman he'd been shown ... then lying here, holding her this way, was the stupidest thing he could do. Because it made him

want more, and it made his heart go soft when it had been a solid lump of granite for such a long time. And he couldn't let himself care for her. He couldn't.

Because if this fairytale were true, he already knew the ending. And it wasn't happily ever after.

He laid awake, bathed in her warmth and her nearness, telling himself to leave her alone and holding her tight in his arms, for the rest of the night.

"Adam . . . ?"

Brigit lifted her head from the firm, warm, male cushion beneath it, and realized it was Adam's naked chest. Her first impulse was to return her head to that wonderful pillow, after trailing her lips over it to see how it would taste.

Fortunately, she came a little more fully awake before giving in to that impulse.

"Oh," she whispered, and then, more softly, "oh."

His eyes were opened, clear, and focused on her face with a mingling of concern and awareness. "Yeah. You can say that again."

They were incredibly dark this morning, his changeable eyes. Like the needles of a blue spruce on a cloudy day.

She remembered last night. The smell of smoke . . . the waking nightmare. And Adam, coming to her, holding her and making it all disappear. Her eyes widened as she thought of her book. The *Fairytale*. But a quick glance confirmed she'd tucked it back under her pillow as she did every night. She sighed and sat up, then

belatedly clutched the blanket to her chest. Her choice of sleeping attire hadn't been exactly modest.

"Too late, Brigit. I already have intimate knowledge of that nightie."

She lowered her eyes, feeling her cheeks burn.

"Don't be embarrassed. You look . . . incredible in it."

"This shouldn't have happened." She spoke quickly, softly, keeping her eyes averted.

"Nothing *happened*, Brigit."

"I slept in your arms."

"Yeah. And I was warm until you moved away. Now I'm freezing." He flung back the covers and surged to his feet, heading toward the wide open French doors. She couldn't take her eyes from his scantily clad body . . . those hair-smattered thighs, hard as tree trunks, that small, compact butt covered only by a thin pair of boxers. The broad, smooth width of his shoulders. The way his golden hair touched his nape. The way it curled slightly there. The way she wanted to touch it.

He closed the French doors, and turned to face her. And the color of his eyes turned darker still. They took on a gleam she hadn't seen before. He took a step toward the bed.

"I . . . I'm sorry," she said softly. "About last night."

"Don't be." He took another step.

She met his gaze, held it, and very slightly, she shook her head. "I can't . . ."

He stopped in his tracks, blinking as if snapping out of some trance state. He lowered his chin to his chest, blew all the air from his lungs.

Then he came the rest of the way to the bed and sank onto the foot of it. No longer the predator. She wasn't afraid of him now.

"Tell me something, Brigit," he said, and he ran two hands back and forth through his hair roughly, as if it would somehow invigorate him. All it did was make the hair stick up like feathers. Make her long to smooth it down again. "How old were you when you got trapped in that fire?"

She closed her eyes. He knew it was real, and not a dream. There was no use denying it. She already knew he could see right through her lies. So she opened her eyes again, and met his. "Eight or nine."

"Jesus." He lifted his brows then, not asking, just waiting.

"It was an orphanage. St. Mary's, in New York. Sister Mary Agnes . . . she was the one who used to tell me the story . . . she died that night."

He was searching her face. For what, she wondered?

"But you got out."

She nodded. "A homeless man who spent most of his time in the park across the street came into that hell and carried me out."

"No kidding?"

"No kidding," she whispered. And as she did, she thought of Raze, and all he'd done for her. She adored him. There was nothing in this world she wouldn't do to keep him safe.

And unfortunately, that included betraying the man who sat in his underwear on the foot

of her bed, staring into her eyes as if he were
seeing her for the first time.

Adam had left her in the bed. He still wasn't
sure how he'd worked up the will to do that,
but he had. She'd been lying there looking
sleepy and vulnerable, and very much as if
she'd rather he stayed.

Right. And she'd told him things, things she'd
been holding back before. And now maybe he
had a jumping-off point. He had to know everything about her. He had to find a way to deter-
mine once and for all if there were even the
slightest possibility she was . . . what he suspected she was. God, he couldn't even complete
the thought without feeling ridiculous.

But he had to know the truth. Before she destroyed him. Because if that was her goal, inten-
tional or not, Adam was sorely afraid she was
going to succeed.

Funny how a woman he was afraid would destroy him could manage to heal him while he
awaited the killing blow. Because that's what
she was doing. He realized it this morning. It
was the damnedest thing. She seemed to have
the same effect on his heart that she had on his
houseplants.

Pure, impossible magic.

Facts. He needed facts.

He sat in a booth at Hal's Deli right now,
across from the man who could get them for
him.

"Don't worry about the money, Adam. Look,
you paid me plenty for trying to track down that
lousy wife of yours, even though I offered to do

it as a favor, and even though I wasn't able to find her for you."

"Successful or not, you put a lot of time into tracing her, Mac. What kind of friend would let you do all that for nothing?"

"Yeah, well, I'm doing better now. The business is thriving. Anything you need I'll do at no charge." He looked Adam in the eye, his expression intense. "I mean it. You offer me a dime, I'll blacken your eye. You're my best friend. Just tell me what you want."

Adam nodded, admitting defeat. "Thanks, Mac."

"So what's up?"

He sighed, feeling inexplicably guilty for what he was about to do. "She goes by the name of Brigit Malone," he said finally. "And she spent some time in a shelter called St. Mary's, in New York. I take it she was an orphan. She mentioned that she might have a twin sister, but that she doesn't know for sure. There was a fire at St. Mary's while she was there. Burned the place to the ground. Now she owns a shop on the Commons. Akasha. And that's just about every goddamn thing I know about her."

Except, he added silently, that she loves the rain. And that having her around seems to make dying houseplants thrive. And that her eyes . . .

He gave his head a shake. He also knew her address. And that she'd lied about the construction going on there. He gave Mac the former.

"But you'd like to know more?"

He nodded, and took another sip of the best coffee in the state of New York. "Yeah. Everything you can dig up, okay?"

"You got it, Adam. It would help if I could see her. Do you have a photo?"

"No." *But I have a painting,* he added silently.

"Well, could you arrange for us to run into each other somewhere?"

"You could come to the house," Adam suggested, barely following the conversation. Why, when she was the one lying to him every time she opened her pretty mouth—probably—was he feeling guilty for asking a P.I. to check her out? Why?

"Oh, that'll work," Mac said. "Assuming she's brain dead."

Adam frowned, trying to get his mind on the matter at hand. "Hmm?"

"If she's plotting something, she'll have reason to be suspicious of me, Adam. And if she is, and she has something to hide, she might take measures to *keep* it hidden."

"Oh."

"So take her out somewhere. Some university function or other. There's always something going on, isn't there?"

"Yeah. There's always something."

"Adam, are you okay?"

He met the other man's eyes, and nodded. "So far."

"If you're so sure she's lying to you, why the hell don't you just toss her out?"

He shook his head. "I can't. I can't explain it, Mac, but—"

"Don't put yourself through this again, pal."

He met his best friend's eyes. The concern he saw there was genuine. He wished he could tell

Mac everything, but he knew he'd sound totally insane.

"Look," he said at last, changing the subject. "There's a thing tonight. Cocktail party for university alumni, to kick off a fund raiser. Starts at nine. Okay?"

Mac sighed, but shrugged in resignation. "Okay. Meanwhile, I'll see what I can find out about her."

"Thanks."

Mac slid out of the booth, apparently out of reasons to stay and try to talk some sense into Adam. He could be overprotective of his friends. It irritated some of them, but Adam saw it for what it was. Genuine caring. The guy felt things deep. Especially loyalty. His friends were lucky people.

Adam lingered after Mac had gone. He still had time left on his lunch break. Customers came and went, sat and ate, chatted and read their newspapers. But he wasn't seeing them. More and more, he saw only one face in his mind. A face far too innocent to be involved in trickery or deceit. Maybe too beautiful even to be merely mortal. If she'd lied her way into his life, then it was only because he'd let her. And he would let her remain, because he was so desperate to find out her true connection to the tale that seemed to have been a part of her childhood as much as his own. And *its* connection to the painting that hung over his mantel and haunted his thoughts.

He still had to know those things. But now . . . he had to know them before she managed to lie—or to enchant—her way right into his heart.

It scared the hell out of him to admit, she already had a pretty decent start.

The way it was going, she'd be finished within a day or two. Brigit was more careful when she carried the canvas up the stairs this time. She'd worked on it most of the day, and barely given the paint any drying time at all before she'd had to move it. Dangerous, lugging a wet painting around like this. It could smudge or smear.

But it didn't. Not this time.

She heard a car out front, and looking down at her paint stained fingertips, she panicked. But then she narrowed her eyes, tilted her head, and listened closely. And she knew the sound wasn't coming from Adam's Porsche.

Wiping her hands with a soft rag, she continued down the curving staircase, hearing the doorbell now. She dropped the rag on a table as she passed, and went to open the front door.

Zaslow stood there leering at her.

Brigit gasped. "What are you doing here?"

His smile was slow and deliberate. "Came to check on your progress, Brigit. Wouldn't want to think you were pulling one over on me."

Brigit ignored him, her gaze shooting past him to where his car sat in the driveway.

"Raze isn't there. You think I'd be stupid enough to bring him along?"

"Where is he? Is he all right?"

"Relax, Brigit. He's fine. And as long as you do what you're told, he'll continue to be fine." His hands snatched hers without warning, and his grip was unnecessarily cruel as he lifted

them, turned her palms up, and examined her fingers. She tried to pull free, but he was too strong. And he smiled at the paint stains still visible on her fingertips.

"Looks like you've been a good little forger, Brigit. How much longer?"

"Let go ... dammit, Zaslow, you're hurting me. I said let go!" Her words were firm, and delivered as commands as she tried to twist her hands free of his grip.

He smiled fully, but the smile died a second later. A large hand came down on Zaslow's shoulder, jerking him backward, out of the doorway, so he stumbled on the stairs. He released his grip on her, more out of surprise, she thought, than anything else. She was surprised herself.

"Adam," Brigit breathed.

He didn't look at her. His eyes blazed with midnight-blue fire, and they were all Zaslow's. At some point, she wasn't certain when, he'd grabbed a handful of the other man's shirt, and held it now, bunched in his fists.

"When a lady tells you to let go," he said, his voice dangerously soft, "you let go. Got it?"

"You misunderstood, mister. Brigit and I are old friends ..." Zaslow tried to wrest himself free. Adam finally let go, but did so with a little shove that sent Zaslow the rest of the way down the front steps.

Adam glanced her way, one brow lifted in question.

"Tell him, Brigit," Zaslow said, and she grimaced, ready to declare that the very sight of him made her skin crawl. But before she got a word

out, he added, "Raze wouldn't want you to bad-mouth me. You know he wouldn't."

The fury that had been bubbling inside her froze, and slowly turned into fear. The bastard had her firmly in his control. She had to say and do exactly what he told her, or dear, sweet Raze would suffer for it. Damn Zaslow for using a helpless old man this way. Damn him for this!

She saw Adam watching her, saw his eyes narrow.

She lifted her chin, swallowed hard. "We're old friends," she confirmed with a slight nod. "Just had a slight disagreement."

"That's right. A slight disagreement. But we've settled it now."

A muscle worked in Adam's jaw. He held her eyes captive, refusing to look away. Merciless in his probing and searching. And there wasn't a doubt in her mind that he knew she was lying. For once, she was glad. She didn't want him to think she'd have anything this vile as a friend.

"Brigit doesn't need friends like you," he said, never turning to look at Zaslow, never taking his intense stare from her. "If you darken my door again, you'll have to be carried out of here."

Zaslow's icy eyes flared with anger and maybe a hint of fear. The way Adam delivered the threat left no doubt he meant every word of it, even without eye contact. And though Zaslow was the bigger of the two, Brigit found herself believing Adam could and would do exactly what he'd said he would.

Zaslow never answered, just turned and headed down the driveway, got into his car, and drove off, spitting gravel in his wake.

Brigit closed her eyes, her breath escaping her in a rush, her back bowing a little.

Adam came inside and closed the door. He stared down at her. She could feel his intense gaze even before she opened her eyes.

"He's no friend, is he Brigit?"

"No."

"Lover, then? Or a former one?"

Her eyes flared wider. "No!"

Adam nodded thoughtfully, pursing his lips. "You called him . . . Zaslow?"

She only nodded.

"He has some kind of hold over you. That much is obvious."

She held his gaze, said nothing.

"But you don't want to tell me about it."

Drawing a long, deep breath to battle her constricting throat, she whispered, "Yes I do, Adam. I want that more than I've ever wanted anything, I think. But . . . I can't."

Adam frowned, searching her face, waiting.

"I'm sorry," she added, finally forced to lower her gaze from the power of his.

He was silent for a long moment, and she knew his eyes were still probing and searching her face. Finally, he sighed, and turned away. "Do you like parties, Brigit?"

Frowning, completely thrown by his change of topics, she looked up quickly, turning to stare after his retreating back. "Parties?"

"Boring faculty thing. Lots of pretentious fools, sipping punch and spouting intelligencia to anyone who'll listen. A string quartet. Dancing." He turned around, sent her a wink and a sheepish smile. "Hell, it's free food, if nothing

else. My attendance is pretty much required. It might be a little more bearable if you'd come with me."

She just stared at him, and she knew she must be gaping, but she couldn't move or speak.

"If you don't want to, that's—"

"No. I mean, yes, I want to." Oh, why had she said that? She should have stayed here. It would have given her more time to work on the painting. "When?" she heard herself asking.

He glanced at his watch. "Two hours."

She had a feeling she'd regret this. "I'll be ready."

"Good." He turned as if their conversation were over, resumed walking toward the study.

"Adam?"

He stopped, not turning around.

"Thanks . . . for not pushing me about . . . about Zaslow."

"Don't thank me, Brigit. That conversation isn't over yet." Then he walked into the study, closing the doors behind him.

He grated his teeth, closed his eyes, and told himself he was a hundred kinds of fool. He'd been shaking with anger. *Shaking* with it. It had taken every ounce of will he'd had in him to keep from knocking that bastard on his ass when he'd come in and seen the way he was manhandling Brigit.

Zaslow. She said his name was Zaslow.

It was ridiculous to feel so protective of her. Stupid, when she obviously knew the man, and when the man obviously knew things about her that she hadn't shared with Adam. Hell, he was

a fool. For all he knew this Zaslow might be in on whatever plot Brigit was working here.

His instincts, though, balked at the notion that Brigit would willingly have anything to do with the brute. He obviously had something on her. Something powerful enough to make her lie for him. She'd been ready to spew venom when he'd claimed to be her friend. And then he'd said something cryptic. Adam bit his lip, trying to recall it exactly as Zaslow had said it. "Raze wouldn't want you to bad-mouth me."

So who or what was Raze? What was Zaslow's hold on Brigit? What was her true reason for being here, in Adam's house? And what did Zaslow have to do with it?

Damn, the longer he knew the woman, the more questions he had about her. No answers. Just more and more questions.

He was turning into a freaking basket case. And in his rush to get to the house to see who the hell the stranger in the doorway was, he'd left his briefcase in the car. Yup. A basket case.

He left the study, headed through the foyer to the door. As he passed the marble-topped pedestal table at the base of the stairs, he glanced at the now-thriving houseplant there, wondering again at her green thumb—or was it fairy dust? Then he absently snatched the wadded rag from the stand's surface, thinking Brigit must have been dusting and forgot it.

He stopped, opening his hand and staring down at the soft bit of cloth on his palm. It was smeared with colors. Greens and blues and gray here and there. He lifted it to his face, sniffing.

Paint.

He furrowed his brows and sent a questioning gaze up the stairs, but Brigit was nowhere in sight.

Paint.

And a slimebag of a man holding something over her head, something deadly.

And knowledge of a forest that had existed only in his own imagination.

And the ability to make him forget all of it, just by looking into his eyes.

"Just what in the hell are you up to, Brigit Malone," Adam whispered, staring up the staircase she'd just ascended. "Just what in the hell am I going to do about you?"

Chapter Eight

"WHY DID I say I'd go with him? Why, why, why?"

Brigit could have slapped herself for idiocy. She'd blurted her acceptance before giving it any thought. So here she was, going to a party, while poor Raze was God only knew where . . . afraid and alone . . .

Someone should knock her upside the head for her foolishness.

Deep down inside, she knew she couldn't have painted anymore tonight, anyway. Even if she'd stayed. She'd poured every ounce of . . . of . . . juice, for want of a better word . . . into the work today. She'd wielded those brushes until she was completely dry. She couldn't find another drop of whatever it was that made her able to reproduce perfect likenesses on canvas. Creative energy. Magic. She didn't really know what it was. But she'd tapped it to the bottom of her toes today, and there just wasn't any more. So she'd stopped.

There would be more *juice* tomorrow. She

wasn't afraid there wouldn't be. But she still felt guilty for going out with Adam when Raze was in such dire straits.

Maybe because she was afraid she was going to enjoy it too much.

Too late now, though. She'd agreed, right or wrong. So she supposed she might as well make the best of it.

She wore a green skirt that was made up of countless long strips. Its tendrils reached to the middle of her shins, and rippled and swirled like leaves in the wind when she moved. And brown sandals with thongs that criss-crossed their way up her legs. Her top was a forest-green body suit with a scooped neck. And of course, her pewter fairy, caressing the glittering quartz point, hung around her neck.

She was sitting at the vanity, rebraiding her hair nice and tight, when she heard a soft tap, and then her bedroom door opened.

She met Adam's gaze in the mirror. His expression was speculative.

"Am I late?" she asked.

"Not yet. But you will be if you continue with the braid."

She turned around, but he was already coming forward. He stopped when he stood right behind her, and then he gently turned her face back to the mirror. His fingers dove into her half-done braid, and she felt them moving there, separating, smoothing. Part of her wanted to close her eyes and revel in the feeling of his hands in her hair. There was something so intimate about it. Another part wanted to pull

away and rapidly bundle her hair back into its accustomed style.

He shook it loose, then bent to reach past her for the brush, without asking permission. He ran the brush through her hair, slowly, right from the top of her head, all the way down to the middle of her back where it ended. Over and over again. His free hand followed the path the brush took, and finally, she sighed, tipped her head back, and let her eyes fall closed.

The brushing stopped. And she felt her glasses being gently removed from her face.

Her eyes flew open. She came face to face with the wild little girl she'd been. Only she was a woman now. Sensual and wanton and impulsive.

She saw him in the mirror, standing behind her, staring at her as if he couldn't do otherwise. This man from her dreams with his honey-gold hair and wide-set, almond-shaped wizard's eyes. This man with the hollows in his cheeks giving him a haunted expression, even when he smiled. This man who moved her like no man ever had.

"Why do you hide?" he whispered.

She stiffened, her gaze shifting lower, skimming over his lips, drawn there by their movement when he spoke. She brought her eyes up to meet his again in the mirror. "I don't know what you mean."

"Yeah, you do." He held her gaze, and his was probing in search of secrets. "You're not this prim and proper lady you pretend to be."

She swallowed, but her throat remained dry. "Why do you say that?"

"Because it's true. I see it right there, in those bottomless eyes of yours." He leaned a little closer, so his breath fanned her neck as he spoke, and his head was close beside hers.

Impulsively, she closed her eyes, fearing this man who could see all her secrets. "You're imagining things, Adam. There's nothing in my eyes except—"

"Fire." His voice had lowered. It was little more than a whisper now, but somehow more powerful than it had been before. "Your eyes damn near boil over with passion, sometimes. Your skin . . . it just about simmers. I feel it when I'm close to you . . . like this."

He was close. Too close. And she did feel as if her skin were on fire. Her breathing quickened, and her lips parted. The one inside grew stronger.

"I think, Brigit Malone, that deep down inside, you're a hellion."

Her eyes fell closed again. Her head tipped back of its own accord. Or maybe not. Maybe it was the hellion he'd seen so clearly controlling her movements now. Her hair slipped back, away from her shoulders, and she felt his warm breath on her neck. The fire burned hotter. His lips moved closer. She knew without looking. And then his mouth touched her skin, and he had to feel the wild thudding of her pulse just beneath his lips. He mouthed the skin of her neck as if tasting it, slowly parting and closing his lips again and again.

The power of her desire for him was beyond anything she'd ever known, and it left her trembling and weak with longing when he lifted his

head. She lowered hers, meeting his gaze in the mirror again. Her own eyes were heavy lidded, passion glazed.

His lazy smile did little to disguise the hunger in his own. "See? There's the real Brigit."

She shook her head in silent denial.

His hands came down to her shoulders, kneading gently. "It's true. I think you're just afraid of her."

"I'm not . . ." She blinked at the reflection of the two of them; the sight of his hands on her bared shoulders, those long fingers moving so slightly against her skin, brought the flames roaring back to life, and she couldn't suppress a small shudder. "Maybe . . . maybe I am, a little."

"It's okay," she said softly, as his fingers splayed over her flesh. "I am, too."

She turned a little to look up at him. "I'm not sure I believe that. It's hard to imagine you afraid of anything."

His gaze roamed her face. "Oh, I am. I'm afraid of you, Brigit." His hands rose, and his fingers moved slowly through her hair. "And I'm even more afraid that in another few seconds, I'm not going to be the least bit interested in going to this thing tonight."

She bit her lip, because she was rapidly losing interest in going out as well. "You said your attendance was required."

"It is."

She clasped his hands in hers, and pulled them gently from her hair, holding them, looking down at his long, slender fingers as they twined with hers. "Then we should go."

"If you insist." He closed his hands around hers and pulled her to her feet.

"I can't go like this." She glanced over her shoulder at the mirror once more.

"Sure you can. In fact . . . I dare you."

"Y—you *dare* me?" It was difficult to speak when he was looking at her that way. The touch of those blue eyes on her skin was doing odd things to her pulse and her breathing all over again. All it took was a glance . . . at least, when he was looking at her the way he was looking at her right now.

"Yeah. I dare you. What do you say?"

His words, his breaths, caressed her lips because they stood so close, and a brand new shiver worked through her. Only the slightest movement would bring their lips together. And God, what would *that* be like?

Forcing her gaze up, away from his mouth, she saw the mischief and the challenge in his eyes. It touched something inside her. Her own wall of mischief, she supposed. And she smiled. "Let's go."

Adam was bored. His eyes had a glazed-over look about them as he stood, the obligatory glass in his hand, discussing admissions policies with a stuffy-looking man who was thirty pounds overweight. The place made Brigit feel inferior, to say the least. Educated, sophisticated types lingered everywhere. The very rich and the very literate. They sipped champagne from fluted glasses and spoke about politics and travel.

On a raised platform, a string quartet played classical music, and she couldn't begin to imagine anyone dancing to it. Dainty round tables

stood at strategic points, laden with tiny and nearly inedible lumps that claimed to be hors d'oeuvres. Very nice to look at, but worthless as sustenance. There were bowls of nonalcoholic punch scattered here and there. Neon-colored stuff. Green, yellow, and blood red. Yum, she thought.

The women in the room represented the woman she'd always wanted to be. Sleek and polished. Not a hair out of place. Beautiful, smart, successful women who always knew what to say and what to do. How to act. Which fork to use. They were respected. They were admired.

And Brigit felt more like the homeless, dirty-faced street kid she'd been than she had in a very long time. She stood rigid, back ramrod stiff, chin high, and she tried to pretend. Maybe, she thought, she could fool them. Maybe they wouldn't see the street brat beneath the facade. Maybe. If she were very careful and very quiet.

"Anything wrong?"

She glanced up at Adam, startled by his voice coming so close to her ear. The man he'd been talking with had wandered off, leaving them alone together in this crowd of glitter and wealth and intelligence.

She shook her head, looking down. "I don't fit in here, Adam. I shouldn't have come."

He smiled. It surprised and then shook her. He was so handsome when he smiled. And he looked incredible in his dark suit. His shoulders even broader, his waist narrower than before. He fit in here. He was born to this kind of gathering.

His hand closed around hers. "You're right.

You don't fit in here. Everyone here is a phony, Brigit. Hiding behind a mask. Using either their money or their degrees to make up for their lack of character. Or even soul. Look around."

She did. And as she did he nodded toward a couple who stood near the ghoulish green punch. "Those two like their cocaine more than their money. They're probably high right now."

Her eyes widened, but he was already steering her gaze elsewhere. "And there's Jack. Alone tonight. Probably gave his wife a few bruises she couldn't hide with makeup."

"No."

"Yes. And the fat guy over in the corner?" He nodded in that direction. "He's only been out of prison for six months. Embezzling. And see that incredibly intelligent-looking woman by the stage? The one with the slicked-back hair and the glasses? She likes sleeping with her freshmen students."

Brigit gave her head a shake.

"And the guy who just went—"

"No. I don't want to hear any more."

"Okay. Point is, Brigit, they're just people. Good and bad in all of them. Brains and money don't make them any better than you."

He wouldn't think that if he knew the truth. That she was a thief. A criminal. A woman out to steal, even from him. She lowered her chin to her chest in abject shame.

His forefinger caught it, lifted it, and his eyes probed hers in that way that made her tingle all over. "You're the most beautiful woman here tonight, Brigit. That's why they're all staring."

She shook her head in denial, felt her cheeks burn.

"You are."

"Adam? Aren't you going to introduce me?" The deep voice came from just behind her, and Brigit turned too fast, as if caught doing something she shouldn't, when in fact, all she'd been doing was drowning in Adam's eyes.

"Hello, Mac," Adam said, pumping the man's hand, and turning to Brigit. "Brigit Malone, meet Mackenzie Cordair. Mac, for short. He's an old friend of mine."

Brigit offered her hand and Mac took it. He smiled at her, but there was something in his eyes. Some questioning, searching kind of interest that made her uncomfortable. He wanted something. She could feel it.

"Good to meet you, Brigit," he said.

"Likewise." She narrowed her eyes, peering into his, seeing goodness and honor there. A strong sense of loyalty. No menace or evil. Then why this feeling? She felt he was a threat to her.

"I've heard a bit about you," Mac said, snatching a drink from a passing tray. "You're Adam's new boarder."

"Yes." She took a sip of her own drink, and its sweetness made her grimace. "And what do you do, Mr. Cordair?"

His brows went up as if the question had taken him by surprise. Adam cleared his throat, and Mac seemed to hesitate before he answered. "I'm a teacher, like Adam. Only, I teach over at the elementary school, instead of here at the university."

"How nice."

He was not being honest with her. She didn't know what he was hiding, but there was something, and the knowledge scared her.

So find out what he's up to, the wild one inside whispered. *You know you can.*

She shouldn't, though. She shouldn't. He was Adam's friend.

A friend who's lying through his teeth. Check him out, for heaven's sake. Don't be such a wimp.

Her fingers inched nearer to his pocket, while she distracted them by gesturing with her other hand, and commenting on the music and the food. Inside, she felt the old excitement welling up. It had always been a challenge to try and a thrill to succeed. And damn, but that wild thing inside was getting a charge out of this.

The wallet practically fell into her hand, and she couldn't restrain her satisfied smile. She'd just check his i.d., and then she'd know . . .

Adam was staring down into her eyes when she looked his way. Staring at her with a hunger that frightened her, and something else that looked a little like trust.

God, he couldn't let himself trust her. Not when she was about to steal from him.

Guilt swelled like a tidal wave, and over-whelmed her wariness of Mac Cordair and his motives. She bent over, straightened up again, and held out the wallet. "I think you dropped this."

Mac's eyes widened in shock, then narrowed on her. As if he knew full well he hadn't dropped the wallet.

The place was stifling all of a sudden, and that knowing look in Mac Cordair's eyes frightened

her. She had to get out. "You two go ahead and catch up," she managed. "I'm going to find the powder room."

And before either of them could say another word, she turned and lost herself in the crowd. She didn't go to any powder room though. Instead she made her way to the nearest exit, and slipped outside, into the parking lot. The fresh, night air on her face revitalized her, gave her a little more sanity and strength.

She leaned back against the cool wall of the building, staring up at the star-speckled sky and trying to shake the feeling of impending doom that had settled over her in there.

And she heard the door open and swing slowly closed, and she knew it was Adam who'd come to join her.

"Will you promise not to laugh if I tell you something?" She said it without turning to look at him.

He came closer, stood beside her, one arm sliding around her waist to draw her tight to his side. "I can't imagine I'd laugh at anything you had to tell me, Brigit. But yeah, I promise."

Biting her lower lip, she worked up her nerve. "I . . . I hate crowds. Mainly because . . . because I *know* things about people. When I look into their eyes, I can see . . ." She closed her eyes and simply blurted it. "I can see inside them. What they're feeling. Who they really are."

"You see inside them?"

She expected ridicule, but there was only confusion.

"Your friend, Mac, he wasn't being honest. I don't know why, because he seems like an hon-

est man. but he was keeping something from us
. . . or at least, from me."

She dared a peek up into Adam's eyes. He
was looking at her as if she'd told him that pigs
could fly. And she lowered her face. "It's always
been that way. I'm weird, Adam. I'm not like
normal people. Never have been. I don't—"

"What do you see when you look into my
eyes?"

Her head snapped up sharply. The question
startled her.

"Tell me."

Oh, God, why had she confided in him like
that? He couldn't possibly believe her. Never
would. He was playing along now, because it
amused him. Nothing more.

"Tell me," he said again, and she made the
mistake of looking at him. Right into those dark
sapphire eyes, with the occasional fleck of turquoise. So changeable.

Mesmerizing and so very sharp.

"I see goodness," she heard herself whisper,
as if she couldn't help but answer him. "Under
a mountain of anger and rage. A mountain built
on pain. That's what I see most of in your eyes,
Adam. A pain that never dies."

He blinked as if she'd slapped him.

"I want to make it better," she whispered. Her
hand drifted upward, and her fingertips stroked
his corded neck. And then she realized she'd
spoken her thoughts aloud, and her eyes widened. She started to turn away, mortified, but he
caught her shoulder, stopping her.

"I have a feeling," he whispered, "that you're
only going to make it worse."

She closed her eyes, shook her head in denial, but knew he was right. And how on earth could he know that she'd hurt him in the end?

"Problem is, I don't have brains enough to let that bother me."

She hadn't noticed the change in the music, the way it had got suddenly louder as someone opened a window. But Adam had. And before she'd given her consent, his arm crept around her waist, and he drew her close to him. His fingers twined with hers, and he turned in a circle.

She put her hand on his shoulder, lifted her head, eyes widening in surprise. He drew a breath, expelled it as a sigh, and shook his head. "What the hell am I gonna do with you, Brigit Malone?"

She didn't answer. She couldn't, because being in his arms this way was too potent an experience not to rob her of her powers of speech. She clung to him, and they danced. And it seemed to Brigit that he held her a little closer, and then a little closer still.

The music wove a spell around her as magic as anything Akasha had to offer. And by the time the song ended, her head was resting against Adam's chest. She could feel the pounding of his heart beating in perfect time. Her arms had curled around his neck, and his clasped her waist tightly, so their bodies were pressed together from hip to head. She felt him bend a little, felt his face pressing into her hair. She was in a dream, floating amid an ocean of stars. And no one existed, no crowd filled the room on the other side of the nearby door. She was alone in

a glittering galaxy, wrapped in Adam's arms, and she'd be content to stay right there forever.

Someone cleared a throat, very loudly, and she felt Adam stiffen. He stopped moving. But she clung tighter, keeping her eyes closed and having no desire to leave his arms.

"Angel, the song's over." He spoke near her ear, one hand stroking her hair. "From the way everyone seems to be emerging from the building and staring, I'd say the party is, too."

"Mmm." Then his words sank in, and her eyes flew open. She stepped away, whipping her head around, seeing several pairs of eyes glued to the two of them, and her face burned. People made their way to their cars, gawking at the couple who'd still been dancing to music only they could hear.

"Can we leave now, Adam?" she whispered, head lowering.

"Damn right we can." His voice was coarse and a little choked.

He didn't know what the hell was happening. It was . . . it was almost like magic. While he'd been dancing with Brigit, he'd lost track of where he was . . . of *who* he was, for Christ's sake. The music had died away. The ground beneath his feet had dissolved. He'd closed his eyes, but he'd still been able to see. He and Brigit had been floating, dancing and floating, in a midnight-blue sky that sparkled with diamond-like stars.

Not a feeling. Not a daydream. No way in hell, this had been as freaking real as . . .

As his trip to the forest of Rush when he'd been seven years old.

He didn't know what kind of spell she was weaving around him. He didn't know much of anything right now. Except that he wanted Brigit. He wanted her so much he was shaking with it. And it didn't matter that he had no idea who, or for that matter *what*, she really was or what the hell she was up to or why she'd wormed her way into his life. He wanted her. She could be an ax murderer and he'd still want her.

And he'd tell her so, too. The second he got her home.

He was silent in the car, and that was okay. She was, too. And she supposed he might be lost in the impossible task of making sense of their momentary lapse back there at the university. Or maybe he hadn't lapsed at all. Maybe it was only her, and maybe he'd just been humoring her.

She'd always been able to tune out the world. To lose herself utterly in her own place. A magical place of twinkling stars and rainbow glimmers flashing sporadically. A place without gravity or sound or thought.

Usually, though, it was up to her to make it happen. To close her eyes and focus on tranquility and peace, and to find that place. This time it had been spontaneous. It had happened as if on its own, without warning. Like . . . like magic.

Why?

God, for those few moments she hadn't even thought of Raze

Adam twisted the key and the car's engine died. Only then did she realize they were back at the house. And fear made her throat narrow to the size of a piece of straw. It made her stomach into a small, hard chunk of ice. That dance had altered things. She'd revealed her innermost fantasies . . . her secret desires. She was sure she had.

Without a word, she shoved her door open and got out, heading for the front door more quickly than she should. Ashamed of running from him without explaining herself. But too afraid to do anything about it.

Her sandaled feet made little tapping sounds on the steps, and she gripped the latch, only to yank in vain.

She let her head fall down until her eyes focused only on her own bare toes, and didn't even turn when he came up behind her, reached past her to insert his key in the lock. He twisted the key, then hesitated. His warm breath fanning her neck was almost more than she could bear.

She nearly collapsed in relief when he finally opened the door and stepped back. But instead she managed to remain standing. Even to walk into the house. And he stepped in behind her, closed the door, and said, "Are you really magic, Brigit? Is that what it is?"

His hands closed on her shoulders from behind, turning her slightly, and then he pointed. She looked up. The chandelier's crystal prisms were on fire, bathed in moonlight that slanted in through the wall of windows. They sparkled, throwing beams of gem-colored light like the

storm god hurling lightning bolts. Flashes of red and green and gold bounced from the walls, danced on the floors, caught and blazed in the mirrors.

"It's never looked like this before," Adam whispered. And the tone of his voice was like a child's . . . filled with wonder. So she turned to see him, and a blaze of green painted his eyes. Both eyes, making them flash unnaturally. "A lot of things are like they've never been before, Brigit. Since you came through that door."

She shook her head.

"It's true." His hands came up to cup her head, fingers spreading tingles of awareness over her nape and down her spine. "What is it about you that has my dying plants looking as if they could grow into an entire rain forest?" He searched her face, his eyes still glowing, sparkling, catching and holding hers until she couldn't look away. "What is it about you Brigit . . . that makes me feel . . ."

She caught her breath as he drew her, gently, inexorably closer. Until he held her the way he'd been holding her when they'd danced.

". . . makes me feel I'll wither and die unless I kiss you . . . right now."

He kept his eyes opened, kept her captive in their depths. One hand continued to cradle her head, but the other slid down, curled around her waist, and pulled her tighter. So tight she felt every ripple of muscle in his chest. And then his head came down and he kissed her.

His lips touched her mouth, tasted, testing, she thought. And she surrendered with a small

sigh. Her entire body melted in his arms as she opened her mouth in gentle invitation. Sweet surrender.

And she knew she'd never be the same.

Chapter Nine

HE WAS DROWNING. And the same sensation overcame him as before, when they'd danced. That almost out-of-body experience that she seemed to instigate. He wasn't here. There was no floor beneath his feet, no ceiling. The glimmering lights from the chandelier's prisms became palpable. Warm, pulsing as they painted his face. The focal point of his entire existence became Brigit. Her lips beneath his, her body in his arms. The soft sounds of surrender she made.

Every whisper-soft touch of her fingers in his hair was as powerful as a 220-volt shock. Every breath passing from her parted lips into his, carried the very essence of the woman he held. Every touch of his tongue as it pressed through the moist barrier brought a taste so sweet it was beyond description. Drugging. Addictive. So that he pressed deeper, seeking more. The very heat of her body was a song . . . music he could hear only in his soul. Blending and mingling with his own. He wanted to devour her!

When her knees seemed no longer able to support her, Adam bent and scooped her into his arms, never taking his mouth from hers. And somehow he moved through the glittering night that surrounded them, swimming through space thick with rainbow flashes that he could now hear as well as touch. And then he was lowering her to the floor he couldn't feel. Like a cloud under her back, and he was lying there with her, on top of her, kissing her because he couldn't seem to stop.

And she was kissing him back just as eagerly. Her arms twined around his neck and her hands threaded in his hair, and her body moved beneath his, rubbing against him, pressing closer. But still not close enough.

His hands slid beneath her hips, pulling her tighter to him, and he ground his hips hard against her softness.

And all at once she twisted her face to the side, and their lips came apart. She was gasping for air, and her words came out desperate and hoarse.

"No more, Adam. We can't . . ."

Like ice water, those words.

Adam blinked rapidly, and as if the spell had suddenly been broken, the room came into focus. They were in the study, on the Oriental rug near the barren hearth. There was no music. And part of him thought that was because the music had been her . . . or the two of them, together. But that was foolishness. Fantasy. The flashing prisms had lost the supernatural glow . . . the one they'd never really had in the first place.

And he was lying on top of Brigit with one knee wedged between her legs, holding her so tight he was surprised she could breathe. She had to feel how hard he was. How could she *not* feel him pressing into her? Or his heart hammering like a runaway train? Or his ragged breathing?

What the hell had happened to his brain? His mind? He'd never lost himself like this. It was only sex for Christ's sake. He'd always thought about it ahead of time, planned a time when he wouldn't be interrupted or rushed, made sure he had a condom or two nearby.

It had never been desperate and mindless and crazed! On a floor for Christ's sake! A floor. She must think he was some kind of animal.

He rolled off her, glanced at her face, expecting to see revulsion in her eyes. Maybe even fear.

But she wasn't looking at him. She was staring up at the painting that hung above the mantel. And she was crying.

"Brigit? What's . . . Jesus, tell me I didn't hurt you."

She brought her gaze to his, levering herself up onto her elbows. "You didn't hurt me. I was as carried away as you were," she whispered, and there was pain in her voice that belied the words. He *had* hurt her. Maybe not physically, though.

"Then why—"

She only shook her head, and he didn't have a clue what the hell to say to her. She got to her feet, turned toward the stairs. "You don't want

to get tangled up with a woman like me, Adam. You really don't."

She was right. He knew she was right. He didn't *want* to get tangled up with her. It just didn't seem to Adam that he had much of a choice in the matter. He shook his head, pushing his hands through his hair in frustration. "Why don't you let me be the judge of that?" He rolled to his feet, came up behind her, and settled his hands on her shoulders. "I don't know what the hell this is, Brigit, but it's powerful."

"It's madness."

He lowered his head, intent on kissing the crook of her neck, but she danced away before his lips could taste her skin again.

"I'll only hurt you, Adam. Destroy you, maybe. I don't want to do that, but if you touch me . . . if you kiss me once more . . . I might not be able to help myself."

And before he could reply, she ran from him. Right up the stairs, and he heard her bedroom door slam. Imagined he heard the lock turning.

Damn!

What was happening to cool, calm, analytical Adam Reid? The man who'd decided he wanted nothing more to do with conniving women? This one all but *admitted* she was up to no good. Told him not to trust her, promised she'd hurt him . . . destroy him, maybe. And what does he do but hunger for her all the more!

And how was it that her words of warning mirrored those spoken to him by that fairy he'd encountered as a child? God, the longer he knew her the more inclined he was to believe it was all true. And if it were true, she *had to* leave him.

And there was nothing he could do to prevent it. Hell, he was supposed to *help* her to leave him.

It would kill him.

No. No, he couldn't let this go on. No way. He had to get past this obsession with Brigit Malone. He had to find a way.

Turning in a slow circle, he pushed both hands through his hair.

Soon.

She'd always known she didn't fit in . . . always felt there was something different about her, something lacking.

She hadn't realized what it was until tonight. But now she suspected the reason for her oddness was the lack of a single shred of decency. If she hadn't been able to tell another thing about Adam, she knew these two facts. He was good. And he was hurt. Injured . . . perhaps beyond repair. Betrayed again and again by people he trusted.

She was about to betray him, as well. She was going to steal from him . . . steal what she knew to be his most precious possession. How could she let herself make matters worse by . . .

If that man were to come to care for her, her guilt would be compounded.

It was bad enough, wasn't it . . . that she'd let herself begin to care for him?

The phone was ringing. It woke him from a fitful sleep, filled with dreams of having hot, frantic, insane sex with Brigit. And he was coated in sweat and panting like a goddam ad-

dict in need of a fix. Trembling. Gooseflesh crawling over his arms and thighs.

Jesus!

He snatched up the phone and growled hello in a voice that sounded totally unlike his own. Barbaric and raw. Like his yearning for her.

"Adam? It's Mac. You all right?"

He cleared his throat but his voice wasn't a hell of a lot more civilized when it emerged. "Fine."

"Sounds like you've been wrestling a bear. Well, I have a shitload of information on your lady friend. Interesting stuff, too. You want to meet me?"

Adam sat up straighter. Information. On Brigit. Yes, that was what he needed. Maybe he could figure out what she wanted from him, besides to drive him out of his mind. "Just tell me. What did you find out?"

"On the phone?"

"Yes on the freaking phone! Talk, already!"

"Okay, okay. Jesus, you wake up cranky, Reid."

Adam rolled to his feet, fumbling in the nightstand for a pad and pen in case he wanted to make a note. He heard Mac shuffling papers, then the man cleared his throat.

"I got most of this before last night, Adam, but I couldn't very well blurt it out right there in front of her."

"Go on."

"Before I start, there's something else."

"What?" Adam's patience was down to its ragged edges.

"I did not drop that wallet last night."

Adam frowned. "What the hell are you trying to say, Mac?"

There was a thoughtful pause. And then, "Nothing. Never mind. Listen, here's the rundown on your girlfriend. There was only one child by the name of Brigit who was at St. Mary's at the time of the big fire. Brigit Doe, they called her. Last name unknown. Mother unknown. No birth certificate was ever on file for her. None that was found, anyway."

"What, she just appeared at the shelter one day with no past, no story?" Adam was beginning to think his friend was doing shoddy work. Then again, who could blame him? He was working gratis, after all. And then he gave himself a mental kick for doubting Mac's integrity. Man, what was happening to make him think this way?

"Oh, she had a story all right," Mac said, unaware, apparently, of his friend's treasonous thoughts. "But there's no verification to speak of. Whatever records existed were destroyed in the fire. All I have is word of mouth. The reminiscences of an old nun in a nursing home."

"Tell me what you have, Mac. I don't give a damn if you heard it from a talking jackass."

Mac sniggered, then stopped himself when he seemingly realized Adam was not making an attempt at levity. "Ahem ... All right. Here it is. One morning the parish priest, a Father Anthony Giovanni, walked into the church to find two babies at the altar. Twins, maybe, but not identical. The other one was blond. Anyway, there was a note, but that gave them nothing. Just said to take care of the girls, and was signed

John. The only other clues were a pair of identical, handmade storybooks. One was tucked in beside each kid, and each book had a name on the inside cover. The names were Brigit and Bridín."

The last vestiges of doubt were rapidly disintegrating. Funny, how they felt the same way the ground would feel if it were crumbling beneath his feet. "You're *shitting* me?"

"No, I'm not. The old nun said there were pendants inside the books as well, though she couldn't remember exactly what they looked like."

Adam knew what they looked like. At least, he knew what *one of them* looked like. A pewter fairy twined around a quartz point. The one Brigit never took off.

"This retired nun says she knew both Sister Mary Agnes and Brigit, and that she got the story straight from Sister Mary Agnes," Mac continued. "Anyway, the twins were taken to the children's shelter attached to the church. The nun—Sister Ruth—says Bridín was adopted right away. Brigit was sickly, though, so no one wanted her. She lived with the sisters until the night of the fire."

Adam tensed. "And after that?"

"Never seen again. Someone said she'd gone back into the flames after Sister Mary Agnes. The old nun died in the blaze, but no sign of the girl's remains were found. Two eyewitnesses reported seeing an older man rushing into the burning building. From the descriptions, the local cops i.d.'d him as a transient who went by the name of Razor-Face Malone."

"Malone?" *R. F. Malone. My God, not her husband. But an old bum who'd saved her life once? Is it possible?*

Raze wouldn't like you bad-mouthing me. Zaslow's words rang in Adam's ears. What the hell did it mean? Had this *Raze* turned against her? Was he working with Zaslow? Did he have something to hold over her head?

"I told you it was interesting," Mac went on.

"Was it arson, Mac?"

"Nope. Faulty wiring. No question about that. Besides, old Razor-Face wasn't a firebug. Just a little delusional. According to police records, the few times he was picked up for vagrancy he'd done some talking about fairy princesses and some enchanted forest. Rush, he called it."

"Jesus H. Christ." Adam mouthed the words, but no sound emerged. Icy chills raced up and down the back of his neck, and he rubbed it with one palm to chase the feeling away.

"That's it for now, pal. But you know, you're onto something here. Until now no one knew the woman going by the name of Brigit Malone was the same kid who disappeared in that fire. The question is, why?"

"Why," Adam repeated stupidly.

"I still have feelers out on this, Adam. Looking for anyone who knew Razor-Face Malone. And I'm still pulling in tidbits about Brigit Malone, the businesswoman. Trying to see what came between the night of the fire, and the day she turned up in town. Nothing earth shattering so far. I'm trying to track down the missing twin sister, too. You want me to keep on this, right?"

"What?"

"I said, should I keep digging? Or do you have enough?"

Adam gave his head a shake. He could no longer feel his lips, and there was a loud buzzing sound in his head that seemed to be drowning out Mac's voice. "Yeah," he managed. "Yeah, keep digging."

"Are you *sure* you're all right, Adam? You sound . . ."

"I'm fine. Listen, check out a guy named Zaslow, too." He didn't wait for an answer, just hung up the phone, vaguely aware that the pad and pen he'd been holding had fallen from his suddenly numb fingers. "I'm fine. Unless you count the fact that I'm ninety-nine percent sure I'm living with a real live fairy, that is. Other than that . . . I'm fine."

She hadn't slept well. Couldn't. There was still a faint trace of wood smoke in the air, clinging . . . like a specter from the past trying to haunt her dreams. Before dawn, she rose. She needed good, clean, dawn-fresh air. Earth under her feet.

She dressed quickly, pulling on an ancient pair of faded, frayed cutoffs and an oversized t-shirt that had been tie-dyed and trimmed in beaded fringe. She wondered for a moment why she'd brought these things. She hadn't worn them in years. Hadn't intended ever to wear them again. They clashed with her role as a normal, respectable businesswoman. They would give her away as a phony.

But she didn't really feel as if it mattered anymore. If anyone had ever bought the act, it was

a miracle. She couldn't play the part anymore. Hell, for a while, she'd even fooled herself.

But she knew what she was. She was strange. A misfit wherever she went. She'd been more at ease living in that condemned, rat-infested heap of bricks with Raze and the other homeless people, than she'd ever been moving among "civilized" types. She was wild and wanton, constantly at war with desires so hot they burned her at night. She'd dreamed of Adam last night. Dreamed of him as she'd never dreamed of him before. All night, images of the wild sex she wanted to have with him had drifted through her mind, in vivid, electrifying detail.

She might as well stop fighting the wild one inside. Because the wanton was a part of her she could no longer deny. And this morning, she felt more like that wild child than ever. She finally admitted that she'd be more content to feel her bare feet sinking into soft brown earth or lush grasses, than she could ever be in high-heeled shoes, clicking over shiny parquet. She was filled with nervous energy. She wanted to run like an untamed thing. A mustang filly, kicking her heels up behind her as she raced until her lungs burned. She wanted to dance and jump and spin and cartwheel.

She just wasn't normal. And it was high time she stopped trying to pretend she was.

She slipped out the back way, not bothering with shoes, leaving her glasses behind and her hair flying free. She took her time. The sunrise would be incredible. She could smell it in the air. Already, out over the lake, the midnight-

blue sky was paling, and there was a narrow ridge of pink lining the mountains where they made love to the sky.

Oh, and the water! Look at the water!

There was a path, a jagged path fraught with loose stones, bordered by boulders and so steep it seemed impossible to travel by. She would try it later, she decided. But for now, the cliffs were her destination. That beautiful outcropping of rock where she and Adam had sat together in the rain. She'd watch the sunrise from there.

As soon as she sat down on the cool stone, she felt stronger. Not a bit happier about what she had to do, and certainly no clearer about her own lost identity. But physically better. The morning breeze and the waves crashing below seemed to rinse away the exhaustion of a sleepless night, taking it with them back out into the depths to leave it there. And the sun's upper lip was fiery orange as it kissed the sky . . .

As it rose, she remembered the way Adam had kissed her. Gently, then deeper. Parting her lips with such care and tenderness, working his way inside . . . just the way the sun slowly worked its way into the sky. And finally, taking, possessing, filling her. Transforming her into something . . . something she didn't know or recognize. Or freeing that part of herself she'd been fighting for so long. Fully formed now, it seemed. The wanton. The wildness raged in her now, and she wondered how she'd ever cage it again.

God, why couldn't she be like other women? Cool and sleek and in control?

The sun beamed its full force down, warmth

and light washing over her ... through her. The headache burned away. She was strong again. But no more knowledgeable than she'd been before. "Who am I," she whispered, and choked away her tears to voice the question again, louder. "Who am I, dammit? Where do I belong? What cruel god created me, and why, for heaven's sake? What the hell am I *doing* here?"

Each question was louder than the one before, and the final one was shouted as she shook her fists at the sky. Fury and rage and confusion all exploding from her in the form of questions she already knew had no answers. Questions that had plagued her even at St. Mary's. And then she had to be rid of it. All of it. She stood up, filled to brimming with nervous energy and anger, and sick to death of worry and remorse. She didn't want to think about it anymore.

For the first time in years, Brigit only wanted to feel alive. She wanted to feel wild and free, and filled with reckless abandon the way she used to feel before she'd decided to become responsible and respectable. She wanted to do something utterly thrilling.

She looked down at the waves rolling to shore below, and slowly, she smiled. "Yes," she whispered. Then she turned around, and walked several yards. When she faced the lake again, she drew a breath, and the wild one inside her grinned. She ran right up to the edge, stretched her arms up over her head, bent a little at the knees ... and then she dove.

God, it was wonderful! Just like flying. She pointed her body like an arrow, and watched the stone walls speeding past her in a blurred

gray rush. The air whistled past her ears, whipping her hair up behind her, whooshing over her body. Then she punctured the lake. Stabbed into it, torpedoed down deep. And she arched her back, and pushed with her arms, and shot up toward the surface. Her head broke through, and she flung her hair backward, tipping her chin to the sky and inhaling the fresh morning air until her lungs were filled to bursting.

It felt good to be wild again. She'd stifled herself for too long. She'd lived calmly and quietly and become staid and complacent. No more, dammit! The turmoil inside her needed release, and a little wildness was exactly the way she ought to vent it.

And since she still had a lot of venting to do, she began swimming away from shore, burning all the energy that had been pent up inside her for so long.

She swam faster, harder, and her heart pumped and her muscles burned. But it felt good. It felt good to take her anger out this way. She had every right to be angry with the way things had turned out.

Growling with effort, she paddled onward. Raze had been taken from her, was being used to force her to lie and steal one more time. And she slashed her hands through the water as if Zaslow's evil face were there on the surface. She took out her fury toward him on the lake.

When she was too tired to swim another stroke, she slowed, and floated on her back, rising and falling with the swells of the blue water. And she knew the source of her anger as well as she knew her own reflection in the mirror.

She cared deeply for Adam Reid. And she was being forced, against her will, to betray him.

"I don't want to do this," she whispered, and the waves gained strength until she couldn't float anymore. So she rolled over, still breathless, panting, and just treaded water. "I don't want to betray Adam."

A wave slapped her face, sloshing water into her mouth, and she realized that her anger and her energy were spent. Only remorse for what lay ahead of her remained. Tears fell to blend with the waters of Cayuga. "I . . . just . . . don't . . . want to."

But you know you have to.

Another wave slapped her. She swallowed more water, and turned to look back toward the shore. And then her heart skidded to a halt in her chest, because she'd swum so far the shore was a hazy outline in the distance.

She blinked in shock. "Oh, God, what have I done?"

Closing her eyes, she called on that wild one inside, knowing instinctively *she* was the stronger one. The braver one. "Have to try," she told herself, and she began swimming shoreward.

Ten strokes . . . twenty. Why didn't the shore look any closer? Forty . . . fifty. She paused to catch her breath. The water's caress was chilling her overheated flesh, and her lungs were beginning to ache. A sob tore at her breastbone, but she battled it into submission, and launched herself shoreward once more. But she knew her progress was minuscule at best. Before she'd made it halfway, she was too exhausted even to

keep her head above water. Damn, she'd been an idiot. A fool. She'd let the caged one take control, and it was going to cost her. Her longing gaze swept the shoreline once more. "It's too far . . ."

Try!

Slap! She spit water out of her mouth, and nodded tiredly. She had to keep trying. She was a lot of things, but not a quitter. Not a coward. She began paddling again. But her muscles screamed in protest, and burned with every movement. Another wave splashed her, pushing her under. She fought to the surface, choking and spitting, and then another swept her under. Her arms ached and her legs cramped when she broke surface yet again, straining onward. A few more strokes . . . and that was all. She tried, but it was simply impossible to go any farther. Impossible. And she'd given it her best shot.

Numbly, she lifted her arms again, tried to kick her feet, but the merciless water pulled her into its cool embrace, and closed over her head.

He'd almost reached her when she went down for the last time. Dammit! It was all but impossible to keep an eye on her with the morning breeze rippling the surface, and those swells out there where she was. He'd been looking for her, intent on telling her what he knew and asking her what the hell was really going on.

But she hadn't been in the house, and when he'd looked outside, he'd heard her. Her anguished cries to a deaf god had blasted the anger from Adam's mind. *Where do I belong? What the hell am I doing here?* Pain arcing through the

dawn sky so clearly it hurt to hear it.

And the questions . . . he didn't want to analyze them now. He told himself that it was normal for a person who'd never known her parents to feel an identity crisis now and then. He didn't believe that was the case, here, but he told himself he did, and focused on getting to where she was. Talking to her.

Taking her pain away . . .

No. Not that. Just . . . just . . .

He followed the sound of her voice . . . catching sight of her just as she dove from the cliffs like an eagle swooping down on its prey.

"Jesus Christ . . . Brigit!"

He ran to the ledge as well. Crying out in anguish when he saw her body pierce the lake, holding his breath while she was hidden from view by the sapphire waters, and then nearly collapsing in relief when she surfaced again.

Like a mermaid when her head emerged. Like a pagan goddess as she tipped her head skyward, eyes closed as if to receive the kiss of the sun.

And then she began swimming. Adam shook his head in disbelief. Then realized he shouldn't. He'd sensed from the beginning that the staid, reserved Brigit was only a mask she wore. That the real woman within was a hellion. Well, he'd been right. Though even then, he'd underestimated her.

He caught sight of her again, diving under the waves. She surfaced some yards out, and dove again. And again. And again, each time swimming farther from the shore.

"Brigit," he said softly, wondering if she were

even aware how far out she'd gone. "Brigit! Can you hear me?" He shouted, cupping his hands around his mouth. She didn't respond, didn't look back. Damn, she hadn't looked back since she hit the water. Not once.

Okay . . . there . . . she was stopping, floating. Resting. Maybe she was okay. But, damn, she was a long way out. He turned his body, not his head, and started heading toward the path that led down to the shore. Keeping his eyes on her as he decided to swim out in case she needed help.

But then a wave hit her and swept her under. She came up sputtering, and he knew she'd finally seen how far away the shore was. He couldn't see the panic in her face. But he could feel it. He could feel it as surely as if it were his own. And he didn't even stop to wonder how the hell that was possible.

She stroked toward shore and was swept underwater again. And Adam didn't hesitate. He turned back toward the cliff, heeled off his shoes, and ran, peeling the shirt over his head as he went, and letting the wind take it from his hands. The jeans stayed where they were. No time for those now. He hit the edge running and pushed off hard. And then his body was knifing downward at what felt like the speed of light. Icy-cold water met him head on, engulfing him, chilling him through to the bone by the time he curved up to the surface again. And then he poured every cell into making his strokes powerful, making each movement of his body propel him forward as fast and as far as possible.

And he'd just about reached her when she

vanished beneath the surface. Like a rebellious mermaid struggling against her fate, only to be yanked into the depths by some overbearing sea god. And then he was diving down, deeper, stroking madly, eyes wide and straining to see her through the ever-darkening water.

And then he did.

Stroking straight down, he caught her under the arms, yanked her to him, got his legs under him again. His lungs burned. He couldn't hold his breath much longer, but he wouldn't let her go. He wouldn't. He might not find her again. His legs pumped. He moved his entire body to propel himself upward. And finally his head emerged in an explosion of droplets . . . and hers with it.

Holding her from behind, he maneuvered her head onto his shoulder as he dragged gulps of air into his starved lungs. His legs still working to keep them afloat, he gripped her chin with one hand, turned her head a little, stared down at her beautiful face. Satin skin. Huge eyes, closed now, thick long lashes beaded with lake water. Rivers of it running down over her throat.

He put his lips to hers, tried to breathe for her. It was awkward, all but impossible to do while trying to tread water. Three breaths. Then he struck out for shore. And in a few seconds, he paused to force his own breath into her body again. Then swam some more.

He'd nearly reached the shallows when she choked and began twisting in his arms.

He only held her tighter, and stroked onward until his feet reached bottom. They were still a

hundred yards from the shore, but he could walk now. He got his footing and picked her up, carrying her the rest of the way.

They emerged from the water like that. Adam still searching her face for the signs of life that had subsided into stillness again, still frantic for her. And Brigit just lying in his arms, head thrown backward, long hair trailing in the water as were her arms.

He laid her on the shore. No sand. Cayuga's shore was grassy down here, rocky in other spots. With barely time to catch his breath he bent over her again, covered her mouth with his, pushing air into her chest until it rose.

Seconds ticked by, and then he felt her moving. Her hands came up, threaded into his hair, tugging gently until he lifted his head away. She rolled weakly to one side, choking, gagging, spewing lake water into the grass. And then she sat there, head hanging down between her braced arms.

"Are you all right? Do you need an ambulance?"

She said nothing. Her back to him.

"What the hell were you trying to do, Brigit?" Silence.

He gripped her shoulder, pulling her around to face him. "Talk to me, dammit! What the hell is going on with you! You could have got yourself killed out there! Or is that what you wanted?"

Her eyes seemed to recapture a bit of life then, and her chin came up a little. "I was coming back. I was coming back . . . I just couldn't make it."

"Why?" His grip on her shoulders tightened, and he shook her a little. "*Why*, Brigit?"

She shook her head slowly. "It was stupid . . . but it wasn't what you think."

"Jesus, Brigit, at this point I don't even *know* what I think." He wrapped his arms around her in abject relief, held her hard to his chest, and ran his hands over her wet skin. "I'm just glad you're okay."

She straightened away from him, and a worried frown puckered her brows. Her palms came up to run slowly down either side of his face. "Adam," she said, and it was no more than a whisper. "Don't care about me. Whatever you do . . . don't care . . ."

And then her back bowed with a spasm of coughing, and her shoulders shook with it. He pulled her to his chest again, and just held her there. "What the hell made you think I cared, Malone? Adam Reid doesn't care about anyone except Adam Reid. Anything else is freaking lunacy." He only wished to Christ it was the truth.

He scooped her up in his arms and headed back for the house, taking a longer but safer path up the steep, rocky hillside. And he didn't bother trying to silence the voice inside that told him every word he'd just uttered was a goddamn lie. And had been, since the first day he'd laid eyes on her.

Turmoil. So much of it in his eyes. And his face. Even his hair showed signs of stress. It stuck up a little crazily from the many times he'd shoved his hands through it. He was sitting in a leather armchair, just staring at her, when

she awoke some hours later. Those eyes seemed to be eating holes through her, intense. Burning. He sat slouched, one elbow propped on the chair's arm, and his hand buried in his hair.

He'd put on dry clothes. A pair of pleated black trousers with knife-sharp creases. A clean white t-shirt, and a black suit jacket. The jacket hung open. He had classes today, she realized. But he was waiting . . .

He hadn't shaved yet this morning. Soft golden bristles coated his face. A shade or two darker than his hair. He looked tired. So tired.

Brigit blinked, realizing she'd been staring at him as intently as he was still staring at her. She looked away, tried to take stock of herself instead of him. Her lungs hurt. Her throat hurt. Her head hurt.

Her clothes were damp. He'd laid her on the sofa in the study, built up a fire in the hearth. But he hadn't undressed her. Just wrapped her in so many blankets she couldn't help but feel warm.

She looked at him again, and trembled because he was still staring at her that way. Disturbing.

"You should change."

His voice coming so suddenly amid the silence made her jump.

"I'd have done it myself, but . . ." His lips thinned and he shook his head. "I think we both know what would happen if I were to undress you. With my hands, I mean, instead of just with my eyes."

Her face burned. She brought her hands to it.

"Why are you here, Brigit Malone? What the hell are you trying to do to me?"

"Adam . . ."

"No. No more lies. Just tell me. Dammit, Brigit, just open your mouth and tell me." He closed his eyes, laughed just a little, a bitter, harsh sound. "Jesus, Brigit, did you really think you could convince me you were some kind of supernatural being? A *fairy* for Christ's sake?"

She sat up straighter on the sofa, fear somersaulting in her chest. He wasn't making sense. "I never said I was—"

She stopped speaking when he pulled her book, her *Fairytale*, from behind his back, and laid it gently on the coffee table. "Never said it. But set it up so I'd find all the clues. What did you do, Brigit, throw my old plants out and replace them with new ones when I wasn't looking? Hmm?"

"Adam, I don't know what you're—"

"So I was supposed to see the suddenly thriving plants and immediately think of that Celtic text. I was supposed to remember how it said animals and plants respond to the presence of fairy folk, and I was supposed to wonder."

She frowned at him, shaking her head slowly from side to side.

"And that story someone planted with the old nun. Now that was the kicker, that really was. Brilliant. Did you think of that, too, Brigit?"

She felt her eyes narrow. "Old nun?"

"Oh, come on, you had to know I'd check up on you. You had to know . . . That's why you left that story with the nun, for me to find. No mother. No birth certificate."

"You checked up on me?"

"I had a P.I. do it."

She was stunned, shaken right to the core. But she knew, at once. "Mac Cordair," she whispered.

"He talked to this old nun, Sister Ruth . . ."

"Sister Ruth," she echoed, her voice a choked whisper.

"So old she's easily persuaded to forget about the privacy laws. She told the story of twin girls with apparently no past, left at the altar of a church. Twin girls . . . who just happen to have the same names as the ones in the fairytale you told me. The motherless fay princesses whose mortal father brought them to the human world."

She shook her head, slowly getting to her feet and letting the blankets fall to the floor around her. Automatically, she grabbed her precious book and held it to her chest. "I told you the story, Adam. I told you myself . . . but what difference does any of it make? It was just a story. It wasn't real."

He shook his head, looking as if he wasn't entirely in agreement with that statement. "If it isn't real, then someone went to a lot of trouble to make me think it was. It's almost as if this thing has been planned from the day you and your sister were left at that . . ."

He stopped speaking at the thump her book made when it hit the floor. His gaze went from it, up to her face, and she tried to close her mouth, tried to stop her eyes from watering. She lifted her hands to him, gripping his t-shirt in trembling fists. "I have a sister?" She searched

his face, trying to see, no longer caring about anything else, breathless and hurting, but desperate to know. "A *sister?*"

"You didn't know?"

She blinked, choking on tears. "I . . . Sister Mary Agnes told me . . . things . . . about a sister. But I thought . . . I thought it was something she just tacked onto the *Fairytale*. Something to make it more real to me. She pretended to believe I was one of them. I guess she thought . . ." She released his shirt, lowered her head. "I believed it . . . for a while. Once I was old enough to realize it was only a story, I thought *all* of it was a story." Lifting her eyes to meet his once more, she went on. "I tried checking my records once, but the lawyer I spoke with said it was impossible. They're sealed—"

"Your records were destroyed in the fire, Brigit. But according to a retired nun who claims she was there at the time, you had a twin sister who was adopted almost immediately."

His voice had lost the accusatory ring. And his eyes had taken on a wide, wondering expression. She sank backward, until she was sitting on the floor. "A sister."

"You really didn't know. You really didn't make any of this up, did you?"

She said nothing, just sat there, stunned. Adam rose and came forward. He stood close to her, towering over her, his hands on her shoulders. "Why are you here, Brigit? Why did you come to me?"

She blinked and lifted her eyes. "I can't tell you that."

"Then—"

"No. I can't leave, either. Adam . . ." She drew a breath, fought for strength. "You saved my life today. And now you've given me . . . given me a reason to go on . . ."

"Your sister."

She nodded. "I—" A sob interrupted her, but she fought it and began again. "God, I can't believe it. Bridín is real. She's real."

"Brigit—"

"I won't hurt you, Adam. I swear . . . whatever my intent was . . . I won't. I can't. B-but I need to be here."

"Why?"

"J-just for a few more days. Just until I figure out what to do."

"Why, Brigit?"

She gripped his lower arms and pulled herself to her feet. She stood so close to him that she could feel the warmth of his body. Feel every breath, almost every thought. And she tipped her head back, staring into his eyes, wishing with everything in her that he would let her stay. She'd find a way to solve this thing without hurting him or getting Raze killed. She *would*.

Pouring her heart into her eyes, and from them, into his, she whispered, "Please don't make me go, Adam. *Please*."

In her eyes is the power to bend a man to her will. The words from the ancient text whispered through Adam's mind as he stared at Brigit's ebony eyes.

"Okay."

The word slipped through his mouth without

warning. He didn't think about it first, because she was so close that all he could think about was holding her, warming her, healing her. She could have died out there today. Hell, she'd stopped breathing. That had been no act, and neither was this.

My God, it was true. This woman was the child in the *Fairytale*. The one he'd been shown long ago. The daughter of a fay queen. No. Yes! And it was Adam's destiny to help her . . . and then to let her go.

He closed his eyes in misery, but quickly shook off the self-pity. Because there was more going on here. She didn't seem to realize who she really was, let alone what she was supposed to do about it. She had her own reasons for coming to him. And whatever she was up to, he had to believe she didn't want to do it. Someone was forcing her. And when he thought about that, he thought about the creep he'd found here yesterday. Zaslow, and this mysterious Raze, the mere mention of whose name had forced Brigit to lie. What the hell was he to her? What was Zaslow? What were they up to?

Sweet Jesus, she was in trouble. Or she'd convinced him that she was. And instead of feeling bad for her, he felt good. For himself. Selfish bastard. All he could feel was gratitude that whatever deceptions she'd committed, she'd been forced to commit. He was sure of that, now.

He searched her face, fell into her eyes, and ended up holding her tight against him. His hands dove into her hair, stroking and untan-

gling it. "Dammit, Brigit, why won't you open up to me? Why won't you let me help you?"

"I can't," she whispered. "This is my problem, Adam. Mine. And only I can solve it."

Chapter Ten

ADAM LEFT, BUT she could tell he wasn't happy with her answers. Or . . . her lack of answers. And she had a feeling he was somehow letting her stay here quite against his will. As if he were being blackmailed the way she was. Or . . . or maybe as if he were being hypnotized into doing what she wanted. But he wasn't.

He'd wanted to throw her out. At least, part of him had. So why hadn't he?

Didn't matter. She had to get in touch with Zaslow. Since her recent communion with her "other self," the wild one, she'd found a bit more courage and strength. Enough, she thought, to try again to fight Zaslow. To take her life back again. To regain control. She had to find a way to make Zaslow give this whole idea up. She had to . . .

But how?

Brigit paced the study, her eyes going often to the painting on the wall above the marble hearth. Watering each time they met those dark, mysterious eyes peering at her from amid the bushes.

She had a sister. God, even with all this garbage going on, she couldn't get past the wonder of it. The joy of it. All this time, not knowing. All this time, wondering, wishing, hoping. Dreaming of her sister.

Her perfect, golden sister. Bridín. Brigit wondered if Bridín could be as wonderful as she'd dreamed. Oh, but she had to be! She would be!

Brigit owed Adam more than she could ever repay, she realized sadly.

And that brought her back to the matter at hand. Her impending betrayal of Adam Reid, the man who'd given her a dream come true. A sister.

She had no idea what was going on with Adam. Why he would accuse her of trying to convince him she was some kind of fairy or something. His anger confused her, and his words this morning . . . God, she'd lost track of when he was speaking about her *Fairytale* and when he was speaking about her real life.

Except for the part about a sister.

Brigit closed her eyes and tried not to dwell on that aspect of this mess. Not right now. Right now, her only goal was to convince Zaslow to let her off the hook. She had to find a way.

Money. The man was greedy, and he was doing this for money. He'd told her he was being paid a hundred thousand dollars for the painting. So if she could find a way to give him an equal amount . . .

Oh, but how? Where the hell was a formerly homeless street brat going to come up with a hundred grand?

She blinked in surprise as the answer came to

her. The shop. Akasha. It had been just another condemned heap when she'd discovered it. The city had been about to tear it down to put up something new and shiny, when Brigit had come along with her plan to repair it, to make it into something special and new.

Other business owners on the Commons had jumped onto Brigit's bandwagon, and the local students had joined her in her campaign to save a building that turned out to be over 150 years old. And after that the loans had come easily. With the money she'd already saved up from her former career as an art forger, it was enough to get Akasha up and running. And when her business had thrived as she'd known it would, the loans had been repaid on time and with interest, and the entire city won.

It had been a lonely street brat's dream come true. But it wasn't half as important to Brigit as Raze was. Or as her sister was.

Or as important as Adam Reid had suddenly become to her.

It was the only way.

With trembling hands, Brigit picked up the telephone, and dialed the number Zaslow had warned her to use only in an emergency.

Zaslow was there. He answered on the third ring.

"It's me." Why was her voice shaking so much?

"Is it done?"

"N-no. Not yet."

"Then why the hell am I hearing your voice?"

Brigit licked her lips, cleared her throat. "I have a deal to offer you."

"We already have a deal, Brigit. Finish the damned painting and I won't kill your friend."

"I know . . . I know . . . but . . ."

"But?"

He sounded ominous. Her hand was sweaty, making the receiver slick. So much riding on her words. Raze's life. Her own future. She had to be careful.

"If I were to sell the shop, Zaslow, I could get at least a hundred grand. Maybe more. I'll give it to you. All of it, if you'll just let Raze go."

Silence. Dead and heavy. Lengthening.

"Please," she whispered.

He sucked in a slow breath. "It's Reid, isn't it? You sleeping with him, Brigit? You getting soft?"

"No!"

"I had a man watching you at that little snob-fest last night, honey. I have a man watching every move you make. He's got his eyes on you right now. I heard all about your little dance with Reid. Seems the two of you were so into it, you forgot to stop when the music did."

She swallowed, but almost choked on it.

"Did you take him to bed when you got home, Brigit? Did you show him all the tricks you learned on the streets? Hmm?"

Fear made her heart trip over itself. But anger set it right again. "If you have someone watching my every move, as you say, then you already know."

He laughed and it made her skin crawl. "You apparently don't understand how this works, Brigit, love. But don't worry. I'll make sure you get the point. This is life and death, honey. You

cooperate, there's life. You give me bullshit like
this, and there are gonna be some corpses turning up in odd places."

"What do you mean by that?"

Again, that low, evil laughter. "You need a
lesson in obedience, Brigit. A little class in cause
and effect."

"Don't do anything to Raze!" She shouted at
the receiver as panic bubbled in her chest.
"Please, don't hurt him! I'll finish—"

The phone went dead.

Frantic, Brigit dialed the number again. Only
to hear endless ringing. God, what was Zaslow
thinking? What was he going to do?

She paced, wringing her hands until she'd
made red marks all over them. And finally, she
hauled her equipment down to the study, and
she painted. She worked slowly, carefully, tam-
ing her trembling hands by the sheer force of
her will, battling the fear and the imaginary hor-
rors it induced . . . until she finally found that
place where it all faded away. And her mind
floated free as her hands worked.

Free. And images of a sister who looked like
Brigit, only she radiated goodness and purity
and control, and her hair was as golden as the
sun. She was everything Brigit had tried to be,
everything she'd failed to be. If only she knew
her. Bridín. If only she had her here, to talk to,
to confide in.

Maybe . . . maybe someday, they'd find one
another.

And maybe those people who'd adopted Bridín had known what they were doing when
they'd chosen not to take both babies. Maybe

they'd somehow sensed that Brigit was less than worthy of a family's love and of a sister like Bridín. Maybe she didn't deserve to find her twin. It might be fate.

She came back to herself with a start when she heard vehicles out front. "Oh, God, Adam!" Whirling, she stared at the sun slanting low through the study windows. Late afternoon. He was back. And he wasn't alone.

She grabbed the painting and took the stairs two at a time, running full tilt to her bedroom, lunging to the back of that oversized closet. She only paused long enough to place her painting carefully, not smudging the paint or allowing anything to touch the sides. Then she raced downstairs again, dumping the palettes and dirty brushes and uncapped tubes of paint into a heap in the middle of the color-spattered drop cloth, and gathering the entire bundle like a peddler's pack. She slung it over her shoulder and snatched up the tripod under her arm.

Her trip up the stairs was a little slower this time. She kept tripping, and the tripod was awkward, swinging sideways and knocking against her legs every couple of steps. But she made it to the top, and flung everything into the closet. She slammed the door, panting.

Still no sound from downstairs. Adam must be busy with whoever had arrived with him. She ran into her bathroom, cranked on the faucets and scrubbed the still-wet paint from her hands. When stains remained, she used nail polish remover to lighten them.

Good. Barely noticeable.

She turned to head back downstairs, stopping

in the doorway when she heard Adam come in.
"Brigit?"

"Up here," she called, and at the same moment, realized she was still wearing a paint-smattered smock over her clothes. She hauled it over her head, tossed it behind her into the bedroom, and slammed the door just as he stepped into the study and looked up at her.

She forced a smile, and tried to remember if she'd checked her face for paint flecks.

Adam glanced at the stool that stood in the middle of the study, then up at her, then back at the stool again, frowning.

"There was a big cobweb I couldn't reach," she lied, feeling miserable. "I was on my way back to the kitchen with the stool and I got distracted. Sorry."

He only shrugged, looking up at her again. "Can you come down here? There's a package for you."

Brigit felt her brows crease. "A package?"

"Delivery men were just unloading it when I pulled in, so I signed for you. Did you order something?"

She shook her head, running her palm over the cool hardwood rail as she walked toward the stairway, then started down it. "No," she said. "I can't imagine what . . ."

Halfway down the stairs she stopped, recalling Zaslow's evil laughter, his cryptic threats.

"What . . . kind of package?"

"Big son of a bitch," Adam said.

She blinked, forcing herself down the remaining stairs, turning to go out the huge double doors of the study, through the foyer.

The front door felt heavy, the knob, hard to turn. Slow and sloppy. She forced it open and took a single step outside.

The coffin-shaped wooden crate sat on the sidewalk, daring her to step forward, daring her to look inside.

Brigit screamed.

He'd only been a few steps behind her, but when she screamed, Adam shot forward, adrenaline propelling him like rocket fuel.

She'd fallen to her knees on the front steps. Her face covered by her trembling hands, her entire body shaking, she was muttering . . . or maybe praying. "Please . . . nononono . . . please, please, please . . . no . . . no . . . pleeeease . . ."

Adam caught her shoulders. "Easy, Brigit. Come on, get up. Turn around. Look at me."

She tried, but her knees buckled. He had to help her. She was breathing too fast, in short, choppy little gasps. He drew her to her feet, and he turned her, nice and slow, holding her steady. And then he sucked air through his teeth. The woman was terrified. He'd never seen terror etched as clearly and plainly as he saw it now on her stricken face, in her eyes. The color had fled, leaving her skin as smooth and white as bleached linen. Her eyes were wide, her irises distended until the whites were no more than a narrow band encircling the black centers.

Shaking uncontrollably, she clung to him with her hands and with her eyes. Clung to him as if for her very salvation.

"Just what do you think is in that box, Brigit?"

Her lips parted, but only jerky, spasmodic breaths escaped.

Shaking his head in frustration, Adam guided her hands to the railing, and anchored them there. Then he spun on his heel and headed out to the tool shed. He grabbed a pry bar, and hurried back to the front of the house. God knew he didn't dare leave Brigit alone out there for more than a second or two. She was where he'd left her, her eyes glued to that damned box as if she expected a dragon to jump out of it and swallow her whole.

He bent to the wood, pried up a board. Then another. And another. And another. He tossed each one aside, letting them clatter to the ground and then moving on to the next. And then he dropped the bar, looking at the box's contents. When he could breathe again he said, "Come here, Brigit, and take a look. And then tell me what the hell this is all about."

Her frightened eyes met his. She tried to take a step forward, but that was all. "I . . . I can't. J-j-just t-tell me . . ."

He picked a brick from the top of the pile, and held it up.

She frowned, blinking.

"Bricks. A bunch of them."

Brigit moved then. She came off the step as if shot from a cannon, and a second later she was on her knees beside that crate and bricks were flying everywhere. She snatched them up, clawed them into her hands and tossed them aside, one after another, as if she were digging for something.

"Jesus, Brigit, enough!"

He grabbed her wrists when she went on digging. Pulled her hands up, holding them prisoner in his. "Look at this. What the hell is the matter with you?"

He held her hands up in front of her face, so she could see what he did. Her nails were broken, fingertips bleeding from the frantic search. But her eyes were still wide, still jumping wildly from his to that box full of bricks and back again.

"There's nothing there," he told her. "Nothing. Just bricks. Nothing else."

Her breaths quickened, roughened. Her eyes squeezed tight and she clenched her jaw. "Thank God," she whispered through grated teeth. And then, eyes opening, calmer now, but beginning to burn with something . . . anger, maybe. "Damn him, damn him, damn him."

And that was all. She melted into Adam's arms, tears flash-flooding, sobs spasming hard in her chest and wrenching her small body. And he held her. He held her hard. And he felt the sharp angles of her shoulder blades, and winced. He hadn't seen her consume enough to keep a bird alive since she'd moved in, though he hadn't given it much thought until now. And come to think of it, judging by the circles under her eyes, she hadn't slept either. She was an emotional cauldron, and she was damned near bubbling over. Terrified for sure. And yes, trying to pull something on him. Which, for some reason had fallen to the very bottom of his list of things to worry about.

Oh, he had questions all right. He was brimming with them. But the questions would have

to wait. Right now the only thing he wanted was to make this haunted woman's nightmares go away.

Her sobs stopped, and it was several moments before he realized she was unconscious in his arms.

She woke slowly . . . her senses coming to life one at a time. Bit by bit. And the very first was the sense of smell. Even before she was aware of it, she smelled the violets on the air. Sweet honeysuckle. And . . . and sandalwood? Yes. And wax. She could smell the wax. And the so-subtle scent of tiny tongues of flame. Candles, her mind whispered. And floral incense.

Was she dreaming? Was she at Akasha? It felt as if she was.

A touch, gentle and warm on her face, stroking a slow path down over her cheek. Fingertips, tracing the line of her jaw, so slowly. Stopping at her chin, trailing down the arc of her neck, and making her tip her head back further in response. They felt good, those warm fingertips. And when they reversed their path, moving upward again to her cheek, she pressed closer to their touch. Her face found the entire palm, and she rubbed her cheek against it.

"Ah, Brigit . . ."

The voice was deep, and very soft. Barely more than a whisper. A familiar one, though. A comforting one. The hand caressed her face, fingers threading through her hair.

"You're magic, you know. Everything you do . . ."

And then lips—their kiss so light she was al-

most convinced it had only been imaginary—
gently brushing her forehead.

Adam. She wanted to see him. She needed . . .

Her eyes opened about the fourth time she
commanded them to do so. And things were
blurry. She felt lightheaded, fuzzy, drunk.

"Just like Sleeping Beauty," he said.

His face swam into focus, and she saw that he
was smiling, slightly. Just slightly.

"I . . ." She licked her parched lips and tried
again. "I feel . . . funny." She was only gradually
beginning to hear the soft strains of music. And
beyond that, the gentle tinkling sounds of a
wind chime. They came as if from a great distance.

"It's the tranquilizer," Adam told her, and his
hand was moving into her hair now, stroking
up and back, the way he'd stroke a cat. She liked
it.

"Tranq . . . ?" Her mouth refused to shape the
rest of the word.

"You passed out, Brigit. I called an ambulance. When they arrived and brought you
around, you started shaking and hyperventilat-
ing again, so they gave you a shot."

"Oh." She didn't remember any of that.

"You need to relax."

"Mmm." She was nothing if not relaxed. Her
eyes fell closed, but popped open again. She
looked past him this time, saw the foggy halos
of candlelight . . . many of them. And the fiery
red tip of an incense stick. "What . . . is all this?"

Adam shrugged. "I thought it would make
you feel better."

Her lips pulled up at the corners. "It does. It reminds me . . . of Akasha."

His hand came away from her hair. She lifted her own, groping until she found his, closed around it, and drew it slowly back to her. She kept hers over it, saw him smile and begin stroking her hair again.

"Your shop is a special place," he told her. "When I walk in there, I get this instant sense of . . . I don't know . . . peace, I guess."

"Yes."

"I thought you could use a little peace right now."

Oh, he had that right.

"So I tried to duplicate the atmosphere for you."

She frowned a little. "You went to the shop?"

"I borrowed your keys and sent one of my students. Michael. Most trustworthy guy I know. I hope you don't mind."

"I don't."

"I had him bring one of those tapes you always have playing in there, and a set of those chimes. I asked him to pick up some scented candles and floral incense, so I could get the smells right. It was easier than bringing all the plants."

She closed her eyes, again hearing the soft music. No wonder she'd felt so relaxed when she'd awakened. "Enya," she told him as she recognized the hauntingly beautiful voice, in a song called "Fairytale." "My favorite."

"Good."

"You're a sweet man, Adam."

"Not a chance, Brigit."

"You did all this for me . . ."

"Oh, I did more. I undressed you. Or hadn't you noticed?"

She drew a short, sharp breath when he said it, coming a little more fully awake than she'd been. She lifted the blankets that covered her and peered underneath. She was naked, except for the white panties she still wore. Lowering the covers, she met his eyes.

"I told myself it was just to make you comfortable," he said slowly, his eyes pinning hers, holding them prisoner in their depths. "But it was a lie. Before I covered you up, I looked at you, Brigit. I looked at your breasts. I touched them."

Her breath quickened, and she felt her nipples harden in response to his words, and the images those words evoked.

"Thought you ought to know," he went on, still staring into her eyes. "I'm sorry."

She sat up in the bed, very slowly, because she was dizzy, and moving made it worse. The bed seemed to spin in uneven circles. Adam's hands came to her shoulders, as if he'd push her back down to the pillows.

"Don't, Brigit," he told her. "If you want to be away from me, I'll leave. You have to stay here. You need to rest."

"I don't want to rest." She let him press her down, though, too weak to fight him. "I want . . . to know . . ."

His eyes narrowed, searching her face. "To know what?"

"How," she whispered. "How you touched me."

Adam stood beside the bed, staring down at her, his face unreadable. "How?"

Lifting her trembling hands, Brigit caught the blankets at her shoulders, and slowly pushed them down, all the way to her hips, just as far as she could reach. "Show me."

Adam slammed his eyes closed. "Jesus Christ, Brigit . . ."

"I want you to . . ."

"You're drugged! You don't know what the hell you want."

He would have turned away. But her hand shot out to capture his wrist. She held him as tight as she could, and she drew his hand downward. He didn't resist. He let her bring it lower, let her settle his palm on her breast. Her nipple rose, pressing against his flesh, and she knew he had to feel it. She saw him clenching his teeth, his jaw flinching, and she heard the air rush out of his lungs.

She released his hand. When he drew it away, she sat up again, battling the dizziness and winning. "You don't want me, then. Is that it, Adam?"

He stood there, right beside the bed, looking down at her with fire in his wizard's eyes, and candlelight gleaming from his golden hair so that he resembled a pagan god. His hands closed around one of hers, and he drew it closer, until her palm pressed right to the zipper of his jeans. She felt the iron bulge beyond the denim.

"Does it feel to you as if I don't want you?"

"Then why—"

"I don't want to want you, dammit. I don't want to feel a goddamn thing for you!"

She pressed her hand harder to that denim-encased swell. She drew back, lifting her chin, the wanton inside having escaped and taken charge. "You don't have a choice in the matter."

"Witch," he breathed. But he didn't turn away. Her fingers fumbled with the jeans, with the button and then the zipper, and then he was free. He was in her hands.

She looked at him, huge and hard and dark, and so very close to her. She kissed him there, and then ran her tongue from the base to the tip, an incredibly long journey. He shuddered and groaned as if in agony, and she took him into her mouth, working him until he gripped handfuls of her hair and pulled her away.

"Fine," he growled, tearing the covers from the bed with one hand. "You want it so bad, you've got it lady. You've got it."

He kicked free of his jeans, and climbed into the bed with her, his flesh hot, burning. His mouth demanding ... no, enslaving hers when he took it. One hand tore at her panties, ripping them apart rather than sliding them off her. And then that hand cupped her, parted her, invaded her with its calloused fingers. He pinched and he entered and he took. And then he used both hands to press her thighs open, and he settled himself on top of her. His hardness pressed into her, nudged farther, entered her.

Brigit closed her eyes, clutched his shoulders, and gave a soft cry when he slid himself into her body in one sudden thrust.

And that cry galvanized him. He froze, right where he was, his eyes popping open, his face stricken. "Jesus, what am I doing?"

"Adam," she whispered, searching his dark blue eyes, knowing he'd been lost for a few moments. But he was back now. And this was what she wanted. Him. Not his body, but him.

She threaded her fingers into his hair, and drew his head downward. But he resisted.

"Brigit . . ." he whispered, searching her face. "I'm the first for you . . ."

"Yes," she told him. "I've waited a long time to find you, Adam Reid." And she kissed him. One second. Two. Three, and more. And then he kissed her back. His lips moved, nuzzled, tasted, and his body rocked slowly with hers. His arms cradled her tightly and closely, and he made slow, exquisite love to her. He kissed a hot path down her jaw, over her neck, and sucked the skin between his teeth, nibbling, tasting.

"My God, Brigit," he whispered as their hips met again and again. Not roughly, the way he'd begun. But with such exquisite tenderness it brought tears to her eyes.

"You taste so sweet . . . so sweet . . . so good . . ."

He was kissing her again, then. Her neck, her shoulders, her chest, her arms. Her breasts. He couldn't seem to get enough of kissing her skin. And as he kissed he moved, and she moved with him, bringing him deeper and deeper inside her. Every thrust sent her spiraling higher, her insides seeming to twist tighter, in preparation for the final release.

When it came, it blinded her with its intensity. She screamed aloud, clinging, clawing him, her entire body convulsing and her mind vanishing

in the chaos of sensation. And Adam moved faster, plunged deeper, arched his back and growled her name out loud, before he slowly relaxed and sank on top of her.

He gathered her into his arms, and she held on tight, kissing his face.

He rolled her onto her back, and laid beside her, propping himself on one elbow. His eyes took their time, roaming up and down her utterly naked body, and there was a look of confusion and wonder about him.

He shook his head. "I shouldn't have done that. Dammit, Brigit, I shouldn't ... but damn you, you made it impossible. Jesus, where do you get this power over me? This freaking magi ..." He stopped speaking, and she saw his gaze skid to a halt, focused on her abdomen. His eyes widened, and he shook his head, blinked, and stared some more. "What the hell is that?"

Brigit sat up fast, defensive, and looked down at herself, wondering what he'd seen to shock him so. "What?"

His hand came forward, forefinger tracing the little red mark just above the triangle of jet curls. "This."

She frowned harder. "Adam, it's only a birthmark."

"In the shape of the crescent moon," he whispered. "And it's blood red."

"So?"

He lifted his gaze slowly, met her eyes, his own narrowing, searching. "Brigit?"

"What?"

He licked his lips, swallowed hard. "Brigit, you told me that when you were a child, you

believed in that *Fairytale* of yours. That you believed it was true, and that you really were—"

She shook her head quickly. "A childhood fantasy, Adam. That's all it was. A silly dream."

"What if it wasn't?"

Brigit frowned at him, shaking her head in confusion. "What do you mean, what if it wasn't? It had to be. There are no such things as fairies. Everyone knows that."

"But what if there were? What if you really—"

She shook her head hard, and started to turn away from him. But he slipped his hands into her hair, and gently made her face him. "Have you ever really considered the possibility, Brigit? Have you ever put it to the test?"

Her lips thinned. "Sure I have, Adam. I check behind me every day for wings, but so far—"

"I'm being serious here."

She didn't want him to see the tears forming in her eyes, but he wouldn't let her turn away, so see them he did. And he leaned closer, to kiss the tears away. "Why does the thought of it make you cry, if you're so sure it's all nonsense?" he whispered.

"Because I believed so strongly once, Adam. And when I found out the truth it was like someone took away my heart. It hurt to grow up, and face reality, and put fantasy away where it belongs. In a little box of childhood memories. But I did it. I don't want to have to do it all over again."

He blinked and shook his head as if trying to shake water from his hair. "Okay," he said softly, stroking her hair with his soothing hands.

"Okay, I won't push it. Not now. Not if it's gonna make you cry. But . . ."

"But, what?"

He shook his head slowly. "Nothing. Never mind."

She didn't want to "never mind." She wanted to ask him if he were actually considering what he'd said to be a possibility. And she would have . . . except that she wasn't sure she was ready to hear his answer.

Chapter Eleven

❦

HER MIND WAS clearer when she woke, some-time later. And the sensation that had drawn her out of sleep's warm embrace was one of loss, of emptiness, of coldness.

Blinking in the newborn sun's soft amber light, she struggled for memories. Her eyes shot wider when she found them. She'd fallen asleep wrapped tightly in Adam Reid's arms. Right after making incredible love to him.

"Oh, no," she whispered, scanning the room in search of him, not seeing him, feeling her face heat anyway. "God, tell me I didn't." But she did. She knew perfectly well she did. And she'd been so determined not to. Not to let him too close. Not to let him care.

She could only hope it had been no more than physical to him. She could only pray he hadn't let himself develop any feelings, not even a passing fondness for her. Because she might be forced to betray him in the end. She closed her eyes, bit her lower lip hard. Not "might be," she told herself with brutal honesty. She would be

forced to betray Adam. She'd tried buying Zas-low off, and his response had been that . . . that horrible delivery last night. That coffin-shaped box. His message, delivered loud and clear, as to what could so easily happen, should she resist his plan in any way.

What a cruel, malicious bastard to torture her that way! For a few unbearable seconds she'd believed Raze lay still and cold in that box. God, the feeling that had swamped her then—the very thought of that sweet, gentle man dying at the hand of one so evil . . .

She slammed her eyes closed as that desolate image crept into her mind.

Fight him, said the one inside. *Don't let that bastard do this to you!*

No, she couldn't fight Zaslow again. Not while he still had Raze. She *would have* to betray Adam. And he didn't deserve to be hurt like that. Not again.

She knew what lay at the heart of Adam's old pain. The one she saw in his eyes, shadowing his soul, never leaving him. She knew it was centered on betrayal. The betrayal felt by a boy whose own father turned on him like some vicious animal. The betrayal felt by a husband whose own wife takes everything he has and slips away like a thief in the night. The kind that was the most deadly. That which came from someone he loved. Trusted. Believed in.

He might seem tough and hard-nosed, but she could see through that shell to the man inside. He was fragile right now. It wouldn't take much to do him in.

She hoped to God the killing blow wouldn't

be the one she had to deliver. And she assured herself it wouldn't be. Not as long as he hadn't let himself care.

Where was he?

Frowning at the new thought, Brigit got out of the bed. His bed. The pillow beside her was still sunken where he'd laid his head. Everywhere there were signs of Adam. His scent filled the room, and his clothes lay strewn on the floor. Golden strands of his hair clung to the brush on the dresser, glimmering like fire in the morning sunlight.

But Adam wasn't here.

She snatched his robe from the bedpost and wrapped it around her as she hurried to the French doors matching those in her own bedroom. She pushed the latch down, stepped out onto the deck to look up and down its wrought-iron length. But he wasn't out here, either.

And then she saw him. He was standing on the outcropping of rock where they'd sat in the rain. The one where she'd given in to the wildness inside, and dove into the lake on a whim. And nearly got herself killed for her trouble.

He stood there, just staring out over the water toward the fiery ball of the rising sun. And he seemed . . . God, he seemed tortured. The wind came rushing off the lake to whip his pale hair into chaos. He stood, braced against it, facing it. His hands shoved into his jeans pockets, his eyes distant. Staring out over the wind-tossed waves, but, she thought, not really seeing anything there.

Oh, Lord, what had she done?

Ducking back inside, she raced to her own

bedroom, yanking a pair of black stirrups on just because they were the first things she grabbed when she opened the dresser. No time for the hairbrush. She snatched an oversized gauzy black shirt from a hanger in the closet and pulled it on, fastening the big gold buttons with trembling fingers. Black tails, front and back, reached to her knees. She stuffed her feet into her favorite leather thong sandals and ran into the hallway and down the stairs.

Outside, the air still held the chill of night. But dawn's warmth was already invading. The breeze drew goosebumps to the surface of her skin, but the sun on her eyelids warmed her. She folded her arms over each other and ran along the path that skirted the house, just in time to see Adam disappearing in another direction. He hadn't taken the path that led down to the lake's grassy shore. Instead, he'd gone off into the woods nearby. A steep hillside, thick with pines, rose regally on the western side of the house. State land, she knew. Not Adam's own. He headed up the hill, and vanished as soon as he passed the first row of thick-needled sentries.

Where in the world was he going?

Brigit licked her lips, tilted her head to one side, and debated with herself for no more than a minute. Then, her decision made, she started after him.

Adam could no longer see the old path. The one he'd followed as a small, adventurous child. It hadn't been made by man, anyway. Probably a deer trail or something. And deer changed paths all the time, to keep a step ahead of their

predators. There were new paths trodden into the mossy forest floor. Mazes of them, going off in a hundred directions, and criss-crossing themselves often along the way.

Where was it? And how the hell was he supposed to fulfill his destiny—to show Brigit the way home—if he couldn't even find the trail that had once led him there?

He remembered crossing a stream. And there'd been a rise within the hillside, a hump of sorts. He'd had to climb it. He'd had to do that on hands and knees, he recalled, because the hump had been wearing a coat of blackberry briars. The cave was partway down a grassy slope on the far side of that briar-riddled hill.

If there ever had actually *been* a cave. Adam had long ago convinced himself—with a lot of help from his father—that there hadn't been. That it had all been in his imagination. But now, he'd swung the other way. He'd decided that he'd been right all along. Even as a child. He really had found some kind of mystical doorway to some enchanted realm. He really had talked to a fairy there, who'd shown him his fate.

And his fate really was the woman he'd made love to last night. The woman he'd left sleeping like an angel in his bed. His fate, it seemed, was to have his heart broken by that beautiful half-fairy enchantress, and he'd likely waste away with longing for her the rest of his life, just the way Keats had tried to warn him he would.

Too bad he hadn't listened.

He'd got out of bed this morning, determined to get it over with. If he could find the spot in the woods, he'd show it to her, take her through

to the other side, and be done with it. The longer he put it off, the more it was going to hurt. He was getting too damned used to having her around.

But now he faced another roadblock. One he hadn't even considered before. What if he could never find that place again?

It felt good, in a way, to let himself explore the possibility that his childhood fantasy had been real. That he really had crossed some invisible threshold into a fantasy world called Rush, and he really had met a fairy princess there, a pregnant one, who'd shown him his future. He hadn't realized how much he'd missed believing in fantasy until he'd started to let himself do it again. And it was all because of Brigit.

Her presence made his houseplants thrive, and she could tell a man was lying to her by looking into his eyes . . .

Goddamn, but that was something, wasn't it? The way she took one look into Mac's eyes and just knew. Just like that. She knew he was lying. Goddamn.

Her footfalls always seemed soundless and she could predict the weather. And that birthmark . . . only, it was more than just a birthmark, wasn't it? It was the mark of the crescent moon that was talked about in that old Celtic text. The sign that marked her as a fairy of royal blood.

God, he could barely believe he'd let himself be convinced by all of this. But he had. And in doing so he'd regained something he'd thought he'd never find again.

And it had driven him to come out here. He hadn't trusted in his own mind enough to do so in nearly thirty years. He'd try now. Maybe, the

small part of his mind that remained stubbornly skeptical told him, maybe being here again, in this forest where it had all started, would trigger something in his memory. Some logical explanation that would account for everything. All of it.

Or maybe he'd find that doorway he'd been trying for so long to believe had never existed.

Her skin was sweet.

He stopped in his tracks, frowning as the realization hit him right between the eyes. He'd kissed her, he'd kissed her all over. He'd tasted her skin. And it had truly seemed as if there was a flavor to it. A sweetness.

Honey. Just like in that Celtic text.

"Christ," he muttered, and forced himself to continue walking. But after an hour trudging through the woods, he realized he wasn't going to find the place. Not now.

And for some reason, even that didn't convince him that it had never existed in the first place. It only made him worry that he'd be unable to complete his destiny, and to give Brigit the help she wasn't even aware she needed. Or maybe it simply wasn't time yet. That fairy had told him he had to show Brigit the way to her sister, and *then* the way back home. Maybe he had to do this in the proper order, if it were going to work at all.

Or maybe . . . maybe he really *wouldn't* be able to find it again.

Sighing in defeat, he sank down onto a damp, rotting stump and wondered what the hell his next move should be. Hell, if he couldn't find

the doorway, did that mean he could keep her here, with him?

"Whatever it is, Adam, you can get past it."

He jerked his head up at the sound of her voice, squinting in disbelief when he saw her. Her sudden appearance there seemed to add even more credence to his theory. No normal woman could follow a man through the forest without making a sound, could she?

She came closer, sank down onto the forest floor, hooking her elbows on her knees, feet crossed at the ankles. "When I'm in a place like this, it reminds me how insignificant our troubles really are. I mean, what do they matter, in the scheme of things? We could disappear tomorrow, and the world would keep right on turning. The wind would still blow . . ." She closed her eyes, tilted her head back, and inhaled nasally. ". . . Mmm. And forests would still smell like no other place can smell. And the pines would still whisper their secrets to one another . . ."

He frowned, but found himself listening in a way he never had before. And suddenly he heard them. As the wind brushed through the needled boughs it seemed as if the trees themselves were whispering in a million hushed voices. He'd been able to hear them once. He'd been in on those secrets, a long time ago. It had been . . . magic.

He lowered his head, caught her staring at him.

"I'm sorry about last night, Adam. I . . . know you didn't want anything to happen between us. And I . . . pushed you into it."

He was surprised at her heartfelt apology, and he couldn't stop himself from smiling at the embarrassment in her huge, ebony eyes. The color in her cheeks. Her take on what had happened between them . . . What had happened between them had been incredible. It had been beyond anything he'd ever experienced with a woman.

"It wasn't exactly rape, Brigit. I don't recall begging for mercy."

She dipped her head, gnawing on her lower lip.

"I wanted it as much as you did," he said, and his voice tightened and roughened. "I still do."

Her head came up, eyes glittering. "No you don't, Adam. It was a mistake and I—"

"Don't tell me what I want. I know. I've been lusting after you since I laid eyes on you. Maybe even longer than that."

"How—"

He gave his head a firm shake. "Don't ask. Believe me, angel, you don't want to go there."

She looked alarmed, frightened for him, as she searched his face. "I didn't come out here for this. This isn't what I—"

"The point is," he said, interrupting her deliberately, "I resisted everything my body was screaming for, for one simple reason."

She tilted her head, waiting.

"I didn't trust you, Brigit."

He saw the flash of guilt in her ebony eyes, the remorse, but the truth, too. Right there. She didn't duck it or try to hide it. She took his direct hit, and she never even flinched.

"I know you're up to something. I know

you're keeping the truth from me . . . about a lot
of things. From who you really are, to what you
expected to find in that crate yesterday. But
knowing all that doesn't stop me from wanting
you." He shrugged, wishing she were sitting
closer. Wishing he could touch her. "So there's
my dilemma."

Without meeting his eyes, she whispered,
"I'm sorry."

"I was afraid. See, I've trusted the people I
care about before. And I've been hurt before. I
was afraid it would happen again if I let myself
feel anything for you."

She said nothing, only sat there looking as if
she were in abject misery.

"Problem is, I can't stop myself from feeling
something for you."

She gasped, parted her lips to argue with him,
but he didn't give her time.

"I don't even know what it is, exactly. But
there's definitely something. Something powerful. Something . . ." He reached out across the
distance between them, cupping her chin and
lifting her gaze to his. "Something I've never felt
before," he finished, and he felt a little sick to
his stomach. "So the whole caution thing is really a moot point. The choice has been taken
right out of my hands."

She shook her head. "Adam, don't—"

"It's a relief, really. I don't have to struggle
against it anymore. I'm sort of left with no
choice but to go with this thing."

"I don't want to hurt you."

She sure looked as if she meant every word
of it. But she was going to. She didn't realize it

yet, but she had no choice in the matter. Before she did, though, he was going to get to the bottom of whatever she was up to and confront her about it, and make her tell him why.

There was a powerful reason motivating her. He knew that as well as he knew everything else. A reason that had to do with the fear he'd seen in her eyes yesterday. And he suspected, with the creep who called himself Zaslow. These were things he knew, beyond doubt. Not like those other things. Those fairy things that he couldn't begin to understand.

"I believe that," he told her, because he did.

"Adam, I'd tell you everything if I could. I swear it."

"I know."

Tears brimmed in her eyes, and he found himself wanting to change the subject. He could see the agony this one was causing her. She wanted to tell him the truth. He knew she meant it when she said that she did. But she couldn't, and the conflict was tearing her apart.

Interesting.

"Adam—"

"Shhsh." He stroked her hair, studied her face. "I want to tell you something." He saw her press her lips together, and she nodded for him to continue. Adam drew a deep breath and let his hand fall away. He took his gaze from her, and looked around at the pines and the myriad paths twisting through them. "I used to come out here when I was a little boy. But I haven't been back in almost thirty years."

Her brows lifted, in interest, he supposed, but

mostly, in surprise that he'd changed the subject
rather than grilling her.

He got off his stump and sat on the ground
in front of it, leaning his back against the uneven
bark. He lifted his arms toward her, waiting.

With a little sigh of disbelief, she came closer,
curling into the V between his open legs, and
laying her side against his chest. He closed his
arms around her. It felt good to hold her there.
It felt right.

"Why did you stay away so long?"

"My father forbade me to ever come back
here. And I knew better than to disobey the old
bastard."

"He was a monster, Adam." She snuggled
closer to him as she said it, and her arms tightened around his waist. "It wasn't your fault,
what he did to you. You know that."

"It's taken a long time, but yeah. I know that."

She lifted her head, scanning his face with
eyes that seemed to see more than they should.
When he looked away, she lowered her head
again. "Why didn't he want you out here?"

"Because . . . I thought I saw something out
here. Something . . . that couldn't have been real.
And I guess the old man thought he was making
sure I knew the difference between fantasy and
reality."

"No," she whispered. "No one believes beating a child will keep him sane. No one who
abuses their own child does it for the child's
own good. Though I imagine they all say they
do." She sat up, looked him in the eye. "He did
it because he was sick, Adam."

It was as if she sensed the bolt of pain that

shot through him when he remembered. And she deftly pulled that bolt out again, snapped it in two, and tossed it aside.

Brigit's hand ran over his nape, the warmth of her fingertips infusing him.

"Damn," he said softly. "You're good for me, Brigit."

"That's what friends are for," she whispered.

"Is that what you are? My friend?"

She lowered her eyes, licked her lips. "I care about you, Adam. No matter what else happens, don't doubt that."

She turned sideways again, as she'd been before, tucking herself against his body. And he closed his arms around her almost automatically. It was such a natural thing to embrace her, to hold her, to talk to her this way.

"So, why did you come out here this morning, after staying away for so long?"

He stiffened a little. "That gets back to what I was starting to tell you before. About what happened the last time I came up here."

"Thirty years ago," she whispered. "What did you see, Adam?"

He drew his brows together, glancing down at the top of her head, which told him nothing. "What the hell. You deserve to be warned, Brigit. Hell, you're living with me, *sleeping* with me . . . though you might change your mind about that soon enough." He licked his lips, trying not to realize how important her reactions to his revelations would be to him. "You might as well know the worst. I found a cave out here, somewhere. And I crawled through it and emerged . . . somewhere else."

She sat up, eyes sharp and probing as they met his. "Where?"

"Rush." He blurted it before he could think better of it, waited for the fear or the sympathy to fill her eyes. He never saw it. He saw something more like childish excitement and wonder, instead.

"The forest of Rush?" she breathed. "The one in the painting? God, Adam, the one in my *Fairytale*?"

He shrugged. "Yeah. It was exactly like the one in the painting. And . . ." He closed his eyes, letting his voice trail off.

"That's incredible."

"In-credible. Meaning not credible. That's exactly what it was. A kid's daydream. Nothing more. At least, that's what I thought . . . until I saw that book of yours."

She sat up straighter. "It looked like the Rush in my book?"

He only nodded.

"What happened there?" She was all but bouncing up and down as she spoke. "Did you see anyone? Talk to anyone? How did you find your way back?"

"Slow down. Are you sure you want to hear this? You said before—"

She stopped speaking, eyes narrowing. "Well, just because I want to hear it doesn't mean I have to believe in it again. Please tell me the rest, Adam." Like a little girl pleading for a bedtime story. He couldn't have resisted if he'd wanted to.

"All right. But . . . brace yourself. I met a woman who claimed to be a fairy. I . . . she had

. . . wings. And . . . Jesus, Brigit, she said her name was Máire."

Brigit went stiff, looking up at him slowly. She pressed both hands to her chest, fists clenched until her knuckles whitened. Her eyes . . . God, they were wider than he'd ever seen them. "Don't," he whispered. "Don't look like that. There's a chance I heard some version of your fairytale somewhere, and just transferred it to my dream. Maybe."

She blinked, gave her head a shake, and finally nodded. "I know. I know none of it can be real. For a second I just . . . let myself forget. You know, when I was a little girl, I honestly thought of Máire as . . . as my mother."

"Ah, Jesus, Brigit, I shouldn't have—"

"Go on," she whispered, and he thought she was holding her breath. "I want to hear the rest. Please, go on."

He swallowed hard, licked his lips. "You're sure?" She nodded, and he began again. "In this . . . this daydream or whatever the hell it was, Máire told me she'd show me the way home, but first she wanted to know if I'd like to see my fate, because she'd seen it the second she'd looked into my eyes."

"Yes," Brigit whispered. "That's the same question she used to ask me . . ."

Adam looked at her sharply.

"I used to dream about her, too, Adam. But go on," she told him. "Did you say yes?"

"Yes." He wanted to ask questions, but he was compelled to get the entire story out. Here and now. No more hiding from it.

Brigit blinked fast, and he thought there were tears trying to work into her eyes.

"What did she show you?"

"You," he said, and the single word slipped from between his lips without his consent, and fortunately, without a sound. She never heard it. He hoped she never saw it. He was confessing enough as it was.

Brigit shook her head hard, but he went on. "She pushed aside some bushes and told me to look through. I did, and I saw a woman, bathing in a pool, all but hidden by rushes."

"Like the painting?"

"Not *like* the painting. It *was* the painting. Only . . . real. And then she told me the woman was my fate. That my destiny was to show her the way home, and that I mustn't let myself fall in love with her, because she would break my heart. And then she let the bushes come together again. When I looked up at her again, she was gone. I pushed the bushes apart again, but there was no lake, no woman. Just more trees. I turned around, and there was the cave, right in front of me, though it hadn't been there before. So I crawled inside, and, I don't know, I guess I fell asleep there. When I woke later and came out again, I was in these very ordinary woods, not far from my house." He smiled at her, seeing her confusion, and decided to give her a way out, in case she wasn't ready to swallow all of this. "It took me a while to realize I'd probably fallen asleep the first time I entered the cave, and that the rest was just a dream."

"You really believe that?"

He was surprised she would ask the question.

He thought she'd already made up her mind that none of this could be real.

"What else could it have been?"

She blinked, looking a little dazed. "I know ... it had to be a dream. What else could it be? It's just that ... Adam, you have a painting of what you saw, hanging in your study. Unless you painted it yourself ..." She lifted her brows, waiting.

"No. I found it in a shop on the Commons. The Capricorn."

"Then how can you dismiss all of that so easily?"

"I don't know. Anything can be explained if you try hard enough. Say ... the painting is only *similar* to that childhood fantasy, and when I saw it, I subconsciously substituted it for the image I'd seen in the dream."

"But you don't believe that. Do you, Adam?"

He wasn't sure he should tell her what he believed. So he shrugged, drew a breath. "Lately ..."

"Lately, what ... ?"

He wanted to tell her. He wanted to see if he could scare her into running from him, because he'd already decided he couldn't run from her. He didn't have the strength let alone the will.

But he couldn't do it. He couldn't deliberately drive her out of his life by telling her the thoughts he'd been having about her. Not now.

Or ... not yet.

Maybe it would be better to let her see that Celtic text. See if she saw the parallels that he did. See if maybe it stirred something in her.

He shook his head. "Doesn't matter."

She stepped closer, ran her fingers through his hair, searched his face. "Why did you tell me all of that?"

"I'm not sure," he told her, in all honesty. He wrapped his arms around her waist to hold her close to him. Seemed he couldn't get enough of having her close to him. "Maybe so you'd know my deepest, darkest secret, Brigit. Maybe I thought it might make you feel a little safer, later, when you're ready to tell me yours."

She closed her eyes, as if afraid he might see it written right there, in neon ink. "I will tell you," she whispered, and the words carried the force of a vow. "Very, very soon. I promise, Adam."

"But not yet."

"No." She lowered her head to his chest, but not in time to hide her fresh tears. "Not yet."

Chapter Twelve

HE WAS HURT that she couldn't tell him the secrets she was keeping. And that she was still holding herself at arm's length from him. She could feel his pain. And while she could strive to keep her heart set aside, she couldn't physically put a distance between them. When he slid his arm around her shoulders and drew her close to his side for the walk back to the house, she didn't resist. Didn't pull away. Couldn't.

"I don't want to worry about it anymore," he whispered, leaning close to her ear. "I don't want to think about anything bad. Not until I have to."

"But, Adam, I—"

He silenced her with a finger to her lips. And then he replaced it with his mouth. He kissed her deeply, thoroughly, and his hands cupped her backside, pulling her tight against him.

"You're good for me, angel," he whispered against her neck, as his mouth moved there. "You make me feel like I've never felt. And I want to feel that way again."

"We shouldn't—"

"I need you, Brigit."

It was a confession that was wrung from him, she realized. And it was her undoing. The next thing she knew, she was the one kissing him. Holding him so tight her arms ached, wishing she never had to let go. He did need her. She'd always known that. She was the one who could heal his old wounds. And God, how she wanted to do that. There was nothing she wanted more.

His kisses became feverish, and hers responded in kind. They made frantic love on the forest floor, with the blue sky overhead and the music of birds playing in time with their breathing and their whispers and their kisses and the gentle slapping of their bodies, one against the other.

And when it was over, and he scooped her into his arms and carried her naked, back to the house, she realized it wasn't over. Not at all. It was only beginning.

The entire day, and long into the night, they spent together. Talking and laughing and making love, over and over again.

It was, Brigit thought, the most perfectly wonderful day of her entire life. And the most perfect night. She wished to God it didn't have to end.

But it did. The next morning, when Adam headed out to the university. She kissed him goodbye, and pretended to believe he'd come home that night, and the magic would begin all over again.

But the magic was make-believe. And the time for her betrayal came again. Her heart felt as if

it were made of lead, this time, when she took out the canvas, and the paints, and set up the tripod in the study. And it took a lot longer to achieve the state she needed in order to work. But she did it. Because Raze's life was hanging in the balance, and because she had no choice.

She felt like the lowest, most vile being on the planet.

And even then, she let her mind wander back to the story Adam had told her out there in the woods. And his earlier questions. What if it were all true? What if she really was the little girl in the *Fairytale*?

Impossible.

And yet, here she stood, wielding paintbrushes without looking, letting some other force control her hands. The ability had been a part of her life for so long, she'd simply accepted it as natural. The way some people can do acrobatics, and some can run like the wind, and some sing like angels. But now, she wondered if maybe that thing, that *juice*, as she called it, might go by another name. Like "magic."

Silly. Ridiculous.

And what about her green thumb? Sure, lots of people were good at growing things. That was no big deal. But often, when a plant seemed to be in trouble, she'd instinctively go to it, and rub its leaves between her fingers while envisioning it healthy and strong. She'd done that automatically. Without forethought. The way one pets a dog. But every time she did, the plant would begin to thrive within a day or two. More than thrive. Those formerly ill subjects often grew better than any other plants in the shop.

And then there was the way she could read a man's heart by looking into his eyes. Another talent she'd grown accustomed to. So much so that she never questioned it.

But now she wondered if there were the slightest chance . . . the tiniest possibility that . . .

No. No, letting herself believe again would only bring disappointment.

Inside, the wild one called Brigit a fool for refusing to see what was staring her in the face. But Brigit ignored her, and she painted all the same.

Adam didn't actually sit down. He was knocked there, hard, right into the chair facing the desk in Mac's shoddy little office. Mac's words, his information, hit him like a fist, and Adam simply collapsed, the wind whooshing from his lungs in response to the imaginary blow.

"That's not possible. It can't be . . ."

Mac crooked one eyebrow. "Jesus, Adam, don't tell me this woman means something to you." When Adam didn't answer, Mac, came around the desk, staring down at him, looking scared. "Dammit, this is exactly what I was afraid of. Adam . . . Adam, talk to me. Are you all right?"

Adam shook his head, but couldn't speak. Words deserted him. Pain took their place. Pain so intense there had never been its equal. His muscles went limp. He was drunk with pain.

"You *knew* she was scamming you!" Mac tugged off his tie, whipped it to the floor, and began pacing the office in quick, angry strides.

"You knew it right from the first day, Adam. How could you let yourself—"

"Doesn't matter." He managed to speak the words, but they were muffled, dull. "Doesn't matter at all, does it?"

He flipped open the file folder he'd slammed shut only seconds ago, looked at the police mug shot of the man who'd been at the house. The man who called himself Brigit's old friend. Ernie Zaslow was only one of his many aliases. The man was into many scams, but his favorite, it seemed, was brokering stolen art. He'd served eight years when he'd tried to sell a stolen Picasso to an undercover fed. The police had suspected him of many similar acts of fencing, but had been unable to prove many of the charges.

Most interesting of all was his m.o. Zaslow had got away with his crimes for so long, because his victims rarely knew they'd been robbed. He replaced each stolen painting with a duplicate so perfect even the owners had trouble telling the difference.

But Zaslow was no forger. He'd been working with a partner. And that partner had never been caught.

Adam recalled that paint-smeared rag he'd found on the marble pedestal stand the other day, and he felt sick all over again.

"What could she be after, Adam? Come on, you have to snap out of it. You want to catch her, don't you?"

Adam lifted his head, but it seemed too heavy. Did he? He wasn't sure.

"The only painting I have that's worth anything is 'Rush.' " He shook his head slowly. "I

can't believe she'd be involved in a plot to steal it. She knows . . ."

"Knows what?"

Adam didn't answer aloud. Internally, though, he was kicking himself. Brigit knew how much that painting meant to him. How could she be plotting something like this? How? And why?

He remembered the stains on her fingertips, and the faint aroma in the study . . .

. . . and the look in her eyes when he made love to her. And the feel of her skin under his hands, and the smell of her hair.

God!

"But 'Rush' isn't valuable, is it? It wasn't done by a master . . ."

"It's anonymous. Unsigned. Art dealers speculate all sorts of theories about it, but none have been proven. It's the mystery that makes it so valuable. But not priceless. It's only priceless . . . to me."

How could she . . . after what they'd shared? He'd let himself believe in her, let himself begin to care.

"What are you going to do, Adam?"

Adam shook his head. "I don't know."

"According to the FBI files, Zaslow is only a broker. A fence, if you want to call it that. He had a forger that was never named, and he had a talented burglar by the name of Melvin Kincaid who made the switches for him. He and Kincaid both did time. They went up for a heist they pulled in seventy-eight. And either of them could have reduced their sentence by naming the forger, but neither would do it."

Seventy-eight. God, Brigit couldn't have been much more than a teenager back then. A teenage art forger? How much sense did that make?

He looked up at Mac, who was still pacing. "So why do you think they didn't turn her over, pal? Loyalty. Honor among thieves?"

"Her?" Mac stopped walking and stared at him. "You think Brigit's the *forger*?"

Adam nodded.

Mac swore. Then he walked to the window and swore some more. "With Mel, it might have been loyalty. From what I've dug up on him, he was goddamn likeable, if a little light-fingered. Adam . . ."

Adam looked up, coming alert at Mac's tone.

"Adam, I tried to check these two out. Mel Kincaid is dead."

Adam blinked. "How?"

"He was tied to a chair and beaten to death with a baseball bat. They found him in an abandoned apartment building in Brooklyn. The day he was killed was the same day Ernie Zaslow hopped a commuter flight into Lansing."

Adam's devastation was compounded now. By fear. "You think Zaslow murdered him?"

Mac shrugged. "If he did, he's one dangerous son of a bitch, Adam. Your Brigit Malone has herself mixed up in some bad company. She's either in league with a killer, or in danger from him. Either way, you have to get the hell away from her. Throw her out, Adam, before she drags you down with her."

The thought that she might be in danger sent cold chills racing up his spine, and slapped a little more sense into Adam. He grimaced at his

own idiocy. He'd known for days that Brigit was up to something, and suspected almost from the start that she was being forced, somehow, to do whatever it was she was doing.

So nothing had changed, had it? Except that he now knew what it was she was being forced to do.

He was angry. Yes, he was still very angry at the thought that this morning Brigit had kissed him goodbye, and then she'd gone into the study to work on her forgery. And he was furious that she hadn't trusted him enough to tell him the truth. Didn't she know that he'd have given her the damned painting if she'd asked?

He closed his eyes tight.

"Adam?"

"I know," he said softly, though he didn't know. He didn't know anything anymore.

"So what are you going to do?"

He only shook his head.

Mac sighed, impatience making him grimace. "You're not going to ask her to leave, are you?"

Adam blinked. "No. Not yet."

"Adam, wake up! You go home, right now, and you toss her out the front door, bag and baggage. You tell her you're onto her little con game, and if she ever darkens your door again, you'll turn her in to the cops so fast she won't know what hit her. You got it?"

Adam looked up into his friend's concerned eyes and simply said, "I can't do that."

"Then what are you going to do?"

Adam rose, surprised to find his legs unsteady. The pain was hardening, changing. "I don't know. But I know she's not a criminal.

Maybe once, Mac, but not anymore."

"This isn't enough to convince you? Jesus, Adam, I never thought you were gullible."

Adam almost laughed out loud. If Mac had a clue the kinds of things that had been dancing through Adam's mind, he'd have thought the term gullible far too mild. He had to convince Brigit to trust him. Had to make her let him help her out of this mess. And then . . . and then he had to let her go. He knew that. Had known it from the start. He had to let her go.

Even though it would tear his heart out.

Mac sighed long and hard, but went to his desk and unlocked a drawer. He withdrew what looked like a marking pen, brought it over, and tucked it into Adam's pocket. "The ink only shows up in a black light, pal. Take my advice and mark the back of your painting. At least take that precaution."

"All right."

"Adam . . ."

Adam looked at Mac, and knew his friend was genuinely afraid for him. "I'll be okay," he said, but even to his own ears, it lacked conviction.

"If you need me . . ."

"Yeah."

She stopped painting earlier than usual, and put her things away. The juice just wasn't flowing today.

Adam's manuscript had been sitting on the desk in the study, and something . . . some force she didn't pretend to understand, had drawn her to it. It felt as if, from the second she'd

stepped into the room, that book had been calling to her.

And she'd never been one to ignore her instincts. So she went to the desk, and she looked
at the leather-bound translation of some ancient
Celtic text.

And then she stood motionless, blinking in
shock because the words on the pages had a
magical cadence, a lilt of sincerity. They rang
true, somehow, as they outlined the characteristics of fairy folk. Especially those of the feminine ilk. It told of their affinity with nature, and
the way plants and animals thrive when a fairy
is near. It told of how a fairy could read a man's
soul by looking into his eyes, and how she could
capture the soul of a mortal man, and enslave
him forever.

Breathless with wonder, Brigit sank into the
chair behind Adam's desk, and continued to
read. And when she came to the pages describing the crescent moon birthmark and what its
color might signify, she was trembling all over.
Head to toe. Goosebumps traveled up and down
her arms and chills tumbled over her spine.

What in the name of God was this?

"Interesting reading, isn't it?"

Her head came up fast at the sound of Adam's
voice. She stared at him, not really seeing, heard
him, but wasn't really hearing.

"Where did you get this?" she asked softly.

Adam tilted his head, sniffed the air. "What's
that smell?" he asked, and his face was hard. No
hint of a smile touched his eyes. "Almost smells
like paint. Ridiculous, isn't it, Brigit?"

She blinked, shook her head, wondered why

he seemed so . . . so empty. So sad. Glancing down at the book on the desk, she jerked in surprise when he spoke again.

"It's a translation of a text uncovered in an archaeological dig in Ireland. They figure it's around nine hundred years old."

He spoke as if that bit of information held some particular relevance, but she didn't know what. "Adam . . . this is uncanny. The . . . the birthmark . . ."

He lowered his head, no longer looking her in the eye. "Yeah. It blew me away when I saw it on you. But, dammit, Brigit, that isn't important right now. What's important is that you don't trust me. After everything . . . everything I've told you . . . you still can't be honest with me."

He was angry! He'd been angry before he'd ever spoken to her, and she would have realized it if she hadn't been so shocked by what she'd read. "Adam, what's the matter? What did I do?"

He opened his mouth but snapped it closed again, apparently changing his mind. He lowered his chin, shook his head. "Nothing. Nothing at all."

She came from behind the desk, moving toward him. "Talk to me."

Shaking his head, he started to turn away.

"Adam, please. This is scaring me."

She saw his back stiffen, his head come up, though he didn't turn to face her. "You're scared?"

"Of course I'm scared! How can I not be?"

He turned then, slowly, his eyes narrow and wary, and hurt.

"Adam, how long have you known about this," she asked, pointing at the book on the desk.

"Almost a year."

"Then you knew ... about these similarities. You already knew ..."

"Knew what, Brigit?"

"The ... the things that book says ... they're so similar to ..."

He averted his eyes, biting his lower lip, nodding. His every movement showing his cynical doubt of what she said.

"Adam, there's a way to explain it. There has to be. Maybe my birthmark is just ... just a coincidence. Or maybe ..."

"Or maybe what? Come on, Brigit, tell me what you're really thinking. Don't keep lying to me."

It was her turn to narrow her eyes, search his face. "Why are you so angry with me, Adam?"

He blinked twice, gave his head a shake, and turned away from her.

She ran around him, stopping in front of him, blocking his exit. "Please ..." It was a faint whisper, a hoarse plea. "Don't walk away without telling me why."

"You know why."

She nodded slowly, understanding coming to her in waves that nearly knocked her breathless. He'd had enough of her lies. He was tired of waiting for her to trust him with the truth.

"It's almost over, Adam. I swear, it won't be long now, and I'll be able to tell you everything. Please, don't give up on me. Not yet."

He started to walk past her, and anger surged through her more forcefully than it had ever done.

"No!"

She yelled it at the top of her voice, sending the force of her fury into the word. Adam stopped dead as if he'd slammed into a brick wall.

He blinked in shock, his eyes widening.

Brigit paid little attention to that. She was too busy searching for answers, fearing the worst. God, did he know then? Had he somehow found out that she was about to steal his painting?

It didn't matter. She had no choice but to go through with her plan. She couldn't risk Raze's life. But when it was over, maybe when she explained what she'd done, and why she'd done it, maybe he'd understand. Maybe he'd find some way to forgive her. Maybe . . .

But she knew better, didn't she? Maybe another man would be able to forgive this kind of betrayal. But not Adam. And it would be wrong of her to even ask him to.

She tried to stifle her sobs as she turned away, and ran through the study and up the stairs to her room.

Adam stood precisely where he was, not moving, not even breathing.

Something had just happened here. Something that defied explanation—well, defied every explanation except one. When Brigit had shouted at him . . . she'd hit him. Hard. Only . . . she hadn't moved.

A solid blast of hot anger had slammed into Adam's chest as palpable as a wrecking ball. He'd been heading for the door, and it had stopped him in his tracks. Wham!

And it had vanished just as suddenly.

He lowered his chin to his chest, shook his head. No more room for doubt. It had happened. And he was either completely insane, which he knew damned well he wasn't, or Brigit Malone was a fairy.

And she doesn't know, he thought in stunned silence. Hell, she was probably more confused by all of this than he was.

Brigit Malone. Fairy or thief? Or both. Somehow, in some twisted-up way, she must be both.

He'd stick it out for a few more days. Watch her every move, and find out for himself.

She tossed in the bed, twisting and writhing until the sheets had tangled around her legs like boa constrictors. God, what had come over Adam?

He must have been checking up on her. It was the only answer. He must have been trying to verify the lies she'd told him. About her reasons for not being able to stay in her house. About her past. Could he have found the truth? No one knew why she was really here. No one but Zaslow. How could Adam have found out?

He didn't trust her anymore. Not the way he had. And it was killing her. It was tearing her apart not to have him here, to hold her the way he had before. It was too lonely, now, in this bed without him. She sat up, wrenching the covers

from her body, dashing the tears from her eyes
with the back of one hand.

She'd go to him, right now, and tell him
everything. Maybe he'd understand. Maybe
he'd help her find another way out of this mess.
Maybe . . .

She whirled, uttering a little squeak of surprise when there was a tap on the French doors.
And then her eyes widened and her pulse skit-
tered wildly, just beneath the skin of her wrists.

The doors were flung open, and Zaslow
stepped through them, shaking his head slowly.
"Sleeping alone, tonight, are you? What happened? Trouble in paradise, Brigit?"

She shook her head rapidly, backing toward
the door.

"Is he onto you, Brigit?"

"No." Her back pressed to the cool wood, her
hand rose behind her to grasp the knob.

"You're not going anywhere, darling. Not unless you want Raze's heart delivered to you in
a candy box."

Swallowing the sandy feeling in her throat,
she lowered her hand. She was shaking all over,
fear making her feel as cold as if she were standing naked in a snowstorm.

"Why are you alone? Tell me, and tell me the
truth, or I'll hurt your old friend. And I'll enjoy
it."

She shook her head rapidly. "I don't know! I
swear, Zaslow. He . . . he came home in a bad
mood. I . . . I don't think it has anything to do
with me." It was a lie, but one she hoped he
wouldn't see through. Brigit knew damned well

that Adam's mood had everything to do with her.

"Make up with him."

She blinked, not understanding, and Zaslow rolled his eyes, sighing loud and long. "Show me the painting, Brigit. I want to verify you haven't stopped working on it."

"I haven't."

"Show me," he growled. And she felt her teeth chatter.

Keeping her back to the wall, she sidled toward the closet, only edging nearer him when she had no choice but to go around the chestnut vanity beside her bed. She opened the closet door, reached inside to turn on the light. Inclining her head she said, "It's in the back. Don't smear it."

Zaslow's eyes narrowed on her face. "You leave this room, Brigit, or call out or do *anything* other than stand there, and you can kiss your friend Malone goodbye. I didn't leave him alone."

And then he ducked into the closet, and she stood there. Trembling. Impotent with fear for Raze. Enraged that she was so helpless.

But you're not helpless, you fool! came the all-too-familiar voice of her wild side. *Something happened downstairs tonight. When you yelled at Adam, he stopped as if he'd walked into an invisible wall. You did that.*

No. That was impossible. It made no sense.

So what in your life ever made sense?

She frowned, refusing to believe, not wanting to believe. But her anger at Zaslow came bubbling up, and she had the feeling that the wild

one inside was deliberately rousing it. Brigit looked into the closet where that self-assured bully stood examining the painting, and she recalled the sight of that coffin-shaped box, and the fear that had nearly paralyzed her. And she got angrier. With her eyes tightly closed, she wished with everything in her that she could hurt Zaslow. Make him pay for what he was putting Raze through. Pain, she thought. The man deserved severe pain.

"Dammit!"

A muffled thud accompanied his cry, and Brigit jerked rigid, her eyes flying open. Zaslow emerged from the closet, pressing three fingers to his forehead. Blood trickled from beneath the fingers, trailing down onto his nose, a single droplet dangling from the tip.

Wide-eyed, Brigit backed away from him . . . from the undeniable evidence. "What—"

"Nothing," he snapped. "A box fell from a shelf." With his free hand he jerked tissues from the dispenser on the vanity, and swiped the blood away, then pressed the wad to the cut on his head. Taking the wad away, he looked at it, then pressed it back again. "The painting looks nearly finished."

She couldn't stop staring at the cut on his forehead. Couldn't slow her racing heartbeat, or the new knowledge that was slowly making itself a home in her mind. "It is," she whispered. "Almost done, that is."

"How much longer?"

She shrugged, lowering her gaze to the floor, shaking her head in wonder.

"Three days," he told her. "Three days, Brigit.

It will either be the length of time it takes to finish the painting, or Raze's expected life span. Do you understand?''

"It's not enough—"

"It's more than enough. Meanwhile, you'd better take your pretty backside down the hall and wiggle it for Mr. Reid. You'll never finish the painting if he throws you out, will you?"

She lifted her head, glared at him. "You son of a—"

"Seduce your way back into his good graces, Brigit. You can do it. You managed it the first time around."

"It wasn't—"

"Good night." He tossed the tissues into the wastebasket, and walked back out the French doors, the same way he'd entered.

And she stared after him, and thought about trying to see if she could wish him to fall on his head from the deck. Only the fear of never knowing where Raze was, of him dying slowly because she couldn't find him, kept her from experimenting on Zaslow just then.

Brigit wondered how he'd managed to get up there in the first place, whether he had a rope ladder dangling from the deck outside or what.

And then it no longer mattered. She was exhausted, physically, emotionally, and mentally. This was too much. Too damned much for anyone to go through. Not just Zaslow and his threats, but this feeling that was slowly encapsulating her entire soul. That maybe she'd never felt as if she belonged here, because she *didn't*. Maybe she belonged somewhere else. Like Rush.

God, it was too much to take in all at once. Especially alone. She sank down to the floor, giving in to the turmoil, letting the tears come at last.

"God, Adam," she whispered. "I need you. I just need you to hold me so much. Can't you just hold me?" And she lifted her head, looking toward the wall that separated his room from hers, and she closed her eyes. "If there's any magic in me at all . . . let it bring you here to me, tonight. Because I don't want to spend the night alone."

Chapter Thirteen

SHE WAS STILL lying to him. Even now.

She was a beautiful woman, who smiled with her eyes whenever he looked into them. She touched him in a way no other woman ever had, in a way he sensed no other woman ever would.

After what they'd shared—the things he'd told her, things he'd never shared with anyone, and the hours of lovemaking so intense and soul-deep it had to be supernatural—she still couldn't bring herself to trust him enough to tell him the truth. Hadn't it meant a damn thing to her? Had it all been an act? If she cared in the least, wouldn't she have opened up to him by now?

And did it matter? Because he still wanted her. He wanted her all the time, day and night, asleep or awake, at home and at work. She was never far from his mind. He couldn't stop thinking about the way it felt to hold her, to kiss her. The taste of her skin. Those honeyed kisses. The loss of himself when he'd been inside her. God!

She was plotting to steal his most precious

possession, even knowing what it meant to him. And he didn't care! He'd rather burn the thing in the fireplace than lose her now.

That was the problem. He cared. He hadn't meant to. He'd been warned not to. And he had to resist her. He had to stop himself from getting any closer to her, because he knew she'd leave him. He knew. And knowing made every breath he drew sheer hell.

He had to stay away from her. Help her, yes, but somehow keep a distance. Keep his emotions safe. He had to . . .

She was in trouble. In so much trouble she couldn't find her way out. And . . . and she needed him.

Adam flung back the covers, sitting up in the bed. He gripped his pillow in his fists and he shook it the way he felt like shaking her when she refused to talk to him. Damn, damn, *damn!*

He wanted her.

Slamming himself out of bed, he paced the floor. Plush carpeting cushioning his bare feet. Warm summer air greeting his naked flesh. He was hard, and she wasn't even in the room. He was hot and he was lonely for her soft, silken body. For her wet lips and for those little sounds she made down deep in her throat when he . . .

Damn!

Five steps to the French doors. He stopped there only briefly, then turned on his heel. Twelve steps past the foot of the bed, to the closed door that led to the hallway. And he stopped there a little longer. A second longer. Long enough for his hand to touch the door-

knob. Long enough for him to curse himself for being an idiot.

He turned again. Ten steps to the bathroom door, four through it, and a cold shower was within reach. It was also the last thing he wanted.

He *wanted* Brigit.

How many steps, he wondered, were there between his room and hers? Only a few. And he'd be there, with her. He could have her.

Keep your distance, you idiot! You're walking right into heartbreak!

She was longing for him, aching for him, right now. Calling to him, somehow. He could feel her calling out to him, though he couldn't hear her. A psychic lure tugged at him. Teased him. Tempted him. Its touch was physical, palpable. Something very real, dammit, had twined around him and pulled tight, so that he felt like a fish caught in a net. And he didn't bother struggling because he thought it might kill him. The net pulled tight, so there was no chance of escape, and then it drew him across that soft carpet. It drew him right up to his bedroom door.

Through it.

He was hauled in by this mental net, and it was against his will. Against everything he knew to be practical and smart and necessary. She would hurt him. Again. She would lie to him, and she would leave him. And yet he walked a little faster, instead of fighting the current that carried him through the hall. He twisted the doorknob, flung her bedroom door open, and stepped inside. And then he stood

there, naked and aroused, just inside her bedroom. And she was on the floor, by her bed. Her legs curled underneath her, tears scalding her cheeks.

She looked up, met his eyes. "Adam . . ."

"I didn't want to come in here," he whispered, and his voice sounded ragged and broken. And even as he said it he was dropping to his knees, clasping her shoulders, running his fingertips over her skin.

"I was wishing for you, Adam."

"I heard you," he said, and he covered her mouth with his, pushed his tongue inside, thrust deep. His breathing was ragged and his hands were pushing the thin straps of the camisole down from her shoulders.

Her hands came around him, and her fingers dove into his hair. She leaned back, opened her mouth wider, and he devoured her, unable to help himself. He moved his mouth sideways, over her face, and down her neck. He tugged the camisole lower, and tasted her breast. The rounded, firm flesh, and then the succulent center. He sucked on her nipple until he felt it throbbing under his tongue. And then he moved to the other side.

He'd pressed her onto her back now. He was pulling the camisole down with him as he moved lower over her body, taking huge bites of her waist, gnawing and licking his way over her abdomen as she clawed and tore at his hair. She twisted, panted, cried, trembled. He had to know her, all of her. He had to experience every sensation, every nuance, every inch of her. It was a compulsion. An obsession. A perversion,

maybe, or perhaps an addiction to that honeyed flavor. He kissed a wet trail over her thighs. He lapped a path down the backs of her calves, tasting the hollows behind her knees. He traced the shapes of her ankles with his tongue, and then kissed the very soles of her small feet, and every toe, before working his way back up again. Higher, until he shoved her legs wider and made his way to the very heart of her.

"Do you want it?" he demanded, blowing hot breath on her, watching her quiver.

"Yesss . . ."

He pulled her apart, and drove his tongue into the feast that awaited him. She tasted so good. Salt and feminine spice. And that honey. That sweetness that belonged to her alone. And he craved more of her, more than he ever could have. He couldn't tell her that, couldn't give words to a need so fierce, so powerful. So he used his mouth to show her. And his tongue and his teeth. Until she screamed his name at the top of her voice, clawing at his shoulders as her hips thumped the floor in convulsive motions.

He crawled back up her body. All the way up her body. He straddled her chest. And he didn't have to tell her. She lifted her head, staring at the erection in front of her with passion glazed eyes. And then she took it into her mouth. Adam lifted his hips. He caught her head in his hands, and he moved against the delicious suction. Her hands crawled around to cup his backside, and then her nails sank into his flesh and she took more of him. Deeper and faster and harder. Until he was the one screaming in sweet

agony, spilling his passion into her, watching her take it, savor it.

And when he wanted to collapse on top of her, he couldn't. Because he needed more. *He needed more.* There would never be enough. So he sank sideways, and he turned so he was on his back beside her. He wrapped his arms tight around her body and pulled her on top of him. She settled herself over him, lowered herself slowly, closing her eyes as she did. She remained upright, and when she opened her eyes again, it was to stare straight down into his. And he saw the wildness in her eyes. The part of her he'd sensed her struggling against so often. It was loose now. And dammit, he was glad. Slowly, she moved lower. Too slowly. He captured her hips in his hands, and then pulled her down fast and hard so he impaled her. Her mouth opened in a silent groan. Her head fell backward and her eyes closed.

His hands at the small of her back pulled her forward though, and then down to him, so he could kiss her and taste her mouth as he made love to her. And he didn't want it to end. Not ever. And it didn't matter that she was lying to him, or that she was going to leave him in the end. Because there was something bigger than both of them, something that seemed to be pushing them together. A force neither of them could understand, let alone overcome. He couldn't resist her. He could try. He could hate her, for all it mattered. He'd still have to be with her like this.

Worst part was, he didn't hate her. Not at all. She held him inside her, and she moved with

him. His tongue trapped in her mouth and his body held tightly inside her body. And when she drew the release from him this time, he felt an emptying of his very soul, flowing into hers. Mating with it, entwining in a knot that could only be eternal.

God, she owned him now. What the hell hope was there for him after lovemaking like this? He'd sold his soul, and Brigit was the new owner. And the deed she held was one he'd handed over without hesitation. Her hold on him was greater than anyone's had ever been. Greater than Sandra's. Greater even than that of his own father when he'd been just a child. Brigit owned him, because he'd surrendered his heart and soul. He'd shared everything with her, unable to do otherwise. Simply sitting there like a duck at a carnival game, waiting for her to do her worst. Praying she'd have mercy. Knowing she wouldn't . . . *couldn't*. Because the choice wasn't hers.

When she left him, when she took the blade that fate had forced into her hands, and drove it straight through his heart, it was going to be the killing stroke. He'd given her too much of himself, now. There was no getting it back. She'd destroy him. She'd utterly destroy him.

And he'd let her.

He was intense, and energetic, but not rough. He might have intended to be. He might even have wanted to be. But he couldn't. It wasn't in his gentle soul to be less than tender with her, though his tenderness was ablaze with passion. It stirred something in Brigit's heart to know she

was capable of stirring so much reaction in him. So much need. It seemed a miracle to her that he would come to her even though he didn't want to.

But it was no miracle. It was magic. And she felt terribly guilty for using it on him. Moreover, she was afraid she wouldn't be able to resist the urge to do it again.

Poor Adam. So sure she was dishonest, so sure she was no good, and yet unable to stay away. She should leave here. That would end his misery. She should go away and just let him alone.

But she couldn't. If she did, the man she loved—the other one—would die.

She stirred. They'd been lying in silence for a long time, he on his back beneath her. She collapsed atop him. Naked. Without covers to hide under. Slowly, though, the love languor faded, and she became aware of how still he was. Not relaxed stillness, either. She felt the tension in every bit of him. He lay stiff, and his arms were on the floor at his sides, rather than around her as they had been.

Slowly she lifted her upper body, so she could look down into his face. But the expression he wore was one she'd rather not have seen. Self-disgust. Regret. Despondency. All so clear in his eyes. Eyes she'd always been able to read.

She shook her head slowly. What could she say? She couldn't assure the poor man that he'd been wrong about her, that she was honest and faithful and true. She wasn't. She was exactly what he thought she was. A liar. A thief.

She lowered her chin in shame and slid off

him, ending on her knees beside him. She watched as he sat up and got to his feet. He looked down at her once, closed his eyes as if in horrible pain, and then he left her. Alone. To face the night and her fears alone. Just as she'd had to face them before. Their passion had been a fire in the night. But all that remained now were ashes.

She showered quickly before crawling into the bed, pulling the covers over her head, and burying herself there. She only wished she'd never have to emerge. But she did. Eventually. And when she did, Adam was gone.

Adam didn't go to the university that morning. Instead, he made a call, early, while Brigit was still sound asleep. He'd made sure of that before calling. He'd crept along the deck outside her bedroom, and peered in through the French doors, like a burglar in his own home, and he'd seen her. Lying naked on the bed, swathed in white fabric. With her raven curls spread around her and her coal-black lashes resting gently on her cheeks. The contrast of honey-smooth skin, and brilliantly white sheets, and her pitch-black hair, was magical. She looked more like an angel than ever. A dark angel. A passionate angel. An angel who could love a man to the brink of madness.

La belle dame sans merci.

It had been a long time before he'd been able to tear his gaze from her, there, sleeping. Spellbinding.

Interesting choice of words, he thought now. He felt as if *he* were under a spell, caught in a

magical web too sticky to allow him to get free. She'd *made* him come to her last night. He'd wanted to stay away, but she'd worked some kind of magic on him. And he had the feeling she knew it. She'd admitted it, when he'd gone to her. "I was wishing for you, Adam." Worst of all, he wasn't even sure he minded all that much. Self-denial wasn't so painful if you were given no choice in the matter.

No matter what he believed about Brigit, he couldn't stop himself from wanting her. From . . . from *liking* her. More than that. Caring about her. And more than *that*, too, though he refused to give a name to what else he felt. No matter how conniving he believed her to be, he couldn't help enjoying her. Thinking about her when he wasn't with her. Reveling in her company when he was. And worrying about her involvement with a murderer like Zaslow.

Maybe there was still some part of his mind that wasn't convinced of her intentions. Maybe after today, that would change. Because once he saw what she was doing with his own two eyes, he couldn't doubt any longer. Could he?

He didn't leave. Instead, he drove his car a short distance away from the house, and walked back. And then he stationed himself just beyond the bank of windows in the study, and he waited, and he watched.

He didn't have to wait long.

Brigit came into the room, lugging more equipment than a woman of her slight build ought to be able to manage. He peered around the corner from outside, frowning hard as she dumped everything on the floor. She spread

drop cloths over the carpeting, and set a tripod in their center. She disappeared again, only to return with tubes and brushes and a palette. And then once more to come back with the stool from the kitchen. She wore stirrup pants and an oversized, paint-smattered white smock.

Her duplicity was like a blow. It hurt, though it shouldn't. He should have been prepared. He was only seeing what he'd known he was going to see.

He continued watching, unobserved.

Brigit headed upstairs one more time, and this time she returned with the canvas. She took her time with it, holding it with the flats of her fingers to its very edges. She set it on the tripod with extreme care. And then she stood poised over it for a time, gnawing her lower lip as she eyed it critically.

Adam's eyes narrowed. He moved farther to the left to get a better view, and when he finally did, he stood there gaping like a fish. God Almighty, it was perfect! It was freaking *perfect!* She'd captured everything from the original. He couldn't spot a single flaw, except for the parts that remained unfinished. And those, he saw with regret, were surprisingly few.

She was a fast worker.

His gaze jumped from the painting to her face again, and he frowned and tilted his head. She stood utterly motionless, seemingly mesmerized by staring up at the original. The one hanging over the mantel. For a very long time, she stood that way, her eyes fixed and unblinking. But odd-looking. Unfocused maybe, as if she were not just looking at the painting, but into it. Or

. . . or something. It seemed to Adam as he watched her that her breathing got slower, and deeper. He could see her lungs expand and contract in a long, drawn-out rhythm. She looked—he sought for an apt description—like a sleepwalker. Yes, that was it, exactly. A sleepwalker. Eyes opened, but not seeing. They seemed glazed-over, cloudy.

And when she finally did begin to move, it was with the slow, almost awkward motions of a somnambulist. Her hands rose in slow motion and worked the tubes of paint and balanced the palette. She never looked at them. And while the movements seemed clumsy, she didn't drop anything. It was all done with an unconscious ease. And then she lifted the brush. And the whole time, her eyes never left the painting on the wall.

Adam blinked, gave his head a shake, narrowed his eyes. Her actions didn't change, though. She painted without looking. And for a long time, he couldn't see what the results might be, because he was unable to take his eyes off her face and her hands as she worked. As he watched, she wielded the brushes faster, and with more confidence. Never blinking, never even peeking at the work in progress.

It was eerie. Watching the scene sent chills right down his spine, but he couldn't look away. Seemed he became as immersed in staring at her as she'd become in staring at "Rush." The spell was only broken when her movements slowed, became more lethargic. And her eyelids drooped, as if the entire exercise had exhausted her. Her shoulders slumped a little. It was ob-

vious she was trying now. Putting forth an effort to keep going. Working at getting it right. The frown lines between her brows appeared, where before she'd seemed utterly relaxed. And then she gave her head a little shake, and set the brush down.

She rubbed her eyes with her fingertips, then finally, she surveyed what she'd done. And so did Adam. He looked from her canvas to the one on the wall several times, and he gaped in astonishment, not only at the sheer perfection of the work, but at the amount she'd accomplished in a single session.

As he looked on, she conducted a similar survey, looking anxiously from one painting to the other. From the original to the forgery. And she nodded in apparent approval. But her face held no joy, no excitement. It seemed sadness was all she felt.

And finally, she began the process of recapping the paint tubes. She gathered up the brushes and took them away, moving off in the direction of the kitchen. Probably to clean them.

Only then was Adam able to focus on anything besides Brigit and what had been happening inside that room. It occurred to him, as it no doubt should have much sooner, that he was too warm with his light jacket on. The sun burned over his back, heating him right through it, and when he wiped the back of a hand across his brow, it came away damp. Frowning, he glanced down at his wristwatch. Three hours! Three hours he'd stood here, all but motionless, lost in watching her. Three hours she'd re-

mained bent over that canvas, with her eyes focused elsewhere.

It was one more thing about Brigit Malone that defied explanation. How the hell did she do what he'd just seen her do? He wondered how *she* explained it to herself. Maybe she thought she was channeling the work or something. He just didn't see how she could do the things she did, and not realize it was . . . it was magic.

And beyond all of that was the fact he had to face. Not possible to doubt it anymore. He'd been right about Brigit's intentions. She'd lied to him all along, with the intention of stealing a painting she knew meant more to him than anything else he owned. She was going to do it despite what they'd shared, or what *he'd thought* they'd shared. Despite what she'd come to mean to him.

God, if she knew him at all, she'd know he wouldn't care about that. About her inability to be honest with him, yes. That hurt. But she could take the damned painting. Hell, if the idea were to switch the forgery for the original, he'd rather have the forgery. Because it was hers. Something she'd done. Why couldn't she see that?

Maybe because he was the only one who felt that way. Maybe because this caring was all on his side. Maybe because he didn't mean a damn thing to her.

Brigit came back into the room, drying her hands on a rag. She carefully lifted the canvas from the tripod, and he almost winced. Moving it while it was still wet was risky . . . and after all that work? He supposed, though, she saw

that as necessary. She had to keep what she was doing a secret, after all. It wouldn't do to have Adam waltz in one afternoon to see it sitting there, big as life.

He had to crouch down low to see her head up the stairs, and then crank his neck uncomfortably to watch her enter her bedroom. So she kept this masterpiece hidden somewhere in her room, then. Okay. Fine. He'd know that much at least. Meanwhile, he decided it would be a damned good idea to mark the original with that pen Mac had given him. Not because he wanted to prove her guilty. Not even in hopes of recovering the work. But just in case she disappeared from his life before he got his answers, he'd need to know, for his own peace of mind, whether she'd gone through with this or not. And because if all he had left of her ended up being the painting she'd created through her own, incredible magic, then he at least wanted to know he held her copy, and not the original. From the looks of things, if Brigit went ahead with her plans, the original wouldn't be hanging there much longer.

Finished. The painting was finished. And so was Brigit. Done for. She wanted to save Raze. She needed to find her sister. And she was in love, deeply, madly in love with Adam Reid. No matter the risk, she couldn't betray him. She couldn't.

Zaslow had given her three days. And that was good, because that would give the paint plenty of time to dry. She had no choice, the way she saw it. There was nothing else she could do.

She'd have to leave Adam, because it wasn't fair to stay. But she'd tell him the truth first. Everything. Everything. She pulled a sheet of paper from her bedside stand, and began her letter to him.

Adam waited until he was certain she was asleep. Then he crept out of bed and downstairs into the study. He carefully removed his painting from its spot above the mantle, and set it on the floor. Then he wrote a single word on the back, in the lower right-hand corner. *Rush*. He watched as the letters faded before his eyes, until only a trace remained.

Then nothing.

Why, he wondered, was he still doubting Brigit's true intent here? Why was there this one, stubborn, stupid part of him that was hoping against hope she would change her mind? Why did he have even a kernel of doubt she'd go through with her plan to betray him?

But he knew why he held on to that tiny shred of hope. He knew perfectly well why, didn't he? He was in love with the goddamned woman. He loved her with every part of him, and if she'd just reconsider, if she'd just turn to him instead of away from him, trust him enough to be honest and let him help her . . .

. . . Who was he kidding? It wouldn't matter. Because in order to help her, he had to try to help her find her sister, and then he had to let her go. In the end, he'd lose her, either way.

There was nothing left for him, was there? He didn't honestly think his heart would survive a single day once she finally left him forever.

The telephone rang, and he picked it up before it could do so again, with a weary, "Yeah?"

"I've found the sister," Mac said without preamble. "And, buddy, you're not gonna believe it."

Chapter Fourteen

THE SITUATION WAS dire.

Darque paused in his rooms—the ones he used on those seldom occasions when he could be here to watch over his captive in person—to stare through the two-way mirror at Bridín.

She'd grown into a stunning young woman. She sat up straight, her posture regal and proud, in the chair beside the bed. Eyes closed, that deep, rich voice of hers as serene as ever as she sang one of the old songs. Such a solemn woman. So resigned to this existence.

Or so she'd convinced him. He'd only recently become aware of what she'd done. While he'd been away seeing to matters in Rush, trying to quell yet another of those constant uprisings, she'd created a painting, and sent it home with her nurse, Kate, who, in turn, had sold it to an art gallery in Ithaca. No coincidence, that. Darque had dealt with her kind too often in the past not to know this had some hidden meaning. And there was only one he could think of. That the painting was meant as a message of

some sort, a message from Bridín to her missing twin. A message which would bring that other one to him. And if he wasn't careful, the two of them might escape. Together—only together—they might well make their way back to Rush, and stir a full-scale revolt. His hold on the throne could be in serious jeopardy.

Naturally, he'd tried to nip Bridín's attempt in the bud, by going to this gallery himself. But he'd been unable to so much as touch the painting. She'd placed an enchantment on it.

As furious as he was with her, he couldn't help but admire her cunning. Despite the frequent tranquilizers, and the constant confinement, she'd managed to hold on to her magic. Gods, it must be stronger than he'd guessed.

And the painting . . . the painting was utterly mesmerizing. He'd stood in that gallery—as close as he could get to the thing—and stared at it, lost in its beauty for hours.

And then he'd decided to try another approach. He'd hired a reputable art thief to steal it. Once the thief did so, Darque would order him to destroy it . . . right there, where Darque could watch, and be assured it was done. Bridín's sister must never see that painting.

Never.

It was only with this most recent trouble that Darque had installed the mirror, so he could watch Bridín at all times. He'd be aware if she tried creating any more magical messages.

It was dangerous for him to be here, now. The kingdom was quiet for the moment, but he knew too well it was only a pause in the chaos that usually reigned. He ought to be there.

And he would be, soon. Just as soon as he saw this painting destroyed, and assured himself the sister remained blissfully unaware of her twin and her heritage, he'd leave.

And this time, he planned to take Bridín with him. With her life in the balance, her people would comply, willingly and completely, at long last. When Bridín, their queen, knelt at his feet, the rest would follow.

All he need do would be to convince her to remove that necklace, and he'd be able to take her. Subjugate her. Make her his servant.

And he was close . . . he was so close to convincing her to remove the pendant. Each night, he went to her while she slept, and used all the strength he had to speak to her mind, to mesmerize it with the power of his own, to bend her to his will. It was exhausting him. Draining him. And it was dangerous. So dangerous, because when he entered her mind that way, he had to open his own to her subtle influence as well.

It was a struggle of wills. But she was beginning to weaken. He was winning. When she learned that the painting had been destroyed, that her sister had never received the message meant for her, her devastation should be the final blow. Her will would be broken, and she would be his to command.

And command her, he would.

As he watched, already savoring his victory, Bridín rose with the grace of . . . of a fay queen. And stood there, with the windows at her back. The setting sun behind her cast fiery red light through the thin nightgown she wore, so that

there was nothing of her body Darque couldn't see.

His throat went dry. He averted his face quickly, knowing the one weapon of the fairy female, that no man, mortal or otherwise, could hope to fight.

But his eyes were drawn back to hers.

"I know you're watching me, Dark Prince," she said slowly, and somehow, though he knew she couldn't see him, her eyes met and melded with his. "I know what you're thinking right now."

Gods, that voice! Deep and smooth and soft. Like velvet stroking him. He put his palms to his ears, closed his eyes. But still he heard her.

"You think you'll own me. That I'll be your slave, as well as your prisoner soon."

"Shut up," he yelled, turning away from the glass.

"But you're wrong, Dark Prince. It is I who will own you. Body and soul. Unless you release me, my handsome, ruthless, evil captor... *you're doomed.*"

Darque grated his teeth as he stormed out of the room, down the stairs and out of the house. Damn her! Damn her, she'd pay. She would pay for that impertinence, and pay dearly.

Chapter Fifteen

THERE WAS SOMETHING on Adam's mind. Something important.

Adam had changed since she'd moved into his life. He'd lost weight. His face seemed drawn and taut, and he rarely smiled. His eyes had lost their sparkle and their life. And they sported circles beneath them. The spring had gone from his step, and Brigit would have been blind if she'd believed it wasn't because of her.

He'd gone and let himself care for her. The fool. The poor, wonderful fool.

He sat, now, in the study, staring into the dying embers that glimmered cherry red in the hearth. He'd gone off to the university this morning, just like always. And with the painting finished, Brigit had spent the day at Akasha, tending to the plants that had been a bit neglected these last few days. She'd tried to get back that old feeling of peace the shop usually gave her. She'd slipped a Clannad CD into the stereo, adjusted the music nice and low. She'd set a few sticks of vanilla incense aglow. She'd

opened a window to admit the autumn breeze, just enough to set all the wind chimes tinkling.

But it hadn't worked. Nothing could ease her mind. Not now. And she knew why. For a brief space in time, she'd been allowed to touch paradise. Adam had let her in, admitted her to that secret place inside his heart.

It had been over too soon. For some reason she could only guess at, he'd changed his mind. He'd tossed her out and locked the iron door to the room where he kept his heart prisoner. And she didn't think he was going to let her back in again.

It had been bad enough before she'd known how sweet it felt to love someone the way she loved him. Now . . . now it was nothing short of sheer torture.

She hadn't expected to see him waiting up for her when she'd come home from Akasha. It was almost midnight, after all. And she winced again as she noticed the marked change in him, since she'd first met him. He sat just as tall, there in the leather chair nearest the hearth. His shoulders were every bit as wide as before. But he seemed wounded. Someplace so deep it didn't show. Except to her. She could see him bleeding.

"Sit down, Brigit. I have to talk to you."

She came forward, realized her knees were shaking, and weak. If he were going to ask her again for her reasons . . .

"I have something for you," he said softly, not even meeting her eyes as he took the slip of paper from his pocket. She took it from him as she passed him on her way to the sofa. But her feet stuttered to a halt when his fingertips touched

hers. And she saw him close his eyes, and she felt the shaft of pain that shot through him.

An answering bolt of guilt assaulted her. God, she was so glad this would soon be over. A few more days. Long enough for the paint to dry thoroughly. And then she'd be gone.

And that was a damned lie. She wasn't glad. Because she knew that once she left him, she could never see him again. For his sake, she had to get out of his life.

She took the paper, unfolded it, and read aloud. "310 Park Street, Binghamton, New York." Her vision blurred as she skimmed the next line, and she didn't feel herself sinking to the floor. She just ended up there, legs folded beneath her, the paper trembling in her hands.

"Bridín McCallister," she whispered, and she felt dizzy. "Bridín . . ."

"Your sister was adopted by Rebecca and James McCallister in 1969," Adam said softly, slowly. "But they were killed in an auto accident ten years later. James's brother, Matthew, took custody of Bridín after that, but something went wrong."

Brigit looked up at him, met his eyes. She parted her lips to question him, but no words emerged. Through her tears she saw the struggle in his eyes. The indecision. And finally he sighed, and reached out a hand to stroke her face.

"I can wish I'd never set eyes on you until hell freezes over. You know that, Brigit? But even then I can't stand to see you hurting."

She sniffed, blinking her vision clear. "You . . . you've found her? You know where she is? Je-

sus, Adam, you've found my sister?" she whispered, then shook her head in disbelief.

Adam's lips thinned, and it seemed he had to force himself to continue. "Yeah. I know where she is. But like I said, Brigit, something went wrong." He closed his eyes and sighed. "Maybe I shouldn't be telling you any of this." He opened his eyes, stared hard into hers.

"I've been dreaming about Bridín all my life," she whispered, still unable to coax her voice to full life or any real volume. Unable to force any solid sound through the tightness of her throat. "You have to tell me."

He nodded, bit his lip. "She started having dreams, right after the accident that killed her adoptive parents. Only, she called them visions, and began insisting her parents had been murdered by some supernatural force. She started talking about her memories of her true home, 'on the other side.' Kept claiming she was only half-mortal. That the other half . . . was fay."

Brigit shook her head slowly. It seemed all she was able to do as she let the information sink into her brain and felt a blade slice her heart.

"Her uncle thinks she's . . . not right. He has her under constant care in his home, though he's rarely there himself. She's not allowed to leave. He didn't let her attend school, had her tutored instead."

She blinked as if he'd slapped her, her body jerking in response to the blow. Brigit closed her eyes.

"And, Brigit, she's still there . . ."

She felt her facial muscles contort as grief overwhelmed her. God, all these years she'd

wondered, dreamed even, of having a sister. That possibility of Bridín being real. The ideal image of her that Brigit had built up in her own mind. To learn this ... it was worse than learning Bridín had never existed.

The book. If her poor sister was mentally ill, it was because of that stupid *Fairytale*! Whoever gave those books to two unsuspecting babies ought to be horsewhipped. Didn't they know the kind of confusion that would have to result?

She hadn't been aware of curling up against Adam's legs, or of lowering her head to his lap, or of the way her tears were soaking through his pant legs. But then he was stroking her hair, and calming her. Helping her. She didn't deserve this. And she lifted her head to tell him so.

"How do you know all of this?" was the question that came out instead. And then she answered it herself. "That private investigator you had checking me out. It was him, wasn't it?"

Adam nodded. "Mac's good, and he has low friends in high places. His methods aren't always ... ethical, but he gets the information he needs." He licked his lips. "He used to date a woman who knows the nurse who cares for Bridín."

She blinked, sniffling.

"When he found out that this twin of yours was probably real, I asked him to keep digging."

"Why?"

He shrugged. "Because I think I was supposed to. And because you'd told me ... how much it meant to you. I just ..."

"And what about me? Is he still investigating me?"

Adam shook his head. "I told him to drop it."

"Why, Adam? Why would you do that, when you know . . ."

"Know what, Brigit?" He got to his feet and stepped away from the spot where she sat on the floor, then he faced her, accusation and a dull ache in his eyes. "That you're still lying to me? Still keeping things from me?"

She flinched away from the accuracy of his words. But he held her eyes, dove into them, probing and searching. "Maybe I'm hoping it won't matter. Maybe I just don't want to know anymore. Dammit, Brigit, maybe I'm hoping you'll forget about this whole thing, whatever the hell it is, and just . . . just start over."

Her tears brimmed anew, and she had to avert her face. She knew he was waiting for her reply. But she couldn't lie to him again. She wouldn't.

He sighed, turning away from her and tugging at his hair. They stood that way, afraid to face each other, for a long, tense moment. Moments in which Brigit could barely contain the urge to fling herself into his arms and tell him she was sorry.

Finally, Adam cleared his throat. "Either way, I think you ought to see your sister."

She gave her head a fast, firm shake. "Not now, Adam. Not yet."

"It's a short trip, Brigit. God, we could drive there in a couple of . . ."

She climbed to her feet, feeling more tired than she ever had in her life. Physical and emo-

tional exhaustion tugged at her. "I don't want her . . . involved. Not until . . ."

"She's been locked up like a prisoner for most of her life, Brigit. If she doesn't belong there, even one more day is too long."

Brigit stopped and stood motionless in front of the fireplace, her eyes scanning the hot coals for answers. "She thinks she's a character from a *Fairytale*, Adam. How can she not belong there?"

He didn't answer. He went silent, and when she turned, she saw the way he was stroking the lush green leaves of the geranium on the end table, the way his eyes danced over the riots of ruby blossoms that had exploded to life overnight. The wonder in his face. The childlike wonder.

"I think maybe she is exactly what she thinks she is. And I think you know it. You must know it by now, Brigit. Don't you?"

She blinked at him, unable to believe he was actually saying what she'd been thinking, afraid to voice. "She can't be," she whispered. "I can't be. It isn't . . ."

"You made me come to you last night," he said softly. "You touched this plant and made it flourish. You taste like honey. You have the mark—"

She held up her hands. "It doesn't matter. I can't deal with this right now. Not yet."

"We could visit her for an hour or two. Drive right back. It would barely qualify as a trip."

She licked her lips, fear twisting around her heart.

"She's your *sister*," he told her. "And I think

you two need to touch base. I think there's probably a lot more riding on it than you could even imagine."

She frowned at him. "Adam, what could you possibly know about this?"

"I just—"

"No. Not now. I'll see her . . . but later . . . after . . ."

"After what Brigit? After you steal the painting for Zaslow?"

She stood there as long as she could, holding that gaze. And then a storm of emotion washed over her. She burst into tears, and she shook all over. Sobs tore at her breastbone.

She heard him swear, his voice loud and harsh, and then he was there, pulling her against him, holding her so hard and so close she felt he'd never let go. His palms slipped over her back, and up to her nape beneath her hair. His mouth moved over her face, dropping kisses and whispers at the same time.

"I'm sorry, Adam. I never meant to hurt you. God, I'm so sorry . . ."

"I don't care, Brigit. Can't you get that through your head? Hmm? Take the painting if you have to. It doesn't matter to me. Just let me help you. Tell me what's happening and let me help, dammit." His hold on her tightened still further. "Let me take the damned painting to Zaslow. Or be there, beside you, when you do. I'll protect you, I promise. That bastard won't ever hurt you again."

"No." She sniffed, and straightened away from him, brushing at her eyes with the backs of her hands, getting her sobs under control.

"Adam, he's already threatening to kill one man I care about. I can't risk him hurting you, too."

"Raze?" Adam asked.

She nodded. "How did you know?"

"Doesn't matter. Is he holding the old man, is that it? And threatening to hurt him unless you get the painting?"

"Yes." She hugged him harder. "Yes, Adam, but please don't get involved in this. If you care about me at all, don't get involved. If he hurt you, too, it would kill me. Just let me handle it."

"When do you deliver the painting to him?" Adam asked, tipping her chin up and searching her face.

"Two more days," she told him, and she saw in his eyes that he wasn't going to stay out of it. He wasn't. He was going to try to be a hero, and probably get himself killed, and that was something she couldn't let him do.

So it would have to be sooner. It would have to be . . .

. . . tonight.

Tears welled in her eyes again. This would be the last night for them. Even if she pulled this off, and got Raze back in one piece, Zaslow would never leave her alone. Not now. She'd have to run, change her name, start again somewhere else and pray he'd never find her. But she'd always know he was only a few steps behind.

She wouldn't put Adam through that.

Before she disappeared, though, she'd do as Adam suggested, and see her sister. At least that one dream could come true. And maybe Bridín would know something more about these ap-

parent . . . powers. Where they came from. What they meant.

But for now . . . it was her last night in Adam's arms, and she was going to make the most of it. She tipped her chin up, and let him cover her mouth with his, and she tasted her tears on his lips.

"I don't deserve this," she told him, when she paused for a breath. And Adam's troubled eyes caressed her face. "You're so good to me, Adam. But I'm not. I'm no good at all."

"Shhsh." He pushed her hair out of her eyes, kissed her forehead. "Don't."

And he kissed her again.

Adam recognized the desperation in her kisses. He knew it well, because he felt it himself. He made love to her. Right there on the floor in front of the hearth. And it was different. Yet another facet of what he felt for her. Because this time it was a healing. A comforting. And a sharing that he'd never experienced before.

And when she'd started to claim her unworthiness, and he'd told her "don't," he'd been silently saying so much more. Don't ruin my fantasy by reminding me you're going to leave me in the end. Don't destroy me, Brigit, because you can. With just a flick of your fingers, you can.

It didn't matter. Adam's obsession was complete. He was captivated by her, and until she broke him to bits, he'd go on being her willing worshipper. He'd do anything for her, go anywhere. He'd protect her, and God forbid he got his hands on the man who was hurting her this

way—this Zaslow creep—because he'd probably murder the bastard.

And when Brigit walked away, as she must, she'd be leaving behind a mannequin. A body without a soul. A man with a heart pulverized to dust. And he knew it, and there was not one damn thing he could do about it.

Two more days. For two more days, he could love her.

And then he'd personally see to it that Zaslow got his precious painting. And he'd keep the one Brigit had made, and love it all the more. He'd see to it that old Raze was safe and sound, and then he'd reunite Brigit with her sister. And somehow, he'd find the ability to lead them to that place in the woods he wasn't even sure he could find anymore. And somewhere, he'd find the strength to let her go.

She couldn't wait. She couldn't put this off. Not any longer. Not now that she knew Adam would try to intervene. To protect her. He'd get himself killed.

He'd never forgive her for going ahead without him. She knew that. But the way she saw it, she had little choice. Raze's life was hanging in the balance and so would Adam's be, if she waited.

She had to get this over with, and the sooner the better.

The thought of hurting Adam by leaving this way twisted her insides into hard knots. He'd found her sister. He'd given her something more precious to her than anything in the world. He deserved so much more in return.

She slipped away from him late that night.

They'd made love for hours, with the French doors open wide, so they could hear the soft, swishing sounds of the lake in the autumn breeze. He was exhausted, now, and lay sleeping soundly as she tiptoed across the floor, through those doors, and over the deck to slip into her own rooms.

And for one fanciful moment in time, she wished that cave Adam had imagined in the woods would turn out to be a real one. Because she'd like to go there. She'd like to crawl through it and find herself in another world. A fantasy world without such things as hurt and betrayal.

Was there such a place? Could there be? Would she ever see it?

She went to the closet to check the painting one more time. She'd make sure it was perfect before she continued in this dangerous plan. She opened the closet door, and brought her painting out. She held it at arm's length, her eyes running over its familiar colors and swirls.

And then they halted on something she hadn't seen before. She squinted, still unsure. It might just be a twig, or a falling, misshapen leaf.

But no, it couldn't be. She set the painting down and took her glasses from where she'd left them on the dressing table. She slipped them on, picked the painting up again, and studied it intently.

The shape rested in a spot that would be right about the breastbone of the woman who stood in the water. Though that part of her body was hidden by leaves and rushes. The pendant shone through. No more than a darker shadow amid

the greenery. But there, all the same.

Brigit lifted her hand, her fingertips clasping her own pewter fairy and quartz crystal.

"No," she whispered, blinking in shock. "It can't be . . ."

But it was. She knew, deep in her gut where you knew things despite what made sense and what didn't—she knew. That fairy in the painting, the one who looked so much like Brigit, only untamed and wild, wore the same necklace. "How?"

The telephone's shrill call made her jerk her head around. Her eyes widened at the thought of its noise waking Adam, and she laid the painting across the bed, snatching the thing up before it could jangle again.

"Brigit?"

She grated her teeth at the sound of Zaslow's voice. "What do you want?"

"Is it done?"

"It's done." She closed her eyes, the finality of her words weighing heavy on her shoulders.

"Good. We can make the exchange—"

"Tonight," she said quickly. "I want this over with, Zaslow. The sooner the better."

"Good."

She thought about Adam, thought about how hurt he'd be when he realized what she'd done.

"Maybe . . . maybe tomorrow would be—"

"No. Tonight, like you said. Don't try changing your mind, now."

"But—"

"Raze is sick, Brigit."

The blood left her head in a rush that made

her dizzy. Her stomach convulsed at the words. "What do you mean?"

"I mean what I said. He's sick. Feverish. Talking crazy and thrashing around in his sleep. He has the shakes."

"Get him to a hospital, Zaslow. Do it now. Call an ambulance and—"

"Not on your life, honey. Listen and listen good. Make the switch. Do it tonight. Bring the original to Binghamton. You know where that is, don't you? About an hour south of you."

She gave her head a shake at the shock that rippled through her at his words. Binghamton. That was where her sister was . . . "Why there?" she whispered, unable, suddenly, to speak in a normal tone of voice.

"Because my client is meeting me there later. Bring the painting to the ball park, Brigit. Raze says you know where that is."

She knew, all right. She and Raze had gone there often to watch the local double-A team play baseball.

"The place will be deserted this time of night. There's a chain-link fence between the diamond and the parking lot. You know where I mean?"

She nodded and said yes, tears scalding her cheeks as she heard a hoarse moan in the background that had to be Raze.

"Meet me there in two hours," Zaslow went on.

"One hour," she shot back. "Sooner if I can make it. Bring Raze, Zaslow. Bring him with you or I swear I'll slash that damned painting to ribbons."

"I'll bring him all right. And if you try to pull

anything on me, Brigit, I'll be the one doing the slashing."

The phone clicked in her ear. Brigit drew a deep, shuddering breath, and replaced the receiver. Then, trembling all over, she stepped out onto the deck and crossed to Adam's doors, to peer inside.

He thought he heard the phone, but he fell back into a contented doze so fast, he was never sure. And moments later, he vaguely recognized her scent. That intoxicating, roses and honey aroma she seemed to exude, and he relaxed again. Good, he thought, in the mists of his slumber. She's coming back to bed. I just want to hold her. Forever. Two days will never be long enough.

She came close, very close. He felt her presence as surely as he felt the cool breeze rushing in through the open doors, even in his half-asleep state. And then he felt her lips on his cheek, feather-light, so brief. Barely lifting away from his skin, they moved, and her whisper was no more than a fairy's breath in his ear, barely audible. Perhaps he even imagined it. Because it couldn't be real. She couldn't have just whispered, "I love you, Adam Reid."

And like the autumn breeze, she blew away. The doors closed, and that sense of her was gone.

Adam waited, groggily expecting to feel her body rolling up against his, her arms wrapping around his waist as she came back to bed. But he didn't. And gradually, that lonely feeling woke him up. He rolled over, sat up in bed, his

lips forming her name, though he didn't speak it aloud. His body shook, and his throat tried to close itself off. Where was she? What was going on?

Drawing a shaky breath, Adam tried to tell himself the feeling of foreboding that crept up his spine was imaginary and didn't mean a damned thing. He tossed the covers aside and put his feet down on the soft carpeting. Imagination took wing, telling him he could feel the warm imprints her bare feet had made in the pile. Foolishness, of course.

He half-turned, reaching for the lamp, but something glimmered there on the pillow, and he paused, frowning. And then he saw it and drew in a sharp breath. The necklace. The one she never took off, lay there on his pillow. My God, she'd left it for him. And that could only mean she didn't plan to come back.

Adam's heart sank in a quagmire, even as he lunged from the bed. His hand closed around the dainty fairy as he lifted it, held it front of him and stared for a split second, as it swung from its chain. Moving automatically now, and quickly, he fastened the thin chain around his own neck. The pain constricting his heart was almost crippling. But somehow, he managed to get moving. To pull on the jeans he'd left tossed on the floor. To stuff his feet into shoes. He didn't even bother with a shirt.

He couldn't let her leave. He just couldn't. Not like this. Not until he talked to her, told her . . .

He yanked the bedroom door open and stepped into the hall. From where he stood he

had a clear view of the study below. And he saw the stepladder under his painting of Rush—or was it hers? And he heard the door slam, and then a car spitting gravel as it tore away.

Jesus Christ. She was going ahead with this thing alone! He raced down the stairs, pausing at the bottom to snatch his keys off the stand where he always left them. But they weren't there. Instead, there was a note.

And he picked it up, his hands trembling.

I don't know what I am, Adam. But thanks to you, I think I might be more than I'd ever believed I could be. You gave me back my childhood dreams, and I'll always be grateful to you for that.

I don't know what's going to happen to me tonight. I only know that I love you too much to let you follow me, and end up getting hurt or killed because of the foolish mistakes I made in the past. You deserve so much more, and a woman far better than I've ever been. Find her. Do it for me.

I'm sorry, but I've taken both sets of your car keys. If I can, I'll mail them to you when this is over.

I'll always love you, Adam. Always. No matter what.

                                        Brigit

Adam turned in a slow circle, frustration burning a hole through his chest as liquid heat swam in his eyes. Tears. Goddamn, he hadn't

shed a tear since he was seven years old. Hell,
Brigit had accomplished the impossible. She'd
taught him how to cry again.

And how to love.

Chapter Sixteen

SHE'S CLOSE TO you now! Closer than ever!

Bridín woke to those words ringing through her psyche. She lay still in the familiar bed; the bed she'd slept in for most of her life. But in her soul, she knew this would be the last time she'd wake here. Her battle of wills with the Dark Prince would end today. But the war would be far from over. Just beginning, in fact.

Things would change then. No more would he look in on her when he believed her to be sleeping. No more would she be the helpless prisoner, locked in his castle tower and totally dependent on him for her every need. No more.

Once she returned to Rush, she'd be restored to power. And she'd be obliged to destroy him.

It occurred to her then that she didn't even know his given name. She never had. When his family had been banished to the dark side centuries ago, the name had been outlawed. No one could utter it in Rush ever again. His family were the dark ones, and the name he used in this realm, Darque, was only an extension of that.

Not that it mattered. Not now. Her time had come. All these years she'd awaited this day, and now it was here. She knew . . . it was time.

The Dark Prince must sense something was about to happen. She could feel his nervousness, hear him pacing in the room beside hers. He would not be an easy man to trick. His keen mind would spot the slightest flaw in her performance. But she suspected she held the weapon that would make her the victor in this particular battle.

He couldn't hurt her. And not just because of the pendant she wore. There was more. All these years he'd held her prisoner, watched her grow and change, as she'd watched him remain the same. Dark, charismatic, and utterly evil. But he'd never been cruel to her, despite that she was his sworn enemy. And she'd been sure to look deeply into his eyes whenever he approached her. She knew she possessed that fairy allure, so dangerous to mortal and fay males alike. And she'd focused that allure on the Dark Prince, praying he'd be susceptible as well. That she could soften his barren, black heart toward her . . . just a little bit. Just enough.

She'd soon find out whether her attempts had been successful.

She relaxed her body, muscle by muscle, and focused on a single spot on the white ceiling above her. She concentrated, waiting for the knowledge to come to her. She'd know what to do. She'd know exactly what to do.

Staring at the ceiling, but not seeing it, she pictured her sister's beautiful face, put Brigit foremost in her mind, just the way she had

imagined her. The way she'd painted her. And she concentrated. When she'd focused every part of herself, mind and spirit on her sister, she consciously relaxed, letting her mind open like the petals of a flower in the sun. And she knew what she had to do.

She had to get sick. Very sick. Sick enough so they'd take her from this place to a hospital. She wasn't sure why she was supposed to do that, or even if she could do it, but she would certainly try.

Her focus shifted. She concentrated now on the physical rather than the spiritual. And as she willed it, so it happened. Her state altered, and her breathing slowed. Her heart rate followed suit, and her body temperature dropped.

Yes. That's it. But more. Just a bit more.

Focus. She tapped the strength of her will, used all the power she had. And consciousness began to recede. Not enough oxygen now, she supposed, to maintain it. She reached for the lace doily on her bedside stand, caught it, and tugged until the lamp that rested atop it crashed to the floor. That done, she rolled onto her side, close to the bed's edge. Teetering now. This experiment could kill her. She must be careful.

She leaned a little farther, heard the door open just as all thoughts faded away. She felt her body falling from the bed, felt the crushing impact on her right side when she hit the floor.

Darque reached Bridín's bedroom door at the same time as Kate, the nurse. He flung the door open, surged inside . . . and paused there as the blood drained from his face. Bridín lay on the

floor, amid the litter of broken glass. Her face as lily white as that of a corpse. Her eyes closed.

"Gods, why now?" he snarled as he moved forward, instinctively bending over to pick her up, then hesitating. The pendant. He couldn't lay his hands on her as long as she wore that pendant.

And then Kate was crouching beside him, pressing her palms to Bridín's face the way Darque had intended to do.

"Lord, she's cold as ice!" The nurse caught Bridín's wrist in her hands, and shook her head. Her eyes widened as she looked up at Darque.

He scowled down at the beautiful woman on the floor. "Damn you, Bridín, your timing couldn't be worse." He stood straight and paced away from her, rubbing his forehead with his fingertips. At any moment now, Zaslow would be taking possession of that damned painting. And Darque had to be there when that happened. He had to be sure it was destroyed, at once, before Bridín's sister ever set eyes on it. He had to witness it burning with his own eyes. He couldn't trust this to Zaslow. It was too important. And he couldn't wait.

Nor could he leave Bridín here in this condition. She looked as if she were at death's door. Gods, he couldn't just let her die.

He turned abruptly, saw Kate maneuvering Bridín's limp form back into the bed, stroking her hair, muttering softly. He could care less if she died, he reminded himself. It wouldn't matter to him in the least, except that he needed her. He needed her to secure his hold on the throne of Rush.

"What's wrong with her?" he demanded.

Kate turned on him, wide-eyed.

"You're a nurse, dammit. What's causing this?"

"I don't know."

Sighing in disgust, Darque paced toward the bed, stood beside it, looking down at Bridín's ivory face, the dark circles even now beginning to form around her eyes. The way her hands trembled against the white sheets.

Kate's head lay upon Bridín's breast for a moment. When she straightened, she faced him. "I don't have a stethoscope here, but I think her heartbeat is irregular. And it looks as if her blood pressure is falling dangerously. We need to get her to a hospital, Mr. Darque."

He narrowed his eyes and moved closer. Without taking his gaze from Bridín, he said, "Go downstairs and call an ambulance. You're to ride in it with her. You're to stay with her at all times, Kate. Do you understand?"

Kate nodded and started toward the door.

"I'll join you at the hospital soon. I have something I have to do first, but I'll come there directly. Don't let her out of your sight for an instant, Kate, until I get there."

"I won't," she said. "I'll take care of her. Don't worry, Mr. Darque." And then she left the room.

Darque bent over the bed, lifted his hand as if to touch her face, but caught himself, and drew it away again. "I'm warning you, Bridín of Rush, if this is some kind of a trick . . ."

His words trailed off as her eyes fluttered, and then opened, mere slits, unfocused and watery.

But they caught his and held them, and her pale, trembling hand rose slowly, reaching for his face.

He couldn't touch her. But she could touch him with no ill effects if she wanted to do so. It surprised him when her chilled palm settled on his cheek, and her eyes, dulled though they were, still managed to pierce his.

"Before I . . . go . . ." she whispered. "I wish to know . . . your name."

His name? The Dark Prince blinked in shock. "You're not going to die, Bridín," he assured her. "You'll live . . . long enough to serve my purposes, at least. But since you asked, my name is the same as my father's before me, and his before him, and many before them. I am Tristan of Shara." He held her gaze and added, "Ruler of Rush."

Her chilled hand fell away from his face, and he saw in her eyes that his barb had struck its target. And then they fell closed, and she said no more.

Tristan of Shara felt his stomach lurch, and wondered at it. But he lifted his hand, and spoke the words that would remove the invisible barrier which kept the fairy from passing.

And then he sat down in the chair beside the bed, and he stared at her a while longer.

Chapter Seventeen

THE POUNDING ON the front door came just as Adam reread her letter for the fourth time, while racking his brain to figure out where she'd gone. How he could reach her in time to protect her when he didn't even know where she'd gone. The interruption irritated the hell out of him.

"Dammit, Adam, open up!"

The voice was not one to be ignored. Mac wasn't the type to yell and pound on a door at this hour unless something was very wrong. Adam clasped the letter in his hand, went to the door, and yanked it open.

"What the hell are you doing here?"

"Sticking my nose in where it doesn't belong." Mac shoved Adam aside and came in, heading straight for the study. "You're going to knock me right on my ass for this, buddy, but do us both a favor and save it for later, okay?"

Adam shook his head in confusion. "Look I don't know what you're talking about, and I don't have time to find out. And since I need to borrow your car, I'm not likely to knock you on your ass just now."

"Good, because I tapped your phones."

"You . . ."

"Tapped your phones. Illegal as hell. I could lose my license."

Adam blinked. "Why?"

Mac's face twisted into a grimace. "Because you're my friend and I was worried about you. Afraid you were about to walk into another scam perpetrated by another woman. Jesus, Adam, I was with you last time, remember? I didn't want to watch you go through all that again." He tilted his head, surveying Adam's face. "Or am I already too late? Is she gone, Adam?"

"Yeah, and I have no idea where."

Mac sighed in disgust, stomped straight through into the study, and reached for the painting. With a quickness that made Adam cringe, he jerked the painting off the wall, flipped it around, and scanned the back. "Did you do what I told you? With the marking pen?"

Adam nodded, moving forward quickly and restlessly, wishing he knew what to do to help Brigit. "Yeah. But there's no sense looking for it. She switched them, Mac. Took the original with her, and I don't even give a damn. It's her I want, not the freaking painting."

Mac's head came up sharply. "You *knew* she'd switched them?" At Adam's nod, he rushed on. "And you just let her go? Just like that? What's got into you, Adam, you lost your mind or what?"

But even as he spoke, Mac was scanning that canvas again, yanking a flashlight the size of a

pen from his shirt pocket, flashing its purplish glow over the back in search of the ink.

"I didn't just let her go! She told me she had two more days, and I was planning to be there with her when she delivered the damned painting to this Zaslow jerk. But she left early, took my keys so I couldn't follow. She's meeting the bastard alone and there's not a damned thing I can do about it."

"Yeah, well you ought to know, Adam, that I just eavesdropped on a phone call from Zaslow. The jerk didn't *ask* her to pull this scam. He didn't give her any goddamn choice. Sounds as if he's holding the old man, just to be sure she complies."

"I know all that. She came clean, Mac, told me everything."

"He's a sadistic bastard," Mac went on. "Told Brigit that old Raze was sick, started listing symptoms and sounded like he was enjoying it. I thought I heard a moan in the background, but—"

"Jesus Christ. No wonder she took off in such a hurry."

"Ah, hell, Adam," Mac's words held a new urgency, and Adam looked up fast. Mac stood, staring at the lower right-hand corner of the painting, and shaking his head. "She didn't do it, pal. She didn't switch them. This is the original."

"What?" Adam lunged forward. A rush of adrenaline flooded his veins, and it propelled him, pushing him.

He looked over Mac's shoulder to see the

word, scrawled in Adam's own hand, illuminated by the ultraviolet glow. *Rush*.

"Brigit . . ." Adam breathed, almost limp now with relief. She *hadn't* betrayed him. Even with all the pressure on her to do it, and even when he'd told her he didn't care about the damned painting, that he'd willingly hand it over to Zaslow himself, she'd been unable to go through with it.

"This Zaslow is no slouch. He's an expert. She might have pulled it over on him if she'd waited a few days, let the paint dry. But man, he's gonna see through this so fast he won't have to look twice." Mac frowned hard. "And we both know this bastard has killed before."

Adam blinked, shock seeping through his bones, and the need for action making every nerve ending in his body twitch and jump. "Tell me you know where she's meeting him, Mac."

"Oh, yeah," Mac said, with a hard nod. "You bet your ass I know. An hour from here. Binghamton. At the double-A ball field there. We can call the cops and have them—"

"No cops." Adam headed for the front door at a run. "You leave your keys in the car?"

"Yeah, but Adam, we have to notify—"

"No cops, Mac." He stopped with his hand on the knob, his palm itching and shaking to send a glance back over his shoulder. "They'd connect her with the other forgeries . . . the ones in the past. She'd end up in prison."

"If she's guilty—"

"She was a kid, Mac. You said yourself, she couldn't have been much more than a teenager when those other heists went down."

Mac's lips thinned, but he nodded. "Okay. All right. It's your call. But I'm coming with you. You can't take on a thug like Zaslow alone."

Adam shook his head. "No way, pal. This is my fight." Adam started through the door.

"Jesus, Reid, aren't you even going to put a shirt on first?"

Adam didn't answer. He jumped into his friend's car and twisted the key.

She couldn't do it. She couldn't betray Adam that way, not when she knew how often he'd been hurt in the past. It didn't matter that he'd told her he didn't care. *She* cared. She'd tried to make herself switch the paintings. She'd gone so far as to take the original off the wall. But she'd never removed it from its frame. Adam had done too much for her. He'd taught her how to love. And there was no room in that love for betrayal. She ended up hanging the original back on the wall, and leaving the house with the copy.

She'd brought the forgery, its paint still tacky, to the meeting place. It rested in the back seat of her car as she paced the ground in front of the vehicle. The moon was waning, but bright. A lopsided half circle of goodness and light, spilling down on the grassy diamond. The place was abandoned tonight. The season recently over, the bleachers empty. The grass needed mowing, she thought, and the chalk lines had faded. She looked through the link fence that stretched around this end of the field, to the deserted dugouts. And she thought about Raze, and how much he loved to come here and watch

the Binghamton Mets. How he'd order a hot dog with extra relish and a Cherry Coke every time, like some kind of ritual. How he knew every player by name, and could predict which ones were destined to get called up to the major leagues.

She loved that old man. She'd never loved anyone as much as she loved Raze. Until now.

Zaslow's van rolled in, and Brigit went stiff. The vehicle pulled up beside hers, the headlights went out, and the motor died.

Zaslow's door opened and he stepped out, came around to stand near its nose. She remained where she was, standing nervously at the front of her own car. Both vehicles were aimed at the fence and the field. As if they were sitting there awaiting the first pitch.

"Well? Where is it?"

She lifted her chin, felt the wind whipping tendrils of hair around her face. "I want to see Raze first."

Zaslow tilted his head, shrugged. "Fair enough. Let's just get on with this, Brigit. My client was in touch right after I talked to you, and he's running out of patience."

Zaslow stepped between her car and his, to open the van's passenger door. Brigit moved to stand beside him, and when the interior light came on, she saw Raze, slouched in the seat. His careworn face was relaxed, head tilted to one side. He slumped there, so still she jerked in shock at first, thinking he was dead. But then she saw his chest rise and fall, slightly, but enough, and she drew a steadying breath. She'd

take care of Raze. Right now, nothing mattered but that.

She started forward, but Zaslow stepped right in front of her, blocking her path. "Not so fast, Brigit." He closed the van door. "The painting."

She glanced past him, through the window of the van at his back. In the pale moonlight, she could see a set of keys dangling from the switch. Hope surged in her chest.

"It's in the back seat," she said, inclining her head toward her car, three feet behind her. "Go ahead, take a look."

She stayed where she was as Zaslow moved past her to bend to the car and open the back door. She saw him lean in, reach out, and she lunged around the van's nose, reaching for the driver's door, just as she heard him yell, "Bitch!"

A gunshot rang out even as she was about to wrench the door open. Brigit ducked instinctively, covering her head with her hands, pressing her face to the cool metallic door.

"You lying, cheating little witch! Did you really think you could—could..." His voice trailed into silence.

Why? What... Brigit straightened just a little, and leaned forward to peek around the front of the van. But Zaslow wasn't looking at her anymore. He was staring through the chain-link fence at the baseball diamond. Blinking in confusion, she followed his gaze, only to see a dark, menacing form standing out on the field, right between home plate and the pitcher's mound. Where had he come from? How had he managed to walk out there without either of them noticing? But there he was, standing still as

stone, so completely enshrouded in shadow that only his outline was visible. But even without seeing him, Brigit knew he stared straight at Zaslow.

She couldn't make out a single detail about the man. It seemed he wore a black coat, with a caped back that swayed in the wind. The collar was turned up, and his face was completely hidden in the shadow of a black felt hat.

"Enough, Zaslow," the form said, only Brigit got the creepy sensation that no part of him moved to issue the command. Not even his lips.

Danger washed over her like a cold breeze. She could smell it, *taste* it in the air, and her heart chilled in her chest.

"Mr. Darque," Zaslow said, and his voice had gone from shaking with rage, to quivering in fear. "What are you doing here this early? I'm not supposed to meet you for another hour."

"You told me my painting would be here, Zaslow. I came to collect it. Though it doesn't matter now."

"I—I d-don't under—"

"I paid you to steal the painting. Not to have it copied."

"Oh, that. Don't worry about that, Mr. Darque. It's the best way to do these things," Zaslow blustered, but his voice was far from steady. "I thought—"

"I did not employ you to *think*, Zaslow. Nor to make copies. That painting should never have been seen, especially by *that one*." When he said that last part, he turned toward where Brigit crouched beside the van, afraid to stand up and

show herself. "Your *thinking* has ruined my plans, Zaslow."

He cocked his head toward Brigit's car, where Zaslow still stood near an opened rear door. The dark man lifted one hand and pointed a finger. A bolt of blue fire shot from it, blasting through the chain link as if it were butter. The bolt hit Zaslow dead center of his barrel chest. He howled in undisguised agony, his body hurtling backward through the air. He landed on the blacktop of the parking lot, rolling over and over before coming to a dead stop. And then he lay still. A thin spiral of smoke rose from his chest.

The scream she'd intended to emit died of fright and never emerged. She swallowed the air she'd sucked in, and looked back toward the dark form in the field. And she saw the blackened hole in the chain link, where that bolt had blasted through.

She had to get away from here. She had to get Raze away from this thing. She straightened from her hunched position on the ground, gripping the van door, ready to tug it open and jump behind the wheel, her eyes never leaving that deadly being.

He looked right at her and she got an awful feeling of impending doom. The hand pointed in her direction. Her heart slammed against her ribs, and she dove away from the van even as the blue fire raced toward her. She hit the ground, somersaulted, tried to breathe. God, what if he missed her and hit Raze? The fire—or whatever it was—had burned into the ground near her head, hitting like a bolt of lightning, and leaving bare, charred earth and wisps

of smoke. As she whipped her gaze back to that evil, perhaps inhuman form, its hand took aim again. She scrambled to her feet and ran for cover, heading away from the van, toward the hulking bleachers, thinking she could hide behind or under them. And blasts rocked the ground with their impact, practically at her heels all the way.

"Brigit!"

Shocked, she twisted her head at the sound of Raze's voice, but her ankle turned, and she went down hard. Pain shot from the injured ankle up into her leg. Panting, she looked back to see Raze, levering himself out of the van on the driver's side.

"The pendant," he rasped.

His feet hit the ground, and he gripped the door for support, only to fall to his knees all the same. God, what had Zaslow done to him to make him this weak?

"Use the pendant!"

Raze sagged forward, and then he was still.

Automatically, Brigit reached up to clasp the pewter fairy, but she found nothing there, and belatedly remembered leaving it on Adam's pillow. An act of love. No less.

"If she were wearing her pendant, old man, I wouldn't be foolish enough to take aim at her."

That deep, calm voice floated through the night, and chills raced up Brigit's spine. She looked up, saw that thing lifting his hand toward her again, and knew he had her this time. If she twitched, that fiery spear would run her through. And if she didn't, it would do so anyway. And there was nowhere to go.

*   *   *

Adam saw it. He didn't believe it, but he saw it. Some black enshrouded wizard or something, hurling lightning bolts at Brigit as she ran for her life. And he didn't know why, or what this was all about. He only knew he had to protect her, if it meant his life.

Adam ran over the blacktopped parking lot to the grass at the edge of the diamond. He poured all his strength into running toward the scene unfolding there. He saw Brigit struggle to her feet, and turn to face her attacker. He saw her stand a little straighter as she realized she was trapped. Nowhere to run. He ran faster, harder, his lungs burning. And then, just as that thing lifted its deadly hand toward her again, Adam launched himself. He growled with physical effort as he pushed off with his feet. And his body arrowed into the space between Brigit and the dark thing. Like a diver, only there would be no water to cushion the landing, he thought vaguely. And maybe it wouldn't matter anyway, because by the time he landed, he didn't think he'd be feeling much of anything. He saw the fire leave the dark man's fingertips as he sailed through the air. And he had a second to wonder at it, just before the blue lightning hit him in the chest, hot and hard and sizzling. Like a shotgun. Like a sledge hammer. He felt his ribs crack under the impact, felt his body driven backward. Its voltage had his nerves screaming aloud, and the burn! God the burn was like a brand in the center of his chest. He hit the ground so hard he couldn't draw a breath. But he saw what happened. He saw that blue fire

double over itself, as if ricocheting off his chest, and he saw it shoot back to its source.

Adam's eyes followed. The blue bolt smashed into the man on the mound, and he vanished. Just like that. Gone.

And Adam felt himself slipping away, too. But he knew Brigit was okay, just by the way she whispered his name as she fell to the ground beside him. The way she stroked his face, kissed him. And he didn't regret what he'd done for a second.

God, that burning. Grating his teeth, he lifted one hand and grasped his sternum. His palm closed on something that seared it. He gripped the item anyway, tearing it from his chest and letting it fall into the grass at his side. Blackness descended on him. And he found his only regret in leaving this world, was that he was leaving her. He loved her, and he'd never even told her so.

Brigit stared, blinking in disbelief. The shape burned into the center of Adam's chest was a familiar one. She searched the grass and found it. Her pewter fairy. He'd been wearing it. He'd found it there on his pillow, and he'd put it around his own neck.

Tears threatened, and she swallowed hard. She reached out to retrieve her pendant from the grass, only to draw away fast when it burned her fingertips. Frowning, she looked closer. The once-clear quartz point held lovingly in the pewter fairy's embrace was blackened now, charred as if something had burned it. And she realized that somehow, the bolt of fire had hit

the crystal. She'd seen it rebound back to anni-
hilate its owner. Had her pendant somehow
been responsible? But how? Was that why Raze
had been yelling at her to use . . .

Raze!

She twisted her head to see him lying on the
ground beside the van. So still. And again, she
leaned over Adam, shaking him gently. Torn in
two.

Tires skidded on pavement, and a door
slammed. Footfalls pounded toward her, and
she heard a man swearing out loud. Then he
was kneeling beside her, and she frowned in
confusion.

She knew him. The man Adam had hired to
check up on her, the private investigator. Mac
Cordair. It didn't matter why he was here.
"Help him," she whispered. "Please, help him."

His fingers pressed to Adam's neck, and then
his head lowered to Adam's chest. His lips thin,
he faced her. "There's a phone in my car, Brigit.
No, not the one I came in. That's . . . borrowed.
The one Adam was driving. Find it, and call an
ambulance. Hurry."

She staggered to her feet, saw him bending
over Adam's body, positioning his hands over
Adam's chest again. And she spun, and raced
away to make the call.

Bridín rested in the hospital bed, waiting, and
listening with scarcely veiled amusement to the
hospital nurse's puzzled tone.

"Her pulse was barely there when she arrived, doctor. Weak, and thready. Heartbeat er-

ratic. Respirations slow and shallow. Body temp way down. I don't understand it."

"Odd. Her vitals are normal now."

Yes, but don't think about sending me back, because I can re-create those symptoms if I have to.

"We'll run some tests, keep her overnight for observation, see what the blood work turns up."

"Yes, doctor."

Lovely, the way they talk about me as if I'm not even in the room. Do they think I'm deaf as well as insane?

"Nurse, is this patient considered dangerous? Prone to violence?"

"Not according to what her private nurse told us."

"A suicide risk, then?"

"No, doctor."

"Hmm. Then why the apes outside the room? They worried she'll try to run off?"

They referred, of course, to the sentries outside her hospital room. Two of Darque's oversized hulks. She considered them prison guards. They'd followed the ambulance, at Darque's orders, no doubt.

"I asked," the feminine voice replied. "Her nurse says she doesn't have a history of running away."

"Let's send them on their way, then. They're making the staff nervous and scaring the hell out of the patients. You'd think we had Charles Manson in here the way they're watching her."

Bridín heard the smile in the nurse's voice as she replied, "Yes, Doctor. I'll do that right away. No doubt they'll argue the point, but I'm sure Security can handle them. And then I'm taking

that nurse of hers a cup of coffee. Poor woman is worried sick."

"You just be sure she stays in the waiting room. I don't want anyone bothering this young lady until we get to the bottom of these symptoms."

Perfect. And not a moment too soon, either. Brigit is here!

Brigit paced the emergency room, and she couldn't stop crying. Mac stood in a corner, looking a little shell-shocked and staring into a cup of coffee he hadn't yet tasted. Brigit had been all but hysterical by the time he'd had a chance to question her about what had happened. And she didn't suppose her story about a man in black hurling lightning bolts at them had made much sense to Mac as he'd driven her to the hospital, behind the ambulance with its flashing lights and screaming siren.

It still made no sense to her.

She only knew what she'd seen. And what she'd seen had been Adam, throwing himself in front of her, saving her life.

She had held herself together until they'd bundled him and Raze into an ambulance. Another had arrived a few seconds later. They'd taken Zaslow away in a black vinyl bag.

Despite his confusion, Mac had convinced Brigit to tell the police she'd arrived after the fact. That she'd seen nothing, and had no idea what had happened.

They were busy right now at the field, with a team of electricians, trying to find the source of the high-voltage charge that had killed one man

and put another in the hospital. When they found nothing, they'd probably attribute it to summer lightning, blasting down from a clear sky.

Brigit jumped to attention when the doctor emerged from Adam's room. She nodded in Brigit's direction and Brigit hurried forward.

"Is he . . ."

"Alive, but still unconscious," the woman said softly, and she placed a gentle hand on Brigit's shoulder. "He took a powerful jolt, Miss . . ."

"Malone. Brigit."

"Brigit," she repeated. "His heart rate is normal now, steady, and he's breathing on his own, but he might be out for quite some time."

"But is he going to be all right? When he wakes up, will he—"

The hand on her shoulder tightened. *"If* he wakes up, Brigit. I have to be honest with you. Right now, we can't even be certain he will. He could slip into coma. And if he does come around, there could be brain damage."

"My God," she whispered. "My God."

"Then again, he might be just fine. There's no way to be sure of the extent of the damage, right now. We'll know more in a day or so. I'm sorry the news isn't better."

Brigit tried to keep her knees steady. Tried not to sink to the floor. It was an effort she wasn't certain she'd be able to sustain very long.

"As for the man who was brought in with him, Mr. uh . . ." She flipped a chart open, scanned it. "That's right. Malone, same as you. He's sleeping off the effects of a pretty potent

tranquilizer. Other than that, he's just fine."

Brigit's head came up. "He's not sick?"

"No. Just sleepy."

So Zaslow had been lying to her about that. Torturing her. And probably enjoying it. He'd deserved that blue bolt to the chest. Her knees gave, caught again. She swayed just a little, and steadied herself.

She hadn't realized Mac stood just behind her until she felt his arm settle around her shoulders.

"I want to see Adam," Brigit managed to whisper.

The doctor—Dr. Evans, she recalled belatedly—nodded. "You can go in, sit with him for a few minutes."

She turned to glance up at Mac.

"Go on," he urged. "He'd want you there. I'll see him later."

Dr. Evans stepped aside, held the door open for her, and Brigit, drawing a deep breath, walked through.

Adam lay still on the bed, eyes closed, but he didn't look ill or weak. He looked wonderful, only sleeping.

She moved slowly toward him, blinking back her tears, and she sat right on the edge of the mattress, her hand running over his face, tracing his cheekbones, and the line of his jaw. She bent lower, retracing that path with her lips. "Adam . . . I'm so sorry. God, I never meant for this to happen. I never wanted you to be hurt."

Her fingers sifted his hair. Stroked it. "I love you, Adam. I never said it out loud, but you knew, didn't you? You know it's true, even now.

I love you. I want you to come back to me, so I can tell you. I want to be able to look into your eyes when I say it. Okay?"

Her tears dampened the skin of his face. She brushed her lips over his, and tasted them. "Please, Adam," she whispered. "Please . . ."

The soft, steady beeping sound jumped and quickened. The pace of the sounds picked up, and a second later, Dr. Evans was leaning over her, gently tugging her away. "Come on, Brigit. That's enough for now. We have to be extremely careful with him right now."

She sniffed, knuckling her eyes dry. "Yes. Okay, whatever's best for Adam."

And she let the other woman lead her back into the hall, into the waiting room. She sank into a chair, feeling apart from herself. As if all of this were happening to someone else, and she was no more than a bystander, looking on.

But it wasn't happening to someone else. It was happening to Adam. If he died . . . God, if he died, how could she possibly live with herself? All of this was her fault. She should have found another way. Some other way to end it all.

One thing was certain. Right or wrong, it was over now. Zaslow was gone. Raze was going to be all right. She hadn't gone through with her plan to betray Adam.

The only question was, would he survive? And if he did, would he ever want to look at her again?

Chapter Eighteen

FINALLY! BRIDÍN MELTED in utter relief. All these years of planning, of waiting for the time to come when she could be free of the Dark Prince! Free of her rooms, and her nurse, and the ever-present guards! Free to do what she'd been born to do.

The painting had done its work. It had brought her sister to her, and tonight, she'd see her twin for the first time since infancy.

Thank the fates, Bridín thought. Rush needed her now. She sensed it with every part of her. The situation there must be dire, and it was high time she return and take her place as ruler. High time she oust the dark encroacher who'd taken her grandfather's throne, and whose father had murdered her mother, and driven her own father into exile. Rush was calling. Rush needed Bridín. And Bridín needed Brigit, because only together could they cross through the doorway. Assuming Bridín could even *find* the doorway. But she would. She had to. She needed her sister to . . .

But wait.

Bridín tilted her head to one side, listening to her heart, feeling it twist painfully in her chest.

"Brigit?" she whispered.

Frowning, she tossed the sterile-smelling sheets aside and got to her feet. This was unexpected. Brigit ... her sister, was in need right now, too. She was alone, and afraid, and her heart ... her heart was breaking in two.

Bridín closed her eyes, wishing it wasn't so. For many years, she'd been without any sort of emotional attachments. She'd been the prisoner of the Dark Prince. Her nurse and her guards worked for him and were under his control. By necessity, her relationships with them had been stilted, formal. Except for Raze, she'd never allowed herself to feel anything for anyone.

But this was her sister. Her twin. Her Brigit, whom she'd locked away in a room in the back of her mind; a room reserved for things she couldn't have. Things she'd someday have. Her dreams of Rush. Of the man she'd choose to rule beside her. And of her beautiful dark-haired, ebony-eyed twin sister.

Now Brigit was here, within reach. And Bridín was afraid she'd forgot how to behave with someone she loved. Maybe, she'd forgot how to love at all.

She squeezed her eyes shut tight, and her throat closed off. No tears came, though. No tears for Bridín. She often thought she had none.

She'd think of more practical matters now. Like how to get upstairs to the Intensive Care Unit, where Brigit was waiting. She'd been without drugs for hours and hours now, and she felt

stronger. Clearer. A little magic, then, to help her on her way.

She'd be checked on by nurses at every shift change, she knew. It had just been done. She had time. The guards had been ousted, and her own nurse, Kate, was in the waiting room, sipping coffee. She focused, closing her eyes, willing those who met her to pay no attention, to ignore her as if she were not even there. Invisibility was not a physical state, but a mental one. One she hoped she'd achieved as she opened her door and stepped into the hall, toward the elevators.

"All right," Mac said, and he gave Brigit's hand a squeeze. "All right, I'll go for now. But only to the nearest motel. I'll call in, leave my number at the nurses' station."

Brigit nodded. "And I'll call you if there's any change," she promised.

"Or if you need me. For anything. And I mean it, Brigit," he said, stepping into the elevator, turning to face her. "I love that oaf in there like a brother. And *he* loves . . ." He stopped speaking all of a sudden, frowning as his gaze shifted to something behind her. His eyes changed, altered, took on an entranced quality.

Brigit turned to see what had captured his attention so thoroughly. A woman stood there in the all but deserted hallway, looking around uneasily.

The elevator doors slid closed. The line of his vision was broken. Mac was gone. And the woman's eyes found Brigit, and then she blinked as if in surprise or shock or something.

She was beautiful. Her golden blond hair framed her delicate face and spilled down over her shoulders, all the way to her waist. She was slight, short, and fragile-looking, like Brigit, but with an inner strength that showed in her topaz-blue eyes.

She took a step closer, lifting a hand as if reaching out. "Brigit?"

Brigit blinked hard and rapidly. It couldn't be. It couldn't possibly be . . . but something inside her was saying that it was. "Bridín?"

"Is it really you, Brigit?"

Brigit stepped toward her, shaking her head in wonder. "My sister," she whispered in blatant disbelief. And then she saw the pendant around the woman's neck. The pewter fairy, twined around a quartz point. "Bridín . . ." Brigit's voice gave out. But she moved faster, and her sister did likewise, until they were clinging to one another in the center of the waiting room.

Brigit's arms held tightly to her sister's body, and she felt her frailty. The petite build, the apparent fragility, but she felt the strength underlying all of that, too. She held her hard, trembling all over, and when she finally backed away, her tears made it hard for her to see clearly.

"I can't believe this," she said, sniffing, and brushing at her cheeks. "Bridín, what . . ." Her words died, as she remembered what Adam had learned about her sister. And she looked again at what she was wearing. "Are you a patient here? Are you sick?"

Her almost-smile was so perfectly sane. So knowing. Her eyes were filled with emotion, but

remained dry. "I only pretended to be sick, so they'd bring me here. I knew you were coming, Brigit. I had to see you."

A little chill ran up Brigit's spine, and she licked her lips. "How could you know I was coming here tonight?"

But Bridín was scanning the waiting room. "Where's Raze? I thought he'd be with you."

"Raze?" How could she know Raze?

The blue eyes widened. "He's not sick, is he? Gods, I never thought of that! Is he all right?" She swung her head, looking around frantically.

"He's fine," Brigit said, touching her shoulders to calm her. "Raze is fine. He's just sleeping off a tranquilizer."

"Then why are you here?" Bridín asked, her body relaxing, her face returning to its placid, calm mask as she faced Brigit once again. "This is the Intensive Care Unit, Brigit. What's going on?"

"It's . . ." But before she could answer, Bridín's hand was touching her face. Her chilly palm cupped Brigit's cheek, rested there, still, steady. As if she were *feeling* something there.

Eyes closed, Bridín said, "Oh, Brigit . . . you could have been killed. It was so dangerous, to go there. And the man . . . the man . . . who tried to destroy you when he realized you'd seen my painting . . . didn't you recognize him? He's the Dark Prince. His family murdered ours, Brigit. They were the reason we had to flee Rush. And he's kept me his prisoner all my life. He'll do anything to stop me from going back."

Her arms closed again around Brigit, and she held on with surprising strength. "He wanted

the painting because he knew it was my message to you."

"The painting?" Brigit felt her blood run cold.

"Yes. I painted it for you, Brigit. I gave it to my nurse, as a gift, but I knew she wouldn't keep it. I knew it would make its way to you, somehow, and bring you here to me. And it did. But I'm sorry it nearly got you killed." Her sigh was deep and ragged. "Thank goodness your Adam was there," she said softly, and still there was surprisingly little emotion in her voice.

Brigit shook her head, trying to digest what all of this meant. And eventually, Bridín's grip eased, and she backed away. "You think it's true, that I'm insane, don't you, Brigit?"

Brigit shook her head. "No. It's obvious you're not. You know about Adam . . . and about that . . . that dark being . . ." She lifted her head, her eyes wide with wonder. "He's dead, I think. He tried to kill me, and Adam jumped in the way and—"

"Yes, I know. Adam was wearing your pendant. And the Dark Prince's blast was reflected right back onto him. But he isn't dead. I'd sense it if he were. That blast wasn't a killing one. Seems our enemy balks at the murder of beautiful fay princesses. Lucky for him he intended to show mercy, not to obliterate you, or it would have certainly destroyed him. As it is, I believe he's gone back to Rush. The blast put him in nearly as bad a shape as it did Adam. I sense . . ." Her brows knit together. "I sense he's weak, and in pain. But not dead. Not that one."

Brigit blinked, slowly letting her mind absorb

the truth, reeling, because she could no longer deny or doubt it.

"It's all so simple," Bridín told her. "Brigit, the *Fairytale* is real. You don't know about Rush because you don't need to. I remember everything because I must. I have to fight Darque for the throne, and I have to restore our kingdom. Brigit, it's time for me to go back there."

Brigit lifted a hand to stroke her sister's hair. "I've only just found you again, Bridín. I don't want you to leave me now. Not yet."

Bridín smiled gently. "I won't leave you. I can't. The only way either of us can pass through the doorway to the other side, is if we enter it together. Unless you come with me, Brigit, our kingdom is lost."

Brigit backed away, shaking her head. "But . . . I can't. I can't go back with you, Bridín. I'm sorry, but—"

Bridín's head jerked up, and for the first time, real emotion became apparent in her expression. Anger colored her eyes a shade darker, and her lips thinned, jaw clenched. "You have no choice in the matter. It's our destiny to return to Rush! We must go back. Our people are depending on us."

"Your people, you mean. God, Bridín, I don't even remember this place. There has to be a way you can go back without me."

"There isn't." Bridín inhaled nasally, so deep her chest expanded. Her chin came up. "So I have to find a way to convince you. My own sister."

"You don't have to convince me of anything, Bri—"

"This man. The one who saved you. He's in there?" She jerked her head toward Adam's room.

Brigit nodded.

"And you fear he's dying?"

"No . . ." Brigit sighed, lowering her chin to her chest. "I don't know. Maybe."

"Come on, then."

Bridín struck out across the waiting room, her steps fast and purposeful. Brigit ran after her when she realized her intent, but before she caught up, Bridín had burst into Adam's room, and was at his bedside. She leaned over him, touching his face, just the way she'd touched Brigit's earlier.

Bridín pressed her palms to either side of Adam's face, as Brigit rushed over to her side, scared half to death. Then Bridín went utterly still and her mouth fell open.

"What is it," Brigit asked, searching her sister's face.

"It's him," Bridín whispered. "He's the one I'm supposed to find."

"What?"

"He knows the way," she said softly. "This man knows the way back to Rush. He's been there, Brigit. I saw him in a dream. He's the one who's going to show us the doorway back home."

"Bridín, you don't understand. He's the reason I can't go back with you. I love this man."

"We can't let him die."

"No, we can't let him die," Brigit said softly. Then she narrowed her eyes and looked up at her sister.

"I thought you said it wasn't a killing blast?"

"For a fairy, it wouldn't have been. For a mortal . . ." She shook her head sadly.

"Is there a way we can . . . help him?"

Bridín stared into Brigit's eyes. "I can help him. But if I do, you have to promise to come back with me. I want your word. Give it to me, and I'll save your Adam's life."

Brigit's heart twisted into a hard little knot. But she looked down at Adam, so still in that bed, and she knew she had no choice. She couldn't let him die. Brushing a tear from her cheek, she nodded. "Yes. I promise. If you help him, I'll go with you."

Bridín seemed to sag a bit in relief. Then she bent over Adam, laying her palms on his temples, closing her eyes. Seconds ticked by, and Brigit waited, watching, praying.

And right before her eyes, the crystal point dangling from Bridín's neck, hovering just above Adam's face, began to glow very softly. A gentle white gleam suffused the quartz. And it beamed downward, touching Adam's face, bathing it.

Brigit blinked and rubbed her eyes, but the apparition didn't go away. Not until Bridín shook her head, and stood straight again. "I'm not strong enough. Not by myself. There are still too many of their chemicals floating around in my bloodstream, diluting my magic. You'll have to help me, Brigit."

"M-me?"

Bridín looked at Brigit's neck, frowned. "Where is your pendant?"

"I . . ." She gave her head a shake, and thrust

a hand into the pocket of her jeans, pulling out the pewter fairy, with its broken chain and blackened crystal.

"Well, it's no good like *that*," Bridín said. "Cleanse it. And hurry up. We don't have all night."

Brigit frowned, just staring at her.

Bridín's eyes softened. Her tone gentled. "I'm sorry, little sister. It's so vital to me to get back. I've been waiting so long for this day. I . . . I'm being impatient and short-tempered with you, forgetting you don't understand the ways . . ."

She stepped closer to Brigit, took her hand, and laid it across her own upturned palm. "But you know you have magic in you, don't you Brigit?"

Brigit nodded. "Yes. I know. I think a part of me has always known. But I didn't understand . . ."

"Close your hand around the pendant, little sister." And as she said it, she closed her own, delicate hand around Brigit's, so the pendant was trapped in their fists. "Close your eyes, and work up your energy. Get mad. Think about the Dark Prince and the way he hurt Adam."

Still unsure she could control her own abilities, Brigit complied. She closed her hand tighter and squeezed her eyes simultaneously. As if summoned against her will, that scene at the ball park came rushing back to her. And she did feel angry, despite the distractions at hand.

"That's it. Now, focus all that anger on the evil caught in your crystal. It's his evil, Brigit. Aim your anger at it and fire, just the way he did when he hurled his evil at you. Use your

anger as a weapon, and your goodness to blast that evil out of the crystal."

That odd state of focus that always came over her when she was painting began to steal over Brigit again, right now. Only instead of fixating on an image she wanted to reproduce, it was all directed toward that evil creature that had hurt Adam.

"Send it back where it came from, Brigit."

From the tips of her toes, a wave of *something* rose, up through her body, filling her, rushing upward tingling every nerve ending like an electrical charge. Her lips parted and it escaped, bursting from her in the form of a shout. "Get out!"

And then the feeling was gone, and she felt weak, as if she'd just run a mile.

Bridín's hand over her fisted one eased, and with her free hand, she gently pried Brigit's fingers open. When Brigit looked down at the necklace resting in her palm, the quartz point was as clear and as sparkling as a flawless diamond. She blinked down at it, then up at her sister.

"Magic," she whispered. "You'll get used to it. Now, you have to do it again. For Adam."

Her gaze went to Adam, lying so near death in that bed, and her heart tripped over itself with the force of what she felt for him.

"Come on, Brigit. Help me bring him back. We have to hurry. As soon as the Dark Prince recovers his strength, he'll be back here. And his henchmen will be looking for me soon as well." Bridín took the pendant out of her hand and put it around Brigit's neck, tying a knot in the chain

because the clasp was broken. "Now, go stand over there."

Brigit moved to the opposite side of the bed. She felt as if she were in a dream. Everything was out of focus and surreal. Dazed, she watched her sister, imitating her every move. When Bridín leaned over Adam and placed her hand against his left temple, Brigit leaned over and pressed her palm to his right one. Her cheek touched her sister's, and their pendants met, the chains twisting together right over Adam's face.

"Now," Bridín whispered, "Make him live."

Strength surged through Adam's body, shooting out into his limbs and zinging through his veins more potent than that electrical charge had done.

"Live!"

That command, spoken more fiercely than any drill sergeant's meanest bark, rang in his ears. And it took him a full minute to recognize that beloved voice.

"Live, Adam! Be all right! Dammit, *live!*"

Soft, warm hands were pressed to either side of his head, and Brigit was shouting in his face. He thought he'd better respond soon, before she slapped him or something.

"Adam, wake up!"

"All right, all right," he rasped, forcing his eyes open. "Give a guy a break, would you?"

"Adam . . ." she croaked.

She leaned over him, and her beautiful black eyes brimmed with tears. Her lips trembled into a half-smile as she searched his face. "Adam?"

Lifting one hand to the back of her head, he

pulled her closer, kissed her mouth, tasted her tears. And when he let her go, and she straightened away from him, his vision was a little clearer, his body a little stronger, as if he'd drawn sustenance from that kiss. Damned if he didn't believe he had.

And then he saw the other woman standing nervously near the door, peering out on occasion.

She was beautiful, the other one. Not a nurse. A patient, by the way she was dressed, and . . .

Ah, but what did it matter?

He met Brigit's eyes again, and all that had happened came rushing back to him. He shivered a little, shook his head. "Brigit, what in hell has been going on here?"

The door opened and another woman came in. This one, a doctor. Obvious by the white lab coat and the stethoscope around her neck.

"Brigit, I know you want to be near him," she began, "but he needs to rest and—" She broke off, looking at Adam as if seeing a ghost. And then she said a word that Adam was pretty sure she hadn't learned in med school.

"Brigit?" Adam prompted.

"I . . . I'm not sure."

The doctor finally snapped out of her state of shock, and came further inside, gripping Adam's wrist, flicking a pen-light into his eyes, muttering under her breath.

Glancing around at Brigit, the doctor said, "You two are going to have to step out while I examine him."

"No, Dr. Evans," the strange, golden, rail-thin woman in the hospital gown said softly. "I'm

afraid we can't do that. Adam's leaving. Right now, and so are we."

Every eye in that room turned to the woman who spoke with such quiet authority. And for some reason Adam couldn't figure out, he agreed with her.

"Who are you?" Dr. Evans asked. "Are you a patient here, or—"

"No," Brigit said quickly. Maybe a little *too* quickly for Adam's peace of mind. "She's my sister."

Your sister! He sat up straighter in the bed.

"She wanted to take a nap and a nurse gave her that hospital gown to wear."

As Brigit spoke, the blond woman surreptitiously moved one hand behind her back. But not before Adam had seen the i.d. bracelet on her wrist. He also saw the pendant she wore, and realized at least part of what Brigit had said was true. She was her sister. The mysterious, elusive Bridín had somehow materialized in his hospital room. And that meant—his heart began to crumble into tiny bits of dust. That meant that his time with Brigit was just about over. She'd found her sister, or her sister had found her. And it was time for them to fulfill their destiny, and for him to fulfill his, if he could.

Maybe he was still unconscious. Maybe this was all a dream. A nightmare.

Brigit looked at him, with an unmistakable plea in her eyes. And he responded, doing what he knew she wanted, just as he always seemed to do.

He took the doctor's attention away from Brigit's sister. "I'm all for getting out of here."

Adam distracted them all by getting out of the
bed. Brigit looked relieved. She pushed past the
flustered doctor to yank open a closet and pro-
duce his jeans and running shoes.

"Mr. Reid," Dr. Evans said, "a few hours ago
you were clinically dead. We had to electrocute
your heart three times to get a rhythm. We
weren't even sure you were going to pull
through. There is no way you can simply walk
out of this hospital and—"

"Look, doc, no offense, but I'd really rather
see my own M.D. It's a short drive, really." He
pulled on his jeans, snapped them, tugged up
the zipper, and stuffed his feet into his shoes.

Bridín closed her eyes, seemingly intent on
something. Then Adam heard that universally
cloned, hushed voice come over the P.A.: "Dr.
Evans to E.R., STAT. Dr. Evans to E.R., STAT."

Dr. Evans blew a sigh. "Nobody leaves," she
said. "I'll be back shortly and we'll discuss this."

She waited until Adam shrugged and sat
down on the bed. "All right, if you insist."

"I mean it," she said. And then she left.

Adam got up. "I'm assuming there's a reason
for the hurry."

The P.A. fired up again. "Security to the sixth
floor. Security to the sixth floor. Code green."

"That would be the reason," Bridín said.
"One missing patient, who might be a little bit
off in the head."

Adam paused, staring from one to the other.

"It's all right, Adam. She's right. We really do
need to get out of here."

"Of course you do," Bridín said. "The man
you met earlier knows exactly where you are.

He'll make us both his prisoners if he finds us, and probably kill you, Adam."

Adam met Brigit's eyes. God, there was so much he wanted to say to her, to tell her and to ask her. But he saw the urgency there. He'd find time to tell her . . . to tell her everything, before she left him for good.

And then he'd proceed to spend the rest of his life aching for her.

The three of them slipped out of the room, moving fast toward the elevators.

"We have to get Raze," Brigit whispered as they hit the elevator button.

"I already did that," her sister said softly.

"What do you mean? You've been with me the whole time." Brigit went silent when the elevator doors opened to reveal a skinny, white-haired, stubble-faced man, grinning sleepily.

"My girls," he said, arms opened wide. When they both hugged him, Adam knew he had to be the legendary Razor-Face Malone.

Brigit insisted they couldn't go back to Adam's place. Or to her own. She even felt it wouldn't be safe to go back to Ithaca. Nor was it, she insisted, to remain in Binghamton.

They wound up renting suites at a hotel in nearby Vestal, and they sat around in one of them until the wee hours became dawn. Raze and Bridín filled Adam and Brigit in on everything. How they knew each other. Why Bridín had painted Rush in the first place, and how she'd put an enchantment on the painting before sending it out to find her long-lost sister. Which was why the Dark Prince couldn't just destroy

it himself, and why he'd hired Zaslow to do it
for him. But Bridín's magic had been strong, and
the painting had done its job. It had brought the
sisters together again.

"The *Fairytale* is true," she told Adam. "And
now Brigit must return with me to Rush."

Brigit looked right into his eyes, and he saw
the tears pooling in hers. He wouldn't make this
harder on her. "I know," he said softly. "I've
known all along she had to go back." He
reached across the table, took Brigit's hands in
his. "It's okay," he told her, because he knew
she was hurting as much as he, and he wanted
to make it easier for her to leave him. "It's okay.
I'll be all right."

Raze cleared his throat, and sent Bridín a silent message. She nodded, and they both rose
and went to their own rooms. Brigit got to her
feet, and stumbled into the bathroom, closing
the door behind her, and Adam knew she'd
gone in there so he wouldn't see her crying. She
wanted to spare him from knowing how much
this was hurting her, the same way he'd been
trying to spare her seeing his pain.

Damn, if this didn't kill him, he didn't think
anything ever would. After a while he heard the
shower running. He sat on the bed, telling himself he could get through this, knowing it was a
lie.

Brigit came out of the bathroom, wearing one
of the complimentary hotel robes, and all of a
sudden, it didn't matter. He'd fall apart. He
knew damned good and well he would. But not
until after she'd gone.

She stood there, right beside the bed, and she

stared down at him, and her heartache was in her eyes. He held up his hand, and she took it.

"Come here," he told her.

She crawled onto the bed beside him. Snuggled into the crook of his arms, pressing close. Her damp, dark hair was cool against his chest, and he didn't care.

"Adam, I don't want to leave you. But I promised her. She said she'd save your life if I did, so I promised."

"It's all right, angel," he whispered. "You have to go back. I know that. I've always known."

"How?" She lifted her head, searching his eyes.

"Máire told me. She told me not to fall in love with you, that you had to leave me in the end. That my job was simply to show you and your sister the way back."

"I'm so sorry, Adam."

"I tried to listen to her," he whispered. "God knows I tried. But I couldn't do it, Brigit. I started falling in love with you the second I laid eyes on you, all those years ago, in that vision your mother showed me. And I never stopped."

He drew her closer, kissed her lips. "And I never will."

"I'll never stop loving you, either, Adam. Maybe . . . maybe someday—"

"I'll live for that someday, Brigit." He ran his hands through her satin hair.

"I still can't get used to it. I'm . . ."

"A fairy princess," he finished for her. "An enchantress who stole my heart."

Her smile was tremulous and sad. "The pendants glowed, Adam."

He rubbed her shoulders, held her closer, so that she lay down again. "Will you do something for me, angel?"

He felt her lashes brush his chest when her eyes closed, felt the heat of her breath when she whispered, "Anything."

He swallowed hard, his heart swelling. "Will you put it all out of your mind for just a little while? We don't have much time left together. Right now . . . all I want to do is be with you. I want to hold you and love you. I want this night . . . because it's going to have to last us awhile."

"Yes." She turned her face to his chest, and pressed her lips there. "But first I need to tell you . . . what I was, in the past. What I did."

"The forgeries. I know already. We all make mistakes, Brigit."

"You knew?" She stared at him, her eyes wider and rounder than he'd ever seen them. "You knew what I'd been . . . that I'd forged paintings for Zaslow?"

"Yes."

"Adam, I had to do it. Raze was so old and frail and sick. We were living in a condemned building, stealing or begging just to eat. He would have died—"

He held her tighter. "I know you wouldn't have done it unless you felt you had no other choice, Brigit. But it doesn't matter now. I don't care what you've done in the past, you understand that?"

"But . . ."

"When you left last night, why didn't you

take the painting? I told you it didn't matter to me." He continued stroking her hair as he asked the question.

She sat up again, and stared so deeply into his eyes he thought she could see his soul. "I couldn't. You've been betrayed so often, Adam. By your father, and then your wife. I couldn't hurt you that way. I wanted you to know that you could trust someone and not have it blow up in your face. I wanted to give you that, if nothing else, so that you could find someone worthy of you, someone who deserved a man like you. Someone to love."

His throat swelled, because her words were so dead on. She hit his sore spots with speeding bullets. But they were shots that healed. Warmed him through and through. Made him know that he was all right. He could think about the past, about his father and his wife, and he could deal with it. Because of her. All because of her.

"Well, you succeeded, then. I learned to trust someone. I trusted you, angel, and you didn't let me down."

She closed her eyes. "I'm glad."

"But I'll never be able to find some other woman to love." He shook his head slowly as he looked into her eyes. "Because I love you. And there's never going to be anyone who can make me feel the way you do, Brigit. Not ever. You're magic." He closed his eyes because he felt tears threatening, and he didn't want her to see them.

"I feel the same," she told him. "There will never be anyone else for me, Adam. I'll live for-

ever on the love you and I had between us."

He cupped her head at the base of her neck. "I want to make sweet love to you, angel. I want this night to be the one you remember when you think of me."

Her answer was a single teardrop, which he promptly kissed away.

Chapter Nineteen

AS SHE RODE with Adam in his car on the drive back to Ithaca, Brigit couldn't stop thinking about the future. It loomed before her like a gaping black hole, devoid of life. Devoid of happiness. Devoid of anything good at all.

Because it would be devoid of Adam.

She'd find a way to get back to him. She would, someday. Though her sister had said the battle to regain control of Rush might take years, Brigit was determined.

And afraid. Terrified that the time when she could find her way back to Adam would never come. Or that by the time she finally was free of her promise to her sister, it would be too late. He would have found someone else.

He held her close to his side, driving one-handed. His arm tight around her as if he didn't want to let her go.

At Bridín's gentle insistence, she and Raze followed in the other car, Brigit's car. Bridín had known Brigit wanted to be with Adam. Known she'd *needed* to be close to him, especially now,

when she was so very close to losing him forever.

And Bridín had known other things, too.

Early this morning, while Adam had been sleeping after making love to her all night long, Brigit had been unable to rest. She'd left the hotel, slipping through the lobby and going outside to put her bare feet in the cool grass. To feel the morning dew on her toes and the morning air in her lungs and the morning sun on her face. To be sure everything hadn't turned black and withered and died the way her heart felt as if it were doing right now.

And her sister found her there. She'd come up softly, so Brigit hadn't heard her approach. And she'd settled herself down in the wet grass beside her.

Brigit tipped her head to the side, resting it on her sister's shoulder. "I love you, you know."

"I know," Bridín said, and rested one hand in Brigit's hair. "And I love you, too, little sister. I wish . . . I wish I could go back without you. I wish I didn't have to hurt you this way. If there were another way—"

"I know." Brigit closed her eyes to prevent her tears. "Is there . . . is there any way he could go with me?"

"Give up all he knows, his entire world, to enter one at war, where he could be killed at any moment? Would you ask it of him?"

Brigit lowered her head, ashamed.

"No, sister, there's no way for him to come along. The doorway allowed him to pass once . . . because he needed to see it, so it would be burned forever into his memory. It was his fate

to guide us back there. But it won't let him
through again. Very few mortals are ever allowed to pass. And never more than once in,
and once out again. It's that way for our people's protection."

Brigit sniffed, and brushed a hand over her
eyes. "I should have known you would have
suggested it yourself if it were possible."

"I would have."

Lowering her eyes, Brigit sighed. "I don't deserve him, that's why this is the way things are
turning out. I haven't been a good person."

Bridín's hand clasped Brigit's. "You are good,
Brigit. You are. Don't doubt that anymore.
You've risked everything you cherish, even your
own life, to be sure the people you love most
are cared for and safe. There's nothing bad
about that."

"But the paintings—"

"You have a gift," Bridín told her, echoing the
words of Sister Mary Agnes so long ago. "So do
I. Our mother had it, too, Brigit. She painted all
the illustrations in the books she made for us."

Brigit hadn't thought about that before, but
realized now it went right along with the rest of
the story. Their mother had painted those vellum pages. So naturally she had inherited the
talent from her. From Máire.

"You don't have to copy other people's work,
you know," Bridín went on. "If you just imagine
the image you want to paint, just fix it in your
mind . . . Whatever it is you want to create, create it in your mind first, and keep it there. Focus
on it the way you do on another painting. And
paint, Brigit. It will work. You'll see."

It did sound as if it would work. That Brigit had never had the confidence or maybe the desire to try it before, surprised her. Why hadn't she seen what was so obvious to her sister?

"You are going to paint a storybook for your own little one. Carry on the family tradition."

"My own . . . ?"

Bridín ran one hand over Brigit's belly, and for the first time she smiled fully.

Brigit choked. "You mean I'm. . . ."

"You mustn't tell Adam. He'll never let you go back to Rush if you do."

Brigit's joy in her sister's revelation died a slow, painful death. Her first thought had been of sharing this with Adam. But she knew her sister was right. Telling him would only give him more reason for grief in the coming months and years.

And yet keeping the truth from him was just as wrong.

"Adam is waking, Brigit. He'll be worried about you if he finds you gone. Go on. Go to him."

Brigit swallowed hard. Her eyes were watering as she gave her sister a ferocious hug, and then hurried back to her room.

Now, in the car beside Adam, she told herself again and again that she might be able to survive without him, after all. Because she was carrying Adam's child, and so she'd have a part of him with her always.

It was a solemn group that marched through the woods to the spot Adam had visited as a child. He wasn't certain he could find the way

back there, and part of him, most of him, actually, hoped he wouldn't be able to. Hoped it simply wasn't there anymore.

But he had a sick feeling in the pit of his stomach that it would be there. Just the way he remembered it. And he was about to lose the woman he loved forever.

Yet he stoically forced himself to do what he knew he must do. He loved Brigit too much to deprive her of returning to Rush. To her own world, her own people. He knew fully well she'd never felt as if she had fit in here, in the mortal world.

He'd already asked Bridín about going with them, and he'd known the answer before she'd explained. He'd known it in his heart. This was the end.

He led the way, as the four of them hiked up the hill behind his house, and into the woods. And his muscles seemed lumbering and slow, and his chest felt heavy. His feet barely dragged over the uneven ground, and with every step, his throat tightened more and made it harder to breathe. His eyes burned like fire every time he looked at Brigit.

God she was beautiful. The sun slanted through the trees, setting her ebony hair on fire. Her eyes glimmered when she glanced his way, and she was battling tears, too, though they brimmed more deeply each time their eyes met.

"I love you," he said, for no other reason than that he had to.

"I love you," she replied in a tortured whisper, and she squeezed his hand.

God, how the hell was he going to live without her?

"Are we close?" Bridín called from behind.

Adam shook his head, looking back over his shoulder at her. Her blue eyes glittered with anticipation, but he saw the sympathy there, too. She didn't like doing this to her sister. Even old Razor-Face seemed to be battling tears.

"Bridín, I have to warn you," Adam said, though he had to clear his throat several times in order to make his words audible. "I came out here not too long ago, trying to find the spot, but I couldn't do it."

"Of course you couldn't. You came here a bitter, untrusting, cynical man. Your heart was older than Raze's whiskers."

"My whiskers and I resent that remark, Bridey." Though Raze's tone was light, Adam could hear the sadness in his voice.

"Today," Bridín went on, "you come with the heart of a child, Adam. Today, you'll be able to see the path as clearly as a four-lane highway. For though you're crying inside, your heart is filled with love and goodness."

He looked down, shaking his head from side to side. And then he stopped, because he *did* see it. A wavering trail, and it was so much more vivid than any other animal path in the woods, so different. "Dammit," he muttered.

"Adam?" Brigit seemed worried.

Bridín stepped forward. "You see it, don't you?"

He nodded, but his eyes were on Brigit, not her sister. And he saw his own heartbreak reflected there as her tears began spilling over.

"Lead on, Adam," Bridín said.

He did. Gently, he pushed Brigit behind him, and crouched down when they came to the berry briars. None of those fragrant white blossoms, this time. Instead the branches were heavy with fat blackberries.

"We have to crawl from here," he told them.

"So, crawl then," Bridín said.

As the three of them stood watching, Adam self-consciously dropped down on all fours. He crawled along into the arched tunnel of berry briars, and he wished he'd never emerge. He wished he could grab Brigit and run off into these woods and never be seen or heard from again.

But that wouldn't be fair to her, would it? He'd be denying her the chance to fulfill her destiny. He kept going, peering behind him to see Brigit crawling in the same way he was. And he knew the others followed as well. The ground swelled, and he crept over the rise.

Finally, he emerged from the briar patch. And he blinked, because he was on the far side of the same grassy hill he remembered. Despondency thickened his blood until he thought it crawled through his veins like molasses. He walked halfway down the miniature hillside. And then he stopped and just stood, staring into the dark mouth of the cave.

Shaking his head in wonder, he turned and watched the others emerge from the briars, one by one. Brigit hurried to his side, and slid her arms around his waist, burying her head against his chest as a loud sob escaped against her will. He held her close.

Bridín came next, and then Raze. There was a long moment of silence, while they all stood staring.

"Well," Bridín said at last. "This is it, then."

Raze moved toward her, put his hand on her shoulder. "I'm going with you, Bridey."

She shook her head. "It will be dangerous."

"Bridey, girl," Raze said, and then he turned to Brigit. "You girls need to know something. Your father, John, he asked me to watch out for you. Way back when you were just babies. I was no more than a bum. Hell, what did I know about caring for little girls? I was the one who left you at St. Mary's, and delivered your father's note, 'cause I knew they'd care for you there. And when you got separated, I went with you, Bridey, because I sensed you were the one who needed me most. I lost myself for a short time, when that Dark Prince got me under his spell, but I came around soon enough. I'd sworn to be guardian to both of you, for as long as I could. This doorway will open for me, Bridey. Your father promised me it would."

Brigit clung to Adam as Bridín hugged the old man hard.

"Aside from you girls, I got no ties. And there's nothing in this world I'll miss." He touched Bridín's shoulder. "I want to go there, Bridey. I want to see it."

Smiling gently, Bridín nodded.

"It's just a cave," Adam whispered, closing his eyes as he held Brigit still harder. "Maybe there's nothing on the other side. We don't even know—"

"You know," Bridín told him. "It shows in

your eyes, Adam Reid. Come along, and walk us to the gateway. It's time."

Brigit clung harder for a second. But then she slipped out of Adam's embrace. Bridín bent over and crawled into the cave, Raze behind her. Grating his teeth, Adam followed with Brigit close to him, all the way. Inside, they found the larger, roomlike area where he'd played as a child, and he ran his hands over the stone to feel the spot where he'd carved his name such a long time ago.

"Come," Bridín said. She led them once around the room, and then back to the entrance. And then she was scuttling back through the passage, toward the gleaming yellow light at its end.

Adam crawled behind her, his stomach knotting, his pulse pounding. He kept telling himself it wouldn't be there. It wouldn't. It couldn't.

And he emerged, and stood just in front of the cave's entrance. Before him there was a wall of dense vapors—a wavery film of something that looked the way heat waves look when they rise from hot pavement. And he put his hand on it, but couldn't push it through.

"Rush," Brigit whispered, as she emerged from the cave and straightened. She turned in a slow circle, looking all around her, and Adam knew she didn't see the barrier. For her, it wasn't there. Just as it hadn't been there for him when he was a child. She could pass through . . . but he'd be unable to.

His heart contracted painfully.

Brigit threw herself into his arms, sobbing

aloud now, clinging to him with surprising strength.

"It's going to kill me, Adam. God, I don't want to leave you. I love you. I love you!"

"I know." His tears flowed freely now, and he stroked her hair, kissed her face. "I know, baby. I love you, too. This is the hardest thing I've ever done."

"Look there," Raze said, pointing, and everyone followed his gaze.

Castle spires stood beyond the trees in the distance. Softly gray and silver, mingling with the clouds.

"The Kingdom of Rush," Bridín whispered.

She turned then, touched Brigit's shoulder, drawing her away from Adam just a little, and pointing. And Brigit looked toward those towers, and her eyes widened a little, in wonder.

Bridín's eyes filled with tears as she stared at those spires, and Brigit reached out with a shaking hand, to brush them away.

"Leave them," Bridín told her. "I haven't been able to cry since I left here."

"Bridín . . ."

"I have to go, Brigit. It's my destiny. You know that."

"I know. I'm coming." She turned back to Adam, and he held her once more, knowing the time had come to let her go. He loved her, God, how he loved her.

He dipped his head, and kissed her long and deep. And then he straightened away from her. "Just know I love you," he told her. "Never forget that, Brigit. Now go, go on."

Covering her face with her hands, Brigit

turned and ran away from him, sobbing out loud, as she passed through that shimmering veil, and disappeared into the forest beyond it.

"You'll be rewarded, Adam Reid."

"I'll be in hell, Bridín. And if you let anything happen to her..." He shook his head slowly, and ducked back into the cave. Into blackness and emptiness. And he knew he'd never emerge from it again. He'd never feel the sunlight. He'd never smile. He'd never be happy again. Not without Brigit.

He made his way to the large room inside, before his strength gave out. His legs wouldn't hold him any longer, so he sank to the floor with his back braced against the cold stone wall, and he broke down. Grief pounded his body like a hurricane, and he wondered if he'd ever find the strength to get up again.

Brigit sank to the ground beneath an odd-looking tree, with pictures in the swirls of its bark, and she sobbed.

"My sister."

She sniffed, shook her head, refusing to look up. "No. It's no good, Bridín, can't you see that? I'm no good to you here. I'll never be any good without Adam. I need him."

"This is Rush, Brigit. This is your home. It's where you were born."

"But my heart isn't here. It's back there, on the other side, with Adam."

She cried softly, and in a second, her sister whispered, "I know."

The serenity in Bridín's voice reached her. She finally lifted her head, met her sister's gaze.

"I'm sorry," Bridín told her, and she lowered herself down to the moss-covered ground, and put her arms around Brigit. "I'm so sorry. But you're right. You'll be no good here. I can see that. And I believe his love is true. Because he loved you enough to let you go. And I believe yours is true as well, because you gave him up in order to save his life."

"What difference does it make now?" Brigit bit her lip, but her tears continued flowing all the same. "I've left him back there. And you said yourself we can't pass through the damned doorway unless we do it together."

"It's true. I needed you to get back. But I do not need you in order to remain. I can do that all by myself. My place is here." She stroked Brigit's hair, leaned close, and kissed her cheek. "I thought yours was, too. I thought once you set foot here, once you breathed the air of Rush, you'd . . ." Her voice trailed off and she shook her head. "But no. Your place is back there, in the mortal realm, with Adam."

Brigit stopped crying. She met her sister's eyes. "But how . . ."

"There's one way, Brigit." Bridín reached up to the back of her own neck, unclasped her pendant. "If one of us has possession of both the pendants . . . either of us may pass through the doorway alone."

Brigit frowned, shaking her head slowly. "I don't understand. Why didn't you say so in the first place, Bridín? I'd have given you the pendant if that's—"

"Giving up your pendant is only symbolic,

Brigit. It stands for a far greater sacrifice. It means giving up your magic."

Brigit blinked in surprise. Giving up the magic? But she'd only just found it.

"I love you, my darling little sister." Bridín bowed her head, and held her pendant in an opened palm. "I give you my—"

"No!" Brigit jerked herself rigid when she realized what her sister meant to do. "No, Bridín. You mustn't. You're the one who needs the magic. You're the one who's going to stay here, and fight this Dark Prince for the throne. No." And she gave a small tug on her own pendant, freeing it, and pressing it into her sister's hand along with the other one. "I'm the one who gives my magic to you. And my pendant. I won't need it where I'm going."

Bridín bit her lip, closed her palm. "Thank you," she whispered.

"I love you, Bridín."

"We'll see each other again," Bridín insisted, nodding hard as if to insure it would be true. "When the kingdom is safe Brigit, I'll come through again."

Brigit hugged her sister hard. "Thank you. Thank you, Bridín."

"Go on. Go back to your Adam."

Brigit straightened away from her, and turned. Raze had been standing nearby, watching with damp eyes and an occasional sniffle. But then he went rigid, and waved a hand to hush them, and Brigit listened, hearing the sound of hoofbeats in the distance. "Someone's coming."

"Go!" Bridín gripped Brigit's arm, pushing

her back toward the cave. "Go on, now before something happens to you."

"You go," Brigit whispered back. "Go, hide in the forest. Hurry."

Bridín nodded, turned away. But she whirled around, once again, to hug Brigit with all her might.

And then Raze grabbed Brigit and kissed her cheek. "I'll watch out for her, my girl. Don't you worry."

"Goodbye, Raze. I love you!"

Raze turned away as the hoofbeats drew nearer. He gripped Bridín's arm and ran off into the trees, and they were soon invisible within the embrace of that mystical forest. The forest that had once been Brigit's home. She stared at it, and at those castle spires beyond, for only an instant.

And then Brigit turned and ran to the doorway without a backward glance. She ducked her head and crouched low as she crept back inside the cave.

She found Adam there. He sat on the floor and his face was wet with tears that shimmered in the darkness. He seemed lost in agony, and he only blinked in confusion when he saw her.

Then he blinked again, and slowly got to his feet. "Brigit?"

"It's all right, Adam," she told him, hurrying to him, pressing herself close as he enfolded her in his strong, trembling arms.

"God, is this real? If it is, Brigit, I'm sorry, but I can't let you go back. I can't let you go. It's impossible, and it can't be right. Not when it feels so damned wrong. Not when—"

"Shhsh." She tipped her head up, and planted a brief kiss on his mouth. "I told you, it's all right. I'm staying."

He just stared in disbelief, shaking his head slowly. "Staying?"

"Yes. Yes, Adam."

Gradually, his lips pulled into a smile, and his eyes widened. "Staying?" he asked again. "Jesus, Brigit, say it again."

"I'm staying, Adam. Right here with you, forever if you think you can stand me that long."

His arms tightened around her waist, and he lifted her right off her feet, turning her in a circle. Then he let her slide down the front of him until her feet touched the ground, and he bent his head to kiss her, and kiss her, and kiss her.

And when he came up for a breath of air, he held her hard, burying his face in her hair and inhaling. "I love you, Brigit. More than anything in the world. I want to marry you." He drew away so he could look down into her eyes. "Say you'll be my wife."

"I think that would be for the best," she told him, and she gripped his hands and brought them down until his palms rested on her abdomen. "Since my sister tells me I'm carrying your son."

He closed his eyes. Bit his lower lip. And she marveled at the tear that rolled down his cheek a second later. "You're not a fairy," he whispered. "You're an angel, Brigit. You're the angel sent from heaven to save my life. To give me *back* my life. And I'm going to cherish you . . ." His hands rubbed her belly gently. ". . . And our baby, for as long as I live. I promise."

"I'm not magic anymore," she told him.

"Oh, yes you are, angel." He dropped to his knees, and pressed a kiss to the part of her that sheltered his child. "'Cause if this isn't magic, I don't know what is."

Then he rose, and kissed her. It was an endless kiss filled with promises, and dreams . . .

. . . and magic.

*Happily
Ever After . . .*

"I especially love that opening page."

The baby in Brigit's arms made a startled sound, and Adam could have sworn he reached for the book.

"Darling," Brigit whispered. "He wants you to read him his story."

The nurse chuckled and handed the book to Adam. Then she discreetly slipped away. Adam sat on the edge of Brigit's bed, and she held little Jonathon up as if he needed a better view of the pictures.

"Once upon a time," Adam began, and if his voice was choked, it was because of his tears. And because of the swelling in his heart. And because he was wondering again, as he often did these days, how the hell he had gotten so lucky. "There was a little boy. His name was Jonathon Adam Reid, and he was the most precious thing in his parents' lives." Adam reached out one hand to stroke his son's glistening black hair. "They gave him all the love in their hearts, because they knew how very much every child in the world deserves to be loved."

Adam paused, leaned down to kiss his wife, and then his son, and then he turned the page. "One day, Jonathon went on a great adventure, and this is the story of that adventure. It happened on *the other side*, in the enchanted land of the fairy folk, the land known as Rush . . .

The End . . . or is it?

"Speaking of which," said one of the nurses, interrupting them. "I brought my own copy. Will you autograph it for me?"

She picked up the huge storybook from where she'd dropped it when she'd rushed in here, hours ago. It was bound in a lovely leather cover. Each and every page had a beautiful, whimsical painting illustrating it. Paintings created by Brigit, with the remnants of magic she seemed to have retained despite the loss of her pendant.

Adam hoped, for Brigit's sake, that the pewter pendant had helped her sister. She hadn't heard from Bridín since she'd left her in Rush, and Adam knew she worried about her. But there was a certainty nestled deep in Brigit's heart, that no matter what might happen to Bridín, she'd be all right in the end. She talked about that feeling often. She'd told him that she clung to that certainty, believed in it with all her heart.

She turned her attention again to the storybook. Within the book's pages was a tale of adventure every child would cherish. All fiction, of course. Or . . . pretty much so. Unlike her sister, Brigit had assured Adam as she'd offered advice on the plot he'd constructed with great care for his son, she had not inherited the ability to predict the future.

"My kids are going to love it," the nurse said softly. "I can't wait for the next book in the series."

Fairytale, the cover said, in elegant golden calligraphy lettering that glittered magically in the overhead lights. *Book I. Written by Adam Reid. Illustrations by Brigit Malone Reid.*

Epilogue

THERE WERE TEARS of joy in Adam's eyes when he leaned over her and gently laid their newborn son into her arms. "His name is Jonathon, after your father," he told her, kissing her face, tasting her tears. He couldn't take his eyes from the wriggling bundle nestled in the downy white blanket. He had his mother's curling, jet-black hair and his father's sapphire eyes. To Adam there was no one in the room other than the three of them. No doctors or nurses milling around, cleaning up, removing latex gloves, commenting on his healthy son. Just him and his wife and little Jonathon.

"And Adam, after you," Brigit said. Her son had a grip on her finger, and it seemed she couldn't look away. "Don't forget. We agreed."

"Jonathon Adam Reid. Just as we agreed."

And he kissed her.

"He chose a good day to be born, didn't he?"

"A perfect day," she replied. "The day the first copies of his own personal fairytale—the one his parents created just for him —hit the shelves. I think he knew."

Discover Contemporary Romances
at Their Sizzling Hot Best
from Avon Books

THE LOVES OF RUBY DEE
by Curtiss Ann Matlock
78106-9/$5.99 US/$7.99 Can

JONATHAN'S WIFE
by Dee Holmes
78368-1/$5.99 US/$7.99 Can

DANIEL'S GIFT
by Barbara Freethy
78189-1/$5.99 US/$7.99 Can

FAIRYTALE
by Maggie Shayne
78300-2/$5.99 US/$7.99 Can

Coming Soon

WISHES COME TRUE
by Patti Berg
78338-X/$5.99 US/$7.99 Can

D0950543